FLAVIUS JOSEPHUS

Selections from His Works

The B'nai B'rith Jewish Heritage Classics

SERIES EDITORS: David Patterson · Lily Edelman

Already Published

THE MISHNAH
Oral Teachings of Judaism
Selected and Translated by Eugene J. Lipman

RASHI
Commentaries on the Pentateuch
Selected and Translated by Chaim Pearl

**A PORTION IN PARADISE
AND OTHER JEWISH FOLKTALES**
Compiled by H. M. Nahmad

THE HOLY CITY
Jews on Jerusalem
Compiled and Edited by Avraham Holtz

REASON AND HOPE
Selections from the Jewish Writings of Hermann Cohen
Translated, Edited, and with an Introduction by Eva Jospe

THE SEPHARDIC TRADITION
Ladino and Spanish-Jewish Literature
Selected and Edited by Moshe Lazar

JUDAISM AND HUMAN RIGHTS
Edited by Milton R. Konvitz

HUNTER AND HUNTED
Human History of the Holocaust
Selected and Edited by Gerd Korman

*Published in cooperation with the Commission
on Adult Jewish Education of B'nai B'rith*

FLAVIUS JOSEPHUS

Selections from His Works

With Introduction and Notes by

ABRAHAM WASSERSTEIN

The Viking Press · New York

UNESCO Collection of Representative Works
Israel Series
This book has been accepted
in the Israel Series
of the Translations Collection
of the United Nations Educational,
Scientific and Cultural Organization
(UNESCO).

To Maca

Preface

In choosing the passages for inclusion in this volume, I have endeavored to keep in mind the interests of the nonspecialist
reader. There is much in the works of Josephus that illuminates
the constitutional, political, religious, educational, and cultural
history of the Jewish people in the period contemporary with and
immediately preceding the great conflict between the Jews and
the Romans. I have given preference to such material over passages bearing on military or topographical detail. I have also included passages that illustrate the character of the author or express his attitude to events and situations both at home in Palestine
and in the wider context of the Roman World.

The selections here included are not arranged in the chronological order of composition. For Section I, I have chosen only
passages bearing on the life of the author, mainly from his *Life,*
but also including relevant passages from the *War.* Section II contains passages in which Josephus writes on Jewish religion and
civilization, in defense of his people against contemporary anti-
Jewish propagandists. These passages are all taken from *Against
Apion.* Section III, containing selections from the *Antiquities,*
offers passages bearing on the post-biblical history of the Jews,

9

preceding the war against the Romans. It is only in Section IV, devoted to the war itself, that I have offered any military detail; but even here I have tried to keep such material to a minimum.

The translation that I have used is not a modern one. It was made in the eighteenth century by William Whiston, then professor of mathematics at the University of Cambridge, and was first published in 1737. Since then it has gone through a large number of editions. It is probably true that this translation (revised and occasionally corrected by subsequent editors) has had more readers than any other. The slightly archaic style is vigorous and racy; it suits the material and is not unfaithful to the original author; by and large, it is accurate. In some places I have tried to correct the translation, and throughout I have ventured to change words and phrases, not from a desire to improve Whiston's style but in order to simplify and modernize the text and to remove possible misunderstandings arising from the ambiguity of an expression or from the change in the meanings of English words since Whiston's day. The edition referred to throughout is that published by Holt, Rinehart and Winston (1957).

All interpolations and notes inserted by me are in italic type.

I owe thanks to David Patterson and Lily Edelman, the editors of this series, for the care and trouble they have expended on the production of this volume. I am grateful for their patience and painstaking attention to detail, and to Mrs. Edelman in particular for many felicitous improvements in the translation. Professor L. H. Feldman has also been kind enough to go through the Introduction and part of the translation, and while I have not always felt able to accept his suggestions, I thank him for having preserved me from many errors and infelicities; those that remain are, of course, my own. I wish also to acknowledge my gratitude to Mrs. Beatrice Shere, staff member of B'nai B'rith's Commission on Adult Jewish Education, for her careful typing of the Josephus texts.

Jerusalem   A.W.
March 1973

Contents

Introduction

For a long period after Alexander the Great's conquests and settlements in the fourth century B.C.E., the culture of vast areas bordering on the coasts of the eastern half of the Mediterranean was Greek. Hellenic art and religion, philosophy and science, statecraft and military technique, and, most of all, language and literature had superimposed themselves on the existing civilizations of the native inhabitants in countries such as Persia, Egypt, and Babylonia with their ancient traditions of power and empire, no less than on the smaller nations that had developed and preserved their own distinctive cultures.

The Jews were no exception: for hundreds of years before the destruction of their state they were powerfully influenced by Hellenism in all aspects of their life. Alexander's successors, the Ptolemies in Egypt and the Seleucids in Syria, asserted and exercised their power over Palestine whenever they could and for as long as they could. Even in periods of political independence or quasi-independence (as, for example, after the Maccabean revolt in the second century B.C.E.) this influence still persisted. It is not by chance that some of the earliest descendants of the Hasmonean family bore Greek names; this is paralleled by the fact that from the very beginning of the rabbinic tradition we find teachers whose names are not Hebrew or Aramaic but Greek (e.g., Antigonos of Socho and his disciple Boethos).

This should not surprise us. Greek influence is visible over the centuries not only in external matters but also in the most fundamental and most intimate departments of Jewish life: in education and lawmaking, in prayer and biblical exegesis, in religious doctrine and in moral teaching, even in the writing of certain parts of the Bible itself. Thus we are told in rabbinic sources that Greek was part of the curriculum in the schools of some of the rabbis contemporary with Josephus. In the generation after Josephus, R. Shimon b. Gamaliel said: "There were a thousand young men in my father's house. Five hundred of them studied Torah, while the other five hundred studied Greek wisdom" (Babylonian Talmud, *Bava Kama,* 83a).

Some of the reforms introduced into Jewish law were designated by Greek technical terms (e.g., the Prosbul of Hillel); Greek was sometimes used for Jewish prayers; the rabbis were not only familiar with the Greek translation of the Bible but on occasion actually quoted from it; in interpreting the Bible they sometimes used the resources of the Greek language and Greek methods of exegesis; the Jewish doctrines of the immortality of the soul and the resurrection of the dead, which, within the framework of Jewish tradition, are of rabbinic, not biblical, origin, are clearly connected with ideas about the fate and nature of the human soul current in the Greek world. The same is true of other moral teachings found in Talmud and Midrash. Indeed, certain portions of the Hebrew Bible itself show clearly that they were written in a period of contact with Hellenism: this is true not only of the Book of Daniel, which on historical grounds can be dated within the Hellenistic period, but even more of Ecclesiastes (Kohelet), in which we find expressions of sentiments and doctrines directly paralleled in Greek literary sources.[1] Again the vocabulary of ancient rab-

---

[1] It is right to mention that the view here given of the late dating of Daniel and Ecclesiastes is at variance with the traditional Orthodox teaching concerning the date and authorship of the biblical books. According to some of the ancient rabbis Ecclesiastes was written by King Solomon, and

binic literature is full of Greek words taken from practically every area of life; and the thought of the rabbis is often formulated in ways which are paralleled in the works of their Greek predecessors and contemporaries.

Thus it is no exaggeration to say that the history of the Hellenistic period determined the character of the Jewish people, its faith, tradition, and culture. An understanding of contemporary and subsequent Jewish history depends on a proper understanding of this fact.

The world of Hellenism, the world of the Eastern Mediterranean, Hellenistic in character even where native cultures still persisted, was chaotic in its politics. War and rivalry between the successor states and dynasties of the empire that Alexander had founded destroyed the ancient certitudes in religion and philosophy, in thought and action, in the character of political and social consciousness. This world, though destined to inform the culture of the Eastern Mediterranean for many centuries to come, was not, in its political framework, destined to last. It was powerfully affected and then transformed by the injection of the unifying force of Roman power. This historical process in its local impact is nowhere more fully documented than in the works of Josephus.

The Life of Josephus

Josephus, the son of Matityahu, was born in 37/38 C.E., the year of Caligula's accession to the throne. He came from a priestly family with aristocratic connections: he tells us that through his mother he was related to the Hasmonean house. He had what was probably the conventional upbringing of the son of an upper-class family. He seems to have studied Jewish law and its rabbinic interpretation; and he tells us that when he was still very young, at the age of fourteen, his reputation for learning had already grown

---

the Book of Daniel by Daniel himself; though other rabbis ascribed the Book of Daniel to the men of the Great Synagogue and Ecclesiastes to King Hezekiah and his companions (see Babylonian Talmud, *Bava Bathra*, 15 a).

to such an extent that the priests and leading men in Jerusalem would come to him to ask for the elucidation of difficult passages in the Law. This boast is curiously similar to a well-known story in the New Testament (Luke 2:46), and it may well be that Josephus embellished his account with the addition of a conventional motif of biographical writing. But there can be little doubt that he is, at least substantially, speaking the truth: his works give evidence of wide acquaintance not only with the biblical text but also with its interpretation by both the rabbis and some of their rivals, though he may have known much of this material only at second hand.

If we are to believe his account, he began at sixteen to study the tenets and practices of the three sects into which, according to him, the Jews were divided: the Pharisees, the Sadducees, and the Essenes. After spending three years in the wilderness with a hermit named Bannus, he returned to Jerusalem. There, at the age of nineteen, he joined the Pharisees, a party of reformers who, in spite of their innovations, were faithful to tradition. They were nationalists who were nevertheless more capable than the other parties of accepting accommodation with the power of the Roman Empire. Though opposed to the exaggerated externalities of assimilation, they yet, more fundamentally than any other sect, received into the body of their doctrines new ideas and concepts that were to transform Judaism in the centuries to come.

What precisely the motive for Josephus's decision was we cannot say.[2] He does not tell us, nor can we be sure that he was guided by ideological considerations. It is possible that even at that early age calculation and a realistic appraisal of his own opportunities may have played a more important role than faith or doctrine. His motives may not have been entirely selfish, however: a man of his accommodating character and realistic temper may well have felt an affinity with the Pharisees going beyond a simple estimate of advantages to be gained. It is also possible that to let oneself be guided by Pharisaic rules was as fashionable, as much

---

[2] Belonging as he did to an aristocratic, priestly family, he might have been expected to sympathize with the Sadducees rather than with the Pharisees.

the "thing to do," in first-century Judea as it was to adopt Stoic principles in contemporary Rome. In both cases adherence to such principles may have been more a matter of literary dilettantism than of real religious or philosophical commitment.

At twenty-six Josephus went to Rome to try to secure the release of some captive Jewish priests whom the procurator Felix had sent there on a trifling charge to be judged by the emperor. It is not clear from his account whether he undertook this journey on his own initiative or at the behest of the Jerusalem authorities. In either case we may regard the mission as evidence of his high standing in his own country and possibly of some influence at the imperial court. When he reached Italy after a hazardous journey, he tells us, he was introduced to the Empress Poppaea, who helped him obtain freedom for the priests.

Josephus returned to Palestine in the spring of 66, to find the country on the brink of revolt. He argued against war and sedition, representing to his compatriots the power of Rome and the danger to their own people if war were to come. Though the governing classes saw little prospect of success in Jewish revolt and war against the might of Rome, popular enthusiasm prevailed over the caution of the Sanhedrin and of men like himself. Like the other leading priests and Pharisees, Josephus reluctantly joined those preparing for battle. Much in the ensuing conflict is confused and of little interest to the modern reader. We hear of battles and massacres, victories and defeats, treachery and sublime heroism. What stands out in this recital, as far as Josephus's own story is concerned, is the fact that in spite of his youth he was appointed commander in Galilee. He was not, however, particularly successful, lacking both the faith in success and the fanaticism of his rival, John of Gischala, whose portrait he draws with venom and hatred. He seems to have been more interested in calming the passions of the Galileans than in arousing them to resistance and hard fighting. It may, indeed, be true that it was the purpose of his mission to Galilee to keep the area quiet and to preserve the peace.

In the spring of 67 the Roman army under the command of Vespasian advanced into Galilee. Josephus was forced to retreat to Yotapata, where he was besieged by the Romans for forty-seven days. He gives us a long and detailed account in *The Jewish War,* Book III, of the fighting; he boasts of his own stratagems and the esteem in which he was held by the citizens. He planned to escape but was foiled by his own men. He remembered dreams in which he had foreseen the downfall of his people and a change in the fortunes of the Roman dynasty. When the Romans took the fortress he was again ready to surrender. He now had a message to deliver—"not as a traitor, but as a minister of Your will, O Lord." Not surprisingly his comrades were unimpressed by his new-found prophetic vocation (did he tell them about it?); they threatened him, and it was only by means of trickery that he escaped being killed by his own men. He suggested that, since there was no hope left, they should kill one another; they were to decide by lot the order in which they were to die, and "either by good fortune or by the providence of God" he was left at the end with one comrade, whom he persuaded to disregard the suicide pact. Then he was taken to the Romans and brought before Vespasian, who wanted to send him as a prisoner to the emperor in Rome. At this point Josephus claims to have requested a private interview with the general, in the course of which he predicted to him that he, Vespasian, would become emperor. Vespasian, who had at first attached little importance to this prediction, seems to have come to believe it (similar predictions are mentioned by other writers, such as Tacitus and Suetonius). At any rate he kept Josephus in his entourage, treating him, as Josephus says, with kindness and solicitude and presenting him with precious gifts.

This extraordinary story may well be entirely untrue; on the other hand, there may be a kernel of fact in it. The case against it can be stated as follows:

1. It fits in well with the dynastic propaganda of the Flavian house. When Josephus wrote his account, he lived in Rome under the patronage of Vespasian, then emperor, and later under the protection of Vespasian's sons Titus and Domitian. The prophecies related by Josephus, like those omens and oracles mentioned by other Roman historians, may well have been invented as part

of a dynastic legend designed to confer the sanctity of divine approval on the accession to the throne of the family of the Flavii.

2. The element of self-exculpation is so prominent, and it is so closely associated with the claim that Josephus had divine sanction for his surrender, that this alone provides a sufficient possible motive for the invention.

3. There is also the odd parallel of some important features of Josephus's account with a story in rabbinic sources concerning R. Yohanan ben Zakkai. That rabbi, one of the leaders of the Sanhedrin, had, like Josephus, counseled caution at the beginning of the rebellion. Like Josephus, he seemed to have made a realistic appraisal of the power of Rome. The story of Josephus's escape by a ruse from Yotapata is paralleled by that of Yohanan's escape, also by a ruse, from beleaguered Jerusalem. We are told that when Vespasian came to besiege Jerusalem he tried to persuade the inhabitants to surrender the city, promising that he would spare their lives and property. Yohanan ben Zakkai counseled compliance with Vespasian's request and trust in his promises. His advice was not accepted. He thereupon asked his disciples to smuggle him out of the city. They placed him in a coffin and pretended that he was dead and that they were going to bury him in the cemetery outside the city gates. Having thus escaped from Jerusalem, he went to Vespasian and predicted that he would become emperor. Like Josephus he gained his freedom by that prediction. Like Josephus he was accorded additional favors by Vespasian; and he made the famous request: "Give me Yavneh and its sages." We have here what may be called the foundation legend of rabbinic Judaism (see Babylonian Talmud, *Gittin,* 56b et al.).

The similarity of Yohanan's story to that of Josephus is unlikely to be fortuitous; if there is a connection between them it is surely a significant one. But what is its significance? Is one of the stories modeled on the other? Have they both a common source? Is one of them true? Or both? Or neither?

What the two accounts, stripped to their bare bones, have in common is simply that both men are said to have escaped from a besieged city by a trick, both men seem to have ingratiated themselves with the Roman commander, in both cases it was claimed that there had been a prediction of Vespasian's accession to the throne, and in both cases freedom and further favors are said to have been granted to the men involved. Yohanan's story is rounded off with an edifying sequel: the continuity of Jewish learning and religious leadership. That of Josephus has nothing edifying in it except the artificial appeal to divine guidance. It is not a pretty story, but we must remember that he tells it himself. What would personal or political enemies have made of it? Indeed what would an enemy of Yohanan's have made of *his* story?

Josephus was now thirty years old: a failure as a statesman, a defeated general, a prisoner of war, hated by his compatriots, probably distrusted by his captors, though he tells us that he was treated well and boasts of the favors shown him.

In 69, when Vespasian became emperor, Josephus was freed— hence his adoption of the name Flavius, indicating his connection with the new imperial dynasty of the Flavii. He accompanied Vespasian to Alexandria and then returned with Titus to the siege of Jerusalem, where he served the Emperor's son possibly as adviser and certainly as a kind of middleman. On a number of occasions Titus charged him to demand the surrender of the city. When the city was taken and the Temple destroyed he was given land in the plain to compensate him for the loss of his estates in the vicinity of Jerusalem. He was also granted a request for the freedom of his brother and some of his friends; he further obtained a gift of copies of the sacred Scriptures.

The war over, Josephus accompanied Titus to Rome. There he lived in Vespasian's house, became a Roman citizen, and was granted a pension. He survived Vespasian and Titus, who both treated him well, as did Domitian, who succeeded to the throne in 81.

According to his account, Josephus married three times. He divorced one wife, seems to have been deserted by another, and lived happily with a third woman, who came from a Jewish family settled in Crete. He had at least three sons. The date of his death is not known; but it is likely that he did not survive long into the second century.

The Works of Josephus

Soon after settling in Rome, Josephus began writing the works on which his fame rests. He began his literary career with *The Jewish War,* an account of the war between the Romans and the Jews. He had written the original in Aramaic, the lingua franca not only of the Jews but of many of the "barbarian" (i.e. non-Greek) native populations of the East; he enumerates the readers to whom he had then been addressing himself as Parthians, Babylonians, the farthest Arabians, the Jews beyond the Euphrates, and the people of Adiabene. The version that has come down to us is in Greek. It has been suggested, though without any really convincing evidence, that the work as revised and translated exhibits a shift toward a more emphatic expression of Josephus's pro-Roman sympathies. What we can be tolerably sure of is that the Greek version is not simply a literal translation of the first Aramaic edition.

For the second redaction of his work, Josephus made use of Greek or Greek-speaking assistants (*Against Apion,* I:9). The work was written and published between the years 75 and 79; its publication was authorized and encouraged by Titus. It was addressed to a different public, neither Jewish nor "barbarian": the Romans themselves and other Greek-speaking subjects of the Empire. Greek was the literary language of the whole of the eastern part of the Empire, and it was well known and much used among the educated classes of Rome. During the siege of Jerusalem, Josephus had made notes both of his observations in the Roman camp and of reports brought by deserters from the city. He also had access to the "commentaries" of Vespasian. He cites his credentials as those of one who at first himself fought against the Romans and who then, as a prisoner, had a good opportunity to observe the war. Other writers, he argues, had no first-hand knowledge; hence their facts are unreliable and contradictory. Or else they write with a view to flattering the Romans and out of hatred for the Jews: these motives, too, lead to a false account of what happened in the war.

It is of course true and indeed blatantly obvious that his own bias is pro-Roman. The very title of the work, *The Jewish War,* indicates that he writes from the point of view of his Roman masters. But for all that his sympathies were not expressed one-sidedly in favor of his people's enemy. He argues (*War,* I:3) that it is precisely by assigning to the Jews their proper greatness and importance that the historian helps magnify the Roman claim to greatness. But the reader comes also to feel that the glorification of the Roman name was not Josephus's only motive; there is national pride here, and also an apologetic intent, an attempt to exculpate, in part at least, the Jewish people. He parades his Roman sympathies; yet in apportioning the responsibility for the war he blames neither the whole nation of Judaea nor the official leadership but rather the Zealots, his own political enemies. He tries to demonstrate the pacific intentions of the Pharisees. While it is true that Josephus seems to be trying to curry favor with the Romans both for himself and, to some extent, for the class from which he sprang and the group to which he belonged, it is also easy to detect his pride in his people's traditions and in the bravery of Jewish soldiers. This becomes evident not only in isolated incidents or in the rhetorical flourish with which he embellishes some of the speeches, but, even more significantly, in the structure of the work as a whole, in the significance ascribed to the war. Indeed he exaggerates its magnitude and importance wildly, but this exaggeration is significant. To call it, as he does (*War,* I:1), "the greatest of all the wars that ever broke out between cities and nations," means more to him than a mere literary reminiscence from Thucydides, who had made a similar statement regarding the Peloponnesian War (*Thucydides,* I:1). It is the Jew speaking, intent on showing how great his nation is, how important in the scheme of things, great and important enough to measure itself against the might and majesty of the Roman Empire.

Josephus claims to be impartial; he boasts of his accuracy, for which he cites Vespasian, Titus, and Agrippa as witnesses; and he contrasts his own impartiality and reliability with the inaccuracy and bias of other historians; he claims that it is his aim to correct and balance the inaccurate and partial accounts of his rivals and predecessors among the historians of the Jewish War. It has rightly been said that his work is the fullest and most accurate account available of the events leading up to the war and of what happened in it. But accuracy in the description of military and perhaps even political events does not necessarily go hand in hand with reliability in the discussion of character and the ascription of motive. It can be said without injustice to Josephus that his work is partly Roman propaganda, partly personal and Jewish apologetics.

Josephus's account of the war—its immediate prehistory, its course, and its consequences—is based on what he saw and heard; he had a part in the events and was in close contact with all the important actors on both sides. His narrative opens with a history of the Jews during the last two and a half centuries of the Second Commonwealth, that is to say, beginning with the Hasmonean Revolt against the Seleucids in Syria and the re-establishment, precarious and temporary as it was, of Jewish independence. Here he had to use literary material, and it is clear that he relied largely on a non-Jewish source, plausibly identified as the *Universal History,* a work now lost except for fragments quoted by other authors, by Nicolaus of Damascus, a Greek writer encouraged by Herod. Nicolaus had included a great deal of Palestinian material in his historical studies. Josephus seems to have used Nicolaus without discrimination or correction of his misconceptions—natural to a non-Jew—about Jewish laws, conventions, and practices, misconceptions which Josephus, well versed as he claims to be in Jewish traditions, should not have had great difficulty in rectifying. He leaves unchanged expressions clearly indicating the distance of the non-Jewish writer from his Jewish material; and he does not, on the whole, introduce into the account culled from his Greek source a Jewish, let alone Pharisaic, religious coloring in matters of historical interpretation.

But this very lack of independence stemming from fidelity to his source makes his account all the more precious; from it we can learn much about the methods and attitudes of an ancient historian otherwise only sparsely known to us. And, most important, we have here better and more fully documented than anywhere else the history of the period between the Hasmonean Revolt and the end of the Second Commonwealth. It must not be forgotten that for this important chapter in Jewish history we have to rely much more on sources written in Greek than on Hebrew (or Aramaic) material. The latter, in so far as it exists, is late, unsystematic, mixed with legendary material, and written for homiletic or similar purposes. This is, of course, true of some of the Greek documents too: one cannot read the Apocrypha, particularly parts of the so-called Books of the Maccabees, without noticing this same mixture and purpose. But this makes the circumstance of our possessing a historical account all the more fortunate for readers interested in history.

After an interval of more than fifteen years Josephus published a second work, *The Antiquities of the Jews.* As in the *War,* Josephus's purpose was partly apologetic, a defense of the Jewish people. His aim was to give an account of the ancient history of the Jews, their origin, their customs and laws, and to show, in the working out of that history, the handiwork of God's providence, the moral nature of that which happens to men as a result of their good or evil acts, their obedience to God's will or their departure from His commandments. The work was again addressed to a Gentile audience. As a Jew he took the biblical account of history as the framework of his story; and though he began with the creation, he saw the origin of the Jewish nation in the legislation given by Moses.

But it was also as a man well versed in Greek and Hellenistic-Roman historiographical method and in its implicit concepts that he wrote *Antiquities.* It has often been pointed out that the title of his work and its arrangement into twenty books were modeled on the work of the Roman historian Dionysius of Halicarnassus, whose *Roman Antiquities* bears a similar title and is numbered similarly. That he tried to imitate Thucydides and Herodotus as well as other writers can be observed not only in his historical method; there are occasions when his model seems to have influenced not only the form of his narrative but, in some curious way, its contents. Even more interesting, the very concept of Moses as the great lawgiver and of his legislation as the decisive event in the history of the nation, though of course not foreign to Jewish ideas, is nevertheless clearly in the mold of the Greek historio-graphical tradition that glorified figures like Lycurgus and Solon precisely because "giving laws" to their people was the central part of their political life.

The framework within which Josephus set his story determined the sources on which he relied: the Bible and its traditional inter-pretation, Midrash (both rabbinic and Alexandrian), apocryphal works, and Philo, the Jewish-Hellenistic philosopher to whose works we owe the greater part of our knowledge of Jewish exegetical ac-tivity outside the mainstream of rabbinic tradition. But Josephus also used external material: Babylonian and Egyptian writers, classical and Hellenistic Greek historical and religious literature, and archival documentation are all pressed into service as testi-mony confirming the veracity of his Jewish sources. Whether he himself was familiar at first hand with the material he quotes is uncertain; he may be quoting only at second hand from earlier au-thors such as Nicolaus of Damascus, whose *Universal History* may well be the source for many of his citations from Gentile writers. It is, however, not altogether unlikely that he used some biblical and rabbinic sources directly. That he had at his disposal a ver-sion of the Septuagint is evident; he himself mentions in *Antiqui-ties* the well-known story of how the Bible came to be translated into Greek. But there are also indications in certain portions of *Antiquities* that he based his account there on the Hebrew original (or possibly on an Aramaic *Targum*) rather than on the Septu-agint. It is the opinion of some scholars, however, that Josephus relied in the main on secondary sources and that in writing *Anti-quities* he hardly ever independently used the primary sources (in-cluding the Hebrew and Greek texts of the Bible) from which he so copiously quoted. This reliance on secondary sources is prob-able even more in the latter half of the work, dealing with post-biblical history. For this latter period he had no generally ac-cepted sacred Scriptures to provide the framework for his story, but was obliged to rely on Jewish-Hellenistic and Gentile Greek literature, even though material is not lacking in *Antiquities* which must have rabbinic tradition as its origin. There is also biographi-cal, documentary, and archival material.

At the end of the last book of *Antiquities* Josephus mentioned his plan to write an autobiography. In that work, *The Life of Flavius Josephus,* which is apologetic and polemical in character, Josephus defended himself against the attacks of those who criticized his military activities as a commander in the war and his literary work since then. The greater part of the autobiography concerns the description of events at the beginning of the war. But this is not a history, and, significantly, he contradicted here some of the statements he had himself made in the *War* about his own role. For example, it would appear from the *Life* that the Jerusalem authorities sent him to Galilee together with two other priests, with the commission to persuade the rebels there to lay down their arms; in the *War* he tells us that he was sent there as a military commander.

In *Against Apion,* probably written before 96, Josephus returned to the national apologetics of *Antiquities.* He tried to demonstrate the antiquity of the Jewish people and the authenticity and reliability of its literary and historical tradition; he defended the Jews against calumnies of earlier and contemporary enemies, and, in a polemical spirit, he compared Jewish with pagan legislation. This work provides valuable information about the nature of and argumentation of ancient anti-Semitism and about the methods employed in Jewish apologetic literature. Josephus's sources here, as elsewhere, were varied; here, too, it is probable that he relied heavily on secondary materials.

Although there is evidence that, even if only in a garbled version, Josephus's works were not entirely unknown to some Jews in later centuries, they were little read and certainly not studied among the Jews of the Dispersion in late antiquity and the Middle Ages. Like the works of the Alexandrian philosopher Philo, those of Josephus owe their survival to the Christian Church. Josephus illumined for Christian readers both the biblical narrative and the period immediately preceding and contemporary with the birth of Christianity. There are, of course, in his works a few references of particular interest to the Christian reader; whether or not these are the result of pious forgery and interpolation, Josephus was regarded as one of the witnesses to early Christian history.

The modern reader will find his reaction to Josephus as man and historian ambivalent. Vanity and egotism; a willingness to depart from the truth all the more deplorable in a corpus of works containing so much of interest to students of ancient history; betrayal of his companions and his people, desertion to the enemy —all these will be held against Josephus, and rightly. But another thread also runs through all his writings: pride in the Jewish people and its traditions, and the wish to defend it against attack and defamation. Treason and desertion are ugly words, and they describe an ugly reality; but it must be remembered that Josephus is the principal witness against himself.

One further point: while it is true that in recounting certain less-than-honorable episodes in his life he tries to embellish them and occasionally even to invest them with divine sanction, he does report them. It is important to understand that ancient conceptions of loyalty and honor may well have been different from ours. Josephus was not the only ancient politician who, after having been prominent in his country's affairs, lived out his life in exile under the protection of the enemies of his country. Such, for example, was the lot of Themistocles, the Athenian statesman, creator of the Athenian navy, hero of Salamis, rebuilder of the walls of Athens; he died in exile, far from his native city, as a vassal of the Persian king. The story of Alcibiades is even more complicated; brought up by Pericles, friendly with Socrates, entrusted by his Athenian fellow citizens with high and important commands, he later went over to his country's enemies, the Spartans; nevertheless, he was welcomed back home, then exiled again, and he died abroad.

Also, many historians wrote in exile. Thucydides, the great Athenian model of ancient historiography, filled a command in the most fateful war of his nation as did Josephus. He also was unsuccessful as a military man and wrote his history of that war in exile. And, nearer in time to Josephus, there was Polybius, the son of a Greek statesman and general. He was taken as a hostage to Rome, where he lived for many years. He wrote the *Histories,* which describe the rise of the Roman Commonwealth to power and greatness, a work which comprehends the period from the beginning of the first Punic war to the end of the third in 146 B.C.E. That same year also saw the end of Greek independence, and the destruction of Corinth by the Romans, an event (or its aftermath) witnessed by Polybius—from the Roman side. Thus the case of Josephus is not isolated.

Any evaluation of the motives, actions, and character of Josephus, a man so far removed from us in time, living in a civilization utterly different from ours, must be cautious and tentative as well, perhaps, as charitable. The truth about him is necessarily complicated; his was not a simple character. He had his virtues: he seems to have been hard-working and energetic, quick and intelligent, capable in diplomacy and promising in warfare; in his own way he had strong patriotic feelings. But he did not possess the nobility and courage of some of his contemporaries and rivals or the insight and modesty of others who, realizing that the state was lost, laid the foundations of the future life of their people in the schools, academies, and houses of prayer.

PART ONE

The Life of Flavius Josephus

My family has descended all along from the priests; and as nobility among several people is of a different origin, so with us to be of the priestly dignity is an indication of family splendor. By my mother I am of the royal blood; for the children of Asmoneus, from whom that family was derived, had both the office of the high-priesthood and the dignity of a king for a very long time.

My father Matthias was not only eminent because of his nobility, but had a higher commendation because of his righteousness; and had a great reputation in Jerusalem, the greatest city we have. I was myself brought up with my brother, whose name was also Matthias. I made great progress in the improvement of my learning, and appeared to excel both in good memory and in understanding. Moreover, when I was a child, and about fourteen, I was commended by all for my love for learning; on which account the high priests and leaders of the city then came frequently to me, in order to seek my opinion about the accurate understanding of points of law; and when I was about sixteen, I had a mind to try out the several sects among us. These sects are three: the Pharisees, the Sadducees, and the Essenes; for I thought that by this means I might choose the best, if I were once acquainted with them all; so I submitted to hardy training, and underwent great difficulties, and went through the three. Nor did I content myself with these trials only; but when I was informed that one, whose name was Bannus, lived in the desert, and wore no other clothing than grew upon trees, and ate no other food than what grew of its own accord, and bathed himself in cold water frequently, both night and day, in order to preserve his purity, I imitated him in those things, and lived with him three years. So when I had accomplished my goals, I returned to the city, being now nineteen, and began to conduct myself according to the rules of the sect of the Pharisees, which is akin to the sect of the Stoics, as the Greeks call them.

But when I was twenty-six years old, it happened that I took a voyage to Rome; and this on the occasion which I shall now describe. At the time when Felix was procurator of Judea, there were certain priests of my acquaintance, and excellent persons they were, whom for a small and trifling reason he had put into bonds and sent to Rome to plead their cause before the emperor. These I was desirous to procure deliverance for; and that especially because I was informed that they were not unmindful of piety toward God, even under their afflictions. Accordingly, I came to Rome, through a great number of hazards; for, when our ship was wrecked in the Adriatic Sea, we that were in it swam for our lives all night until upon the first appearance of the day, I and some others, by God's providence, were taken up into another ship: and when I had thus escaped, and had come to Puteoli, I became acquainted with Aliturus, an actor much beloved by Nero, but a Jew by birth; and through his interest became known to Poppaea, the emperor's wife; and took care, as soon as possible, to entreat her to arrange that the priests might be set at liberty; and when, besides this favor, I had obtained many presents from Poppea, I returned home again.

And now I perceived plans for change had already begun, and that there were a great many who had very high hopes of a revolt against the Romans. I therefore endeavored to put a stop to these unruly persons, and tried to persuade them to change their minds.

I laid before their eyes against whom it was that they were going to fight, and told them that they were inferior to the Romans not only in martial skill but also in fortune, and desired them not rashly and foolishly to bring dangers of the most terrible kind upon their country, their families, and themselves. And this I said with vehement exhortation because I foresaw that the end of such a war would be most unfortunate to us. But I could not persuade them; for the madness of desperate men was too strong for me.

I was then afraid, lest by repeating these things so often, I should incur their hatred and suspicions, as if I were of our enemies' party, and should run into the danger of being seized by them and slain, since they were already possessed of Antonia, which was the citadel; so I retired into the inner court of the Temple; yet I went out of the Temple again after Menahem [1] and the leader of the band of robbers were put to death, and dwelled among the high priests and the chief of the Pharisees; but no small fear seized us when we saw the people in arms, and we ourselves did not know what we should do, and were not able to restrain the seditious. However, once the danger was directly upon us, we pretended we were of their same opinion but only advised them to be quiet for the present and let the enemy go away in order that they might obtain the credit for justly taking up arms in their defense, still hoping that Cestius [2] would not be long in coming with great forces, and so put an end to these seditious proceedings.

But, upon his coming and fighting, he was beaten, and a great many of those that were with him fell; and this disgrace of Cestius became the calamity of our whole nation; for those that desired the war were so highly elated by this success that they had hopes of finally conquering the Romans. Of which war another event was this: Those that dwelt in the neighboring cities of Syria seized the Jews that dwelt among them, with their wives and children, and slew them, even when they had not the slightest complaint against them; for they did neither attempt any resistance or revolt against the Romans, nor had they shown any marks of hatred or

---

[1] Menahem, son of Judah, a Galilean, one of the leaders of the rebellion, was killed by partisans of a rival, Eleazar (see *War*, II: 448).
[2] Cestius, governor of Syria.

treacherous designs towards the Syrians. But what was done by the inhabitants of Scythopolis [3] was the most impious and the most highly criminal of all; for when the Jews, their enemies, came upon them from outside, they forced the Jews among them to bear arms against their own countrymen, which is unlawful for us; [4] and when, by their assistance, they had joined battle with those who attacked them, and had beaten them, after that victory they forgot the assurances they had given their fellow citizens and confederates, and slew them all. Similar miseries were undergone by the Jews of Damascus; but we have given a more accurate account of these things in the books of the Jewish War. I only mention them now because I want to demonstrate to my readers that the Jews' war with the Romans was not voluntary, but that, in the main, they were forced by necessity to enter into it.

So when Cestius had been beaten, the leaders of Jerusalem, seeing that the robbers and rebels had arms in great plenty, and fearing lest they, while without arms, should be in subjection to their enemies—which also came to be the case afterward—and, being informed that all Galilee had not yet revolted against the Romans, but that some part of it was still quiet, they sent me and two others of the priests, men of excellent character, to persuade the evil men there to lay down their arms and to teach them this lesson—that it was better to have those arms reserved for the most courageous men that the nation had, for it had been resolved that our best men should always have their arms ready against future needs, but that they should wait to see what the Romans would do.

There follows an account of Josephus's arrival in Galilee and a description of the political and military situation there, particularly in Tiberias, Gischala, and Gamala. We hear of Justus, one of the leaders of the revolutionary party in Tiberias, who was later to write a rival account of the Jewish War. We read of treach-

[3] Scythopolis is now called Beit Shean.
[4] See Leviticus 19: 16–18; cf. also *Antiquities,* VIII: 223.

ery and massacre, of negotiations and intrigue. Jose-
phus tells of the machinations of his rivals, and of his
own preparations for arming and fortifying the towns
of Galilee. He describes political measures he took
with a view to preserving both the peace with the
Romans and his own authority in the district.

I was now about thirty, at which time of life it is hard for any
one to escape the calumnies of the envious, even though he restrain himself from fulfilling any unlawful desires, especially
where a person is in great authority. Yet did I preserve every
woman free from injuries; and as to what presents were offered
me, I despised them, not standing in need of them; nor indeed
would I take those tithes due me as a priest. Yet do I confess that
I took part of the spoils of those Syrians who inhabited the cities
adjoining us, after I had conquered them, and that I sent them to
my kindred in Jerusalem; although I twice took Sepphoris by
force, and Tiberias four times, and Gadara once, and when I had
subdued and taken John, who often laid treacherous snares for
me, punished neither him nor any of the people forenamed, as the
progress of this discourse will show. And it was on this account, I
suppose, that God, who is never unacquainted with those that do
as they ought to do, delivered me out of the hands of my enemies,
and afterwards preserved me when I fell into those many dangers
which I shall relate hereafter.

Now the masses of the Galileans had such great kindness for
me, and so much fidelity, that when their cities were taken by
force and their wives and children carried into slavery, they did
not so deeply lament for their own calamities as they were solicitous for my preservation.

The preceding paragraph is a typical example of Jose-
phus's unrestrained self-satisfaction. This is comple-
mented by uninhibited denigration of his enemies and
rivals, such as Justus or John of Gischala. The former
is the subject of the following extract. Omitted is the
account of the confused situation and the develop-

ments, both military and political, in Galilee, an ac-
count spiced with stories of plots and stratagems, re-
volts, ambushes, escapes, embassies, speeches, and
prophetic dreams.

And now I have a mind to say a few things to Justus, who has himself written a history concerning these affairs; and also to others who profess to write history but have little regard for truth, and are not afraid, either out of ill will or good will to some persons, to relate falsehoods. These men act like those who compose forged deeds and conveyances; and because they do not fear any corresponding punishment, they have no regard for truth. When, therefore, Justus undertook to write about these facts concerning the Jewish War, that he might appear to have been an industrious man, he falsified what he related about me, and could not speak truth even about his own country; whence it is that, being belied by him, I must defend myself.

And so I shall say what I have concealed till now; and let no one wonder that I have not told the world these things a long time ago; for although it is necessary for an historian to write the truth, yet he is not strictly bound to animadvert on the wickedness of other men—not out of any favor to them, but out of an author's own moderation. How then comes it to pass, O Justus!, most sagacious of writers (I address myself to him as if he were present), for so you boast of yourself, that I and the Galileans have been the authors of that sedition, which your city engaged in, both against the Romans and against the king—for even before I was appointed governor of Galilee by the authorities of Jerusalem, both you and all the people of Tiberias had not only taken up arms, but had made war with the cities of the Decapolis in Syria. Accordingly, you had ordered their villages to be burnt, and a domestic servant of yours fell in the battle. Nor is it I alone who say this; but it is so written in the commentaries of Vespasian, the emperor; also how the inhabitants of Decapolis came clamoring to Vespasian at Ptolemais, demanding that you, who were the culprit, might be brought to punishment; and you would certainly have been punished at the command of Vespasian had not King

Agrippa, who had power given him to have you put to death, changed the punishment from death into a long imprisonment at the earnest entreaty of his sister Berenice. Your political administration of affairs afterward also clearly revealed both your behavior in life, and that you were the cause of your country's revolt against the Romans, plain proofs of which I shall produce presently.

I also have a mind to say a few things to the rest of the people of Tiberias regarding you; and to demonstrate to those that light upon this history that you bear good will neither to the Romans nor to the king. To be sure, the greatest cities of Galilee were Sepphoris and your native Tiberias; but Sepphoris, situated in the very middle of Galilee and having many villages around it and able with ease to have been bold and troublesome to the Romans had they so desired—yet did it resolve to continue faithful to its masters, and at the same time excluded me from their city, and prohibited all their citizens from joining with the Jews in the war; and, that they might be out of danger from me, they, by a wile, induced me to fortify their city with walls; they also, of their own accord, admitted a garrison sent them by Cestius Gallus, who was then in command of Syria, and so held me in contempt, though I was then very powerful, and all were greatly afraid of me; and at the same time that the greatest of our cities, Jerusalem, was besieged, and our Temple, which belonged to us all, was in danger of falling under the enemy's power, they sent no assistance thither, unwilling as they were to have it thought they had borne arms against the Romans; but as for your city, O Justus!, situated upon the lake of Genesaret, and 30 furlongs from Hippo, 60 from Gadara, and 120 from Scythopolis, which was under the king's jurisdiction; when there was no Jewish city near, it might easily have preserved its fidelity to the Romans if it had so desired; for the city had plenty of men and weapons; but, you say, I was then the author of their revolt; and pray, O Justus!, who was that author *afterward?*—for you know that I was in the power of the Romans before Jerusalem was besieged, and before the same time Jotapata had been taken by force, as well as many other fortresses, and a great many of the Galileans had fallen in the war.

It was therefore then a proper time, when you were certainly freed from any fear of me, to throw away your weapons, and to demonstrate to the king and the Romans that it was not by choice but forced by necessity that you fell into the war against them; but you stayed till Vespasian himself came as close as your walls with his whole army; and then you did indeed lay aside your weapons out of fear, and your city would for certain have been taken by force had Vespasian not complied with the king's supplication for you and excused your madness. It was not I, therefore, who was the author of this, but your own inclinations to war. Do you not remember how often I got you under my power and yet put none of you to death?

Nay, you once fell into a tumult against one another, and slew one hundred and eighty-five of your citizens, not out of your good will to the king and the Romans, but out of your own wickedness, and this while I was besieged by the Romans in Jotapata. Nay, indeed, were there not reckoned up two thousand of the people of Tiberias during the siege of Jerusalem, some of whom were slain, and the rest captured and carried off as captives? But you will say that you did not engage in the war, since you then fled to the king! Yes, indeed, you did flee to him; but I say it was out of fear of me. You say, indeed, that it is I who am a wicked man. But then, for what reason was it that King Agrippa, who saved your life when you were condemned by Vespasian to die and who bestowed so much wealth upon you, did twice afterward put you in bonds, and as often obliged you to run away from your country, and, when he had once ordered you to be put to death, he granted you a pardon at the earnest request of Berenice? And when (after so many of your wicked pranks) he had made you his secretary, he caught you in further wrongdoing and drove you out of his sight. But I shall not inquire further into these matters of scandal against you.

Yet I cannot but wonder at your impudence, when you have the nerve to say that you have better related these affairs of the war than all the others who have written about them, while you did not know what was done in Galilee; for you were then at Berytus with the king; nor did you know how much the Romans suffered at the siege of Jotapata, or what miseries they brought upon us; nor could you learn by inquiry what I myself did during that siege; for all those that might offer such information were destroyed in that engagement. But perhaps you will say that you have written precisely about what was done against the people of Jerusalem. But how could that be? for neither were you present, nor have you read the commentaries of Caesar,[5] of which we have evident proof because you have contradicted those commentaries of Caesar in your history. But if you are so hardy as to affirm that you have written that history better than all the rest, why did you not publish your history while the emperors Vespasian and Titus, the generals of that war, as well as King Agrippa and his family, who were men well skilled in the learning of the Greeks, were all alive? for you have had it written these twenty years, and then you might have had testimony of eye witnesses regarding your accuracy. But now, when these men are no longer with us, and you think you cannot be contradicted, you venture to publish it.

As for me, I was not afraid of my own writing, but instead offered my books to the emperors themselves, even while the facts were almost under men's eyes; for I was self-confident that I had observed the truth of the facts; and even as I expected to have their attestation of that truth, so I was not deceived in my expectation. Moreover, I immediately presented my history to many other persons, some of whom were involved in the war, as was King Agrippa and some of his kindred. Now the emperor Titus was so desirous that knowledge of these affairs should be derived from these books alone that he subscribed his own hand to them and ordered that they be published.

As for King Agrippa, he wrote me sixty-two letters, attesting to the truth of what I had therein included; two of those letters I have here subjoined, and you may thus learn if you wish their contents: "King Agrippa to Josephus, his dear friend, sends greeting. I have read through your book with great pleasure, and it ap-

[5] I.e., Titus

pears to me that you have written it much more accurately, and with greater care, than have the other writers. Send me the rest of these books. Farewell, my dear friend."

"King Agrippa to Josephus, his dear friend, sends greeting. It seems by what you have written that you stand in need of no instruction, in order that we may learn everything from the beginning. However, when you come to me, I will inform you of a great many things which are not known." So once this history was completed, neither by way of flattery, which was not agreeable to him, nor by way of irony, as you will say, for he was entirely a stranger to such an evil disposition of mind, Agrippa wrote this by way of attestation to what was true, as all that read my works may do. So much for what shall be said concerning Justus, which I am obliged to add by way of digression.

> *The part of the* Life *dealing with further events of the war in which Josephus had an active part is omitted; these are fully described in the* War. *What is appended here are a few passages from that work relating to Josephus's withdrawal to Jotapata, his capture, his imprisonment, and liberation.*
>
> *In the late spring of 67* C.E. *Josephus left Tiberias for Jotapata. Book III of the* War *contains a full account of how the place was besieged by Vespasian, how it was defended, and how it was captured.*

And now the Romans searched for Josephus, both out of the hatred they bore him and because their general was very desirous to have him captured; he reckoned that once he were captured, the greatest part of the war would be over. They then searched among the dead, and looked into the most hidden recesses of the city; but as the city was taken first, he was assisted by a certain supernatural providence; for he escaped from the enemy while he was in their very midst and leaped into a deep pit, adjoining which was a large den at one side which could not be seen by those above ground; and there in that den he found forty persons of eminence who had concealed themselves, with enough provisions to last many days. So in the daytime he hid himself from the enemy, who had seized all the places; and at night, he emerged from the den and looked about for some way of escaping, taking exact note of the watch; but since all places were guarded everywhere because of him and since there was no way of escaping unseen, he went down again into the den.

Thus he hid for two days; but on the third day, after they had captured a woman who had been with them, he was discovered. Whereupon Vespasian immediately and zealously sent two tribunes, Paulinus and Gallicanus, ordering them to give Josephus their right hands as a security for his life and to exhort him to come up.

They came and invited him to come up, giving him assurances that his life would be preserved; but they did not prevail with him; for he became suspicious out of his certainty that one who had done so many things against the Romans must suffer for it, despite the mild manner of those inviting him. He was afraid that he was being invited to come up in order to be punished, until finally Vespasian sent a third tribune, Nicanor, one who was well known to Josephus, having been his familiar acquaintance in the old days. When Nicanor arrived, he enlarged upon the mildness of the Romans towards those they have conquered; and told him that he had behaved so valiantly that the commanders admired rather than hated him. The general was very anxious to have him brought to him, not in order to punish him, for that he could do even if he did not come voluntarily, but because he was determined to preserve a man of his courage. Moreover, Nicanor added, had Vespasian been resolved to trap him in an ambush, he would not have sent one of his own friends nor put the fairest coloration upon the vilest action by pretending friendship but meaning perfidiousness; nor would he himself have acquiesced to come to him, had it been to deceive him.

Now, as Josephus began to waver over Nicanor's proposal, the soldiers became so angry that they ran hastily to set fire to the den; but the officer, being very anxious to take Josephus alive, would not permit them to do so. And then, as Nicanor pressed Josephus to comply and the latter understood how the multitude of the enemy threatened him, he called to mind the dreams he had dreamed in the night, whereby God had signified to him beforehand both the future calamities of the Jews and the coming events concerning the Roman emperors. Now Josephus was able to offer shrewd conjectures about the interpretation of such dreams as were ambiguously delivered by God.[6] Moreover, being a priest himself and a descendant to priests, he was not unacquainted with the prophecies contained in the sacred books, and he was just then in a trance; and remembering the tremendous images of the dreams he had recently had, he sent up a secret prayer to God, saying, "Since it pleases You, who have created the Jewish nation, to oppress the same, and since all their good fortune is gone over to the Romans; and since You have chosen this soul of mine to foretell what is to come to pass hereafter, I willingly give myself up to the Romans and am content to live. And I take You as my witness that I do not go over to the Romans as a deserter of the Jews, but as Your minister."

Once he had said this, he was about to comply with Nicanor's invitation. But when those Jews who had fled with him understood that he was about to yield to those who were inviting him to come up, they encircled him in a body and cried out, "Nay, indeed, now may the laws of our forefathers, which God Himself ordained, well groan aloud; that God we mean who has created the souls of the Jews of such a temper that they despise death. O Josephus! are you still fond of life; and can you bear to see the light in a state of slavery? How quickly have you forgotten yourself! How many have you persuaded to offer their lives for liberty! You have therefore had a false reputation for manhood, and a similarly false reputation for wisdom, if you can hope for preservation from those against whom you have fought so zealously, and are willing to be preserved by them, if they are in earnest. But even though the good fortune of the Romans has made you forget yourself, we must see to it that the glory of our forefathers not be tarnished. We will lend you our right hand and a sword, and if you will die

[6] Perhaps this is an allusion to the interpretation of dreams by Joseph in Egypt. There are other passages in the works of Josephus in which he tells us of dreams and their significance.

willingly, you will die as general of the Jews; but if unwillingly, you will die as a traitor to them." As soon as they said this, they began to thrust their swords at him, threatening to kill him if he thought of yielding to the Romans.

Upon this, Josephus was afraid of their attacking him, and yet thought he would be a betrayer of God's commands if he died before he had delivered God's message. So he began to talk like a philosopher to them of the distress he was then in, saying to them: "O my friends, why are we so eager to kill ourselves? and why do we set our soul and body, which are such dear companions, at such variance? One says that I am not the man I was formerly. Nay, the Romans understand well enough how that matter stands. It is a brave thing to die in war, but only if it be according to the law of war, by the hand of conquerors. If, therefore, I avoid death from the sword of the Romans, I am truly worthy to be killed by my own sword and my own hand; but if they speak of mercy and would spare their enemy, how much more ought we to have mercy upon ourselves and spare ourselves! For it is certainly a foolish thing to do that to ourselves which we quarrel with them for doing to us.

"I confess freely that it is a brave thing to die for liberty, but only if it be in war and done by those who take that liberty from us; but at present our enemies do neither meet us in battle nor do they kill us. Now, he is equally a coward who will not die when he is obliged to die, and he who will die when he is not obliged so to do. What are we afraid of when we will not go up to the Romans? Is it not death? If so, what we are afraid of? When we but suspect our enemies will inflict it on us, shall we inflict it on ourselves for certain? But, it may be said, we must be slaves. And are we then in a clear state of liberty at present? It may also be said that it is a manly act for one to kill himself. No, certainly, but a most unmanly one, as I should esteem that pilot to be an arrant coward who, out of fear of a storm, should sink his ship of his own accord. Now, self-murder is a crime most remote from the common nature of all animals, and an example of lack of piety towards God our creator: nor indeed is there any animal that dies by its own contrivance or by its own means; for the desire for life is a law engraven in them all; on which account we deem those that openly take it away from us to be our enemies, and those that do it by treachery are punished for so doing.

"And do you not think that God is very angry when a man does injury to what He has bestowed on him? For from Him it is that we have received our being; and we ought to leave it to His disposal to take that being away from us. The bodies of all men are indeed mortal, and are created out of corruptible matter; but the soul is ever immortal, and is a portion of the divinity that inhabits our bodies. Besides, if any one destroys or abuses a deposit he has received from a mere man, he is esteemed a wicked and perfidious person; but then if any one cast out of his body this divine deposit, can we imagine that He who is there affronted does not know of it? Moreover, our law justly ordains that slaves who run away from their master shall be punished, though the masters they ran away from may have been wicked to them. And shall we endeavor to run away from God, who is the best of all masters, and not think ourselves highly guilty of impiety? Do you not know that those who depart from this life, according to the law of nature, and pay that debt which was received from God, when He that lent it to us is pleased to require it back, enjoy eternal fame? that their houses and their posterity are assured, that their souls are pure and obedient and obtain a most holy place in heaven, from whence, in the revolution of ages, they are again sent into pure bodies; while the souls of those whose hands have acted madly against themselves are received by the darkest place in Hades, and God, their father, punishes them in their posterity? for which reason God hates such doings, and the crime is punished by our most wise legislator.

"Accordingly, our laws determine that the bodies of such as kill themselves should be exposed till the sun sets,[7] without burial, although at the same time it be allowed by them to be lawful to bury our enemies. The laws of other nations also enjoin such

---

[7] There is no explicit prohibition in the Pentateuch directed against suicide; Josephus could here be referring to some later legal enactment. The arguments enumerated in the preceding passage against self-destruction are, of course, paralleled in Greek philosophical literature.

men's hands to be cut off when they are dead which had been made use of in destroying themselves when alive, while they reckoned that as the body is alien from the soul so is the hand alien from the body. It is therefore, my friends, a right thing to reason justly, and not add impiety towards our Creator to the calamities which men bring upon us. If we have a mind to preserve ourselves, let us do it; for to be preserved by our enemies, to whom we have given so many demonstrations of our courage, is in no way inglorious; but if we have a mind to die, it is good to die by the hand of those that have conquered us. For my part, I will not run over to our enemies' quarters in order to be a traitor to myself; for certainly I should then be much more foolish than those that deserted to the enemy, since they did it in order to save themselves, and I should do it for my own destruction. However, I heartily wish the Romans may prove treacherous in this matter: for if, after their offer of their right hand for security, I be slain by them, I shall die cheerfully, and carry away with me the sense of their perfidiousness as a consolation greater than victory itself."

Now these and many similar arguments did Josephus use with these men, to prevent their murdering themselves; but, having long ago devoted themselves to dying and desperation having shut their ears, they were irritated by Josephus. They then ran toward him with their swords in hand, one from one quarter and another from another, and called him a coward; and every one of them appeared openly as if he were ready to smite him; but he calling to one of them by name, and looking like a general to another, and taking a third by the hand, and making a fourth ashamed of himself by begging him to stop, and being in this condition distracted with various passions he kept every one of their swords from killing him, and was forced to act like such wild beasts as are surrounded on every side, who always turn against those that last touched them. Nay, some of their right hands were powerless because of the reverence they bore their general in his fatal calamities, and their swords dropped out of their hands; and not a few of them there were, who, even when they aimed to smite him with their swords, spontaneously dropped their weapons.

However, in his extreme distress, he was not destitute of his usual sagacity; but trusting himself to the providence of God, he put his life into jeopardy: "And now," said he, "since it is resolved among you that you will die, come, let us commit our mutual deaths to determination by lot. He whom the lot falls to first, let him be killed by him that has the second lot, and thus fortune shall make its progress through us all; nor shall any of us perish by his own right hand, for it would be unfair if, when the rest are gone, somebody should repent and save himself." This proposal appeared to them to be very just; and when he had prevailed with them to determine this matter by lots, he drew one of the lots for himself also. He who had the first lot laid his neck bare to him that had the next, in the belief that the general would die among them immediately; for they thought death, if Josephus might but die with them, was sweeter than life; yet he was left with another to the last, whether we must say it happened so by chance, or whether by the providence of God; and as he was very anxious neither to be condemned by the lot, nor, were he to be left to the last, to bathe his right hand in the blood of his countryman, he persuaded him to place his trust in him and to live as well as himself.

Thus Josephus escaped in the war with the Romans and in his own war with his friends, and was led by Nicanor to Vespasian; but now all the Romans ran together to see him, and as the multitude pressed around their general, there was a tumult of various kinds; while some rejoiced that Josephus was captured, some threatened him and others crowded around to see him close; but those that were further away cried out to have their enemy put to death, while those that were near remembered his actions, and an amazement appeared over the change in his fortune. Nor were there any of the Roman commanders, however much they had been enraged against him before, who did not relent when they saw him. Above all, Josephus's patience under affliction made Titus pity him, as did also consideration of his age; he remembered that only a short while ago Josephus was fighting, and now he lay in the hands of his enemies. This led Titus to consider the power of fortune, and how quick is the turn of affairs in war, and how insecure is the state of man; he then influenced a great many others to be of the same forgiving nature as himself, inducing them to be lenient with Josephus. He was also of great weight in persuading his father to save him. However, Vespasian gave orders that he should be held with great caution, intending in a short time to send him to Nero.

When Josephus heard him give those orders, he said that he had something in his mind that he wanted to say to the emperor alone. When therefore all were ordered to withdraw, save Titus and two of their friends, Josephus said, "You, O Vespasian, think no more than that you have taken Josephus himself captive; but I come to you as a messenger of greater tidings; for had I not been sent by God to you, I knew the law of the Jews in this case and how it becomes generals to die. You're sending me to Nero? Why? Are Nero's successors, who stand between you and the throne, going to survive? You, O Vespasian, are Caesar and emperor, you, and this your son. Bind me now still tighter, and keep me for yourself, for you, O Caesar, are lord not only over me but over the land and the sea, and all mankind; and certainly, in order to be punished, I deserve to be held in closer custody than I am now in, if I rashly affirm anything of God."

After he had said this, Vespasian did not immediately seem to believe him, but supposed that Josephus was saying this as a cunning trick in order to save himself; but in a short time he was convinced, and believed what he said to be true, for God Himself was raising his expectations of obtaining the empire, and by other signs foreshadowing his advancement. He had also found Josephus to have spoken truth on other occasions; for one of those friends present at that secret conference said, "I cannot but wonder why you could not foretell for the people of Jotapata that they would be conquered, nor could you foretell your own captivity, unless what you now say be a vain thing, in order to avoid the anger that has arisen against yourself."

To which Josephus replied, "I did foretell to the people of Jotapata that they would be captured after the forty-seventh day, and that I would be taken alive by the Romans." Now when Vespasian had inquired of the captives privately about these predictions, he found them to be true, and then he began to believe the ones concerning himself. But he did not yet set Josephus free from guard and chains, but instead bestowed on him suits of clothes and other precious gifts; he continued to treat him also in a very kindly manner, with Titus also expressing interest in the honors done him.[8]

The following passage is the conclusion of the Life.

When the siege of Jotapata was over and I was among the Romans, I was treated under guard with every consideration. Vespasian showed me great respect. Moreover, at his command, I married a virgin from among the captives, yet she did not live with me long; after my being freed from my bonds and going to Alexandria with Vespasian, we were divorced. However, I married another wife in Alexandria, and was thence sent, together with Titus, to the siege of Jerusalem; I was frequently in danger of being put to death—since the Jews were very eager to get me under their power in order to have me punished, and the Romans also, whenever they were beaten, supposed their defeat was occasioned by my treachery, and made continual complaints to the emperor asking him to bring me to punishment as a traitor to them; but Titus Caesar was well acquainted with the uncertain fortune of war, and refused to answer the soldiers' vehement solicitations against me.

Moreover, when the city of Jerusalem was taken by force, Titus Caesar persuaded me frequently to take whatsoever I would of the ruins of my country, saying that he gave me leave so to do; but when my country was destroyed, I thought nothing else to be of any value which I could take and keep as a comfort for my calamities; so I made a request to Titus that some of my fellow countrymen might be given their liberty; I also had the Holy Books by Titus's concession; nor was it long after that I requested of him the life and freedom of my brother, and of fifty friends, and was not denied. When I also went once to the Temple, by permission of Titus, where there were a great multitude of captive women

[8] On the questions raised by this story see Introduction, pp. 18–19.

and children, I arranged for all those that I remembered among my own friends and acquaintances, numbering about one hundred ninety, to be set free: and so I delivered them, without their paying any price of redemption, and restored them to their former fortunes; and when I was sent by Titus Caesar with Cerealius and a thousand horsemen to a certain village called Thecoa, in order to ascertain whether it was a place fit for camp, as I came back I saw many captives crucified, among them three former acquaintances. I was very affected by this, and went with tears in my eyes to Titus and told him of them; so he immediately commanded them to be taken down from the scaffold, and to have the greatest care taken of them in order to make sure of their recovery; yet two of them died under the physician's hands, while the third recovered.

But after Titus had settled the troubles in Judea, and conjectured that the lands I had in Jerusalem would bring me no profit because a garrison of Romans was soon afterward to be stationed there, he gave me another estate in the plains; and as he was departing for Rome, he selected me to sail along with him, and paid me great respect; and when we arrived in Rome, I had great care taken of me by Vespasian; he gave me an apartment in his own house, where he had lived before he became emperor. He also honored me with the privilege of Roman citizenship, and gave me a pension; he continued to respect me to the end of his life, without any abatement of his kindness to me, which very thing made me envied and brought me into danger; for a certain Jew named Jonathan, who had raised a tumult in Cyrene, and had persuaded two thousand men of that country to join with him, was the occasion of their ruin; but when he was bound by the governor of that country and sent to the emperor, he told him that I had sent him both weapons and money. However, he could not conceal his being a liar from Vespasian, who condemned him to die; according to which sentence he was put to death.

Nay, after that, when those that envied my good fortune did frequently bring accusations against me, by God's providence I escaped them all. I also received from Vespasian no small quantity of land as a free gift in Judea; about this time I also divorced my wife, not being pleased with her behavior, but not till she had given birth to three children, two of whom are dead and one whom I had named Hyrcanus is alive. After this I married a wife who had lived in Crete but was a Jewess by birth; a woman with eminent parents, the most illustrious in all the country, and whose character was beyond that of many other women, as her future life did demonstrate. By her I had two sons; the elder's name was Justus, and the next Simonides, who was also named Agrippa; and these were the circumstances of my domestic affairs. However, the kindness of the emperor toward me continued as before; for after Vespasian died, Titus, who succeeded him in the government, maintained the same respect for me which I had had from his father; and frequently when accusations were laid against me, he refused to believe them; and Domitian, who succeeded, still augmented his respects to me, punishing those Jews that were my accusers, and commanding that a servant of mine, my son's tutor, a eunuch and my accuser, should be punished. He also made that estate I had in Judea tax-free, which is a mark of the greatest honor to him who has it; and also, Domitia, the wife of the emperor, continued to do me kindnesses. This is the account of my whole life; let others judge my character as they please; and so, for the present, I here conclude my narrative.

PART TWO

Against Apion

PART TWO

I suppose that, through my books on the antiquities of the Jews, I have made it evident to those who peruse them that our Jewish nation is of very great antiquity [1] and had originally a distinct existence of its own; also, I have therein declared how we came to inhabit this country where we now live. Those *Antiquities* contain the history of five thousand years, and are taken out of our sacred books, but are translated by me into the Greek tongue. However, since I observe a considerable number of persons giving ear to the reproaches laid against us by those who bear us ill will, and will not believe what I have written concerning the antiquity of our nation, taking it for a plain sign that our nation is of a recent date that we are not so much as vouchsafed a bare mention by the most famous historiographers among the Grecians, I therefore have thought myself under an obligation to write briefly about all these subjects in order to convict those that reproach us of spite and deliberate falsehood, and to correct the ignorance of others, and withal to instruct all those desirous of knowing the truth.

[1] Great importance is attached in ancient literature generally to "antiquity" and autochthonous origin of nations, races, states, and families.

As for the witnesses whom I shall produce for the proof of what I say, they shall be such as are esteemed by the Greeks themselves to have the greatest reputation for truth, and to be the most skillful in the knowledge of all antiquity. I shall also show that those who have written so reproachfully and falsely about us are to be convicted by what they have written themselves to the contrary. I shall also endeavor to give an account of the reasons why it has happened that there have not been a great number of Greeks who have made mention of our nation in their histories. I will, however, bring those Grecians to light who have not omitted our history, for the sake of those that either do not know them, or pretend not to know them yet.

And now, in the first place, I cannot but greatly wonder at those men who suppose that we must pay attention to none but Grecians when we are inquiring about the most ancient facts, and must inform ourselves of their truth only from them, while we must not believe ourselves or other men; for I am convinced that the very reverse is the truth. I mean this—if we will not be led by vain opinions but will make inquiry after truth from the facts themselves—we will find that almost all that concerns the Greeks happened not long ago, in fact, one may say, only yesterday. I speak of the foundation of their cities, the invention of their arts, and the setting down of their laws; and as for their care about the writing down of their histories, it is very nearly the last thing they set about. However, at least they acknowledge that it is the Egyptians, the Chaldeans, and the Phoenicians (for I will not now reckon ourselves among them), that have preserved the memorials of the most ancient and most lasting traditions of mankind; for all these nations inhabit such countries as are least subject to destruction from the atmosphere; and these also have taken especial care to have nothing omitted of what was done among them; but their history was esteemed sacred and put into public tables, as written by men of the greatest wisdom they had among them; but as for the place the Grecians inhabit, ten thousand destructions [2] have

[2] Stories similar to the account of the Flood were current among the Greeks.

overtaken it and blotted out the memory of former actions; so that they were ever beginning a new way of living, and each group supposed that it was the origin of the new state.

It was also late, and with difficulty, that they came to know the letters they now use; for those who would advance their use of these letters to the greatest antiquity assert that they learned them from the Phoenicians and from Cadmus; [3] yet is nobody able to demonstrate that they have any writing preserved from the time, neither in their temples, nor in any other public monuments. The time when those lived who went to the Trojan War, so many years afterward, is in great doubt, and great inquiry is made whether the Greeks used their letters at that time; and the most prevailing opinion and that nearest the truth is that their present way of using those letters was unknown at that time. However, there is no writing which the Greeks agree to be genuine among them more ancient than Homer's poems, which must plainly be confessed later than the siege of Troy; nay, the report goes, that even he did not leave his poems in writing, but that their memory was preserved in songs, and they were put together afterward; and this is the reason for such a number of variations as are found in them. [4] As for those who set themselves about writing their histories, I mean such as Cadmus of Miletus, and Acusilaus of Argos, and any others that may be mentioned as succeeding Acusilaus, they lived but a little while before the Persian expedition into Greece. But then for those that first introduced philosophy, and the consideration of things celestial and divine among them, such as Pherecydes and Pythagoras, and Thales, all with one consent agree that they learned what they knew of the Egyptians and Chaldeans, and wrote but little. And these are the things which are supposed to be

---

[3] That the Greek alphabet was derived from Semitic sources was recognized by the Greeks. Cf. Herodotus, V.58. Most letters in the Greek alphabet correspond both in their phonetic value and in their place in the series to corresponding Hebrew letters. Their names are basically the same, and in most cases their *numerical* value coincides with that of their Hebrew counterparts.

[4] This is one of the important passages used in the discussion of the so-called Homeric question.

the oldest of all among the Greeks; and they have much ado to believe that the writings ascribed to those men are genuine.[5]

How can it then be other than absurd for the Greeks to be so proud, and to vaunt themselves to be the only people that are acquainted with antiquity, and that have delivered the true accounts of those early times in an accurate manner! Nay, who is there that cannot easily gather from the Greek writers themselves that they knew but little on any good foundation when they set out to write, but rather wrote their histories from their own conjecture? Accordingly, they confute one another in their own books on purpose, and are not ashamed to give us the most contradictory accounts of the same things.

As for the causes of this great disagreement of theirs, there may be assigned many that are very probable, if any have a mind to make inquiry about them; but I ascribe these contradictions chiefly to two causes, which I will now mention, and still think what I shall mention in the first place to be the principal of all; for if we remember that in the beginning the Greeks had taken no care to have public records of their several transactions preserved, this must for certain have afforded those that would afterward write about those ancient transactions the opportunity of making mistakes, and the power of making lies also; for this original recording of such ancient transactions had not only been neglected by the other states of Greece; but even among the Athenians themselves, who are said to be autochthonous and to have applied themselves to learning, there are no such records extant; nay, they say themselves that the laws of Draco concerning murders are the most ancient of their public records; yet that Draco lived but a short time before the tyrant Pisistratus.[6] As for the Arcadians, who make such boasts of their antiquity, there is no need to speak of them in particular, since it was still later before they got their letters and learned them, and that with difficulty also.

There must therefore naturally arise great differences among

[5] It is a remarkable fact that in the *Greek* reports concerning their sages and philosophers there appear with great frequency acknowledgments of oriental influence.

[6] Pisistratus was tyrant of Athens in the sixth century B.C.E.

writers, when they had no original records to lay for their foundation, which might at once inform those who had an inclination to learn, and contradict those that would tell lies. However, we are to suppose a second occasion besides the former of these contradictions; it is this: That those who were the most zealous to write history were not solicitous for the discovery of truth, although it was very easy for them always to make such a profession; but their business was to demonstrate that they could write well, and make an impression upon mankind thereby; and in what manner of writing they thought they were able to exceed others, to that did they apply themselves. Some of them betook themselves to the writing of fabulous narrations; some endeavored to please the cities or the kings, by writing in their commendation; others fell to finding faults with transactions, or with the writers of such transactions, and thought to make a great figure by so doing; and indeed these do what is of all things the most contrary to true history; for it is the great proof of true history that all concerned therein both speak and write the same things; while these men, by writing differently about the same things, thought they would be believed to write with the greatest regard to truth. We therefore must yield to the Grecian writers as to language and eloquence of composition; but then we shall give them no such preference as to the verity of ancient history; and least of all as to that part which concerns the affairs of our own several countries.

As to the care of writing down the records from the earliest antiquity among the Egyptians and Babylonians: that the priests of the former were entrusted therewith, and employed a philosophical concern about it; that it was the Chaldeans that did so among the Babylonians; and that the Phoenicians, who were mingled among the Greeks, did especially make use of their letters, both for the common affairs of life and for recording the history of common transactions, I think I may omit any proof, because all men allow it so to be; but now as to our forefathers, that they took no less care about writing such records (for I will not say they took greater care than the others I spoke of), and that they committed that matter to their high priests and to their prophets, and that these records have been written down all along to our own times with the utmost accuracy; nay, if it be not too bold for me to say it, our history will be so written hereafter; I shall endeavor briefly to inform you.[7]

For our forefathers did not only appoint the best of these priests, and those that attended upon the divine worship, for that design from the beginning, but took precautions that stock of the priests should continue unmixed and pure; for he who is partaker of the priesthood must propagate with a wife of the same nation [8] without having any regard to money, or any other dignities; but he is to make a scrutiny, and take his wife's genealogy from the ancient tables, and procure many witnesses to it; and this is our practice, not only in Judea but wheresoever any body of men of our nation do live; and even there an exact catalogue of our priests' marriages is kept: I mean in Egypt and in Babylon, or in any other place of the rest of the habitable earth, whithersoever our priests are scattered; for they send to Jerusalem names of the bride, her father, and her more remote ancestors, and signify who the witnesses are also; but if any war breaks out, such as have broken out a great many already, when Antiochus Epiphanes made an invasion upon our country, as also when Pompey the Great and Quintilius Varus did so also, and principally in the wars that have happened in our own times, those priests that survive them compose new tables of genealogy out of the old records, and examine the circumstances of the women that remain; for still they do not admit those that have been captives, suspecting that they had had intercourse with foreigners.[9]

---

[7] Josephus here seems to confuse the keeping of genealogical registers by the priests in the Second Temple period with genuine historical writing. As to the mention of prophets as keepers of historical records, H. St. J. Thackeray rightly points out, in his *Josephus, The Man and the Historian,* that the historical books of the Old Testament are included in the prophetical part of the rabbinic canon. See Babylonian Talmud, *Bava Batra,* 14b–15a, where the authorship of the historical works is ascribed to prophets (Samuel: his Book and Judges; Jeremiah: his Book and Kings; etc.)

[8] See Leviticus, Chapter 21.

[9] Josephus himself tells us that, at the command of Vespasian, he married a captive. He divorced her when shortly afterwards he obtained his release. It may be that the prohibition against a priest (such as Josephus) marrying

But what is the strongest argument of our exact management in this matter is what I am now going to say, that we have the names of our high priests, from father to son, set down in our records, for the interval of two thousand years; and if any one of these have been transgressors of these rules they are prohibited from presenting themselves at the altar, or partaking of any other of our rituals; and this is justly, or rather necessarily done, because every one is not permitted of his own accord to be a writer, nor is there any disagreement in what is written; they being only prophets that have written the original and earliest accounts of things as they learned them from God Himself by inspiration; and others have written what has happened in their own times, and that in a very distinct manner also. Thus, we have not an innumerable multitude of books among us, disagreeing from and contradicting one another, but only twenty-two books,[10] which contain the records of all the past times; which are justly believed to be divine; and of them, five being of Moses, which contain his laws, and the traditions of the origin of mankind till his death. This interval of time was little short of three thousand years; but as to the time from the death of Moses till the reign of Artaxerxes, King of Persia, who reigned after Xerxes, the prophets, who were after Moses, wrote down what was done in their times in 13 books. The remaining four books contain hymns to God and precepts for the conduct of human life.

It is true that our history which has been written since Artaxerxes in every detail has not been esteemed of the same authority as the former, because there has not been an exact succession of prophets since that time; and how firmly we have given credit to those books of our own nation is evident by what we do; for dur-

---

a captive woman played some part in the decision that led to the separation.

[10] We now reckon the number of books in the Hebrew Bible as 24, corresponding to the number of letters in the Greek alphabet. It is interesting that the rabbinic tradition uses a Greek division (compare the epics of Homer) whereas the Alexandrian-Jewish, septuagintal, and Christian traditions in antiquity, like Josephus, follow a Hebrew model. There are, of course, twenty-two letters in the Hebrew alphabet.

ing so many ages as have already passed, no one has been bold enough either to add anything to them or take anything from them, or to make any change in them; but it becomes natural to all Jews, immediately and from their very birth, to esteem those books to contain divine doctrines, and to persist in them, and, if occasion arises, willingly to die for them. For it is no new thing for our captives, many in number and frequently in time, to be seen to endure torture and deaths of all kinds in theaters so as not to be obliged to say one word against our laws and the records that contain them; whereas, there are none at all among the Greeks who would undergo the least harm on that account, no, nor in the event all the writings among them were to be destroyed; for they take them to be such discourses as are framed agreeably to the inclinations of those that write them; and they have justly the same opinion of the ancient writers, since they see some of the present generation bold enough to write about such affairs wherein they were not present, nor had concern enough to inform themselves about them from those that knew them; examples of which may be had in this late war of ours, where some persons, without having been in the places involved, or having been near when the actions took place put a few things together by hearsay and insolently abuse the world, and call their writings histories.

As for myself, I have composed a true history of that whole war, and all the particulars that occurred therein, as having been concerned in all its transactions; for I acted as general of those among us named Galileans, as long as it was possible for us to make any opposition. I was then seized by the Romans, and taken captive. Vespasian also and Titus had kept me under guard, and forced me to serve them continually. At first I was put into bonds, but was set at liberty afterward and sent to accompany Titus when he came from Alexandria to the siege of Jerusalem; during which time there was nothing done which escaped my knowledge; for what happened in the Roman camp I saw and wrote down carefully; and what information the deserters brought I was the only man that understood.

Afterward I was at leisure in Rome; and when all my materials were prepared for that work, I made use of some persons as assistants for the sake of the Greek tongue, and by these means I composed the history of those transactions; and I was so well assured of the truth of what I related that I first of all appealed to those who had the supreme command in that war, Vespasian and Titus, as my witnesses, for to them I presented those books first of all, and after them to many of the Romans who had been in that war. I also sold them to many of our own men who understood Greek learning. Now all these men testified that I had the strictest regard to truth; who yet would not have dissembled the matter, nor been silent, if I, out of ignorance or favor to any side had either given false colors to actions or omitted any of them.

There have indeed been some bad men, who have attempted to calumniate my history, and took it to be a kind of scholastic performance for the exercise of young men. A strange sort of accusation and calumny this since every one that undertakes to deliver the history of actions truly ought to know them accurately himself in the first place, as either having been involved in them himself, or having been informed of them by such as knew them. Now, both these methods of knowledge I may very properly lay claim to in the composition of both my works; for, as I said, I have translated the Antiquities out of our sacred books,[11] which I easily could do since I was a priest by birth, and have studied that philosophy contained in those writings; and as for the History of the War, I wrote it as an actor myself in many of its transactions, an eyewitness to the greatest part of the rest, and not unacquainted with anything whatsoever that was either said or done in it. How impudent, then, those who undertake to contradict me about the true state of those affairs! who, although they pretend to have made use of both emperors' own memoirs, yet could not be acquainted with our affairs who fought against them.

This digression I have been obliged to make out of necessity, desirous as I am of exposing the irresponsibility of those profess-

[11] In those parts of the *Antiquities* that coincide with the biblical account, Josephus is, of course, heavily dependent on the Greek Bible.

ing to write histories; and I suppose I have sufficiently declared that this custom of transmitting the histories of ancient times has been better preserved by those nations which are called barbarians [12] than by the Greeks themselves. I am now willing, in the next place, to say a few things to those who endeavor to prove that our constitution is but of recent date, for the reason that the Greek writers have said nothing about us; after which I shall produce testimonies for our antiquity out of the writings of foreigners; I shall also demonstrate that such as cast reproaches upon our nation do so very unjustly.

As for ourselves, therefore, we neither inhabit a maritime country,[13] nor do we delight in merchandise nor in such a mixture with other men as arises from it; but the cities we dwell in are remote from the sea, and, having a fruitful country for our habitation, we take pains in cultivating that only. Our principal care of all is this, to educate our children well; and we think it to be the most necessary business of our whole life to observe the laws that have been given us, and to keep those rules of piety that have been delivered down to us. Since, therefore, besides what we have already taken notice of, we have had a unique way of living of our own, there was no occasion offered us in ancient ages for intermixing among the Greeks, as they had for mixing among the Egyptians, by their intercourse of exporting and importing their several goods; as they also mixed with the Phoenicians, who lived by the seaside, by means of their love of lucre in trade and merchandise.

Nor did our forefathers betake themselves, as did some others, to robbery; nor did they, in order to gain more wealth, fall into foreign wars, although our country contained many ten thousands of men of courage sufficient for that purpose; for this reason the Phoenicians themselves came soon by trading and navigation to be known to the Grecians, and by their means the Egyptians became

---

[12] I.e., non-Greeks.

[13] Judea was an inland country. It was only in the Hasmonean period that Jewish rule reached the Mediterranean coast. All the biblical evidence confirms Josephus's statement that the Jews were predominantly an agricultural rather than a mercantile nation. Note also the emphasis on education, typical of Jewish life through the ages.

known to the Grecians also, as did all those people whose wares the Phoenicians carried in long voyages over the seas to the Grecians. The Medes also and the Persians, when they were lords of Asia, became well known to them; and this was especially true of the Persians, who led their armies as far as Europe. The Thracians were also known to them by the nearness of their countries, and Scythians by means of those that sailed to Pontus; for it was so in general that all maritime nations, and those that lived near the eastern or western seas, became most known to those desirous to be writers; but such as had their habitations further from the sea were for the most part unknown to them; which things appear to have happened with Europe also, with the city of Rome that has so long been possessed of so much power and has performed such great actions in war, never being mentioned by Herodotus, Thucydides, nor by any of their contemporaries; and it was very late and with great difficulty that the Romans became known to the Greeks.

Nay, those that were reckoned the most exact historians were so ignorant of the Gauls and the Spaniards that they supposed the Spaniards, who inhabited so great a part of the western regions of the earth, to be no more than one city. Those historians also have ventured to describe such customs as were made use of by them which they had never done or said; and the reason why these writers did not know the truth of their affairs was this, that they had no commerce together; but the reason they wrote such falsities was this, that they had a mind to appear to know things unknown to others. How can it then be any wonder if our nation was no more known to many of the Greeks, nor had given them any occasion to be mentioned in their writings, since they were so remote from the sea and had a conduct of life so peculiar to themselves?

Let us now suppose, therefore, that we made use of this argument concerning the Grecians in order to prove that their nation was not ancient, that nothing is said of them in our records; would they not laugh at us all and probably give the same reasons for our silences that I have now alleged, and produce their neighboring nations as witnesses to their own antiquity? Now, the very same thing will I endeavor to do; for I will bring the Egyptians and Phoenicians as my principal witnesses, because nobody can complain of their testimony as false, since they are known to have borne the greatest ill will towards us; I mean this as regards the Egyptians, all of them, while the Phoenicians, the Tyrians, have been most of all similarly ill disposed towards us; yet do I confess that I cannot say the same of the Chaldeans, since our first leaders and ancestors were derived from them; and they do make mention of us Jews in their records on account of the kindred between us. Now, when I shall have made my assertions good, as far as the others are concerned, I will demonstrate that some of the Greek writers have made mention of us Jews also; that those who envy us may not have even this pretence for contradicting what I have said about our nation.

Josephus goes on to quote at length from a number of non-Jewish sources passages testifying to the antiquity of the Jewish nation. He cites, among others, Manetho, an Egyptian priest of the early Hellenistic period who wrote a history of his country (in Greek) in three volumes. In this work he had mentioned the Hyksos (perhaps these are the shepherd kings) who ruled Egypt for a period of some centuries during the first half of the second millennium B.C.E. *They were expelled from Egypt in the sixteenth century* B.C.E. *Josephus sees in them the ancestors of the Jews and identifies the account of their expulsion with that of Exodus.*

Josephus quotes evidence from Phoenician records bearing witness inter alia *to the building of the Temple in Jerusalem by Solomon. He also quotes from Berosus, a Babylonian priest of ca. 330–250* B.C.E., *who wrote in Greek on Chaldean astronomy, philosophy and history. Berosus had mentioned the Flood, the taking of Jerusalem by Nebuchadnezzar, the transportation of the Jewish population to Babylon, and the return from exile under Cyrus.*

In a number of passages quoted from Greek historical and philosophical writers, Josephus finds (or

pretends to find) evidence among the Greeks of early knowledge of Jewish and Palestinian matters.
In one of these passages the following interesting anecdote is recounted.

But now it is easy for any one to know that not only the lowest sort of Grecians, but those held in the greatest admiration for their philosophic improvements, did not only know the Jews but, when they lighted upon any of them, also admired them; for Clearchus, who was the pupil of Aristotle and inferior to no one of the Peripatetics whomsoever, in his first book concerning sleep, says that "Aristotle, his master, related what follows of a Jew," and sets down Aristotle's own discourse with him. The account is this, as written down by him: "Now, a great part of what this Jew said would be too long to recite; but what includes in it both wonder and philosophy, it may not be amiss to discourse of. Now, that I may be plain with you, Hyperochides, I shall herein seem to you to relate wonders, and what will resemble dreams themselves."

Hereupon Hyperochides answered modestly, and said, "For that very reason all of us are very desirous of hearing what you are going to say." Then replied Aristotle, "It will be best first to give an account of the man and of what nation he was." Then said Hyperochides, "Go on, if it so pleases you." "This man then," answered Aristotle, "was by birth a Jew, and came from Celesyria; these Jews are descended from the Indian philosophers; they are named by the Indians Calani, and by the Syrians Jews, and took their name from the country they inhabit, which is called Judea; but for the name of their city it is a very awkward one, for they call it Jerusalem. Now, this man, when he was hospitably treated by a great many, came down from the upper country to the places near the sea, and became a Grecian, not only in his language, but in his soul also; insomuch that when we ourselves happened to be in Asia [14] about the same places whither he came he conversed with us and with some other philosophical persons, and made a trial of our skill in philosophy; and as he had lived with many

[14] Aristotle spent some years in Asia Minor after his master Plato died.

learned men, he communicated to us more information than he received from us." This is Aristotle's account of the matter, as given us by Clearchus, in which Aristotle discoursed also particularly of the great and wonderful fortitude of this Jew in his diet, and continent way of living, as those that wish may learn more about from Clearchus's book itself; for I avoid setting down any more than is sufficient for my purpose.

> *If the following extracts from Hecateus, a Greek historian, fourth–third century, are genuine, we have here an interesting Greek reaction to the Jews and their character as well as early Gentile evidence for the beginnings of Jewish settlement in Alexandria.*

Again, Hecateus says to the same purpose as follows: "Ptolemy got possession of the places in Syria after the battle of Gaza; and many, when they heard of Ptolemy's moderation and humanity, desired to go along with him to Egypt, and to participate in his affairs; one of whom, Hecateus says, was Hezekiah, the chief priest of the Jews; a man of about sixty-six years of age, and in great dignity among his own people. He was a very sensible man, and could speak very movingly, and was very skillful in the management of affairs. Hecateus mentions this Hezekiah a second time, and says that "as he was possessed of so great a dignity, and had become familiar with us, so did he take certain of those that were with him and explained to them all the circumstances of their people; for he had all their habitations and polity down in writing." [15]

Moreover, Hecateus declares again what regard the Jews have for their laws, and that they resolve to endure anything rather than transgress them, because they think it right for them to do so. Whereupon he adds that, although they are ill spoken of among their neighbors, and among all those that come to them, and have often been treated injuriously by the kings and governors of Per-

---

[15] Referring probably to the conditions under which Jews could settle in Alexandria.

sia, yet they cannot be dissuaded from acting as they think best; but that when they are stripped on this account and have torments inflicted upon them and are brought to the most terrible kinds of death, they meet them in a most extraordinary manner, beyond all other people, and will not renounce the religion of their forefathers.

Hecateus also produces not a few demonstrations of their resolute tenaciousness to their laws, when he speaks thus: "Alexander was once at Babylon, and had an intention to rebuild the temple of Belus that had fallen into decay, and in order to do this he commanded all his soldiers to bring earth thither. But the Jews, and they only, would not comply with that command; nay, they underwent stripes and great losses of what they had on this account, till the king forgave them and permitted them to live in quiet." He speaks also of the mighty populousness of our nation, and says that the Persians [16] formerly carried away many ten thousands of our people to Babylon, and also that not a few ten thousands moved after Alexander's death into Egypt and Phoenicia because of the sedition that had arisen in Syria. The same person takes notice in his history of how large the country was which we inhabited as well as of its excellent character, saying that "the land which the Jews inhabit contains almost three millions of arourae [17] and is generally of a most excellent and most fruitful soil."

The same man describes our city of Jerusalem also as of a most excellent structure, and very large, and inhabited since the most ancient times. He also discourses of the multitude of men in it, and of the construction of our Temple, after the following manner: "There are many strong places and villages, says he, in the country of Judea; but one strong city there is, about fifty furlongs in circumference, which is inhabited by a hundred and twenty thousand men, or thereabouts; they call it Jerusalem. There is about the

[16] A mistake for Babylonians. Such a mistake is more easily understandable in a foreign writer than in a Jewish forger of a pseudo-Greek historical work.
[17] An aroura is approximately two-thirds of an acre.

middle of the city a wall of stone, the length of which is five hundred feet and the breadth a hundred cubits, with double gates; wherein there is a square altar, not made of hewn stone, but composed of unworked stones gathered together, having each side twenty cubits long, and its altitude ten cubits. Hard by it is a large edifice, wherein there is an altar and a candlestick, both of gold, and in weight two talents; upon these there is a light that is never extinguished, neither by night nor by day. There is no image, nor anything, nor any donations therein; nothing at all is planted there neither grove nor anything of that sort. The priests abide therein both night and day, performing certain purifications and drinking not the least drop of wine while they are in the Temple." Moreover, he attests that we Jews went as auxiliaries along with King Alexander; after him with his successors. I shall not think it too much for me to name Agatharchides as having made mention of us Jews, though deriding our simplicity, as he supposes it to be.

> *There follows an extract from Agatharchides, a writer of the second century* B.C.E. *Note the interesting reference to the observance of the Sabbath and its consequences.*

"There are a people called Jews, who dwell in a city which is stronger than all other cities, which the inhabitants call Jerusalem, and who are accustomed to rest on every seventh day; at which times they make no use of their arms, nor meddle with husbandry, nor take care of any affairs of life, but spread out their hands in their holy places and pray till the evening. Now it came to pass that when Ptolemy, the son of Lagus, came into this city with his army, these men, in observing this mad custom of theirs, instead of guarding the city, suffered their country to submit itself to a bitter lord; and their law was openly proved to have commanded a foolish practice. This accident taught all other men but the Jews to disregard such dreams as these were, and not to follow similar idle suggestions delivered as a law, when, in such uncertainty of human reasonings, they are at a loss what they should do." Now this procedure of ours seems a ridiculous thing to Agatharchides, but will appear to such as consider it without prejudice a great thing, deserving a great many encomiums, that certain men constantly put the observation of their laws and their religion towards God before the preservation of themselves and their country.[18]

The following extract introduces an interesting account of ancient anti-Semitism.

One particular there is still remaining behind what I at first proposed to speak to, and that is to demonstrate that those calumnies and reproaches which some have thrown upon our nation are lies, and to make use of those writers' own testimonies against themselves; and that in general this self-contradiction has happened to many other authors by reason of their ill will to some people, I conclude, and is not unknown to those who have read histories with sufficient care.

Now the Egyptians were the first that cast reproaches upon us. In order to please that nation, some others undertook to pervert the truth, while they would neither own that our forefathers came into Egypt from another country, as the fact was, nor give a true account of our departure thence; and indeed the Egyptians took many occasions to hate and envy us, in the first place, because our ancestors had had the dominion over their country,[19] and when they were delivered from them and had returned to their own country again, they lived there in prosperity.

In the next place, the difference of our religion from theirs has occasioned great enmity between us, while our way of divine worship did as much exceed that which their laws appointed as does the nature of God exceed that of brute beasts; for so far they all agree through the whole country to esteem animals as gods, although they differ from one another in the peculiar worship they severally pay to them; and, certainly, they are men entirely of vain

[18] There is evidence in the Jewish literature of the period that some rabbis allowed the desecration of the Sabbath in case of military necessity. In any case, rabbinic law recognizes that the duty to save life overrides the obligation of Sabbath observance.
[19] A reference to the Hyksos; see above p. 64.

and foolish minds who have thus accustomed themselves from the beginning to have such bad notions concerning their gods, and could not think of imitating that decent form of divine worship which we made use of; though, when they saw our institutions approved of by many others, they could not but envy us on that account; for some of them have proceeded to that degree of folly and meanness in their conduct as not to scruple to contradict their ancient writings, and yet were so blinded by their passions as not to discern it.

Among other calumnies of Manetho and other writers a story is quoted according to which the ancestors of the Jews were connected with a group of lepers and other polluted persons who were banished from Egypt and who made common cause with the people of Jerusalem.

According to Manetho, Moses himself was an Egyptian priest who was expelled from Egypt because he was affected by leprosy. Among Jewish laws criticized by Manetho was that against idolatry. This is represented by Manetho as a prohibition against divine worship. It is interesting to note that in ancient propaganda against both Jews and Christians monotheism was equated with atheism.

At the beginning of Book II, Josephus proceeds to a refutation of the anti-Semitic calumnies of Apion. This Alexandrian author, a contemporary of Philo, had written a number of literary and historical works, some of which contained anti-Jewish references. Under Caligula he had taken an active part in the agitation against the Jewish population of Alexandria, and he was head of the Alexandrian deputation sent to Rome opposed to the Jewish envoys to Caligula headed by Philo. Josephus argues that Apion was of native Egyptian, not Greek stock. This is, however, not proved by the fact, cited in evidence, that Apion was born in the Great

Oasis in Upper Egypt. Many Greeks resided in various places in Egypt other than Alexandria, and some enjoyed the privileges of Alexandrian citizenship.

This is that novel account which the Egyptian Apion gives us concerning Moses and the Jews' departure out of Egypt, and it is no more than a contrivance of his own. But why should we wonder at the lies he tells about our forefathers when he affirms them to be of Egyptian origin, when he tells the reverse of this lie? For although he was born in the Oasis in Egypt, more Egyptian, one might say, than any, yet he does foreswear his real country and progenitors, and by falsely pretending to be born at Alexandria cannot deny the depravity of his family; for you see how justly he calls those Egyptians whom he hates and endeavors to reproach; for had he not deemed Egyptian to be a name of great reproach, he would not have avoided the name of an Egyptian himself; as we know that those who brag of their own countries value themselves upon the denomination they acquire thereby, and reprove such as unjustly lay claim thereto. As for the Egyptians' claim to be of our kindred, they do so on one of the following counts: I mean, either as they value themselves upon it and pretend to bear that relation to us; or else as they would draw us in to be partakers of their own infamy. But this fine fellow, Apion, seems to broach this reproachful appellation against us [that we were originally Egyptians] in order to bestow it on the Alexandrians as a reward for the privilege they had given him of being their fellow citizen; he also is apprised of the ill will the Alexandrians bear to those Jews who are their fellow citizens, and so proposes to himself to reproach them, thereby including all other Jews also; while in both cases he is no better than an impudent liar.

But let us now see what those heavy and wicked crimes are which Apion charges upon the Alexandrian Jews. "They came," says he, "but of Syria, and inhabited near the harborless sea, and were in the neighborhood of the dashing of the waves." Now, if the place of habitation includes anything that is reproachful, this man reproaches not his own real country [the Egyptian oasis], but what he pretends to be his own country, Alexandria; but all are agreed that the part of that city which is near to the sea is the best part of all for habitation.[20]

Now, if the Jews gained that part of the city by force and have kept it thereafter without banishment, this is a mark of their valor; but in reality it was Alexander himself that gave them that place for their habitation, when they obtained equal privileges there with the Macedonians.[21] Had this man now read the epistles of King Alexander, or those of Ptolemy, the son of Lagus, or met with the writings of the succeeding kings, or that pillar which is still standing at Alexandria and contains the privileges which the great [Julius] Caesar bestowed upon the Jews; had this man, I say, known these records, and yet had the impudence to write in contradiction to them, he would have shown himself to be a wicked man; but if he knew nothing of these records he has shown himself to be a very ignorant man: nay, when he appears to wonder how Jews could be called Alexandrians, this is another instance of his ignorance, for all such as are called out to be colonists, although they be ever so remote from one another in their origins, receive their names from those that bring them to their new habitations.

And what occasion is there to speak of others when those of us Jews that dwell at Antioch are named Antiochians, because Seleucus, the founder of that city, gave them the privileges belonging thereto? In similar manner do these Jews that inhabit Ephesus and the other cities of Ionia enjoy the same name with those originally born there, by the grant of the succeeding princes; nay, the kindness and humanity of the Romans have been so great that they have granted leave to almost all others to take the same name of Romans upon them: I mean not particularly men only, but entire and large nations themselves also; for those anciently named

---

[20] The Jewish quarter in Alexandria was situated in the northeast part of the city, beyond the great harbor.

[21] It appears that Josephus is exaggerating here. Elsewhere (*Antiquities,* XII) he reports that it was Ptolemy Soter who accorded Alexandrian Jews equality of rights (isopolity) with the Greeks. (The Macedonians were, of course, those Greeks who had conquered Egypt under Alexander.)

Iberi,[22] and Tyrrheni, and Sabini, are now called Romani; and if Apion rejects this way of obtaining the privilege of citizenship, let him abstain from calling himself an Alexandrian hereafter; for otherwise, how can he who was born in the very heart of Egypt be an Alexandrian, if this way of accepting such a privilege, of which he would have us deprived, be once abrogated?

Although indeed these Romans, who are now the lords of the habitable earth, have forbidden the Egyptians to have the privileges of any citizenship whatsoever, while this fine fellow, who is willing to partake of such a privilege himself as he is forbidden to make use of, endeavors by calumnies to deprive those of it that have justly received it: for Alexander did not therefore get some of our nation to Alexandria because he wanted inhabitants for his city, on whose building he had bestowed so much pains; but this was given to our people as a reward; because he had, upon careful trial, found them all to have been men of virtue and fidelity.

Of the same mind was Ptolemy, son of Lagus, as to those Jews who dwelt at Alexandria. For he entrusted the fortresses of Egypt into their hands, believing they would keep them faithfully and valiantly; and when he was desirous to secure the government of Cyrene and the other cities of Libya to himself, he sent a party of Jews to inhabit them. And as for his successor Ptolemy, who was called Philadelphus, he not only set all those of our nation free who were captives under him, but gave a great deal of money and, what was his greatest work of all, he had a great desire to know our laws and obtain the books of our sacred scriptures; accordingly he desired that such men might be sent him as might interpret our law to him; and in order to have them well transcribed, he committed that care to no ordinary persons, but ordained that Demetrius Phalereus [23] and Andreas, and Aristeas—the first, Demetrius, the most learned person of his age, and the others such as

---

[22] Josephus's statements here are not quite accurate. But it is true that under the Roman Empire the advantages of Roman citizenship, or some of them, were granted to non-Roman and non-Italian communities.

[23] A fuller account of the origin of the Septuagint, the Greek translation of the Bible, is given at the beginning of Book XII of the *Antiquities*. See below pp. 107–115.

were entrusted with the guard of his body—should take care of this matter; nor would he certainly have been so desirous of learning our law and the philosophy of our nation had he despised the men that made use of it, or had he not indeed held them in great admiration.

> *The Jewish (and Christian) refusal to join their fellow citizens in the worship of their gods was, in pagan eyes, a proof of both their "atheism" and their unsociability. Worshiping the city's gods was one of a citizen's obligations in a Greek city.*

But besides this, Apion objects to us thus: "If the Jews," says he, "be citizens of Alexandria, why do they not worship the same gods with the Alexandrians?" To which I give this answer: Since you are yourselves Egyptians, why do you fight one against another and have great and implacable wars about your religion? Now, if there be such differences in opinion among you Egyptians, why are you surprised that those who came to Alexandria from another country, and had original laws of their own before, should persevere in the observance of those laws? But still he charges us with being the authors of sedition; those that search into such matters will soon discover that the authors of sedition have been such citizens of Alexandria as Apion is; for while the Grecians and Macedonians were in possession of this city, there was no sedition raised against us and we were permitted to observe our ancient solemnities; but when the number of Egyptians therein came to be considerable because of the confusion of the times, these seditions broke out more and more while our people continued uncorrupted. These Egyptians, therefore, were the authors of these troubles, who not having the constancy of Macedonians nor the prudence of Grecians, indulged their evil manners and continued their ancient hatred against us; for what is here so presumptuously charged upon us is applicable, on the contrary, to them; while the majority of them have not obtained the privileges of citizens in proper times, but style those who are well known to have had that privilege extended to them all, no other than foreigners; for it does not appear that any of the kings have ever formerly bestowed those privileges of citizens upon Egyptians, no more than have any of the emperors now; while it was Alexander who introduced us into this city at first, the kings augmented our privileges therein, and the Romans have been pleased to preserve them inviolable forever.

Moreover, Apion would lay a blot upon us because we do not erect images to our emperors, as if those emperors did not know this before or stood in need of Apion as their defender; whereas he ought rather to have admired the magnanimity and modesty of the Romans, whereby they do not compel those that are subject to them to transgress the laws of their countries, but are willing to receive the honors due them after such a manner as those who are to pay them esteem consistent with piety and with their own laws; for they do not thank people for conferring honors upon them when they are compelled by violence so to do.

The Grecians and certain other nations think it a right thing to make images; moreover, when they have painted the pictures of their parents and wives and children, they exult for joy; there are some who have pictures of such persons as are no way related to them; furthermore, some have pictures of such servants as they are fond of. What wonder is it then if such as these appear willing to pay the same respect to their princes and lords? But then our legislator had forbidden us to make images, not by way of denunciation beforehand, that the Roman authority was not to be honored, but as despising a thing that was neither necessary nor useful for either God or man; and he forbade them, as we shall prove hereafter, to make these images for any part of the animal creation, and much less for God Himself, who is no part of such animal creation. Yet our legislator has nowhere forbidden us to pay honor to worthy men, provided they be of another kind and inferior to those we pay to God; with which honors we willingly testify our respect to our emperors and to the people of Rome; we also offer perpetual sacrifices for them; nor do we only offer them every day at the common expenses of all the Jews; but although we offer no other such sacrifices out of our common expenses, no, not for our own children, yet we do this as a peculiar honor to the emperors, and to them alone, while we do the same to no other person whomsoever.[24]

However, I cannot but admire those other authors who furnished this man with such materials; who, while they accuse us for not worshiping the same gods whom others worship, think themselves not guilty of impiety when they tell lies about us and frame absurd and reproachful stories about our Temple; whereas it is a most shameful thing for free men to forge lies on any occasion, and much more so to forge them about our Temple, which was so famous over all the world, and whose sacredness was preserved by us; for Apion has the impudence to pretend that "the Jews placed an ass's head in their holy place"; and he affirms that this was discovered when Antiochus Epiphanes spoiled our Temple, and found that ass's head there made of gold and worth a great deal of money.[25] To this my first answer shall be this, that had there been any such thing among us, an Egyptian ought by no means to have thrown it in our teeth, since an ass is not a more contemptible animal than goats and other such creatures which among them are gods. But besides this, I say further that this whole story is no other than a palpable lie.

The following extract seems to be the original version of the ritual murder libel. After being used in antiquity against both Jews and Christians, it was appropriated by the Church in the Christian persecution of the Synagogue, and it has had an unbroken history throughout the Middle Ages and into modern times.

He adds another Grecian fable in order to reproach us. In reply to which, it would be enough to say that we who presume to speak about divine worship ought not to be ignorant of this plain truth, that it is a degree of less impurity to profane temples than to forge

[24] Josephus is writing as if the Temple in Jerusalem still stood. After the destruction of the Temple sacrifices were, of course, no longer performed.
[25] Similar stories are told by other ancient authors; the accusation was later transferred to the early Christians. It may have its origin in anti-Jewish war propaganda of the Seleucids during the Hasmonean revolt.

wicked calumnies about its priests. Now, such men as he are more
zealous to justify a sacrilegious king than to write what is just and
true about us and our Temple; for when they are desirous of grati-
fying Antiochus, and of concealing that perfidiousness and sacrilege of which he was guilty with regard to our nation when he
wanted money, they endeavor to disgrace us and tell lies even relating to futurities.

Apion becomes other men's prophet upon this occasion, saying
that "Antiochus found in our Temple a bed and a man lying upon
it, with a small table before him, full of dainties, from the [fishes
of the] sea, beasts of the earth, and birds of the air; that this man
was amazed at these dainties thus set before him; that he immediately adored the king, upon coming in, hoping he would afford
him all possible assistance; that he fell down at the king's knee,
and stretched out to him his right hand and begged to be released;
and that when the king bade him be confident and tell him who he
was and why he dwelt there, and what was the meaning of those
various sorts of food set before him, the man made a lamentable
complaint, and with sighs and tears in his eyes gave him this account of his distress; and said that he was a Greek, and that as he
went over this province in order to earn his living, he was suddenly seized by foreigners and brought to this Temple and shut up
therein and was seen by nobody, but was fattened by these curious
provisions thus set before him; and that truly at the first such unexpected advantages seemed to him matter of great joy; that after
a while they brought down suspicion upon him and at length astonishment, what their meaning should be; that at last he inquired
of the servants that came to him, and was informed by them that it
was in order to fulfill a law of the Jews, which they must not tell
him, that he was thus fed; and that they did the same at a set time
every year; that they used to catch a Greek foreigner and fatten
him up thus every year, and then lead him to a certain wood and
kill him, and sacrifice with their accustomed solemnities and taste
of his entrails, and take an oath upon their sacrificing of the
Greek that they would ever be at enmity with the Greeks; and that
then they threw the remaining parts of the miserable wretch into a
certain pit."

Apion adds further that "the man said there were but a few days to come ere he was to be slain, and implored Antiochus that, out of the reverence he bore to the Grecian gods, he would disappoint the snares the Jews laid for his blood, and deliver him from the miseries with which he was encompassed." Now this is a most tragic fable, full of nothing but cruelty and impudence; yet it does not excuse Antiochus from his sacrilegious attempts, as those who wrote it in his vindication are willing to suppose; for he could not presume beforehand that he should meet with any such thing in coming to the Temple, but must have come upon it unexpectedly. He was therefore still an impious person, given to unlawful pleasures, and had no regard for God in his actions.

But while it so falls out that men of all countries come sometimes and sojourn among us, how comes it about that we take an oath and conspire only against the Grecians, and that also by the effusion of their blood? Or how is it possible that all the Jews should get together at these sacrifices, and the entrails of one man should be sufficient for so many thousands to taste of them, as Apion pretends? Or why did the king not carry this man, whosoever he was and whatsoever his name (which is not set down in Apion's book) with great pomp back into his own country, when he might thereby have been esteemed a religious person himself and a mighty lover of the Greeks, and might thereby have procured himself great assistance from all men against that hatred the Jews bore him? But I leave this matter; for the proper way of confuting fools is not to use bare words, but to appeal to the things themselves that work against them.

Apion also tells a false story when he mentions an oath of ours, as if we "swore by God, the maker of the heaven, and earth, and sea, to bear no good will to any foreigner, and particularly to none of the Greeks." [26] Now this liar ought to have said directly that "we would bear no good will to any foreigner, and particularly to none of the Egyptians." For then his story about the oath would

[26] For the formula: "God maker of heaven, earth and sea" compare Psalm 146:6; Nehemiah IX:6; Acts IV:24. Reinach, who quotes those passages, asks: Did Apion know this formula? Or has his text been changed by Josephus or his Jewish source?

have squared with the rest of his original forgeries, in case our forefathers had been driven away by their kinsmen the Egyptians, not on account of any wickedness they had been guilty of, but on account of the calamities they were under; for as to the Grecians, we are remote from them in place rather than different from them in our institutions insomuch that we bear them neither enmity nor jealousy. On the contrary, it has so happened that many of them have come over to our laws, some continuing their observances although others not having courage enough to persevere and so departing from them again; nor did ever anybody hear this oath sworn by us; Apion, it seems, was the only person who heard it, for he indeed was its first composer.

> *An argument against the Jews: their misfortunes prove*
> *that they are an accursed race. This was assimilated*
> *into Christian theology with some New Testament sup-*
> *port and is still, occasionally, heard nowadays.*

However, Apion deserves to be admired for his great prudence as to what I am going to say, which is this: "That there is a plain mark among us that we neither have just laws nor worship God as we ought to do, because we are not governors but are rather in subjection to Gentiles, sometimes to one nation, and sometimes to another; and that our city has been subject to several calamities. Now, a Roman might be permitted to make such a boast. But as for other men, there is no one who would not say that Apion said what he has said against himself; for there are few nations to whose lot it fell, through watching their opportunity, to come upon an empire, but still the mutations in human affairs have put them into subjection under others; and most nations have often been brought into subjection by others.

Now, for the Egyptians, perhaps they are the only nation that have had this extraordinary privilege never to have served any of those monarchs who subdued Asia and Europe, and this because, as they pretend, the gods fled into their country and saved themselves by being changed into the shapes of wild beasts. Whereas these Egyptians are the very people that appear to have never, in all the past ages, had one day of freedom, no, not so much as from their own lords. For I will not reproach them with relating the manner in which the Persians used them, and this not once only but many times, when they laid their cities waste, demolished their temples, and cut the throats of those they esteemed to be gods; for it is not reasonable to imitate the ignorance of Apion, who has no regard for the misfortunes of the Athenians, or the Lacedemonians, the latter of whom were styled by all men the most courageous, and the former the most religious, of the Grecians.

I say nothing of such kings as have been famous for piety; I say nothing of the citadel of Athens, of the temple at Ephesus, of that at Delphi, nor of ten thousand others which have been burnt down, while nobody casts reproaches on those that were the sufferers, but on those that were the actors therein; . . . But now we have encountered Apion, an accuser of our nation, though one who still forgets the miseries of his own people, the Egyptians. Apion is ignorant of what everybody knows, that the Egyptians were servants to the Persians, and afterwards to the Macedonians when they were lords of Asia, and were no better than slaves, while we enjoyed liberty formerly; nay, more than that, have had the dominion of the cities that lie round about us, and that nearly for 120 years together, until Pompeius Magnus.[27] And when all the kings everywhere went to war against the Romans, our kings were the only people who continued to be esteemed as their confederates and friends on account of their fidelity.

"But," says Apion, "we Jews have not had any wonderful men among us, nor any inventors of arts, nor any eminent for wisdom." He then enumerates Socrates, and Zeno, and Cleanthes, and some others of the same sort; and after all, he adds himself to them, which is the most wonderful thing of all that he says, and pronounces Alexandria to be happy because it has a citizen like him in it; for he was the fittest man to be a witness to his own deserts, although he has appeared to all others no better than a wicked mountebank, of corrupt life and ill discourses; on which

---

[27] An exaggeration. The period referred to is that between the Hasmonean revolt in 168 B.C.E. to the entry of Pompey in Jerusalem in 63 B.C.E.

account one may justly pity Alexandria if it should value itself because of such a citizen as he is. But as to our own men, we have
had those who have been as deserving of commendation as any
other whatsoever; and such as have perused our *Antiquities* cannot be ignorant of them.

As to the other things which he sets down as blameworthy, it
may perhaps be the best way to let them pass without apology,
that he may be allowed to be his own accuser and the accuser of
the rest of the Egyptians. However, he accuses us for sacrificing
animals and for abstaining from swine's flesh, and laughs at us for
the circumcision of our privy members. Now, as for our slaughter
of tame animals for sacrifices, it is common to us and to all other
men; but this Apion, by making it a crime to sacrifice them, dem-
onstrates himself to be an Egyptian; for had he been either a Grecian or a Macedonian, he would have shown no uneasiness at it;
for those people vow to sacrifice whole hecatombs to the gods and
make use of those sacrifices for feasting; and yet the world is not
thereby rendered destitute of cattle, as Apion was afraid would
come to pass. Yet, if all men had followed the manners of the
Egyptians, the world had certainly been made desolate as to mankind, but had been filled full of the wildest sort of brute beasts,
which, because they suppose them to be gods, they carefully nourish.

However, if any one should ask Apion which of the Egyptians
he thinks to be the most wise and most pious of them all, he
would certainly acknowledge the priests to be so; for they say that
two things were originally committed to their care by their kings'
injunctions—the worship of the gods, and the pursuit of wisdom.
Accordingly, these priests are all circumcised and abstain from
swine's flesh. Apion was therefore quite blinded in his mind when,
for the sake of the Egyptians, he contrived to reproach us, and to
accuse such others as not only make use of that conduct of life
which he so much abuses, but have also as Herodotus has said
taught other men to be circumcised.

After recounting with glee the pitiful end of Apion, Jo-
sephus turns to the refutation of other writers whose

*accusations he counters by a long account of the Jew-
ish "constitution."*

But now, since Apollonius Molo and Lysimachus and some others write treatises about our lawgiver Moses and about our laws,
treatises which are neither just nor true, and this partly out of ignorance but chiefly out of ill will, while they calumniate Moses as
an impostor and deceiver and pretend that our laws teach us
wickedness and nothing that is virtuous, I have a mind to discourse briefly, according to my ability, about our whole constitution of government, and about the particular branches of it; for I
suppose it will thence become evident that the laws given us are
disposed after the best manner for the advancement of piety, for
mutual communion with one another, for a general love of mankind, as also for justice, and for sustaining labors with fortitude,
and for a contempt of death; and I beg of those who will peruse
this writing to read it without partiality; for it is not my purpose
to write an encomium upon ourselves, but I shall esteem this as a
most just apology for us, and taken from those of our laws according to which we lead our lives, against the many and the lying
objections that have been made against us.

Moreover, since this Apollonius does not act like Apion and
lay a continued accusation against us, but does it only by starts
and up and down his discourse, while he sometimes reproaches us
as atheists and manhaters, and sometimes hits us in the teeth for
our want of courage, and yet sometimes, on the contrary, accuses
us of too great boldness and madness in our conduct; nay, he says
that we are the weakest of all the barbarians, and this is the reason we are the only people who have made no improvements in
human life; now I think I shall have sufficiently disproved all his
allegations, when it shall appear that our laws enjoin the very reverse of what he says, and that we very carefully observe those
laws ourselves; and if I am compelled to make mention of the
laws of other nations that are contrary to ours, those ought de-
servedly to thank themselves for it who have pretended to depre-
ciate our laws in comparison with their own; nor will there, I
think, be any room after that for them to pretend either that we

have no such laws ourselves, an epitome of which I shall present to the reader, or that we do not, above all men, continue in their observation.

To begin a good way back, I would advance this, in the first place, that those who have been admirers of good order and of living under common laws, and who began to introduce them, may well have this testimony, that they are better than other men, both for moderation and such virtue as is agreeable to nature. It has been the endeavor of all nations to have everything they ordained believed to be very ancient that they might not be thought to imitate others, but might appear to have delivered a regular way of living to others after them. Since this is the case, the excellency of a legislator is seen in providing for the people's living in the best manner, and in prevailing with those that are to use the laws he ordains for them to have a good opinion of them, and in obliging the multitude to persevere in them, and to make no changes in them, neither in prosperity nor adversity.

Now, I venture to say that our legislator is the most ancient of all the legislators whom we have anywhere heard of; for as for the Lycurguses and Solons [28] and all those legislators who are so admired by the Greeks, they seem to be of yesterday, if compared with our legislator, insomuch as the very name of a law was not so much as known in old times among the Grecians. A witness to the truth of this observation is Homer, who never uses that term in all his poems, for indeed there was then no such thing among them, but the multitude was governed by wise maxims and by the injunctions of their king. They continued in the use of these unwritten customs for a long time, although they were always changing them; but for our legislator, who was of so much greater antiquity than the rest (as even those that speak against us upon all occasions do always confess), he exhibited himself to the people as their best governor and counselor, and included in his legislation the entire conduct of their lives, and prevailed upon them to receive it, and brought it so to pass that those that became acquainted with his laws did most carefully observe them.

[28] Famous lawgivers of the Spartans and Athenians respectively.

*The following passage deals with Moses, the leader, ed-
ucator, and founder of the Jewish theocracy. The account given in this passage of the teaching of Moses
concerning God, like much in the following passages,
owes a great deal to rabbinic and Hellenistic-Jewish
formulation.*

Let us consider Moses' first and greatest work; for when it was
resolved by our forefathers to leave Egypt and return to their own
country, this Moses took the many ten thousands that were of the
people, and rescued them from many desperate distresses, and
brought them home in safety. And certainly it was here necessary
to travel over a country without water, and full of sand, to overcome their enemies, and, during these battles, to preserve their
children and their wives, and their possessions; on all such occasions he became an excellent general of an army, and a most prudent counselor, and one that took the truest care of them all; he
also brought it about that the whole multitude depended upon
him; and while he had them always obedient to what he enjoined,
he made no manner of use of his authority for his own advantage,
which is the usual time when governors gain great powers for
themselves and pave the way for tyranny, and accustom the multitude to live very dissolutely; whereas, when our legislator was
in such great authority, he, on the contrary, thought he ought to
have regard for piety and show his great good will to the people;
and by this means he thought he might show the great degree of
virtue in him and might procure the most lasting security for
those who had made him their governor.

When he had therefore come to such a good resolution and had
performed such wonderful exploits, we had just reason to look
upon ourselves as having him for a divine governor and counselor;
and when he had at first persuaded himself that his actions and designs were agreeable to God's will, he thought it was his duty to
impress, above all things, that notion upon the multitude; for
those who once believed that God is the inspector of their lives
will not permit themselves any sin; and this is the character of our
legislator; he was no impostor, no deceiver, as his revilers say,
though unjustly, but such a one as they brag Minos to have been

among the Greeks, and other legislators after him; for some of them suppose that they had their laws from Jupiter, while others said that the revelation of their laws was to be referred to Apollo and his oracle at Delphi, whether they really thought they were so derived, or supposed, however, that they could persuade the people easily that it was so; but which of these it was who made the best laws, and which had the greatest reason to believe that God was their author, it will be easy, upon comparing those laws themselves, to determine, for it is time that we came to that point.

Now there are innumerable differences in the particular customs and laws among all mankind, which a man may briefly reduce under the following heads: Some legislators have permitted their governments to be under monarchies, others entrusted them to the mass of the people; but our legislator had no regard for any of these forms, but ordained our government to be what, in a strained expression, may be termed a theocracy,[29] by ascribing the authority and the power to God, and by persuading all the people to have regard for him, as the author of all good things enjoyed either in common by all mankind, or by each one in particular, and of all that they themselves obtained by praying to him in their great difficulties. He informed them that it was impossible to escape God's observation, either in any of our outward actions or in any of our inward thoughts. Moreover, he represented God as unbegotten, immutable through all eternity, superior to all mortal conceptions in pulchritude, and though known to us by His power yet unknown to us as to His essence. I do not now explain how these notions of God are the sentiments of the wisest among the Grecians, and how they were taught them upon the principles that he offered them.[30] However, they testify with great assurance that these notions are just, and agreeable to the nature of God and to

---

[29] This word seems to have been coined by Josephus, unless he found it in his source.

[30] The claims that Greek philosophers and poets learned their wisdom from the Bible seems to have been a commonplace of Hellenistic-Jewish apologetics. It found its way into Christian literature through Philo of Alexandria. In order to substantiate this claim Josephus is forced to describe Greek philosophical systems in terms not really appropriate to them.

His majesty; for Pythagoras, Anaxagoras, Plato, and the Stoic philosophers that succeeded them, and almost all the rest, are of the
same sentiments, and had the same notions of the nature of God;
yet these men did not dare disclose those true notions to more
than a few because the body of the people were prejudiced by
other earlier opinions. But our legislator, who made his actions
agree with his laws, not only prevailed with those that were his
contemporaries to agree with his notions, but so firmly imprinted
this faith in God upon all their posterity that it could never be removed.

The reason why the constitution of this legislation was ever better directed to the utility of all than other legislations were is this,
that Moses did not make religion a part of virtue but he saw and
ordained other virtues to be a part of religion—I mean, justice,
and fortitude, and temperance, and a universal harmony of the
members of the community with one another; for all our actions
and studies, and all our words, have reference to piety towards
God; for he has left none of these in suspense or undetermined;
for there are two ways of coming to any sort of learning and a
moral conduct of life: the one is by instruction in words, the other
by practical exercises. Now, other lawgivers have separated these
two ways in their opinions, and choosing one of those ways of instruction, or that which best pleased every one of them neglected
the other. Thus did the Lacedemonians and the Cretans teach by
practical exercises, but not by words; while the Athenians, and almost all the other Grecians, made laws about what was to be done
or to be left undone, but had no regard to putting them into practice.

Our legislator, however, very carefully joined these two methods of instruction together; for he neither left these practical
exercises to go on without verbal instruction, nor did he permit
the hearing of the law to proceed without the exercises for practice; but beginning immediately from the earliest infancy and the
appointment of every one's way of life, he left nothing of even the
very smallest consequence to be done at the pleasure and disposition of the person himself. Accordingly, he made a fixed rule of

law, what sorts of food they should abstain from, and what sorts they should use; also, what communion they should have with others, what great diligence they should use in their occupations, and what times of rest should be interposed, that, by living under that law as under a father and a master, we might be guilty of no sin, neither voluntary nor out of ignorance. He appointed the law to be the best and the most necessary instruction of all others, permitting the people to leave off their other employments and to assemble together for the hearing of the law and learning it exactly, and this not once or twice, or oftener, but every week; which thing all the other legislators seem to have neglected.[31]

And this very thing is what principally creates such a wonderful harmony of minds among us all; for this entire agreement of ours in all our notions concerning God, and our having no difference in our course of life and manners, creates among us the most excellent concord of our manners that exists anywhere among mankind; for no other people but we Jews have avoided all discourses about God that any way contradict one another, which yet are frequent among other nations; and this is true not only among ordinary persons, according as every one is affected, but some of the philosophers have been insolent enough to indulge such contradictions, while others have undertaken to use such words as entirely take away the nature of God, as some of them have taken away His providence over mankind.[32] Nor can any one perceive among us any difference in the conduct of our lives; but all our works are common to us all. We have one sort of discourse concerning God, which is conformable to our law, affirming that He sees all things; as also, we have but one way of speaking concerning the conduct

---

[31] The weekly reading of the Torah seems to be of late origin; but it is attributed to Moses in the Jerusalem Talmud (*Megillah,* IV).

[32] Providence was denied by the Epicureans. But Josephus himself tells us that the Sadducees, like the Epicureans, denied divine providence, and, indeed, any divine concern with human action. He is here giving an idealized picture of a monolithic, harmonious, unanimous Judaism that is certainly much at variance with the reality of his time. For his account of the Sadducees, see *War,* II, 164–165; *Antiquities,* XIII:173; 16–17.

of our lives, that all other things ought to have piety as their end; and this anybody may hear from our women and servants themselves.

Hence has arisen that accusation which some make against us, that we have not produced men who have been the inventors of new operations or of new ways of speaking; for others think it a fine thing to persevere in nothing that has been delivered down from their forefathers, and these testify it to be an instance of the sharpest wisdom when these men venture to transgress those traditions; whereas we, on the contrary, suppose it to be our only wisdom and virtue to admit no actions nor proposals that are contrary to our original laws; which procedure of ours is a just and sure sign that our law is admirably constituted; for such laws as are not thus well made are convicted upon trial to need amendment.

What are the things, then, that we are commanded or forbidden? They are simply and easily known. The first command concerns God, affirming that God contains all things and is a being every way perfect and happy, self-sufficient, and supplying all other beings; the beginning, the middle, and the end of all things. He is manifest in His works and benefits, and more conspicuous than any other being whatsoever; but as to His form and magnitude, He is most obscure. All materials, let them be ever so costly, are unworthy to compose an image of Him; and all arts are unartful to express the notion we ought to have of Him. We can neither see nor think of anything like Him, nor is it agreeable to piety to form a resemblance of Him. We see His works, the light, the heaven, the earth, the sun and the moon, the waters, the generations of animals, the productions of fruits. These things God has made, not with hands, not with labor, nor as wanting the assistance of any to cooperate with Him; but as His will resolved they should be made, and should be good also; they were made and became good immediately. All men ought to follow this Being, and to worship Him in the exercise of virtue; for this way of worship of God is the most holy of all others.

There ought also to be but one temple for one God; for likeness is the constant foundation of agreement. This temple ought to be common to all men because He is the common God of all men. His priests are to be continually occupied with His worship, over whom he that is the first by his birth is to be ruler. His business must be to offer sacrifices to God, together with those priests that are joined with him, to see that the laws are observed, to determine controversies, and to punish those that are convicted of injustice; while he that does not submit to him shall be subject to the same punishment as if he had been guilty of impiety towards God Himself.

When we offer sacrifices we do it not in order to surfeit ourselves or to become drunken; for such excesses are against the will of God; but by keeping ourselves sober, orderly, and ready for our other occupations, and being more temperate than others. And for our duty at the sacrifices themselves, we ought in the first place to pray for the common welfare of all, and after that our own; for we are made for fellowship with one another; and he who prefers the common good before what is peculiar to himself is above all acceptable to God. And let our prayers and supplications be made humbly to God, not so much that He would give us what is good, for He has already given that of His own accord, as that we may duly receive it, and when we have received it may preserve it. And this is our doctrine concerning God and His worship.

But, then, what are our laws about marriage? That law acknowledges no other mixture of sexes but that which nature has appointed, of a man with his wife, and that this be used only for the procreation of children. But it abhors the mixture of a male with a male; and if any one do that, death is his punishment. It commands us also, when we marry, not to have regard to portion, nor to take a woman by violence, nor to persuade her deceitfully and knavishly; but demand her in marriage of him who has power to dispose of her and is fit to give her away by the nearness of his kindred; not so that he should abuse her, but that she may acknowledge her duty to her husband; for God has given the authority to the husband. A husband, therefore, is to lie only with his wife whom he has married; but to have to do with another man's wife is a wicked thing; which, if any one venture upon, death is inevitably his punishment; no more can he avoid the same who forces a virgin betrothed to another man, or entices another man's wife. The law, moreover, enjoins us to bring up all our offspring; and forbids women to cause abortion of what is begotten, or to destroy it afterward; [33] and if any woman appears to have done so, she will be a murderer of her child, by destroying a living creature and diminishing humankind.

The duty to educate our children.

The law does not permit us to make festivals at the births of our children, thereby affording occasion to drink to excess; but it ordains that the very beginning of our education should be immediately directed to sobriety. It also commands us to bring those children up in learning, and to exercise them in the laws and make them acquainted with the acts of their predecessors, in order to insure their imitation of them, that they may be nourished in the laws from their infancy, and might neither transgress them nor yet have any pretext for their ignorance of them.

Duty to honor one's parents and other precepts relating to social intercourse.

The law ordains also that parents should be honored immediately after God Himself, and delivers that son who does not requite them for the benefits he has received from them, but is deficient on any such occasion, to be stoned. It also says that the young men should pay due respect to every elder, since God is the eldest of all beings. It does not give leave to conceal anything from our friends because that is not true friendship which will not commit all things to their fidelity: it also forbids the revelation of secrets, even though an enmity arise between them. If any judge takes bribes, his punishment is death; he that overlooks one that offers him a petition, and this when he is able to relieve him, he is a guilty person. What is not by any one entrusted to another ought

---

[33] Infanticide (and the exposure of newborn infants) seems to have been widely practiced in pagan antiquity. The reference to abortion here does not seem to be based on a biblical prohibition.

not to be required back again. No one is to touch another's goods. He that lends money must not demand usury for its loan. These and many more of the like sort are the rules that unite us in the bonds of society.

It will also be worth our while to see what equity our legislator would have us exercise in our intercourse with strangers; for it will thence appear that he made the best provision he could possibly, both that we should not dissolve our own constitution nor show a grudging mind towards those that would cultivate a friendship with us. Accordingly, our legislator admits all those that have a mind to observe our laws to do so; and this in a friendly manner, as esteeming that a true union which not only extends to our own stock but to those that would live in the same manner as we do.

However, there are other things which our legislator ordained for us beforehand, which of necessity we ought to do in common with all men; as to offer fire, water, and food to all such as want it; to show them the roads; and not to let any one lie unburied. He also would have us treat those that are esteemed our enemies with moderation; for he does not allow us to set their country on fire, nor permit us to cut down those trees that bear fruit; nay, further, he forbids us to despoil those slain in war. He has also provided for such as are taken captive that they may not be injured, and especially that the women may not be abused. Indeed he has taught us gentleness and humanity so effectively that he has not despised the care of brute beasts, permitting no other than a regular use of them and forbidding any other; and if any of them come to our house, like suppliants, we are forbidden to slay them; nor may we kill the dams together with their young ones; but we are obliged, even in an enemy's country, to spare and not to kill those creatures that labor for mankind. Thus has our lawgiver contrived to teach us equitable conduct in every way, by accustoming us to such laws as instruct us therein; while at the same time he has ordained that those who break these laws be punished, without allowing any excuse whatsoever.

The belief in a future life.

The reward for such as live exactly according to the law is not silver or gold, nor any public sign of commendation; but every good man has his own conscience bearing witness to himself, and by virtue of our legislator's prophetic spirit, and of the firm security God Himself affords such a one, he believes that God has made this grant to those who observe these laws, even though they be obliged readily to die for them, that they shall come into being again, and at a certain revolution of things receive a better life than they had enjoyed before. Nor would I venture to write thus at this time, were it not well known to all by our actions that many of our people have many a time bravely resolved to endure any sufferings rather than speak one word against our law.

> *Praise of endurance. In other nations, even the bravest among them like the Spartans have frequently surrendered to their enemies. It is far otherwise with the Jews.*

Now for ourselves, I venture to say that no one can tell of so many, nay, not of more than one or two, that have betrayed our laws, no, not out of fear of death itself; I do not mean such an easy death as happens in battles, but that which comes with bodily torments and seems to be the severest kind of death of all others. Now I think that those that have conquered us have put us to such deaths, not out of their hatred for us once they had subdued us, but rather out of their desire to see a surprising sight, which is this, whether there be such men in the world who believe that no evil is to them so great as to be compelled to do or to speak anything contrary to their own laws. Nor ought men to wonder at us, if we are more courageous in dying for our laws than all other men are; for other men do not easily submit to the easier things to which we are accustomed; I mean working with our hands, and eating but little, and being contented to eat and drink, not at random, or at every one's pleasure, or being under inviolable rules in lying with our wives, and again in the observation of our time of rest; while those that can use their swords in war and can put their enemies to flight when they attack them cannot bear to submit to such laws about their way of living; whereas our being accustomed willingly to submit to laws in these instances renders us fit to show our fortitude upon other occasions also.

It is not fear of our governors nor a desire to follow what other nations hold in such great esteem that is able to withdraw us from our laws; nor have we exerted our courage in raising up wars to increase our wealth, but only for the observation of our laws; and when we with patience bear other losses, yet when any persons would compel us to break our laws, it is then that we choose to go to war, though it is beyond our ability to pursue it and bear the greatest calamities to the last with such fortitude; and indeed, what reason can there be why we should desire to imitate the laws of other nations, while we see they are not observed by their own legislators?

I omit speaking about punishments, and how many ways of escaping them the large majority of legislators have afforded malefactors, by ordaining that, for adulteries, fines in money should be allowed, and for corrupting virgins they need only marry them; also what excuses they may have in denying the facts, if any one should attempt to inquire into them; for among most other nations how men may transgress their laws is studied art, but no such thing is permitted among us; for though we be deprived of our wealth, our cities or other advantages we have, our law continues immortal; nor can any Jew go so far from his own country, nor be so affrighted at the severest lord as not to be more frightened by the law than by him. If, therefore, this be the disposition we are under with regard to the excellency of our laws, let our enemies make use of this concession, that our laws are most excellent; and if still they imagine that though we so firmly adhere to them, yet they are bad laws notwithstanding, what penalties then do they deserve to undergo who do not observe their own laws which they esteem superior? Whereas, therefore, length of time is esteemed to be the truest touchstone in all cases, I would make that a testimonial to the excellency of our laws, and to that belief delivered us concerning God; for as there has been a very long time for this comparison, if any one will but compare its duration with the duration of the laws made by other legislators, he will find our legislator to have been the most ancient of them all.

We have already demonstrated that our laws have been such as have always inspired admiration and imitation among all other men; nay, the earliest Grecian philosophers, though in appearance they observed the laws of their own countries, yet did they, in their actions and philosophic doctrines, follow our legislator,[34] and instructed men to live sparingly and to have friendly communication with one another. Nay, further, the multitude of mankind itself has had a great inclination for a long time to follow our religious observances; for there is no city of the Grecians, or barbarians, nor any nation whatsoever, where our custom of resting on the seventh day has not come, and by which our fasts and lighting up lamps, and many of our prohibitions as to our food are not observed; they also endeavor to imitate our mutual concord with one another, and the charitable distribution of our goods, and our diligence in our trades, and our fortitude in undergoing the distresses we are in on account of our laws; and what is here matter of the greatest admiration, our law has no bait of pleasure to allure men to it, but it prevails by its own force; as God Himself pervades all the world, so has our law passed through all the world also. So that if any one will but reflect on his own country and his own family, he will have reason to give credence to what I say. It is therefore only just either to condemn all mankind for indulging a wicked disposition when they have been so desirous of imitating laws that are foreign and evil in themselves, rather than following laws of their own that are of a better character, or else our accusers must leave off their spite against us; nor are we guilty of any envious behavior towards them when we honor our own legislator, and believe what he, by his prophetic authority, has taught us concerning God; for though we should not be able ourselves to understand the excellency of our own laws, yet would the great multi-

---

[34] On alleged imitation of biblical doctrines by Greek thinkers, see above p. 85.

tude of those that desire to imitate them justify us.

As to the laws themselves, more words are unnecessary, for they are visible in their own nature, and appear to teach not impiety but the truest piety in the world. They do not make men hate one another, but encourage people to communicate freely what they have to one another; they are enemies to injustice, they take care of righteousness, they banish idleness and expensive living, and instruct men to be content with what they have, and to be laborious in their callings; they forbid men to make war out of a desire of getting more, but make men courageous in defending the laws; they are inexorable in punishing malefactors; they admit no sophistry of words, but are always established by actions themselves, which actions we ever propose as surer demonstrations than what is contained in writing only; on which account I am so bold as to say that we have become the teachers of other men, in the greatest number of things, and those of the most excellent nature only; for what is more excellent than inviolable piety? what is more just than submission to laws? and what is more advantageous than mutual love and concord? and this so far that we are to be neither divided by calamities, nor to become injurious and seditious in prosperity, but to condemn death when we are in war, and in peace to apply ourselves to our mechanical occupations, or to our tillage of the ground; while we in all things, and in all ways, are satisfied that God is the inspector and governor of our actions. If these precepts had either been written at first, or more precisely kept by others before us, we should have owed them thanks as disciples owe to their masters, but if it be visible that we have made use of them more than any other men, and if we have demonstrated that the original invention of them is our own, let the Apions with the rest of those that delight in lies and reproaches stand confuted.

PART THREE

The Antiquities of the Jews

Preface: The Purpose of This Work

Those who undertake to write histories do not, I perceive, take that trouble on one and the same account, but for many reasons, and such as are very different one from another; for some apply themselves to this part of learning to show their skill in composition and to acquire a reputation for speaking finely; others write histories in order to gratify those that happened to be involved in them, and on that account have spared no pains but have rather gone beyond their own abilities in the performance; but there are others who, of necessity and by force, are driven to write history because they are concerned with the facts and cannot excuse themselves from committing them to writing, for the advantage of posterity; nay, there are not a few who are induced to draw their historical facts out of darkness into light, and to produce them for the benefit of the public, because of the great importance of the facts themselves. Now of these several reasons for writing history, I must confess the two last were mine also; for since I was myself involved in that war we Jews had with the Romans, and knew myself its particular actions and its conclusion, I was forced to give the history of it because I saw that others had perverted the truth of those actions in their writings.[1]

[1] He refers here to rival historians, particularly to Justus of Tiberias.

Now I have undertaken the present work, thinking it will appear to all Greek-speaking readers worthy of their study; for it will contain all our [Jewish] antiquities and the constitution of our government, as interpreted out of the Hebrew Scriptures; and indeed I did formerly intend, when I wrote of the war, to explain who the Jews originally were, what fortune they had been subject to, and by what legislator they had been instructed in piety and the exercise of other virtues, what wars they had made in remote ages until their involuntary engagement in this last with the Romans; but because such a work would take up great compass, I separated it into a treatise by itself, with its own beginning and conclusion; but in the course of time, as usually happens to those who undertake great things, I grew weary and went on slowly, it being a large subject and a difficult matter to translate our history into a foreign and to us unaccustomed language. However, there were some persons who desired to know our history, and exhorted me to go on with it. I yielded to persuasions; I was also ashamed to permit any laziness to have greater influence upon me than the delight of taking pains in such very useful studies: I thereupon bestirred myself and went on with my work more cheerfully. Besides the foregoing motives, I had others: that our forefathers were willing to communicate such things to others, and that some of the Greeks took considerable pains to know our nation's affairs.

I found, therefore, that the second Ptolemy [2] was a king who was extraordinarily diligent in what concerned learning and collecting books; he was also peculiarly ambitious to procure a Greek translation of our law and of the constitution of our government contained therein. Now Eleazar, the high priest, equal to any other of that dignity among us, did not begrudge the forenamed king the fulfillment of his wish because he knew our nation's custom to hinder nothing of what we esteemed ourselves from being communicated to others.

Accordingly, I thought it fitting both to imitate the generosity

[2] Ptolemy Philadelphus (283–245 B.C.E.). A full version of the story of the translation of the Hebrew Bible into Greek is given by Josephus in Book XII of the *Antiquities* (paragraph 11 ff.). See below, pp. 107 ff.

of our high priest and to assume there might even now be many lovers of learning like the king; for he did not obtain all our writings at that time, but those sent to Alexandria as interpreters gave him only the books of the law, even though there were vast numbers of other matters in our sacred books. They indeed contain the history of five thousand years, during which time there took place many strange accidents, many hazards of war, great actions of the commanders, and changes in the form of our government.

On the whole, a man who peruses this history may principally learn that all events succeed well, even to an incredible degree, and the reward of felicity is granted by God to those who follow His will and do not venture to break His excellent laws. They may also learn that so far as men any way deviate from their faithful observance, what was practicable before becomes impracticable; and whatsoever they esteemed as good is converted into an incurable calamity. And now I exhort all those that peruse these books to apply their minds to God and to examine the mind of our legislator [Moses] whether he has not understood God's nature, or ascribed to Him such operations as become His power, or preserved His writings from those indecent fables which others have framed,[3] even though because of the very distant time he lived, he might easily have forged such lies. He did live two thousand years ago, at which time the poets themselves were not so bold as to fix even the generations of their gods, much less the actions of their men, or their own laws. As I proceed, therefore, I shall accurately describe what is contained in our records, in the order of time belonging to them; I have already promised to do so throughout this undertaking, without adding to or taking away anything from what is therein contained.

But because almost our entire constitution depends on the wisdom of Moses, our legislator, I cannot avoid saying something about him beforehand, though briefly; otherwise, those that read my book may wonder how it comes to pass that my discourse,

---

[3] Such "indecent fables" as were told about the Greek gods by Homer or the tragedians.

which promises an account of laws and historical facts, contains so much philosophy. The reader must therefore know that Moses deemed it necessary that he who would conduct his own life well and give laws to others should, in the first place, consider the divine nature, and upon the contemplation of God's operations should thereby imitate the best of all patterns, so far as is possible for human nature, and endeavor to follow them; neither could the legislator himself have a right mind without such contemplation; nor would anything he wrote tend to promote virtue in his readers unless they be taught first that God is the Father and Lord of all things, sees all things, and bestows a happy life upon those that follow Him, but plunges those who do not walk in the paths of virtue into inevitable miseries. Now when Moses wanted to teach this lesson to his countrymen he did not begin establishing his laws in the same way as other legislators did—that is, by contracts and other rites between one man and another—but by raising their minds towards God and His creation of the world, and by persuading them that we men are the most excellent of God's creatures on earth. When once he had brought them to submit to religion, he easily persuaded them to submit in all other things; while other legislators followed fables and through their discourses transferred the most reproachful human vices unto the gods, thus offering wicked men the most plausible excuses for their crimes, our legislator, once he had demonstrated that God possessed perfect virtue, assumed that men ought also to aspire toward it; and on those who did not so think and believe, he inflicted the severest punishments.

Therefore I exhort my readers to examine this whole undertaking in that light; for it will thereby appear to them that there is nothing disagreeable there either to God's majesty or His love of mankind; for all things here have a relationship to the nature of the universe; while our legislator enunciates some things wisely but enigmatically, and others allegorically, he does explain plainly and expressly such things that require direct explanation. However, those that have a mind to know the reasons for everything may find here a very curious philosophical theory, of which I shall waive explication for the present; but if God grant me time, I shall set about writing it [4] after I have finished the present work. I shall now betake myself to the history before me after I mention what Moses says about the creation of the world, which I find described in the sacred books.

For reasons of space I give no extracts from the first ten books of the Antiquities, *which overlap with the biblical account of ancient Jewish history. The period inaugurated by the conquests of Alexander the Great and ending with the reign of Nero is introduced in the second half of the* Antiquities.

There are a number of parallel versions of the following story of a meeting between Alexander the Great and the Jews of Jerusalem both in Jewish-Hellenistic and in rabbinic sources. Their character is clearly legendary. It is not even clear that Alexander ever visited Jerusalem. But the story is of interest since it shows how the Jews represented to themselves their first encounter with the Greeks. Note the favorable attitude towards the Jews ascribed to the Macedonian king, and also the Jewish sympathy towards him. The legend may be connected with attempts to derive claims to citizenship in Alexandria from rights supposedly granted by Alexander, or at least his immediate successors.

Now Alexander, after he had taken Gaza, made haste to go up to Jerusalem; and Jaddua, the high priest, when he heard that, was in agony and terror, not knowing how he should meet the Macedonians. He therefore ordained that the people make supplications and join him in offering sacrifices to God, whom he besought to protect the nation and deliver it from forthcoming perils; whereupon God warned him in a dream, which came to him after he had offered sacrifice, that he should take courage, adorn the city, and open the gates; that the rest should appear in white garments,

[4] It seems that this work was never written, or rather, completed. Josephus alludes to it in a number of other places; and H. St. J. Thackeray thinks that "it had taken shape in the author's mind and was actually begun."

but that he and the priests should meet the king in the habits proper to their order, without fear of any evil consequences, which the providence of God would prevent; . . . When he rose from his sleep, Jaddua greatly rejoiced, and declared to all the warning he had received from God. He acted in accordance with his dream, and awaited the coming of the king.

And when he understood that the king was not far from the city, he went out in procession, with the priests and the multitude of the citizens. The procession was venerable and different in style from that of other nations. It arrived at a place called Sapha, whence one has a view of both Jerusalem and the Temple; and while the Phoenicians and Chaldeans who followed him thought they would be free to plunder the city and torture the high priest to death, the very reverse happened; for Alexander, when he saw the multitude at a distance in white garments, while the priests stood clothed in fine linen and the high priest in purple and scarlet clothing, and on his head his mitre, with the golden plate whereon the name of God was engraved, he approached alone, praised God's name, and then saluted the high priest. The Jews also all together, in one voice, saluted Alexander and surrounded him; whereupon the kings of Syria and the others were surprised at what Alexander had done and imagined him disordered in his mind. However, Parmenio [5] alone went up to him and asked how it came to pass what while all others worshipped him, he should pay his respects to the high priest of the Jews.

To which he replied, "It was not him I worshiped but that God who has honored him with his high-priesthood; for I saw this very person in a dream, in this very habit, when I was at Dios in Macedonia; while I was deliberating how I might obtain dominion of Asia, He exhorted me to make no delay but boldly to pass over the sea thither because He would conduct my army and give me dominion over the Persians; whence it is that having seen no other but Him in that habit and remembering that dream and its exhortation, I believe that I bring this army under divine protection and shall with it conquer Darius and destroy the power of the Per-

[5] One of the Macedonian generals.

sians, and that all things will succeed according to plan."

And after he had said this to Parmenio and had given the high priest his right hand, the priests ran along beside him and he came into the city; and when he went up into the Temple, he offered sacrifice to God, according to the high priest's direction, and magnificently treated both the high priest and the priests. And when the Book of Daniel was shown him,[6] wherein Daniel declared that one of the Greeks would destroy the empire of the Persians, he assumed that he himself was the person intended; and as he was then satisfied, he dismissed the multitude for the present, but the next day he called them back and bade them ask him whatever favors they wished; whereupon the high priest expressed the wish that they might follow the laws of their forefathers and pay no tribute in the seventh year.[7] He granted all they asked; and when they entreated him to permit also the Jews in Babylon and Media to follow their own laws, he willingly promised; and when he said to the multitude that if any of them would enlist in his army on condition that they continue following the laws of their forefathers and live according to them, he was willing to take them. And many were ready to accompany him in his wars.

After the death of Alexander the Great in 323 B.C.E., *his empire fell into disorder and was divided by his generals. The crisis of those years and the general lack of security may well have contributed to migratory movements in Syria and Palestine. This may account, though only partly, for the large-scale settlement of Jews in Alexandria. Their numbers there increased rapidly; and the conclusion can hardly be avoided that Egyptian Jewry increased at least as much through proselytism as through immigration. This would ex-*

---

[6] Parts of the Book of Daniel are thought to have been written in the second century B.C.E. The reference here seems to be to Daniel 8:21 and 11:2–3. See also Chapters 7–8 passim.

[7] I.e., in the Shemitta year, in which the Jews were enjoined to let their fields lie fallow. An indulgent ruler might think that the resultant decline in the income of his subjects justified the remission of taxes for that year.

> *plain, incidentally, the need in Alexandria, so early in*
> *that community's history, of a Greek translation of the*
> *Bible.*

Now after Alexander, King of Macedon, had put an end to Persian rule and had settled the affairs of Judea in the forementioned manner, he died; and his government was divided among many: Antigonus obtained Asia, Seleucus Babylon, Lysimachus governed the Hellespont, Cassander possessed Macedonia, and Ptolemy— the son of Lagus—seized Egypt. And while these princes ambitiously fought against one another, each for his own principality, there were continual wars, lasting wars too; and the cities suffered, losing a great many of their inhabitants in these times of distress.

Ptolemy also seized Jerusalem, using deceit and treachery to do so; as he came into the city on a Sabbath day, as if to offer sacrifice, he without trouble captured the city; the Jews did not oppose him because they did not suspect him to be their enemy and on that day they were at rest. And once he captured it, he reigned over it in a cruel manner. Nay, Agatharchides of Cnidus, who recorded the deeds of Alexander's successors, reproaches us for superstition as leading to our loss of liberty, when he says thus: "There is a nation called the nation of the Jews, who inhabit a strong and great city named Jerusalem. These men took no care, but let it fall into the hands of Ptolemy because they were not willing, by reason of their unseasonable superstition,[8] to take arms, thereby submitting to live under a hard master." This is what Agatharchides relates of our nation.

But once Ptolemy had taken a great many captives, from both the mountainous parts of Judea and the places around Jerusalem and Samaria and near Mount Gerizim, he led them all into Egypt and settled them there. And since he knew that the people of Jerusalem were most faithful in the observation of oaths and covenants, he distributed many of them into garrisons, and gave them equal privileges in Alexandria; he only required of them that they

---

[8] The "superstition" referred to is, of course, the Jewish observance of the Sabbath. On rabbinic discussions concerning the bearing of arms on the Sabbath, see note above on p. 69.

take their oaths to remain faithful to the posterity of those committing these places to their care. Nay, there were quite a few other Jews who, of their own accord, went into Egypt, attracted by the goodness of the soil and by the liberality of Ptolemy.

> *The translation of the Bible into Greek. Our main source for this, one of the most important literary events in the history of western man, is the so-called Letter of Aristeas. The Greek Bible was known to, and even quoted by, the ancient rabbis. It is true that, as time went on, the Septuagint (meaning "seventy" and so-called from the number of translators, the number being rounded off from seventy-two) became suspect in the eyes of Jewish teachers, and new translations into Greek were made. These again testified to the need felt to have a Greek Bible. The Septuagint became the Bible for the new Christian Church, the spread of whose gospel among the Greek-speaking population of the Empire was facilitated by the fact that both the Jewish Bible and the New Testament were available in Greek.*

When Alexander had reigned twelve years, and after him Ptolemy Soter forty years, Philadelphus then succeeded to the kingdom of Egypt for forty-one years. He ordered the Law to be translated, and set free those who had come from Jerusalem to Egypt and were in slavery there; they numbered a hundred and twenty thousand. The occasion was this: Demetrius Phalereus,[9] who was librarian to the king, was now endeavoring to gather together all the books on earth, buying whatever was valuable or agreeable to the king (who was earnestly set on collecting books); to this inclination of his, Demetrius was zealously subservient. And when once Ptolemy asked him how many ten thousands of books he had

[9] Athenian statesman and philosopher, born ca. 350 B.C.E., who went to Egypt, where he became influential in political and literary affairs. He seems to have been, for a time, at the head of the famous Library of Alexandria, the greatest institution of its kind in antiquity.

collected, he replied that he had already about twenty times ten thousand, but that, in a short time, he would have fifty times ten thousand. But, he said, he had been informed that there were many books of laws among the Jews worthy of the king's library, but which, being written in characters and a dialect of their own, would cause no small pains to get translated into Greek; the characters in which they are written seem to be like that of the Syrians, and their sound, when pronounced, is also like theirs; and that sound appears to be unique to themselves. Yet, he said, nothing hindered their getting those books translated; for while nothing is lacking for that purpose, we may have their books also in this library. The king thought Demetrius very zealous to procure him such an abundance of books and to suggest what was proper for him to do, and he therefore wrote to the Jewish high priest that he should act accordingly.

Now there was one Aristeas, who was among the king's most intimate friends, and, because of his modesty, very acceptable to him. This Aristeas had resolved for some time to petition the king to set all the captive Jews in his kingdom free; and he thought this to be a convenient opportunity for making that petition. So he discoursed with the captains of the king's guards, Sosibius of Tarentum and Andreas, persuading them to assist him. Accordingly, Aristeas went to the king and made the following speech: "It is not fit for us, O king, to overlook things hastily, or to deceive ourselves, but to lay the truth open; for since we have determined for your satisfaction not only to get the laws of the Jews transcribed but translated also, how can we do this while so many Jews are now slaves in your kingdom? Do then what would be in keeping with your magnanimity and your good nature: free them from their miserable conditions because that God, who supports your kingdom, was the author of their laws, as I have learned through special inquiry; for both these people and we too worship the same God, the framer of all things. Therefore, restore these men to their own country; and do this to honor God because these men pay Him excellent worship. And know further that though I be not related to them by birth, nor of their country, yet I desire these favors to be granted them because all men are the creation of God; and I am certain that He is well pleased with those who do good."

While Aristeas was speaking thus, the king looked at him with a cheerful and joyful countenance, and said, "How many ten thousands do you suppose there are who want to be set free?" To which Andreas replied: "A few more than ten times ten thousand." The king made answer: "And is this a small gift that you ask, Aristeas?" But Sosibius and the others who stood by said that he ought to make an offering of thanks worthy of his greatness of soul to that God who had given him his kingdom. With this answer the king was much pleased; and he ordered that when the soldiers were paid their wages, 120 drachmae should be laid out for every slave. And he promised to publish a decree about the matter they requested, which would confirm what Aristeas had proposed, especially that God's will be done; whereby, he said, he would not only set those free who had been led away captive by his father and his army, but those who had been in his kingdom before, and those also, if any such there were, who had been captured since. And when they said that their redemption money would amount to over four hundred talents, he granted it.

A copy of that decree I have determined to preserve so that the magnanimity of this king may be made known. Its contents were as follows: "Let all those who were soldiers under our father, and who, when they overran Syria and Phoenicia and laid waste Judea, took the Jews captives, made them slaves, brought them into our cities and into this country and then sold them; also all those that were in my kingdom before, and those who have recently been brought here, be set free by those who possess them; and let them accept 120 drachmae for every slave. And let the soldiers receive this redemption money with their pay, and the rest out of the king's treasury: for I believe they were made captives without our father's consent and without justice; and that their country was harassed by the insolence of the soldiers, who, by moving them into Egypt, made a great profit on them. Out of regard, therefore, to justice, and out of pity for those that have been tyrannized over, I enjoin those who have such Jews in their service to set them at liberty upon the receipt of the aforementioned sum; and that no one use any deceit, but obey what is here commanded. And I request that they submit their names within three days after the publication of this edict to those appointed to execute the same, and also to bring the slaves before them: and let every one inform against those that do not obey this decree, and I shall request that their estates be confiscated into the king's treasury."

The king also ordered that the payment, which was likely to be made in a hurry, be divided among the king's ministers and among the officers of his treasury. What the king had decreed was quickly put into action; and this in no more than seven days, the number of talents paid for the captives being over 460; their masters required the 120 drachmae for the children also.

Now after this had been done in so magnificent a manner, according to the king's wishes, he ordered Demetrius to give him in writing his sentiments concerning the transcribing of the Jewish books; for no part of the administration is conducted rashly by these kings, but all things are managed with great circumspection. I have therefore attached a copy of these epistles, and set down the multitude of vessels sent as gifts to Jerusalem and the construction of every one so that the exactness of the artificers' workmanship and the name of the workmen be made manifest, and this because of the excellence of the vessels.

The epistle read as follows: "Demetrius to the great king, When you, O King, gave me a charge concerning the collection of books to fill your library and the care that should be taken about those that are imperfect, I used the utmost diligence. And I informed you that we lack the books of Jewish legislation, plus some others; for they are written in the Hebrew characters, the language of that nation, and are unknown to us. It also happens that they have been transcribed more carelessly than they should have been because they have not hitherto received royal attention. Now it is necessary for you to have accurate copies of them: indeed this legislation is full of hidden wisdom and entirely faultless, being the legislation of God: as Hecateus of Abdera says, the poets and historians make no mention of it nor of those men who lead their lives according to it because it is holy law and ought not to be proclaimed by profane mouths. If then it pleases you, O King, you may write to the high priest of the Jews asking him to send six of the elders from every tribe, those who are most learned in the laws, that we may learn from them the clear sense of these books and an accurate interpretation of their contents, and so have the kind of collection that may be suitable for you."

When this epistle was sent to the king, he commanded that an epistle be drawn up for Eleazar, the Jewish high priest, concerning these matters, and that he be informed of the release of the Jews that had been slaves among them. He also sent fifty talents of gold for the making of large basins, vials, and cups, and an immense quantity of precious stones. He also ordered those who had the custody of the chests containing those stones to give the artificers leave to select the sorts they liked. He then commanded that a hundred talents be sent to the Temple for sacrifices and other uses. I will give a description of those vessels and the manner of their construction after I set down the epistle written by King Ptolemy to Eleazar the high priest.

"There are many Jews who now dwell in my kingdom, whom the Persians, when they were in power, brought as captives. These were honored by my father; some he placed in the army, giving them greater pay than ordinary; to others, after they accompanied him to Egypt, he committed his garrisons and their guarding that they might be a terror to the Egyptians; and when I took over the government, I treated all men with humanity, especially those that are your fellow citizens, of whom I have set free over a hundred thousand who were slaves and paid to their masters the price for their redemption out of my own revenues; and those that are of a fit age, I have admitted into my army as soldiers; and for those capable of being faithful to me and suitable for my court, I have put them in such posts, thinking such kindness a very great and acceptable gift which I consecrate to God for His providence over me; and as I am eager to do what will be appreciated by these and all the other Jews on earth, I have determined to obtain a translation of your law, to have it translated from Hebrew into Greek, and to be deposited in my library. You will therefore oblige me by selecting and sending to me men of good character who are now elders, six out of each tribe. These must be learned in the laws, and capable of making an accurate translation: and once this shall be finished, I think I shall have completed a glorious work; I have sent to you Andreas, captain of my guard, and Aristeas, men whom I hold in very great esteem, by whom I have sent those gifts which I have dedicated to the Temple and to the sacrifices and other uses, to the value of a hundred talents; and if you will let us know what you would further like, you will do a thing acceptable to me."

When the king's epistle was brought to Eleazar, he replied with all possible respect: "We hope you and your queen and your children are well. When we received your epistle, we greatly rejoiced at your intentions; and when the multitude were gathered together, we read it to them, and thereby made them aware of your piety towards God. We also showed them the twenty vials of gold, the thirty of silver, and the five large basins, and the table for the shewbread; also the hundred talents for the sacrifices and for making what shall be needed at the Temple; which things Andreas and Aristeas, your most honored friends, have brought us; and truly they are persons of excellent character and great learning, and worthy of your trust. Know then that we will gratify you in what is to your advantage, though we do what we did not do before; for we ought to reciprocate for your numerous acts of kindness towards our countrymen. We immediately, therefore, offered sacrifices for you and your sister, with your children and friends; and the multitude offered prayers that your affairs may be to your liking and your kingdom be preserved in peace, and that the translation of our law may be brought to the conclusion you desire. We have also chosen six elders out of every tribe, whom we have sent, and the Law with them. It will be up to you, your piety and justice, to send back the Law after it has been translated; and to return those to us that bring it in safety. Farewell."

*After a long description of various gifts said to have
been sent by the king to Jerusalem, the story continues.*

But after Eleazar the high priest had dedicated these gifts to God, and had paid due respect to those that brought them, and had given them presents to be carried to the king, he dismissed them. And when they returned to Alexandria, and Ptolemy heard that they had come and so too the seventy elders, he sent for Andreas and Aristeas, his ambassadors, who came and delivered to him the epistle from the high priest, and answered all his questions. He then made haste to meet the elders that came from Jerusalem to translate the laws; and he commanded that everybody who had come on other business be sent away, which was surprising and not usual for him to do; for those that came there on such occasions used to come on the fifth day, but ambassadors at the month's end. But when he had sent them away, he waited for those sent by Eleazar; but as the old men came in with the presents the high priest had given them to bring to the king and with the scrolls on which their laws were written in golden letters, he put questions to them concerning those books; and when they had taken off the covers wherein they were wrapped up, they showed him the scrolls. So the king stood admiring the thinness of those scrolls and the exactness of the seams, which could not be perceived (so exactly were they connected with one another); and this he did for a considerable time. He then thanked them for coming, with even greater thanks to him that sent them, and, above all, to that God whose laws they bore. Then did the elders and those present with them cry out with one voice, wishing all happiness to the king. Upon which he burst into tears because of the excess of the pleasure he felt, it being natural for men to reveal the same emotions in great joy as they do under sorrow. And once he had bidden them deliver the books to those appointed to receive them, he saluted the men, saying it was but just to discourse of their errand. He promised, however, that he would memorialize this day on which they had come every year through the whole course of his life; [10] their coming proved to be on the very same day as the victory he had gained over Antigonus by sea. He also gave orders that they should sup with him and ordered that excellent lodgings

[10] It is an ironical and, at the same time, melancholy fact that while the king is said to have instituted a feast to celebrate the translation, the later rabbis fixed a date in the Jewish calendar, the eighth of Tevet, as a day of fasting, to commemorate what they regarded as a misfortune.

be provided them in the upper part of the city.

Accordingly, they made an accurate translation with great zeal and pain; and this they continued to do till the ninth hour of every day, after which they relaxed, taking care of their bodies while food was provided in great plenty: besides, Dorotheus, at the king's command, brought them a great deal of what was provided for the king himself. But in the morning they came to the court and saluted Ptolemy, and then returned to their lodgings, where, after they had washed their hands and purified themselves, they betook themselves to the translation. Now once the Law was transcribed and the labor of translation was over (after 72 days), Demetrius gathered all the Jews together and read over the laws. The populace also approved of those elders who were the translators. They commended Demetrius for his proposal, as the inventor of what was greatly for their happiness; and they desired that he give leave to their rulers also to read the law. Moreover, they all, both the priests and the most ancient of the elders and the leaders of their commonwealth, requested that since the translation was happily finished, it might be continued in its present state and not be altered. And they enjoined that if any one observed anything superfluous or anything omitted, he would review it and have it laid before them and corrected; this was a wise action, that when the thing was judged to have been well done, it might continue forever.

So the king rejoiced when he saw his design brought to perfection, to such great advantage; he was delighted with hearing the laws read to him, and was astonished at the legislator's deep meaning and wisdom. And he began to discourse with Demetrius, "How came it to pass that though this legislation was so wonderful, no one, either poet or historian, had mentioned it?" Demetrius answered "that no one dared be so bold as to touch upon the description of these laws because they were divine and venerable, and because some that had attempted it were afflicted by God." He also told him that "Theopompus [11] wanted to write about

---

[11] A famous Greek historian of the second half of the fourth century B.C.E., of whose works only fragments have survived.

them, but was thereupon mentally disturbed for more than thirty days; and during an interval of lucidity, he appeased God, suspecting that his madness proceeded from that cause." Nay, indeed, he further saw in a dream that his distemper befell him when he indulged too great a curiosity about divine matters and was eager to publish them among common men; but as soon as he stopped that attempt, he recovered his sanity.

And after the king had received these books from Demetrius, he was greatly pleased and gave orders that great care should be taken of them that they might remain uncorrupted. He also desired the interpreters to come to him often from Judea, both on account of the respect he would pay them and the presents he would give them; for, he said, it was now only just to send them away, although if, of their own accord, they would come to him hereafter, they should obtain all that their own wisdom might justly require and what his generosity was able to give them. So he sent them away, giving to every one three garments of the finest sort, two talents of gold, a cup of the value of one talent, and other gifts. He also sent with them for Eleazar the high priest ten beds, with silver feet, and the furniture belonging to them, and a cup of the value of thirty talents; and besides ten garments, a beautiful crown, a hundred pieces of the finest woven linen, and also vials and dishes, and vessels for pouring, and two golden cisterns to be dedicated to God. He also requested that Eleazar give the translators permission, if any of them wished, to come to him because he valued highly a conversation with men of such learning and was very willing to lay out his wealth for such men. And this was what came to the Jews, and was much to their glory and honor, from Ptolemy Philadelphus.

A proclamation of King Antiochus III of Syria concerning the Temple in Jerusalem.

He published a decree, throughout his kingdom in honor of the Temple, which read as follows: "It shall be unlawful for any foreigner to come within the limits of the Temple; this is also forbidden to the Jews, except for those who, according to their own custom, have purified themselves. Nor let any flesh of horses, mules, or asses be brought into the city, whether wild or tame; nor that of leopards, foxes, or hares; and, in general, that of any animal forbidden for the Jews to eat. Nor let their skins be brought into it, nor let any such animal be bred in the city. Let them only be permitted to use the sacrifices derived from their forefathers, with which they have been obligated to make acceptable atonements to God. And he that transgresses any of these orders will have to pay the priests three thousand drachmae of silver."

> *A letter by the same king concerning the transportation of two thousand Jewish families from Babylonia to the rebellious province of Phrygia, there to be guardians of his interests.*

"Having been informed that a rebellion has arisen in Lydia and Phrygia, I thought the matter required great care; and upon counseling with my friends, it has been thought proper to remove two thousand families of Jews, with their effects, out of Mesopotamia and Babylon, to the castles and places that are most conveniently located; for I am persuaded they will be well-disposed guardians of our possessions because of their piety towards God, and because I know that my predecessors have borne witness that they are faithful and eager to do what is asked of them. I request, therefore, though it be laborious work, that you remove these Jews with the promise that they shall be permitted to use their own laws; and when you will have brought them to the aforementioned places you shall give every one of their families a place to build a house, and a portion of land for husbandry and the planting of vines; you shall release them from paying taxes of the fruits of the earth for ten years; and let them have a proper quantity of wheat for the maintenance of their servants until they receive bread corn from the earth; also let a sufficient share be given to those who minister to them in the necessities of life so that by enjoying the effects of our humanity they may show themselves more willing and receptive to our affairs. Take care likewise of that nation, as far as you are able, that they may not suffer disturbance from any one." Now these testimonials which I have produced are sufficient to declare the friendship that Antiochus the Great bore to the Jews.

> *The antecedents and beginnings of the Hasmonean revolt. In the year 175* B.C.E., *Antiochus IV, surnamed Epiphanes, had come to the throne. In this account Josephus relies on the First Book of the Maccabees. Note the framework of international power politics within which Judean affairs must be understood.*

About this time, upon the death of Onias the high priest, they gave the high-priesthood to Jesus his brother, for that son which Onias left was still an infant. But this Jesus, the brother of Onias, was deprived of the high-priesthood by the king, who was angry with him, and gave it to his younger brother, whose name was also Onias; for Simon had three sons, to each of whom the priesthood came. This Jesus changed his name to Jason; but Onias was called Menelaus. Now since the former high priest Jesus had raised a rebellion against Menelaus, who was ordained after him, the populace was divided between them. The sons of Tobias took Menelaus's side but the great majority supported Jason; Menelaus and the sons of Tobias were distressed and withdrew to Antiochus, informing him that they wished to leave the laws of their country and the Jewish way of living according to them, and to follow the king's laws and the Grecian way of living; they desired his permission to build a gymnasium in Jerusalem. And when he had given them this, they also hid the circumcision of their genitals so that even when naked they might appear to be Greeks. Accordingly, they discarded all the customs that belonged to their own country and imitated the practices of the other nations.

Now Antiochus, with the peaceful situation of affairs in his kingdom, resolved to make an expedition against Egypt because he condemned the son of Ptolemy as weak and not yet capable of managing affairs of such consequence; so he arrived with great forces to Pelusium, circumventing Ptolemy Philometor by treachery, and seizing Egypt. He then came to the places around Memphis; and when he had captured them, he hastened to Alexandria in hopes of taking it by siege, and of subduing Ptolemy, who reigned there. But he was driven not only from Alexandria but out of all Egypt by the declaration of the Romans, who charged him to leave that country alone. Accordingly, I will now give a special account of what concerns that king—how he subdued Judea and the Temple.

King Antiochus returning out of Egypt, in fear of the Romans, made an expedition against the city of Jerusalem; and when he was there in the kingdom of the Seleucids, he took the city without fighting, those of his own party opening the gates to him. And once he had gained possession of Jerusalem, he slew many of the opposite party; and after plundering it of a great deal of money, he returned to Antioch.

Now it came to pass, after two years, in the hundred and forty-fifth year,[12] on the twenty-fifth day of that month which is called Kislev by us and by the Macedonians Apeleus, in the hundred and fifty-third olympiad, that the king came up to Jerusalem, and, pretending peace, gained possession of the city by treachery; at which time he spared not even those that admitted him because of the riches that lay in the Temple; but, led by his covetous inclination (for he saw there a great deal of gold and many ornaments of very great value), and in order to plunder its wealth, he ventured to break the pact he had made. So he left the Temple bare, taking away the golden candlesticks and the golden altar; nor did he abstain from even the curtains, which were made of fine linen and scarlet. He also emptied it of its secret treasures, and left nothing at all remaining; and by this means he cast the Jews into great lamentation, for he forbade them to offer those daily sacrifices which they used to offer to God, according to the law.

And after he had pillaged the whole city, some of the inhabitants he slew and some he took captive together with their wives and children so that the multitude of those taken alive amounted to about ten thousand. He also burnt down the finest buildings; and when he had overthrown the city walls, he built a citadel in

---

[12] 168 B.C.E.

the lower part of the city because the place was high and over-looked the Temple, on which account he fortified it with high walls and towers, and put into it a garrison of Macedonians. How-ever, in that citadel dwelt the impious and wicked part of the pop-ulace, from whom the citizens suffered many sore calamities. And after the king had built an idol altar upon God's altar, he slew swine on it and so offered a sacrifice neither according to the law nor the Jewish religious worship in that country.

He also compelled them to forsake the worship they offered their own God and to adore those whom he took to be gods; and he made them build temples and raise up idol altars in every city and village and offer up swine on them every day. He also com-manded them not to circumcise their sons, and threatened to pun-ish any that should be found to have transgressed his injunction. He also appointed overseers, who should compel them to do what he commanded. And indeed there were many Jews who complied with the king's commands, either voluntarily or out of fear of pen-alty; but the best men, those of the noblest souls, did not follow him, but were more greatly concerned with the customs of their country than with the punishment he threatened to the disobedi-ent; on which account they daily underwent great miseries and bit-ter torture; for they were whipped with rods, their bodies torn to pieces, and crucified while they were still alive and breathing; they also strangled those women and their sons whom they had circum-cised, as the king had ordered, hanging their sons around their necks as they were upon their crosses. And any sacred book of the Law found was destroyed; and those with whom they were found perished miserably.

When the Samaritans [13] saw the Jews under these sufferings, they no longer confessed that they were of their kindred nor that

[13] The Samaritans, descendants of those inhabitants of Samaria whose claim to be allowed to participate in the rebuilding of the Temple was re-jected by Zerubabel on the return of the Jews from exile in Babylonia. Throughout the Greco-Roman period the Samaritans appear as a distinct community, sometimes claiming kinship with the Jews and at other times denying it. Their temple was on Mount Gerizim near Shechem (modern Nablus).

the temple on Mount Gerizim belonged to Almighty God. This was according to their nature. They now said they were a colony of Medes and Persians; and indeed they were such a colony. So they sent ambassadors to Antiochus, and an epistle, whose contents are these: "To King Antiochus the god, Epiphanes, a memorial from the Sidonians, who live at Shechem. Our forefathers, upon certain frequent plagues, and following a certain ancient superstition, had a custom of observing that day which the Jews call the Sabbath. And when they had erected a temple at the mountain called Gerizim, though without a name, they offered the proper sacrifices on it. Now, upon the just treatment of these wicked Jews, those that manage their affairs, supposing we were kin to them and practice as they do, make us liable to the same accusations, although we are originally Sidonians, as is evident from the public records. We therefore beseech you, our benefactor and savior, to order Apollonius, the governor of this part of the country, and Nicanor, the procurator of your affairs, not to disturb us, nor lay to our charge what the Jews are accused for, since we are aliens from their nation and their customs; but let our temple, which at present has no name at all, be named the Temple of Jupiter Hellenius. If this were done, we should no longer be disturbed, but should be more intent on our own occupation with quietness and so bring greater revenue to you."

The king sent back the following answer: "King Antiochus to Nicanor. The Sidonians, who live at Shechem, have sent me the memorandum enclosed. When, therefore, we were advising with our friends about it, the messengers sent by them informed us that they are no way concerned with accusations related to the Jews, but choose to follow the customs of the Greeks. Accordingly, we declare them free from such accusations, and order that their temple be named the Temple of Jupiter Hellenius." He also sent a similar epistle to Apollonius, the governor of that part of the country.

The story of Mattathias the Hasmonean.

Now at this time there was one Mattathias, who dwelt at Modin, the son of John, the son of Simeon, the son of Asamoneus, a priest of the order of Joarib, and a citizen of Jerusalem. He had five sons: John, called Gaddis, and Simon, called Matthes, and Judas, called Maccabeus,[14] and Eleazar, called Auran, and Jonathan, called Apphus. Now this Mattathias lamented to his children the sad state of their affairs, the ravage made in the city, the plundering of the Temple, the calamities the multitude were under; and he told them it was better for them to die for the laws of their country than to live so ingloriously as they then did.

But when those appointed by the king came to Modin in order to compel the Jews to do what they were commanded, and to enjoin those that were there to offer sacrifice, as the king had commanded, they desired that Mattathias, the person of the greatest character among them, particularly on account of his numerous and deserving family of children, begin to sacrifice because his fellow citizens would follow his example and such a procedure would make him honored by the king. But Mattathias said he would not do it; and that even if all the other nations would obey the commands of Antiochus, either out of fear or to please him, yet neither would he nor his sons abandon the religious worship of their country; but as soon as he had ended his speech, one of the Jews appeared in their midst and sacrificed as Antiochus had commanded. This roused Mattathias to great indignation, and he ran upon him violently with his sons, who had swords, and slew both the man himself that sacrificed and Apelles, the king's general who had compelled them to sacrifice. He also overthrew the idol altar, crying out, "If any one be zealous for the laws of his country and the worship of God, let him follow me."

And after he had said this, he made haste into the desert with his sons, leaving all his possessions in the village. Many others did likewise, fleeing with their children and wives into the desert and dwelling in caves; but when the king's generals heard this, they took all the forces they then had in the citadel at Jerusalem and

---

[14] The etymology of this name is uncertain. It has been connected with the Hebrew (or Aramaic) word for "hammer." Others have tried to derive it from a combination of the initial consonants of the words *Mi Kamocha Ba-Elim Adonai,* "Who is like unto You among the gods, O Lord" (Exodus 15:11).

pursued the Jews into the desert; and after they had overtaken them, they at first endeavored to persuade them to repent and choose what was most to their advantage, and not put them to the necessity of enforcing the law of war against them; but when they would not comply but continued to be of a different mind, they fought against them on the Sabbath, and they burnt them in the caves, without their resisting or so much as closing up the entrances of those caves. And they avoided defending themselves on that day because they were not willing to break in upon the honor owed the Sabbath, even in such distress; for our law requires that we rest upon that day.[15] They numbered about a thousand, with their wives and children, who were smothered and died in those caves; but many of those that escaped joined Mattathias, appointing him to be their ruler; he taught them to fight even on the Sabbath, telling them that unless they do so, they would become their own enemies by observing the law while their adversaries would still assault them on this day, and that then nothing could prevent all of them from perishing without fighting. This speech persuaded them; and this rule continues among us to this day, that in the case of necessity we may fight on the Sabbath. So Mattathias gathered a great army around him, overthrowing their idol altars and slaying those who broke the laws, all he could get under his power; for many were dispersed among the nations round about them out of fear of him. He also commanded that those boys who were not yet circumcised should be circumcised now; and he drove those away who were appointed to prevent such circumcision.

But after he had ruled one year and had fallen into a distemper, Mattathias called for his sons and said: "O, my sons, I am going the way of all the earth; and I recommend to you my resolution, and beseech you not to be negligent in keeping it, but to be mindful of the desires of him who begat you and brought you up, and to preserve the customs of your country and recover your ancient form of government, which is in danger of being overturned, and not to be carried away by those who, either by their own inclina-

[15] See note above, p. 69.

tion or out of necessity, betray it, but to become such sons as are worthy of me; to be above all force and necessity, and so to dispose your souls, as to be ready, when necessary, to die for your laws, aware, by just reasoning, that if God see that you are so disposed He will not overlook you but will value your virtue and restore to you again what you have lost, returning to you that freedom in which you shall live quietly and enjoy your own customs. Your bodies are mortal and subject to fate; but they receive a sort of immortality through remembrance of the actions they have performed; and I would have you so in love with that immortality that you may pursue glory and that, after undergoing the greatest difficulties, you may not hesitate to give up your lives for such things. I exhort you especially to agree with one another; and in what excellency any one of you exceeds another to yield to him and by that means to reap the advantage of every one's virtues. Do then esteem Simon as your father because he is a man of extraordinary prudence, and be governed by him in whatever counsels he gives you. Take Maccabeus as the general of your army because of his courage and strength, for he will avenge your nation and bring vengeance on your enemies. Admit among you the righteous and religious, and augment their power."

When Mattathias had thus spoken to his sons and had prayed to God to assist them and to recover to the people their former consitution, he died shortly afterward, and was buried at Modin; all the people made great lamentation for him. His son Judas took upon himself the administration of public affairs; and thus, by the ready assistance of his brothers and of others, Judas cast their enemies out of the country, and put those of their own country to death who had transgressed its laws, and purified the land of all the pollutions that were in it.

The following extract throws interesting light on the expansionist policies of the Hasmonean Dynasty. The forcible conversion of the Idumeans was perhaps not the only action of its kind. Among the descendants of the Idumeans thus introduced into the community of the House of Israel was Herod.

But when Hyrcanus heard of the death of Antiochus he made an expedition against the cities of Syria hoping to find them destitute of fighting men. He took Medaba and then Samega, and the neighboring places; and Shechem and Gerizim as well. Hyrcanus took also Dora and Marissa, cities of Idumea, and subdued all the Idumeans, permitting them to stay there if they would circumcise their genitals and follow the laws of the Jews; and they were so desirous of living in the country of their forefathers that they submitted to circumcision and the other Jewish ways of living; at which time therefore it befell them that they were hereafter no other than Jews.

Note in the following extract how, even in antiquity, it was necessary for the inhabitants of Palestine to defend themselves against their near neighbors with the help of faraway allies.

But Hyrcanus the high priest was eager to renew their friendship with the Romans; accordingly he sent a delegation to them; and when the senate had received their epistle, they made a league of friendship with them, in the following manner: "Fanius, the son of Marcus, the praetor, gathered the senate together on the eighth day before the Ides of February, in the senate-house. The occasion was that the ambassadors sent by the Jews had something to propose about that league of friendship and mutual assistance which existed between them and the Romans, and about other public affairs, and desired that Joppa, and the harbors, and Gazara, and the springs, and several other of their cities and districts which Antiochus had taken from them in the war, contrary to the decree of the senate, might be restored to them; and that it might not be lawful for the king's troops to pass through their country and the countries of those subject to them: and that attempts Antiochus had made during that war, without the decree of the senate, might be made void: and that they would send ambassadors to take care that restitution be made them for what Antiochus had taken from them, and that they should make an estimate of the country laid waste during the war: and that they would grant them letters of protection to the kings and free people so they might return home quietly. It was therefore decreed to renew their league of friendship and mutual assistance with these good men, who were sent by a good and friendly people."

But as for the letters desired, their answer was that the senate would consult about the matter when their own affairs would allow them, and that they would endeavor, for the time to come, that no like injury should be done them: and that their praetor Fanius should give them money out of the public treasury to cover their expenses home.

> *Conflict between the Hasmonean rulers and the Phari-*
> *sees. There is a parallel account in the Talmud, though*
> *with different names for the main protagonists.*

However, this prosperous state of affairs moved the Jews to envy Hyrcanus; but those who were the worst disposed to him were the Pharisees, one of the Jewish sects. These have so great a power over the populace that when they say anything against the king or high priest, they are immediately believed. Now Hyrcanus was a disciple of theirs, and greatly beloved by them. And when he once invited them to a feast and entertained them very kindly, and seeing them in a good mood, he began to tell them that they knew he was desirous to be a righteous man and do all things whereby he might please God, which was also the profession of the Pharisees. However, if they observed him offending them on any point and departing from the right way, they were to call him back and correct him. They attested to his being entirely virtuous, with which commendation he was well pleased; but still there was one guest there whose name was Eleazar, a man of bad temper who delighted in seditious practices. This man said, "Since you desire to know the truth, if you want to be truly righteous, lay down the high-priesthood, and content yourself with the civil government of the people." And when he desired to know why he ought to lay down the high-priesthood,[16] the other replied, "We

---

[16] It had been one of the Hasmonean innovations to combine the high priesthood with the royal power. The Pharisees seem to have objected to it,

have heard from old men that your mother had been a captive under the reign of Antiochus Epiphanes." This story was false, and Hyrcanus was provoked and all the Pharisees felt great indignation against him.

Now there was one Jonathan, a great friend of Hyrcanus but of the sect of the Sadducees, whose notions were quite contrary to those of the Pharisees. He told Hyrcanus that Eleazar had cast such reproach upon him, according to the common sentiments of all the Pharisees, and that this would be made manifest if he would but ask the question: What punishment did they think this man deserved? The Pharisees answered that he deserved stripes and bonds, but that it did not seem right to punish reproaches with death; and indeed the Pharisees, even on other occasions, were not apt to be severe in punishments. At this gentle sentence, Hyrcanus became very angry, and thought this man reproached him with their approbation. It was Jonathan who chiefly influenced him to the extent that he made him leave the party of the Pharisees, abolish the decrees they had imposed on the people and punish those that observed them. From this source arose that hatred which he and his sons had met from the multitude.

After the death of King Alexander Jannai, his widow, following the king's advice makes peace with the Pharisees.

So Alexandra, after she had taken the fortress, acted as her husband had suggested and spoke to the Pharisees, putting all things into their power, both as to the dead body and the affairs of the kingdom, and thereby pacified their anger against Alexander. She came among the people and made speeches to them, laying before them the actions of Alexander and telling them that they had lost a righteous king; by their commendation they brought themselves to grieve and be in heavy mourning for him so that he had a fu-

---

particularly in this case, since if their story about the mother of Hyrcanus was true, there was here an infringement of the biblical law (Leviticus 21) according to which special purity was required of the wife of the high priest.

neral more splendid than any of the kings before him. Alexander left behind two sons, Hyrcanus [17] and Aristobulus, but committed the kingdom to Alexandra. As for these two sons, Hyrcanus was indeed unable to manage public affairs and delighted rather in a quiet life; but the younger, Aristobulus, was an active and bold man; and as for Alexandra herself, she was loved by the people because she seemed displeased at the offenses her husband had been guilty of.

So she made Hyrcanus high priest because he was the elder, but much more because he did not care to meddle with politics; she permitted the Pharisees to do everything, also ordering the masses to be obedient to them. She also restored again those practices the Pharisees had introduced, according to the traditions of their forefathers, and which her father-in-law Hyrcanus had abrogated. So she was indeed regent in name, but it was the Pharisees who had the authority; for it was they who restored those who had been banished, and set prisoners at liberty, and, to say everything at once, they differed in nothing from lords. However, the queen also took care of the affairs of the kingdom, getting together a great body of mercenary soldiers and increasing her own army to such a degree that she became a terror to the neighboring rulers and took hostages from them; and the country was entirely at peace, excepting the Pharisees; for they disturbed the queen, urging her to kill those who had persuaded Alexander to slay the eight hundred men,[18] after which they cut the throat of one of them, Diogenes; after him they did the same to several, one after another, till the men who were most powerful came into the palace, Aristobulus with them, for he seemed displeased at what had been done; and it appeared openly that if he had an opportunity he would not permit his mother to go on so. They reminded the queen of the great dangers they had gone through and the great things they had done, whereby they had demonstrated the firmness of their fidelity to their master, to the extent that they had received the greatest marks of favor from him. And they begged of her that she not ut-

---

[17] Not the same Hyrcanus as that mentioned in the preceding extract.
[18] One of the cruel acts of the king, for which see *Antiquities*, XIII.

terly blast their hopes, as had now happened, that once they had escaped the hazards that arose from their enemies in war they were to be cut off at home by their private enemies, like brute beasts, without any help whatsoever. They said also that if their adversaries would be satisfied with those already slain, they would take what had been done patiently, on account of their natural love for their rulers; but if they must expect the same in the future also, they implored of her a dismissal from her service; for they could not bear to think of attempting any method for their deliverance without her, but would rather die willingly before the palace gate in the event she would not forgive them. If she was determined to prefer the Pharisees over them, they still insisted that she place every one of them in her fortresses; for if some fatal demon had a spite against Alexander's house, they would be willing to bear their part and live in a private station there.

As these men were thus speaking and calling upon Alexander's ghost in pity of those already slain and those in danger of it, all the bystanders broke out into tears: but Aristobulus chiefly made manifest his sentiments to his mother, using many reproachful expressions: "Nay, indeed, the case is this, that they have themselves been the authors of their own calamities who have permitted a woman who, against reason, was mad with ambition to reign over them, when there were sons in the flower of their age fitter for it." So Alexandra, not knowing what to do with any decency, committed the fortresses to them, all but Hyrcania, Alexandrium, and Macherus, where her principal treasures were. After a short while, she also sent her son Aristobulus with an army to Damascus against Ptolemy, the son of Menneus, who was such a bad neighbor; but he did nothing considerable there, and returned home.

After this, when the queen had fallen dangerously ill, Aristobulus resolved to attempt seizing the government; so he stole away secretly by night, with only one of his servants, and went to the fortresses where his friends, from the days of his father, were settled; as he had been a long while displeased at his mother's conduct, so he was now much more afraid lest, upon her death, their whole family should fall under the power of the Pharisees; for he saw the weakness of his brother, who was to succeed in the government; nor was any one conscious of what he was doing except his wife, whom he left in Jerusalem with their children. He first came to Agaba, where he found Galestes, one of the powerful men mentioned before. When it was day the queen perceived that Aristobulus had fled; but for some time she did not suppose that his departure was for the purpose of making any innovations. But when messengers came one after another with the news that he had secured the first place, the second place, and all the places, for as soon as one had begun they all submitted, then the queen and her adherents fell into the greatest disorder, for they realized it would not be long before Aristobulus would be able to settle himself firmly in the government. What they were principally afraid of was that he would inflict punishment upon them for the bad treatment his house had had from them; so they resolved to take his wife and children into custody, placing them in the fortress above the Temple. Now a mighty conflux of people came to Aristobulus from all parts, to the extent that he had a kind of royal attendance around him; for in a little more than fifteen days, he had captured twenty-two strong places, which provided him the opportunity to raise an army, for men are easily led by the greater number and easily submit to them. Besides, by offering him their assistance when he could not expect it, they, as well as he, might have the advantages that would come from his being king because they had been responsible for his gaining the kingdom. Now the elders of the Jews, Hyrcanus among them, went in to the queen and requested that she disclose her feelings about the present posture of affairs; for Aristobulus was in effect lord of almost all the kingdom, possessing so many strongholds that it was absurd for them to take any counsel by themselves, however ill she was while she was alive, and that the dangers would be upon them in a very short time. But she bade them do what they thought proper; many circumstances still remained in their favor: a nation of good heart, an army, and money in their several treasuries. She had small concern about public affairs now that her strength was already failing.

Now a short while after she had said this to them, she died at the age of seventy-three, after having reigned nine years. A woman she was who showed no signs of the weakness of her sex, for she was sagacious to the greatest degree in her ambition to govern, and demonstrated by her deeds that her mind was fit for action and that sometimes men themselves show the little understanding they have through the frequent mistakes they make in government. She always preferred the present to the future and the power of an imperious dominion above all things, and, in contrast with that, had no regard for what was good or right. However, she brought the affairs of her house to such an unfortunate condition that she became responsible for the decline of its authority, and that no long time afterward, which she had obtained through a vast number of hazards and misfortunes. And this out of a desire that does not belong to a woman, by complying in her sentiments with those that bore ill will to their family and by leaving the administration destitute of a proper support of great men. Indeed, her management during her administration, while she was alive, filled the palace after her death with calamities and disturbance. However, although this had been her way of governing, she did preserve the nation in peace: and this is the conclusion of the affairs of Alexandra.

Dynastic strife in Judea leads to Roman intervention.

When Pompey had come to Damascus, he heard the causes of the Jews and of their governors Hyrcanus and Aristobulus, who were at odds with one another. Also against them both was the nation, which did not desire to be under kingly government; the form of government they had received from their forefathers was that of subjection to the priests of that God whom they worshiped; and they complained that though these two were the posterity of priests, yet they sought to change the government of their nation to another form in order to enslave them. Hyrcanus complained that although he was the elder brother, he was deprived of the prerogative of his birth by Aristobulus, and that he had but a small part of the country under him, Aristobulus having taken away the rest by force. He also accused him of making incursions into their neighbors' countries and of piracies at sea; the nation would not have revolted were Aristobulus not a man given to violence and disorder; and there were no fewer than a thousand Jews, the most highly esteemed among them, who confirmed this accusation. That confirmation was procured by Antipater, but Aristobulus alleged against him that it was Hyrcanus's own temperament, which was lazy and therefore contemptible, which caused him to be deprived of the government. As for himself, he was necessitated to take it upon him for fear lest it be transferred to others; and as to his title of king, it was no other than what his father had taken before him. He also called as witnesses of what he said certain persons who were both young and insolent, and whose purple garments, fine heads of hair, and other ornaments, were detested [by the court], and in which they appeared not as if to plead their cause in a court of justice but as though they were marching in a pompous procession.

When Pompey had heard the complaints of these two, and had condemned Aristobulus for his violent procedure, he then spoke civilly to them and sent them away; he told them that when he came again into their country he would settle all their affairs, after he had first taken a view of the affairs of the Nabateans. In the meantime, he ordered them to be quiet; he treated Aristobulus civilly lest he make the nation revolt and hinder his return; this, however, was the very thing Aristobulus did, for without expecting any further determination, as Pompey had promised, he marched into Judea.

At this behavior Pompey was angry, and taking with him that army he was leading against the Nabateans and the auxiliaries from Damascus and other parts of Syria, with his other Roman legions, he made an expedition against Aristobulus; but as he passed by Pella and Scythopolis, he came to Coreae, the first entrance into Judea when one passes over the midland districts, where he approached a most beautiful fortress built on the top of a mountain called Alexandrium, whither Aristobulus had fled; and thence Pompey sent his commands to him that he should come to him. Accordingly, at the persuasions of many that he should not make war against the Romans, he came down; and after he had disputed with his brother about the right to the government, he went up again to the citadel, as Pompey gave him leave to do; and this he did two or three times, flattering himself with the hope of having the kingdom granted him; he still pretended he would obey Pompey in whatsoever he commanded, although at the same time he retired to his fortress that he might not depress himself too low and that he might be prepared for a war in case it should prove, as he feared, that Pompey would transfer the government to Hyrcanus: but when Pompey enjoined Aristobulus to deliver up the fortresses he held and to send an injunction to their governors under his own hand for that purpose, for they had been forbidden to deliver them up on any other commands, he submitted indeed to do so; but still he retired in displeasure to Jerusalem and made preparation for war.

> *Pompey besieges Jerusalem. Dissension in the city. Jerusalem is taken. Pompey's settlement of Judaean affairs.*

Now after Pompey had pitched his camp at Jericho he marched in the morning to Jerusalem. Hereupon Aristobulus repented of what he was doing and came to Pompey, promising to give him money and receive him in Jerusalem; he desired that he would end the war and do what he pleased peaceably. So Pompey, upon his entreaty, forgave him and sent Gabinius and soldiers with him to receive the money and the city: yet was no part of this performed. Gabinius came back, being both excluded from the city and receiving none of the money promised; Aristobulus's soldiers would not permit the agreements to be executed. Pompey was very angry and put Aristobulus into prison, and came himself to the city, which was strong on every side excepting the north, which was not so well fortified because of a broad and deep ditch that encompassed the city and included within it the Temple, itself encompassed by a very strong stone wall.

Now there was a rebellion of the men within the city, who did not agree what was to be done in their present circumstances. Some thought it best to deliver up the city to Pompey, but Aristobulus's party exhorted them to shut the gates because he was still being kept in prison. Now these latter barred the others, seizing the Temple and cutting off the bridge reaching from it to the city, and prepared themselves for a siege; but the others admitted Pompey's army and delivered up both the city and the king's palace to him. So Pompey sent his lieutenant Piso with an army and placed garrisons both in the city and the palace to secure them, and fortified the houses adjoining the Temple and all those more distant and outside. And first he offered terms of accommodation to those who were inside; but when they would not comply with what was desired, he surrounded all the places thereabout with a wall, with Hyrcanus gladly assisting him; but Pompey pitched his camp within, on the north part of the Temple, where it was most practicable; but even on that side there were great towers; a ditch had been dug and a deep valley surrounded it, for on the parts facing the city were precipices, and the bridge over which Pompey had entered was broken down. However, a bank was raised, day by day, with a great deal of labor, while the Romans cut down materials for it from the places round about; and when this bank was sufficiently raised and the ditch filled up, though poorly because of its immense depth, he brought his mechanical engines and battering-rams from Tyre; and placing them on the bank, he battered the Temple with the stones that were thrown against it; and had it not been our practice, from the days of our forefathers, to rest on the seventh day, this bank could never have been perfected because of the opposition the Jews would have made; for though our law gives us leave to defend ourselves even on the Sabbath against those that begin to fight and assault us, yet it does not permit us to meddle with our enemies when they do anything else.[19]

When the Romans understood this, they threw nothing at the Jews nor came to any pitched battle with them, but raised up their earthen banks and brought their engines into forward positions so that they might go into action the following days; and anyone may hence learn what great piety we exercise towards God and the observance of His laws, since the priests were not at all hindered from their sacred ministrations by fear during this siege but still twice each day, in the morning and about the ninth hour, contin-

[19] Cf. p. 69, note.

ued to offer their sacrifices on the altar; nor did they omit those sacrifices, even when sad accidents took place because of the stones thrown among them. For although the city was taken on the third month, on the day of the fast,[20] when the enemy fell upon them and cut the throats of those in the Temple, yet even then those who were offering the sacrifices could not be compelled to run away, neither by fear for their own lives nor by the number already slain, thinking it better to suffer whatever came upon them, at their very altars, than to omit anything that their laws required of them.

But when the battering engine was brought near, the greatest of the towers was shaken by it and fell, breaking down a part of the fortifications, so the enemy poured in apace; and Cornelius Faustus, the son of Sulla, with his soldiers, was the first to ascend the wall, and next to him Furius the centurion, with those that followed, on the other side, while Fabius, also a centurion, ascended it in the middle, with a great body of men after him; but now all was full of slaughter; some of the Jews were being slain by the Romans, and some by one another; nay, some, unable to bear the miseries they were under, threw themselves down the precipices, or set fire to their houses and burnt them. Of the Jews twelve thousand fell, but of the Romans very few. Absalom, who was at once both uncle and father-in-law to Aristobulus, was taken captive.

And no small sacrileges were committed concerning the Temple itself, which, in former ages, had been inaccessible and seen by none; for Pompey entered it, and many with him also, and saw all that was unlawful for any other men except the high priests to see. There were in that Temple the golden table, the holy candlestick, the pouring vessels and a great quantity of spices; and besides these there were among the treasures two thousand talents of sacred money; yet did Pompey touch nothing of all this [21] on account of his respect for religion; and in this matter also he acted in a manner worthy of his virtue. The next day he ordered those in

[20] 63 B.C.E.
[21] This statement is supported by Cicero, *Pro Flacco,* 67.

charge of the Temple to cleanse it and to bring what offerings the Law required to God; he restored the high-priesthood to Hyrcanus because he had been useful to him in other respects and because he had prevented the Jews in the country from giving Aristobulus any assistance in his war against him. He also cut off those that had been the authors of that war; he bestowed proper rewards on Faustus and those others who had mounted the wall with such alacrity; and he made Jerusalem tributary to the Romans; he took away those cities of Celesyria which the inhabitants of Judea had subdued, and put them under the rule of the Roman governor and confined the whole nation, which had elevated itself so high before, within its own bounds. Moreover, he rebuilt Gadara, which had been demolished a little before, to gratify Demetrius of Gadara, who was his freedman, and restored to their own inhabitants the rest of the cities, Hippos and Scythopolis, and Pella, and Dios, and Samaria, as also Marissa, Ashdod, Jamnia, and Arethusa; these were in the inland parts. Besides those that had been demolished he restored also the maritime cities, Gaza, and Joppa, and Dora, and Strato's Towers. The last Herod rebuilt in a glorious manner, adorning it with harbors and temples; he changed its name to Caesarea. All these Pompey left in a state of freedom, and joined them to the province of Syria.

Reflections on the causes of the disaster.

Now the causes of this misery which came upon Jerusalem were Hyrcanus and Aristobulus and their raising a rebellion against one another; for now we lost our liberty and became subject to the Romans, and were deprived of that country which we had gained by our arms from the Syrians and were now compelled to restore to the Syrians. Moreover, the Romans extracted of us, in a short time, more than ten thousand talents; and the royal authority, a dignity formerly bestowed on those that were high priests by the right of their family, became the property of commoners.[22]

---

[22] Josephus here has in mind the passing of the royal power to the Herodian family.

Antipater's aid to Caesar in the war against Egypt.

Now after Pompey was dead, and after that victory Caesar had gained over him, Antipater, who managed the Jewish affairs, became very useful to Caesar when he made war against Egypt, and that by order of Hyrcanus; for while Mithridates of Pergamus was bringing his auxiliaries and was unable to continue his march through Pelusium but was obliged instead to stay at Askelon, Antipater came to him, conducting three thousand of the Jews, armed men: he had also seen to it that the leaders of the Arabians should come to his assistance; and on his account it was that all the Syrians assisted him also, not being willing to appear slow in their loyalty to Caesar—viz., Jamplicus the ruler, and Ptolemy his son, and Tholomy the son of Sohemus, who dwelt at Mount Libanus, and almost all the cities. So Mithridates marched out of Syria and came to Pelusium; and when its inhabitants would not admit him, he besieged the city. Now Antipater distinguished himself here, and was the first to pluck down a part of the wall and so open the way to the rest, whereby they might enter the city; and by this means Pelusium was taken. But it happened that the Egyptian Jews, who dwelt in the district of Onian, would not let Antipater and Mithridates, with their soldiers, pass to Caesar; but Antipater persuaded them to come over to their side because he was of their same people, and that chiefly by showing them the epistles of Hyrcanus the high priest, wherein he exhorted them to cultivate friendship with Caesar and supply his army with money and whatever provisions they needed; and accordingly, when they saw Antipater and the high priest to be of the same sentiments, they did as they were asked. And when those Jews came over to Caesar, they also invited Mithridates to come; so he came and received them also into his army.

And after Mithridates had gone over all Delta, as the place is called, he waged a pitched battle with the enemy, near the place called the Jewish Camp. Now Mithridates had the right wing, and Antipater the left; and when it came to the fighting, that wing of Mithridates was giving way and seemed likely to suffer extremely, were it not for Antipater's coming running with his own soldiers along the shore after he had already beaten the enemy opposing him; so he delivered Mithridates and put to flight those Egyptians who had been too strong for him. He took also their camp, and continued in their pursuit. He also called back Mithridates, who had been worsted and had retired a great distance away, and of whose soldiers eight hundred had fallen; of Antipater's only fifty had fallen. So Mithridates sent an account of this battle to Caesar, declaring openly that Antipater was responsible for this victory and for his own preservation; whereupon Caesar commended Antipater and made use of him all the rest of that war in the most hazardous undertakings: he happened also to be wounded in one of those engagements.

When Caesar, after some time, had finished that war and had sailed away to Syria, he honored Antipater greatly and confirmed Hyrcanus in the high-priesthood; he bestowed on Antipater the privilege of Roman citizenship and freedom from taxes everywhere; and it is reported by many that Hyrcanus went along with Antipater in this expedition, and came himself into Egypt.

But Antigonus, the son of Aristobulus, came at this time to Caesar, and lamented his father's fate; he complained that Aristobulus had been poisoned and his brother beheaded, and he desired that he take pity on him who had been ejected out of that principality due him. He also accused Hyrcanus and Antipater of governing the nation by violence, and inflicting injuries upon himself. Antipater was present, and defended himself against the accusations laid against him. He demonstrated that Antigonus and his party were given to innovation, and were seditious persons. He also reminded Caesar what difficult services he had undergone when he had assisted him in his wars, and discoursed about what he had himself witnessed. He added that Aristobulus had been justly carried away to Rome as an enemy of the Romans, and could never be brought to be a friend to them, and that his brother had gotten what he deserved having been seized for committing robberies; and that this punishment was not inflicted on him either in violence or with injustice.

After Antipater had made this speech, Caesar appointed Hyrcanus to be high priest, and gave Antipater whatever principality he himself would choose; so he made him procurator of Judea. He also gave Hyrcanus leave to raise up the walls of his own city, as he had requested, for they had been demolished by Pompey. And this grant he sent to the consuls of Rome, to be engraven in the capitol.

Enter Herod.

Now after Caesar had settled the affairs of Syria, he sailed away; and as soon as Antipater had conducted Caesar out of Syria, he returned to Judea. He then immediately raised up the wall which had been thrown down by Pompey; and, by coming thither, he pacified the tumult in the country, by both threatening and advising them to be quiet; if they would be on Hyrcanus's side, they would live happily and without disturbance, in the enjoyment of their own possessions; but if they persisted in hoping for what might come as a result of rebellion, aiming to gain wealth thereby, they would find him a severe master instead of a gentle governor, and Hyrcanus a tyrant instead of a king, and the Romans, together with Caesar, their bitter enemies instead of rulers: they would never allow to be set aside him whom they had appointed to govern. And after Antipater had said this to them, he himself settled the affairs of this country.

And seeing that Hyrcanus was of a slow and slothful temper, Antipater made Phasaelus, his eldest son, governor of Jerusalem and the places surrounding it, but committed Galilee to Herod, his next son, who was then only fifteen years of age; but that youth of his was no impediment to him, and since he was a youth of strong mind, he presently met with an opportunity to demonstrate his courage; for, finding there was one Hezekias, a captain of a band of robbers with whom he overran the neighboring parts of Syria, he seized and slew him as well as a great number of the other robbers with him; for this action he was greatly beloved by the Syrians; for when they were very anxious to have their country freed from this nest of robbers, he purged it of them; so in their villages and cities they sang songs commending him as having procured them peace and the secure enjoyment of their possessions; and on this account he became known to Sextus Caesar, a relative of the great Caesar and presently governor of Syria. Now Phasaelus, Herod's brother, was moved to emulate his actions, envying the fame Herod had thereby gotten; he became ambitious not to fall behind him in merit so he made the inhabitants of Jerusalem bear him the greatest good will because he ruled the city, managing its affairs properly and not abusing his authority therein. This conduct procured from the nation such respect for Antipater as is due kings and such honors as he might partake of were he absolute lord of the country. Yet this splendor of his did not, as frequently happens, diminish in the least the kindness and fidelity he owed to Hyrcanus.

But now when the leaders among the Jews saw Antipater and his sons grow so much in the good will of the nation towards them and in the revenues they received from Judea and from Hyrcanus's own wealth, they became ill-disposed to him; for indeed Antipater had contracted a friendship with the Roman emperors; and when he had prevailed with Hyrcanus to send them money, he took it for himself and purloined the present intended, sending it to them as if it were his own rather than Hyrcanus's gift. Hyrcanus heard of this but was not disturbed by it; nay, he rather was glad of it; but the leaders of the Jews were in fear because they saw that Herod was a violent and bold man, and very desirous of acting tyrannically; so they came to Hyrcanus, accusing Antipater openly: "How long will you be quiet under such actions as are now taking place? Or do you not see that Antipater and his sons have already seized the government, and that you are king only in name? But do not suffer these things to be hidden from yourself; nor think not to escape danger by being so careless of yourself and your kingdom; for Antipater and his sons are not now stewards of your affairs; do not deceive yourself with such a notion; they are obviously absolute lords; for Herod, Antipater's son, has slain Hezekias and those that were with him, and has thereby transgressed our law, which forbids the slaying of any man even though he is wicked unless he has first been condemned to suffer death by the Sanhedrin; yet he has been insolent enough to do this, and that without any authority from you."

Upon Hyrcanus's hearing this he agreed with them. The mothers also of those slain by Herod raised his indignation; for those women came every day to the Temple to persuade the king and the people to bring Herod to trial before the Sanhedrin for what he had done. Hyrcanus was so moved by these complaints that he summoned Herod to come to trial for what was charged against him. Accordingly he came; but his father had persuaded him to come not as a private man but with a guard for his security; and once he had settled the affairs of Galilee in the best manner he could, he should come to his trial, but with a body of men sufficient for his security on his journey, yet not so great as might look like a threat to Hyrcanus, but still such a one as might not expose him naked and unguarded to his enemies. However, Sextus Caesar, governor of Syria, wrote to Hyrcanus, urging him to clear Herod and dismiss him at his trial, and threatened him beforehand if he did not do this. That epistle of his occasioned Hyrcanus to deliver Herod from suffering any harm from the Sanhedrin, for he loved him as his own son; but when Herod stood before the Sanhedrin, with his body of men about him, he frightened them all: and no one of his former accusers dared after that bring any charge against him: there was a deep silence, and nobody knew what was to be done.

When affairs stood thus, one whose name was Sameas, a righteous man and for that reason above all fear, rose up and said, "O you that are assessors with me, and O you who are our king, I neither have ever myself known such a case, nor do I suppose that any one of you can name its parallel, that one who is called to stand trial with us ever stood in such a manner before us; but every one, whosoever he be, that comes to be tried by this Sanhedrin presents himself in a submissive manner, like one in fear of himself, endeavoring to move us to compassion, with his hair dishevelled, and in a black mourning garment: but this man Herod, who is accused of murder and called to answer so heavy an accusation, stands here clothed in purple, with his hair finely trimmed, and with his armed men about him so that if we condemn him by our law, he may slay us, and by overbearing justice may himself escape death; yet I do not make this complaint against Herod himself; he is to be sure more concerned for himself than for the laws; but my complaint is against yourselves and your king, who give him license so to do. However, take notice that God is great, and that this very man whom you are going to absolve and dismiss for the sake of Hyrcanus will one day punish both you and also your king himself." Nor did Sameas err in any part of this prediction; for after Herod gained the kingdom, he slew all the members of this Sanhedrin (and Hyrcanus himself, too), all excepting Sameas, whom he greatly honored on account of his righteousness, and because, when the city was later besieged by Herod and Sosius, it was he who persuaded the people to admit Herod, telling them that for their sins they would not be able to escape his hands.

But when Hyrcanus saw that the members of the Sanhedrin were ready to pronounce the sentence of death upon Herod, he put off the trial to another day, and advised Herod privately to flee the city so that he might escape. So Herod retired to Damascus, as though he fled from the king; and after he had been with Sextus Caesar and had put his own affairs in a sure posture, he resolved to do thus: In case he were again summoned before the Sanhedrin to undergo trial, he would not obey that summons. Hereupon the members of the Sanhedrin felt great indignation at this turn of events and endeavored to persuade Hyrcanus that all these things were a threat to him; he was not ignorant of this state of matters, but his temper was so unmanly and so foolish that he was able to do nothing at all. But after Sextus had made Herod general of the army of Celesyria, selling him that post for money, Hyrcanus was in fear lest Herod make war against him; nor was the result of what he feared long in coming—for Herod came bringing an army along with him to fight Hyrcanus on the grounds of being angry at the trial he had been summoned to undergo before the Sanhedrin; but his father Antipater and his brother Phasaelus met him and dissuaded him from assaulting Jerusalem. They also pacified his vehement temper, persuading him to take no overt action but only to frighten them with threatenings and to proceed no further against one who had given him whatever dignity he had; they also desired him not just to be angry that he had been summoned and obliged to come to trial, but to remember withal how he was dismissed without condemnation, and how he ought to give Hyrcanus thanks for the same. So they urged him to consider that since it is God who turns the scales of war, there is great uncertainty in the issue of battles, and that therefore he ought not to expect victory when he fought against his king who had supported him and bestowed many benefits upon him, and had done nothing in itself very severe to him; for Hyrcanus's accusation, which was derived from evil counselors and not from himself, had the appearance of severity rather than anything really severe in it. Herod was persuaded by these arguments, and believed it sufficient for his future hopes to have made a show of his strength before the nation, and do nothing more—and in this state were the affairs of Judea at this time.

After the death of Caesar.

When Antony came into Syria, Cleopatra met him in Cilicia and led him to fall in love with her. And there came also a hundred of the most powerful of the Jews to accuse Herod and those around him, and set the men of the greatest eloquence among them to speak. But Messala contradicted them, on behalf of the young men, in the presence of Hyrcanus, who was by this time Herod's kinsman by marriage. When Antony had heard both sides he asked Hyrcanus who governed the nation best. He replied, Herod and his friends. Hereupon Antony, by reason of his old hospitable friendship with their father Antipater, made both Herod and Phasaelus tetrarchs, committing the public affairs of the Jews to them and writing letters to that effect. He also bound fifteen of their adversaries and was about to kill them when Herod obtained their pardon.

Yet these men did not remain quiet when they returned, but a thousand Jews came to Tyre hoping to meet Herod there. But Antony was corrupted by the money Herod and his brother had given him, and so he ordered the governor of the place to punish the Jewish ambassadors, who wanted to make innovations, and to put Herod in charge of the government: but Herod went out hastily to them with Hyrcanus (they stood on the shore before the city), and he charged them to go their ways because great mischief would befall them if they continued their accusation. But they did not acquiesce: whereupon the Romans ran upon them with daggers and slew some and wounded others; the rest fled in great consternation: and when the people made a clamor against Herod, Antony was so provoked that he slew the prisoners.

Herod's enemies are supported by the Parthians. He is forced to flee to Idumaea.

While the Parthians were in consultation about what was to be done, for they did not think it proper to make an open attempt upon a person of his character, and while they put off their decision to the next day, Herod was greatly disturbed. Inclined to believe the reports he heard about his brother and the Parthians rather than to heed what was said on the other side, he determined that when the evening came he would use it for his flight, and not delay any longer, since the dangers from the enemy were not yet certain. He therefore moved with the armed men who were with him; he put his wives on the beasts, also his mother and sister, and her whom he was about to marry [Mariamne], the daughter of Alexander, the son of Aristobulus, with her mother, the daughter of Hyrcanus, and his youngest brother, and all their servants, and the rest of the people with him. And without the enemy's knowledge he pursued his way to Idumaea: nor could any enemy who saw him be so hardhearted as not to have commiserated with his fortune as the women carried their infant children and departed their own country, leaving their friends in prison, with tears in their eyes, sad lamentation, and expecting nothing but what was of a melancholy nature.

As for Herod himself, he raised his mind above his miserable state and was of good courage in the midst of his misfortunes; and as he passed along he bade every one be of good cheer and not give themselves up to sorrow because that would hinder them in their flight, which was now their only hope of safety. Accordingly, they tried to bear their calamity with patience as he exhorted them to do; yet he was once almost going to kill himself when a wagon was overthrown and his mother was in danger of being killed; and this for two reasons, because of his great concern for her, and because he was afraid lest, owing to this delay, the enemy overtake him; but while he was drawing his sword and was about to kill himself, those present restrained him, and being many in number, subdued him; they told him he ought not to desert them and leave them a prey to their enemies: it was not fitting for a brave man to free himself from his own distresses and thus overlook his friends who were also in the same distress. Thus he was compelled to abandon that terrible attempt, partly out of shame at what was said to him, and partly out of regard for the great number of those bent on keeping him from doing what he intended. So he encouraged his mother, taking all the care of her time would allow, and proceeded the way he had proposed to go with the utmost haste, to the fortress of Masada. On the way he had many skirmishes with Parthians attacking and pursuing him, and he conquered them all.

Nor indeed was he as free from the Jews as he had been in his flight: by the time he had gotten sixty furlongs out of the city and was on the road, they fell upon him, fighting hand to hand; he put them to flight, and overcame them, not in the manner of one in distress but like one excellently prepared for war and plentifully supplied. And in the very place where he overcame the Jews, he was later to build an excellent palace and a city around it, which he was to call Herodium. And when he came to Idumaea, his brother Joseph met him: and he then held council on all his affairs and what was fit to be done in his circumstances, since he had a great multitude of followers as well as mercenary soldiers: since Masada, where he proposed to fly, was too small to contain this great multitude, he sent away the greater part of his company, more than nine thousand, bidding them scatter and so save themselves in Idumaea and giving them the wherewithal to buy provisions on their journey. But he took with him those who were the least encumbered and most intimate with him, and came to the fortress, settling there his wives and followers, eight hundred in number, there being in the place a sufficient quantity of corn and water and other necessaries, and then going directly to Petra, in Arabia. But when it was day, the Parthians plundered all Jerusalem and the palace, abstaining from nothing but Hyrcanus's money, which amounted to three hundred talents. A great deal of Herod's money was saved, principally what the man had so providently sent to Idumaea beforehand: nor indeed were the Parthians satisfied with what was in the city; they went out into the country and plundered it, demolishing the city Marissa.

And thus was Antigonus brought back into Judea by the king of the Parthians, who took Hyrcanus and Phasaelus as prisoners; but he was greatly cast down because the women he intended to give the enemy had escaped, together with the money he had promised them as their reward: but being afraid that Hyrcanus, who was under Parthian guard, might have his kingdom restored to him by the multitude, he cut off his ears, thereby taking care that the high-priesthood should never come to him because he was maimed, since the law required that this dignity should be bestowed only upon those who had all their members intact. But one cannot but admire the fortitude of Phasaelus, who, perceiving he was to be put to death, did not think death a terrible thing at all; but he did think that dying at the hands of his enemy was a most pitiful and dishonorable thing: therefore, since his hands were bound in order to prevent him from killing himself, he dashed his head against a great stone and thereby took his own life: he thought this the best thing he could do in his distress, thereby putting it out of the enemy's power to put him to death. It is also reported that after he had made a great wound in his head, Antigonus sent physicians, whom he ordered to infuse poison into the wound and so killed him. However, Phasaelus, before he was quite dead, heard from a certain woman that his brother Herod had escaped the enemy, and so approached his death cheerfully, since he now left behind one who would revenge his death and inflict punishment on his enemies.

Herod becomes king of the Jews.

As for Herod, his great misfortunes did not discourage him but made him sharp in discovering surprising undertakings. He went to Malchus, the king of Arabia, to whom he had formerly been very kind, in order to receive some compensation, of which he was now in greater need than ever, requesting that he let him have some money, either as a loan or as a gift, on account of the many benefits he had received from him. Not knowing what had become of his brother, he was in haste to redeem him out of the hands of his enemies, and was willing to pay as much as three hundred talents for his redemption. He also took with him the son of Phasaelus, a child of seven, whom he might offer to the Arabs as a hostage for the repayment of the money. But he was met by messengers from Malchus, who desired him to be gone because the Parthians had laid a charge upon him not to entertain Herod. This was only a pretense he used in order not to be obliged to repay what he owed him; he was further encouraged to do this by the leaders among the Arabians, that they might cheat him of the sums they had received from his father Antipater, and with which he had entrusted them. He answered that he did not intend to be troublesome by coming thither, but that he desired only to discourse with them about certain affairs of the greatest importance to him.

Hereupon he resolved to depart, and did go very prudently the road to Egypt; and then he lodged in a certain temple, where he had left a great many of his followers. On the next day he came to Rhinocoura, where he heard what had befallen his brother. Malchus soon repented of what he had done and came running after Herod, but with no success, for he was a very great way off and made haste into the road to Pelusium; and when the stationary ships that lay there hindered him from sailing to Alexandria, he went to their captains, with whose assistance he was conducted to Alexandria; he was there retained by Cleopatra, but she was unable to prevail upon him to stay there because he was hastening to Rome, even though the weather was stormy and he had been informed that Italy's affairs were very tumultuous and in great disorder.

So he set sail from there to Pamphylia, and falling into a violent storm he was hard put to escape to Rhodes, and only after the loss of the ship's burden; and there two of his friends, Sappinas and Ptolemeus, met him; and as he found that city very much damaged from its war against Cassius, though in need himself, did what he could to bring it back to its former state. He also built there a three-decker ship, and set sail thence, with his friends, for Italy, and came to the port of Brundisium: and when he had gone from there to Rome, he related to Antony what had befallen him in Judea, and how Phasaelus his brother had been seized by the Parthians and put to death; and how Hyrcanus had been taken as captive by them, and how they had made Antigonus king, and he had promised them no less than a thousand talents plus five hundred women from the leading families of Jewish stock; and how he had carried off the women by night; and how, by undergoing a great many hardships, he had escaped his enemies; as also how, since his own relatives were in danger of being besieged and taken, he had sailed through a storm and suffered all these terrible dangers in order to come, as soon as possible, to him who was his hope and only succor at this time.

This account made Antony sympathize with the change that had taken place in Herod's condition; and reasoning with himself that this was a common fate of those placed so high and that they were vulnerable to the mutations of fortune, he was very ready to give him whatever assistance he desired; and this because he remembered the friendship he had had with Antipater, and because of his hatred for Antigonus, whom he took to be a seditious person and an enemy of the Romans. Caesar [23] was also ready to raise Herod's dignity and to grant him whatever assistance he desired, because of the toils of war he had himself undergone with Antipater his father in Egypt, and the hospitality and kindness he had always shown him; he also was eager to gratify Antony, who was very zealous for Herod. So a senate was convened: and Messala first, and later Atratinus, introduced Herod into it, enlarging upon the benefits they had received from his father, and reminding them of the good will he had borne to the Romans. At the same time, they accused Antigonus, declaring him an enemy not only because of his former opposition to them, but because he had now over-

[23] Octavian, later called Augustus.

looked the Romans and taken the government from the Parthians. The senate was irritated by this. Antony informed them further that it was to their advantage in the Parthian war that Herod should be king. This seemed right to all the senators, and so they made a decree accordingly.

And this was the principal instance of Antony's affection for Herod, that he not only procured him a kingdom he did not expect (for he did not come with any intention to ask the kingdom for himself, which he did not imagine the Romans would grant him, since they used to bestow it on some of the royal family: he had rather intended to request it for his wife's brother, who was grandson through his father of Aristobulus, and of Hyrcanus through his mother), but that he procured it for him so quickly that he obtained what he did not expect and departed from Italy in fewer than seven days in all. (This young man [the grandson] Herod later took care to have slain.) But after the senate was dissolved, Antony and Caesar went out of the senate house, with Herod between them, and with the consuls and other magistrates, in order to offer sacrifices and lay up their decrees in the capitol. Antony also feasted Herod the first day of his reign. And thus did this man receive the kingdom.

Herod was now king; but he still had to overcome much opposition in Judea. He married Mariamne, the granddaughter of Hyrcanus, thus, to some extent, at least, legitimizing his claims to the throne.

After Herod's wedding, Sosius came through Phoenicia, having sent his army ahead of him out over the midland parts. He also came himself with a great number of horsemen and footmen. The king also came himself from Samaria, bringing with him no small army, in addition to what was there before, numbering about thirty thousand; and they all met together at the walls of Jerusalem, encamping at the north wall of the city, being now an army of eleven legions, armed men on foot, and six thousand horsemen, with other auxiliaries out of Syria. There were two generals: Sosius, sent by Antony to assist Herod, and Herod himself, in order to take the government from Antigonus, who was declared an enemy of Rome, so that he might himself be king, according to the decree of the senate.

Now the Jews that were enclosed within the walls of the city fought against Herod with great alacrity and zeal (for the whole nation was gathered together); they also gave out many prophecies about the Temple and many things agreeable to the people, if God would deliver them out of their dangers; they had also carried off what was outside the city so as not to leave anything to afford sustenance either for men or beasts; and, by secret sorties, they made the lack of necessities even greater. When Herod understood this, he opposed ambushes in the fittest places against them, and sent legions of armed men to bring in provisions from remote places so that in a short time they had great plenty of provisions. Now the three bulwarks were easily erected because so many hands were continually at work on them; it was summertime and there was nothing to hinder them from raising their works: so they brought their engines to bear, and shook the walls of the city, and tried all manner of ways to get in: yet those within were not afraid but also set up not a few engines to oppose the engines outside. They also sallied out and burnt not only those engines that were not yet completed but also those that were; and when they came hand to hand, their attempts were no less bold than those of the Romans, though they were inferior to them in skill. They also erected new works when the former were ruined, and, making mines underground, they met each other and fought there; and using brutish courage rather than prudent valor, they persisted in this war to the very last: and this they did while a mighty army lay around about them, and while they were harassed by famine and lack of necessities, for this happened to be a sabbatical year.[24]

The first to scale the walls were twenty chosen men; next were Sosius's centurions; the first wall was taken in forty days, and the second in fifteen more, when some of the cloisters around the Temple were burnt, which Herod gave out as having been burnt

[24] The so called Shemitta year (see Leviticus 25:4), every seventh year, during which the Jews were enjoined to let their lands lie fallow. This explains the lack of provisions.

by Antigonus so as to expose him to the hatred of the Jews. And once the outer court of the Temple and the lower city were taken, the Jews fled into the inner court of the Temple and the upper city; but now fearing lest the Romans prevent them from offering their daily sacrifices to God, they sent emissaries, requesting permission to be allowed to bring in beasts for sacrifices. This Herod granted, hoping they were going to yield; but when he saw that they did nothing of what he had supposed but bitterly opposed him in order to preserve the kingdom for Antigonus, he made an assault upon the city and took it by storm; and now all parts were full of those slain, by the rage of the Romans over the long duration of the siege, and by the zeal of the Jews on Herod's side who were unwilling to leave even one of their adversaries alive; so they were murdered continually in the narrow streets, and in the houses, and as they were flying to the Temple for shelter: and no pity was shown for either infants or the aged, nor did they spare so much as the weaker sex; nay, although the king besought them to spare the people, yet nobody refrained from slaughter, but, like a company of madmen, they fell upon persons of all ages, without distinction. And then Antigonus, without regard to either his past or present circumstances, came down from the citadel and fell down at the feet of Sosius, who took no pity on him or the change in his fortune, but insulted him beyond measure, calling him Antigone (i.e., a woman, and not a man); yet he did not treat him as if he were a woman, letting him go at liberty, but instead put him into bonds and kept him in close custody.

And now that Herod had overcome his enemies, his concern was to govern those foreigners who had been his assistants, for a crowd of strangers rushed to see the Temple and the sacred things in it; but the king, thinking victory to be a more severe affliction than defeat, if it meant that any of those things inside the Temple which it was not lawful to see should be seen by them, used entreaties and threats, and sometimes even force itself, to restrain them. He also prohibited the ravage that was made in the city, and many times asked Sosius whether the Romans would empty the city both of money and men, and leave him king of a desert; and he told him that he esteemed the dominion over the whole habitable earth as by no means an equivalent satisfaction for such a murder of his citizens; and when Sosius said this plunder was justly to be permitted the soldiers after the siege they had undergone, Herod replied that he would give every one a reward out of his own money; and by this means he redeemed from destruction what remained of the city; and he did what he had promised, giving a noble present to every soldier, an appropriate present to their commanders, and a most royal present to Sosius himself, so that they all went away full of money.

This destruction befell the city of Jerusalem as if a periodical revolution of calamities had returned since the one that had befallen the Jews under Pompey; for the Jews had been taken by him on the same day, twenty-seven years ago. So after Sosius had dedicated a gold crown to God, he marched away from Jerusalem, carrying Antigonus with him in bonds to Antony; but Herod was afraid lest Antigonus be kept in prison only by Antony, and that once he was carried to Rome by him he might have his case heard by the senate, and might demonstrate, since he was himself of royal blood and Herod was only a private man, that therefore the kingdom belonged to his sons on account of their family, and in the event that he himself had offended the Romans by what he had done. Because of Herod's fear of this, he gave Antony a great deal of money and endeavored to persuade him to have Antigonus slain so that he might be free from that fear. And thus did the government of the Hasmoneans cease, 126 years after it was first set up.[25] This family was a splendid and illustrious one, both on account of the nobility of their stock and the dignity of the high-priesthood, as well as because of the glorious actions of their ancestors for our nation: but these men lost the government by their dissensions with one another: and it fell to Herod, the son of Antipater, who was of no more than a common family and of no eminent extraction but one subject to other kings. And this history tells us was the end of the Hasmonean family.

[25] The chronology here is slightly inaccurate.

*In the great contest between Octavian and Antony,
Herod had supported the latter. At the Battle of Actium (31 B.C.E.) Octavian emerged the victor. This presented Herod with a difficult and dangerous situation.*

Herod's other affairs were now very prosperous, and he could
not be easily assaulted on any side. Yet, after Antony had been
beaten at the battle of Actium by Octavian, there did come upon
him a danger that would hazard his entire dominions: at that time
both Herod's enemies and friends despaired of his affairs, for it
was not probable that he who had shown so much friendship for
Antony would remain without punishment. So it happened that his
friends despaired and had no hope of his escape; as for his enemies, they all appeared outwardly troubled by his situation, but
were privately very glad of it, hoping to obtain a change for the
better. As for Herod himself, he saw that there was no one of
royal dignity left but Hyrcanus, and therefore he thought it to his
advantage not to suffer him to remain an obstacle in his way any
longer; in case he himself survived and escaped the danger he was
in, he thought it was safest to put it beyond the power of such a
man as Hyrcanus to make any attempt against him at such junc-
tures of affairs: and in the event he should be slain by Caesar,
Herod's envy prompted him to desire to slay Hyrcanus, who
would otherwise be king after him.

While Herod had these things in mind, a certain opportunity
was offered him; for Hyrcanus was of so mild a temper that he
desired not to meddle in public affairs nor to concern himself with
innovations, but left all to fortune, contenting himself with what
that offered him: but Alexandra [26] was a lover of strife, and exceedingly desirous of a change of government; she told her father
not to bear forever Herod's injurious treatment of their family, but
to anticipate their future hopes, as he safely might; she desired
him to write about these matters to Malchus, who was then ruler
of Arabia, to receive them and to protect them from Herod, for if
they went away, and Herod's affairs went badly, as was likely be-

[26] His daughter, Herod's mother-in-law.

cause of Octavian's enmity toward him, they should then be the only persons that could rule the government, both because of their royal descent and the good disposition of the multitude towards them. While she used these persuasions, Hyrcanus put off her suit; but since she showed she was a woman, and a contentious one at that, and would not desist either night or day but always went on speaking to him about these matters and about Herod's treacherous designs, she at last prevailed upon him to entrust Dositheus, one of his friends, with a letter declaring his resolve; and he requested the Arabian ruler to send him some horsemen, to receive him and conduct him to the Dead Sea, which is three hundred stades from the bounds of Jerusalem. And he did therefore trust Dositheus with his letter because he was a faithful attendant to him and Alexandra, and because he had no small occasion to bear ill will to Herod; for he was a kinsman of one Joseph, whom Herod had slain, and a brother of those formerly slain at Tyre by Antony: yet even these motives could not induce Dositheus to serve Hyrcanus in this affair; for, preferring the hopes he had from the present king to those he had from Hyrcanus, he gave Herod the letter. So Herod took Dositheus's kindness in good part, bidding him do what he had already done, that is, go on serving him, by rolling up the epistle and resealing it, and delivering it to Malchus, and then bringing back the letter in answer to it; for it would be much better if Herod could know Malchus's intentions also. The Arabian ruler sent back an answer that he would receive Hyrcanus and all that should come with him, and even all the Jews that were in his party: that he would, moreover, send sufficient forces to protect them in their journey and that Hyrcanus should not want for anything. As soon as Herod received this letter, he immediately sent for Hyrcanus and questioned him about the league he had made with Malchus; and when Hyrcanus denied it, Herod showed his letter to the Sanhedrin and put the man to death immediately.

And this account is contained in the commentaries of King Herod: but other historians do not agree with them, for they suppose that Herod did not find, but rather made, this an occasion for putting him to death, by treacherously laying a snare for him; for thus do they write: That Herod had given him no opportunity to suspect he was displeased but put this question to Hyrcanus, whether he had received any letters from Malchus. And when he answered that he had received letters but only those of greeting, Herod asked further, whether he had not received any presents from him. And when he had replied that he had received no more than four horses to ride on, which Malchus had sent him, Herod charged Hyrcanus with the crimes of bribery and treason and ordered that he be led away and slain. And in order to demonstrate that Hyrcanus had been guilty of no offence when he was thus brought to his end, they alleged how mild his temper had been; and that even in his youth he had never given any demonstration of boldness or rashness, and that the situation was the same when he became king, but that even then he committed the management of the greatest part of public affairs to Antipater; and that he was now over fourscore years old and knew that Herod's government was in a secure state. He also came over the Euphrates, leaving those who greatly honored him beyond that river, though he were to be entirely under Herod's rule; and that it was a most incredible thing that he should start anything by way of innovation and not at all agreeable to his temper, but that this was a plot of Herod's own contrivance.

This was the fate of Hyrcanus; and thus did he end his life, after he had endured various turns of fortune in his lifetime; for he was made high priest of the Jewish nation in the beginning of the reign of his mother Alexandra, who held the government nine years; and when, after his mother's death, he took the kingdom himself and held it three months, he lost it because of his brother Aristobulus. He was then restored by Pompey, receiving all sorts of honors from him and enjoying them forty years; but when he was again deprived by Antigonus and was maimed in his body, he was made a captive by the Parthians, and thence returned home again after some time because of the hopes Herod had held out to him, none of which came to pass according to his expectation: but he was still afflicted with many misfortunes through the whole course of his life, and, what was the heaviest calamity of all, he came to an undeserved end. His character appeared to be that of a

man of mild and moderate disposition, who allowed the administration of affairs to be generally done by others under him. He
was averse to much mingling with the public, nor had shrewdness
enough to govern a kingdom; and both Antipater and Herod came
to their greatness by reason of his mildness; and at last he met
with such an end from them as was lacking in either justice or
piety.

Now Herod, as soon as he had put Hyrcanus out of the way,
hastened to Octavian; and because he could not have any hopes of
kindness from him on account of his friendship for Antony, he
had a suspicion of Alexandra, lest she take this opportunity to
bring the people to a revolt, and introduce rebellion into the affairs of the kingdom; so he committed the care of everything to
his brother Pheroras, and placed his mother and his sister and the
whole family at Masada, charging him that if he should hear any
sad news about him, he should take charge of the government; but
as to Mariamne his wife, because of the misunderstanding between
her and his sister, and his mother, which made it impossible for
them to live together, he placed her at Alexandrium, with Alexandra, her mother, leaving his treasurer Joseph and Sohemus of Itu-
rea to take charge of that fortress. These two had been very faithful to him from the beginning, and were now left as a guard to the
women. They also had it in charge that if they should hear any
mischief had befallen him, they should kill them both; and, as far
as they were able, to preserve the kingdom for his sons, and for his
brother Pheroras.

When he had given them this charge, he made haste to Rhodes
to meet Octavian; and when he had arrived at the city, he took off
his diadem but remitted nothing else of his usual dignity; and
when, meeting him, he requested that he let him speak to him, he
therein exhibited a much more noble specimen of a great soul, for
he did not indulge himself in supplications, as men usually do on
such occasions, nor offer him any petition, as if he were an of-
fender; but, in an undaunted manner, he gave an account of what
he had done; for he spoke thus to Octavian: That he had the
greatest friendship for Antony, and did everything he could so
that he might inherit the government; that he was not indeed in

the army with him because the Arabians had diverted him, but that he had sent him both money and corn, which was too little in comparison with what he ought to have done for him; "for, if a man owns himself to be another's friend and knows him to be a benefactor, he is obliged to hazard everything, to use every faculty of his soul, every member of his body, and all his wealth, for him; in which I confess I have been too deficient. However, I am conscious myself that so far I have done right, that I did not desert him after his defeat at Actium: nor after the evident change of his fortune did I transfer my hopes from him to another, but have preserved myself, though not as a valuable fellow soldier to Antony, yet certainly as a faithful counselor, when I demonstrated to him that the only way he had to save himself, and not lose all his authority, was to slay Cleopatra; for once she was dead, there would be room for him to retain his authority and to bring you to compromise with him rather than to continue in enmity any longer. None of this advice would he listen to, but preferred his own rash resolutions, which turned out unprofitably for him but profitably for you. Now, therefore, in case you wonder about me and my alacrity in serving Antony, in view of your anger with him, I confess there is no room for me to deny what I have done, nor will I be ashamed to admit, publicly too, that I once felt great kindness for him; but if you will leave him out of the case, and only examine how I behave with my benefactors in general, and what sort of friend I am, you will find by experience that we shall do and be the same to yourself, for it is only changing the names, and the firm friendship we shall bear you will not be disapproved by you."

By this speech and by his behavior, which showed Octavian the frankness of his mind, he won him over, since he was himself of a generous and magnificent temper, so much so that those very actions which were the foundation of the accusation against him won him Octavian's good will. Accordingly, he restored his diadem again, encouraging him to exhibit himself as great a friend to himself as he had been to Antony, and then held him in great esteem. So once he had received such a kind reception, and had, beyond all his hopes, secured his crown more entirely and firmly settled upon him than ever, he went his way to Egypt, giving presents, even beyond his means, to both him and his friends; and in general he behaved himself with great magnanimity: and he returned to Judea with greater honor and assurance than ever, frightening those with expectations to the contrary, as still acquiring from his very dangers greater splendor than before, by God's favor. So he prepared for Octavian's reception as he was going out to Syria to invade Egypt; and when he came back, he entertained him with full royal magnificence. He also bestowed presents on the army, and brought them provisions in abundance. He also proved to be one of Octavian's most cordial friends, putting the army in array, and riding along with him, with one hundred and fifty men, well appointed in all respects, in a rich and sumptuous manner for the better reception of him and his friends. He also provided them with all they might need as they passed over the dry desert: they lacked neither wine nor water, of which last the soldiers stood in the greatest need; and besides, he presented Octavian with eight hundred talents, procuring for himself their good will because he was attending to them in a greater and more splendid manner than his kingdom could afford; by which he more and more demonstrated to Octavian the firmness of his friendship and his readiness to assist him; and what was of the greatest advantage to him was that his liberality came at a seasonable time also; and when they returned from Egypt, his assistance was no way inferior to the good offices he had already given them.

However, when he came to his kingdom again, he found his house in total disorder, and his wife Mariamne and her mother Alexandra very uneasy; for, as they supposed (what was easily supposed), they were not put into that fortress for their security but as into a garrison for their imprisonment: and they were very uneasy that they had no power over anything, either of others or their own affairs: and Mariamne, believing the king's love for her to be hypocritical, more pretended (as advantageous to himself) than real, she looked upon it as untrue. She also was grieved that he would not allow her any hopes of surviving him, should he come to any harm himself. She also recollected the commands he had formerly given to Joseph, inasmuch as she endeavored to please her keepers, especially Sohemus, being well apprised how all was in his power. And at first Sohemus was faithful to Herod, neglecting none of the things he had placed in his charge. But once the women, by kind words and liberal presents, had gained his affections for themselves, he was overcome by degrees, and at length revealed to them all the king's injunctions, and this principally because he did not expect that Herod would come back with the same authority he had before. He thought he should both escape any danger from him and at the same time gratify the women who were likely not to be overlooked in the settling of the government. Nay, they would be able to make him abundant recompense since they must either reign themselves, or be near to him who would reign. He had further ground of hope also that though Herod should have all the success he could wish for and should return again, he could not contradict his wife in what she desired, for he knew that the king's fondness for his wife was inexhaustible. These were the motives that led Sohemus to reveal what injunctions had been given him. Mariamne was greatly displeased to hear that there was no end of the dangers she was under from Herod, and was very uneasy about it, and wished he might obtain no favors and esteemed it almost an insupportable task to live with him any longer; and this she later openly declared, without concealing her resentment.

And now Herod sailed home, joyful over his unexpected good success, and he went first of all, as was proper, to his wife, and told her, and only her, the good news, preferring her over the rest because of his fondness for her and the intimacy between them: but as it happened, as he told her of his great success, she was so far from rejoicing at it, rather she was sorry about it; nor was she able to conceal her resentment, but, in keeping with her dignity and the nobility of her birth, she returned his salutations with a groan, and so declared that she grieved rather than rejoiced at his success—and Herod was disturbed by the evident signs of her dissatisfaction. It troubled him greatly to see that this hatred of his wife for him was not concealed, but open; and he took this so ill and was so unable to bear it because of his fondness for her that he could not continue long in any one mood, sometimes he was angry at her, and sometimes he became reconciled himself; but by changing from one passion to another, he was filled with great uncertainty, thus entangled between hatred and love, and was frequently disposed to inflict punishment on her for her insolence toward him; but being deeply in love with her in his soul, he was not able to get rid of this woman. In short, though he would gladly have her punished, so was he afraid lest, before he was aware, he should by putting her to death bring a heavier punishment upon himself at the same time.

When Herod's sister and mother perceived that he was in this excellent opportunity to exercise their hatred against her, they provoked Herod to wrath by telling him such long stories and calumnies about her as might at once incite his hatred and jealousy. Now, though he willingly enough heard their words, he had not yet the courage to do anything to her as if he believed them, but still he became more and more badly disposed to her, and these evil passions were more and more inflamed on both sides. While she did not hide her disposition towards him, he turned his love for her into wrath against her; but just as he was going to settle this matter once and for all, he heard the news that Antony and Cleopatra were both dead, and that Octavian had conquered Egypt; whereupon he made haste to go to meet Octavian, leaving the affairs of his family in their present state. However, as he was setting out on his journey, Mariamne recommended Sohemus to him, professing that she owed him thanks for the care he had taken of her, and asked the king for a place for him in the government; upon which an honorable employment was bestowed upon him accordingly. Now, when Herod came to Egypt, he was freely introduced to Octavian, being already a friend of his, and received very great favors from him.

Thus Herod grew more generous, conducting Octavian as far as Antioch; but upon his return, as much as his prosperity was augmented so much the greater were the distresses that came upon him in his own family, chiefly in the affair of his wife, wherein he had formerly appeared to have been most fortunate; for the affection he had for Mariamne was no way inferior to the affections of such as are on that account celebrated in history, and this very justly. As for her, she was in other respects a chaste woman and faithful to him; yet she was somewhat rough by nature, and treated her husband imperiously because she saw he was so fond of her as to be enslaved to her. Nor did she consider that she lived under a monarchy, and was at another's disposal: accordingly she would behave saucily with him, which he usually accepted in a jesting way, and bore with moderation and good temper. She would also openly mock his mother and his sister, on account of the meanness of their birth, and would speak unkindly of them, to the extent that there existed before this disagreement an implacable hatred among the women. And now there were even greater reproaches among them than formerly, which increased suspicion, and lasted a whole year after Herod returned. However, these misfortunes, which had been kept under cover for a long while, burst out all at once on the following occasion: as the king was one day about noon lying down on his bed to rest, he called for Mariamne out of his great affection for her. She came in accordingly, but would not lie down beside him; and while he was filled with desire for her company, she showed her contempt of him, adding, by way of reproach, that he had caused her grandfather and her brother to be slain; and when he took this injury very unkindly and was ready to use violence against her, in a precipitate manner, the king's sister Salome, observing that he was more than ordinarily disturbed, sent in to the king his cupbearer, who had been prepared long beforehand for such a plan, and bade him tell the king how Mariamne had persuaded him to assist in preparing a love potion for him; and if he appeared to be greatly concerned and to ask what that love potion was, to tell him that Mariamne had prepared the potion and that he was only instructed to give it to him; but in case he did not appear to be much concerned about this potion, to let the thing drop; and that if he did so, no harm should thereby come to him. When she had given him these instructions, she sent him in at this time to make such a speech. So he went in, in a composed manner, to give credit to what he should say; and he said that Mariamne had given him presents and persuaded him to give the king a love potion; and when this moved the king, he said that this love potion was one she had given him, whose effects he did not know, which was the reason of his resolving to give him this information as the safest course he could take both for himself and the king. When Herod heard what he said, his indignation grew even more violent; and he ordered Mariamne's eunuch, who was most faithful to her, to be brought to torture concerning this potion, knowing well it was not possible that anything small or great could be done without him; and while the man was under the utmost agony, he could reveal nothing concerning the love potion except that so far as he knew Mariamne's hatred against Herod was occasioned by something Sohemus had said to her. Now, as he was saying this, Herod cried out aloud, and said that Sohemus, who had been at all other times most faithful to him and his government, would not have betrayed whatever injunctions he had given him unless he had had a closer conversation than ordinary with Mariamne. So he gave orders that Sohemus should be seized and slain immediately; but he allowed his wife to take her trial; he got together those most faithful to him and laid an elaborate accusation against her for this love potion which had been charged upon her by way of calumny only. However, he was in too great a passion to judge this matter clearly. Accordingly, when the court was at length satisfied that he was so resolved, they passed the death sentence upon her; but once the sentence was passed he himself suggested, as did some others of the court, that she should not be thus hastily put to death, but be laid in prison in one of the fortresses belonging to the kingdom. But Salome and her party labored hard to have the woman put to death, and they prevailed with the king to do so, advising this out of caution lest the populace become tumultuous should she be allowed to live. And thus Mariamne was led to execution.

When Alexandra observed how things went and that there was little hope that she herself would escape similar treatment from Herod, she changed her behavior to the reverse of what might have been expected from her former boldness, and this in a very indecent manner. Out of her desire to show how entirely ignorant she was of the crimes leveled against Mariamne, she leaped out of her place, reproaching her daughter in the hearing of all the people; she cried out that Mariamne had been an evil woman, un grateful to her husband, and that her punishment came justly for her insolent behavior because she had not made proper returns to him who had been their common benefactor. And after she had for some time carried on in this hypocritical manner, and had gone so far as to tear her hair, her indecent and dissembling behavior, as was to be expected, was greatly condemned by the rest of the spectators, as it was principally by the poor woman who was to suffer; for in the beginning she uttered not a word, nor had been upset by her peevishness, but had only looked at her; she did, out of a greatness of soul, become concerned at her mother's offence, especially because she exposed herself in a manner so unbecoming: but as for herself, Mariamne went to her death with an unshaken firmness of mind, and without changing the color of her face, and thereby evidently revealed the nobility of her descent to the spectators even in the last moments of her life.

And thus died Mariamne, a woman of excellent character, both for chastity and greatness of soul; but she lacked moderation, and had too much contentiousness in her nature, yet she had all that can be said in the beauty of her body and her majestic appearance in conversation; and thence arose the greatest reason why she did not prove so agreeable to the king, nor live so pleasantly with him as she might otherwise have done; for while she was most indulgently used by the king, out of his fondness for her, and did not expect that he could do anything harsh to her, she took too unbounded a liberty. Moreover, that which most afflicted her was what he had done to her relatives; and she ventured to speak of all they had suffered at his hands, and at last greatly provoked both the king's mother and sister till they became her enemies; and the same was true of Herod, on whom alone she depended for her expectations of escaping final punishment.

But after her death, the king's affections for her were kindled more strongly than before: for his love for her was not of a calm nature, nor such as is usual among other husbands; for at its commencement it was of a spontaneous kind; nor was it by their long cohabitation together brought under control; but at this time his love for Mariamne seemed to seize him in such a peculiar manner that it looked like a divine vengeance sent upon him for the taking of her life; for he would frequently call for her, and lament for her, in a most indecent manner. Moreover, he bethought himself of everything he could do to divert his mind from thinking of her, contriving feasts and assemblies for that purpose, but nothing would suffice; he therefore laid aside the administration of public affairs and was so far conquered by his passion that he would order his servants to call for Mariamne, as if she were still alive and could still hear them; and while he was in this state, there arose a pestilential disease that carried off the greatest part of the populace including his best and most esteemed friends, and made all men suspect that this was brought upon them by the anger of God for the injustice done to Mariamne. This circumstance affected the king still more until at length he forced himself to go into desert places, and there, under pretence of going hunting, bitterly afflicted himself; yet he had not borne his grief there many days before he fell into a most dangerous illness himself; he had an inflammation and a pain at the back of his head, joined with madness; and the remedies that were used did him no good at all, but proved harmful and at length brought him to despair. All the physicians also that were around him, partly because their medicines could not conquer the disease, and partly because his diet could be no other than what his disease inclined him to, permitted him to eat whatever he had a mind to, thus leaving hope of his recovery and committing him to fortune. And thus did his illness go on, while he was at Samaria, later called Sebaste.[27]

Now Alexandra abode at this time at Jerusalem; and being informed of Herod's condition, she endeavored to get possession of two fortified places around the city, the one belonging to the city itself, the other to the Temple; and those that could get them into their hands had the whole nation under their power, for without their command it was not possible to offer sacrifices; and to think of leaving off those sacrifices is plainly impossible to every Jew, who is still more ready to lose his life than to leave off that divine

[27] The Talmud also relates legends concerning Mariamne's marriage and death. She is said to have killed herself when she saw that her whole paternal family had been destroyed. Herod had her body preserved in honey (Babylonian Talmud, *Bava Batra,* 3b).

worship which he has been wont to pay to God. Alexandra, therefore, spoke with those who had charge of these strongholds, saying
that it was proper for them to deliver the same to her and to Herod's sons lest, upon his death, any other person should seize the
government; and that upon his recovery none could keep them
more safely for him than the members of his own family.

These words were not at all taken in good part by them; and, as
they had been in former times faithful to Herod, they resolved to
continue so more than ever both because they hated Alexandra
and because they thought it a sort of impiety to despair of Herod's
recovery while he was yet alive, for they had been his old friends.
They sent messengers, therefore, to acquaint him of Alexandra's
plan; he delayed no longer, but gave orders to have her slain; yet
it was with difficulty, and only after enduring great pain, that he
got rid of his illness. He was still sorely afflicted both in mind and
body, and very uneasy, and readier than ever upon all occasions to
inflict punishment upon those that fell under his hand.

Herod introduces pagan customs.

Herod revolted against the laws of his country and corrupted
their ancient constitution, which ought to have been preserved inviolable, by introducing foreign practices: we suffered great harm
because of this, while those religious observances which used to
lead the multitude to piety were now neglected: for first he appointed solemn games to be celebrated every four years, in honor
of the emperor, and built a theater at Jerusalem, and also a very
great amphitheater in the plain. Both of them were indeed costly
works, but in opposition to Jewish customs; for we have had no
such shows delivered down to us as fit to be used or exhibited by
us, yet did he celebrate these games every four years in the most
solemn and splendid manner. He also made proclamation to the
neighboring countries, and called men together out of the whole
nation. The athletes and the rest of those that strove for the prizes
in such games were invited out of every land, both by the hopes of
the rewards to be bestowed, and by the glory of victory to be
gained. So the principal persons who were the most eminent in

those sorts of exercises were gotten together, for very great rewards for victory were proposed, not only for those who performed their exercises, but for the musicians also, and he spared
no pains to induce all persons most famous for such exercises to
come to this contest. He also proposed no small rewards to those
who ran for the prizes in chariot races, drawn by two, or three, or
four pairs of horses. He also imitated everything, however costly
or magnificent, in other nations out of an ambition that his specta-
cle might become famous. Inscriptions also of the great actions of
Augustus, and trophies of those nations which he had conquered
in his wars, all made of the purest gold and silver, encompassed
the theater itself: nor was there any thing that could be subservient to his design, whether it were precious garments or precious
stones set in order, which was not also exposed to sight in these
games.

He also made a great preparation of wild beasts and of lions in
great abundance and of such other beasts as were either of uncom-
mon strength or of such sort as were rarely seen. These were prepared to fight with one another, or men condemned to death were
to fight with them. And truly foreigners were greatly surprised and
delighted at the vastness of the expenses here exhibited, and at the
great dangers that were here seen; but to natural Jews, this was no
better than a dissolution of those customs for which they had so
great a veneration. It appeared also no better than an instance of
barefaced impiety to throw men to the wild beasts for the purpose
of delighting the spectators; and it appeared an example of no less
impiety to change their own laws for such foreign exercises: but,
above all the rest, the trophies were most distasteful to the Jews;
for they considered them to be images included within the armor
that hung round about them, and were sorely displeased because it
was not the custom of their country to pay honor to such images.

Nor was Herod unacquainted with their disturbance; and, since
he thought it unreasonable to use violence with them, he spoke to
some of them by way of consolation and in order to free them
from their superstitious fear; yet he could not satisfy them, and
they cried out with one voice of their great uneasiness at the of-
fences they thought he had been guilty of; although they might

consider bearing all the rest, yet they would never tolerate images of men in their city, meaning the trophies, because this was not in agreement with the laws of their country. Now when Herod saw them in such disorder, and that they would not easily change their resolve unless they received satisfaction on this point, he called the most eminent men among them, and brought them to the theater, and showed them the trophies, and asked them what sort of things they took those trophies to be; and when they cried out that they were images of men, he gave order that they should be stripped of those outward ornaments which were around them, and showed them the naked pieces of wood; which pieces of wood, now without any ornament, became matter of great sport and laughter to them.

When therefore Herod had thus got rid of the multitude, and had dissipated the vehemency of their passion, the greatest number of the people were disposed to change their conduct, and not to be displeased with him any longer; but still some of them continued in their displeasure against him because of his introduction of new customs, and esteemed the violation of the laws of their country as likely to be the origin of very great mischiefs to them: they thus deemed it an instance of piety to hazard themselves rather than to seem as if they took no notice of Herod, who, upon the change he had made in their government, introduced such customs, and that in a violent manner, which they had never been used to before, as indeed in the pretense of a king but in reality in the guise of showing himself to be an enemy to their whole nation. On that account ten men that were citizens of Jerusalem conspired together against him, and swore to one another to undergo any dangers in the attempt: they took daggers with them under their garments for the purpose of killing Herod. Now there was a certain blind man among those conspirators who, because of his indignation against what he heard had been done, though unable to offer assistance in the undertaking, yet he was ready to undergo any suffering with them to the extent that he became a very great source of encouragement to the rest.

Once they had taken this resolution, by common consent, they went into the theater, hoping that Herod himself would not escape them since they should fall upon him so unexpectedly; but supposing, however, that should they miss him, they would kill a great many of those around him; and they took this resolution, though they die for it, in order to suggest to the king the injuries he had done to the people. These conspirators, therefore, standing thus prepared, went about their plan with great alacrity; but one of Herod's spies appointed for such purposes, to fish out and inform him of any conspiracies made against him, found out the whole affair, and told the king of it just as he was about to go into the theater. So when he reflected on the hatred he knew the greatest part of the people bore him, and on the disturbances that arose on every occasion, he thought this plot against him not improbable. Accordingly, he retired into his palace, calling those accused of this conspiracy before him by their several names; and as, with the guards falling upon them, they were caught in the very act and knew they could not escape, they prepared themselves for their ends with all the decency they could and without retracting at all from their resolute behavior, for they showed no shame for what they were about, nor denied it; but when they were seized, they showed their daggers and confessed that the conspiracy they had sworn to was a holy and pious action; that what they intended to do was not for gain, or out of any indulgence of their passions, but principally for those common customs of their country which all Jews were obliged to observe or to die for. This was what these men said, out of their undaunted courage in this conspiracy. They were led away to execution by the king's guards, and patiently underwent all the torments inflicted on them till they died. Nor was it long before that spy who had discovered them was seized by some of the people, out of the hatred they bore him; he was not only slain by them, but pulled to pieces, limb from limb, and given to the dogs. This execution was seen by many of the citizens, yet not one of them would reveal the doers of it. After Herod made a strict scrutiny, using bitter and severe torture, certain women that were tortured confessed what they had seen done; the authors were so terribly punished by the king that their entire families were destroyed for their rash attempt. Yet the obstinacy of the people and their undaunted constancy in defense of their

laws did not make Herod any less harsh with them; he still
strengthened himself in a more secure manner, and resolved to
surround the people in every way lest such revolts end in an open
rebellion.

> *Having recounted examples of Herod's cruelty, Jose-*
> *phus offers his readers an instance of the king's*
> *generosity.*

In this very year, which was the thirteenth of Herod's reign,
very great calamities fell upon the country; whether derived from
the anger of God, or whether such misery returns naturally in certain periods of time; for, in the first place, there were perpetual
droughts, and for that reason the ground was barren and did not
bring forth the same quantity of fruits that it used to produce; and
after this barrenness of the soil that change of food which the lack
of corn occasioned made the people ill, and a pestilential disease
prevailed, one misery following on the back of another; and the
circumstances of being destitute both of methods of cure and of
food made the pestilential distemper, which began in a violent
manner, the more lasting. The destruction of men in such a manner deprived those surviving of all their courage because they had
no way to provide remedies sufficient for their distresses. When
therefore the fruits of that year were spoiled and whatsoever they
had laid up beforehand was spent, no hope for relief remained,
and the misery, contrary to what was expected, still increased; and
this, not only in that year, but what seed they had sown perished
also so that the ground did not yield its fruits the second year.
Their distress made them also, out of necessity, eat many things
never eaten before; nor was the king himself less free from the
distress than other men, being deprived of his accustomed tribute
from the fruits of the ground; and since he had already expended
what money he had in his liberality to those whose cities he had
built, this miserable state of things procured him the hatred of his
subjects; for it is a constant rule that misfortunes are laid at the
feet of those that govern.

In these circumstances, he considered how to procure some seasonable help; but this was a hard thing to do since neighbors had no food to sell them; and his money also was gone, even had it been possible to purchase a little food at a great price. However, he thought it best, by all means, not to leave off his endeavors to assist his people; so he cut off the rich furniture in his palace, both silver and gold, not sparing his finest vessels or those made with the most elaborate skill, but sent the money to Petronius, who had been made prefect of Egypt; and since not a few had already fled to him out of their need, and as he was particularly a friend to Herod and desirous to have his subjects preserved, he permitted them to export corn, and assisted them every way, both in purchasing and exporting the same; so that he was the principal, if not the only person, who offered them help. And Herod, taking care the people should understand that this help came from himself, did thereby not only remove the ill opinion of those that formerly hated him, but gave them the greatest demonstration possible of his good will for and care of them.

Herod takes precautions against disaffected subjects.
His attitude to the Essenes.

At this time Herod released to his subjects the third part of their taxes, under pretense of relieving them because of the dearth they had suffered; but the main reason was to recover their good will, which he now needed; for they were uneasy, because of the innovations he had introduced in their practices, about the dissolution of their religion and the disuse of their own customs; and the people everywhere talked against him; he heavily guarded himself against these discontents and removed any opportunities they might have to disturb him, enjoining them to be always at work; nor did he permit the citizens either to meet together or to walk or eat together, but he watched everything they did, and when any were caught, they were severely punished; and many were brought to the citadel Hyrcania, both openly and secretly, and put to death there; and there were spies placed everywhere, both in the city and on the roads, who watched those that met together; nay, it is reported that he would oftentimes himself don the habit of a private man and mix with the crowds in the night and listen to their opinion of his government; and as for those that could no way be reduced to acquiesce to his scheme of government, he persecuted them all manner of ways; but for the rest of the people, he required that they be obliged to take an oath of fidelity to him, and at the same time compelled them to swear that they would bear him good will and continue certainly so to do in his management of the government; and indeed, a great part of them, either to please him or out of fear of him, yielded to what he required of them; but for such as were of a more open and generous disposition, and showed indignation at the force he used against them, he by one means or other made away with them. He endeavored also to persuade Pollio the Pharisee, and Sameas,[28] and most of their scholars, to take the oath; but these would neither submit to do so, nor were they punished with the rest, out of the reverence he bore to Pollio. The Essenes also, as we call a sect of ours, were excused from this imposition. These men live the same kind of life as do those whom the Greeks call Pythagoreans.

Now one of these Essenes, whose name was Manahem, not only conducted his life in an excellent manner, but also had the foreknowledge of future events given him by God. This man once saw Herod when he was a child going to school, and saluted him as king of the Jews; but the latter, thinking that either he did not know him or that he was jesting, reminded him that he was but a private man; but Manahem smiled to himself, and clapped him on his backside with his hand, and said, "However that be, you will be king, and will begin your reign happily, for God finds you worthy of it; and remember the blows that Manahem has given you as being a signal of the change in your fortune; and truly this will be the best reasoning for you, that you love justice towards men, and piety towards God, and clemency towards your citizens; yet I know how your whole conduct will be, for you will not be such a

[28] Probably Shemaya, president of the Sanhedrin. Pollio is Abtalion; see above, p. 140, where Shemaya is mentioned as speaking against Herod before the Sanhedrin (XIV:172). There are, however, chronological difficulties about the mention of Abtalion here. It may be, therefore, that Josephus meant to write "Hillel and Shammai" instead of "Pollio and Sameas."

one; you will excel all men in happiness, and obtain an everlasting reputation, but will forget piety and righteousness; and these crimes will not be concealed from God at the conclusion of your life, when you will find that He will be mindful of them, and punish you for them."

Now at that time Herod did not at all heed what Manahem said, having no hopes of such advancement; but a little later, when he was so fortunate as to be advanced to the dignity of king, and was at the height of his dominion, he sent for Manahem, and asked him how long he would reign. Manahem did not tell him the full length of his reign; wherefore he asked him further whether he should reign ten years or not. He replied, "Yes, twenty, nay, thirty years"; but did not assign the just limit of his reign. Herod was satisfied with these replies, and gave Manahem his hand and dismissed him; and from that time he continued to honor all the Essenes. We have thought it proper to relate these facts to our readers, however strange they are, and to declare what has happened among us, because many of these Essenes have, by their excellent virtue, been thought worthy of this knowledge of divine revelation.

Herod's last illness and death.

But Herod now fell into a distemper, and made his will, bequeathing his kingdom to Antipas, his youngest son; and this out of that hatred to Archelaus and Philip, which the calumnies of Antipater had raised against them. He also bequeathed a thousand talents to the emperor, and five hundred to Julia, the emperor's wife, to his children, and friends and freedmen.[29] He also distributed among his sons and their sons his money, his revenues, and his lands. He also made Salome, his sister, very rich, because she had continued faithful to him in all circumstances, and was never so rash as to do him any harm. And as he despaired of recovering, for he was in about his seventieth year, he grew fierce and indulged the bitterest anger on all occasions; the cause was that he

[29] It was prudent to make the emperor one's heir or partial heir. One's will was thus more likely to be upheld.

thought himself despised, and that the nation was pleased with his misfortunes; besides which, he resented a revolt which some of the lower order of men incited against him, the occasion of which was as follows:

There was one Judas, the son of Saripheus, and Matthias, the son of Margalothus, two of the most eloquent men among the Jews and the most celebrated interpreters of the Jewish laws, and men well-beloved by the people because of the education of their youth, because those that were studious of virtue frequented their lectures every day. These men, when they found the king's disease incurable, incited the young men to pull down all those works which the king had erected contrary to the law of their fathers, and thereby obtain the rewards which the law would confer on them for such pious actions; it was truly on account of Herod's rashness in making such things as the law had forbidden that his other misfortunes, and this disease also, so unusual among mankind, and with which he was now afflicted, came upon him: for Herod had caused such things to be made which were contrary to the law, of which he was accused by Judas and Matthias; for the king had erected over the great gate of the Temple a large golden eagle, of great value, and had dedicated it to the Temple. Now, the law forbids those that propose to live according to it to erect images or representations of any living creature. So these wise men persuaded their scholars to pull down the golden eagle alleging that, although they should incur any danger which might bring them to their deaths, the virtue of the action proposed to them would appear more advantageous to them than the pleasures of life; since they would die for the preservation and observance of the law of their fathers; since they would also acquire everlasting fame and commendation; since they would be both commended by the present generation, and leave an example of life that would never be forgotten by posterity; since that common calamity of dying cannot be avoided by our living so as to escape any such dangers; that therefore it is a right thing for those in love with virtuous conduct to wait for that fatal hour by such behavior as may carry them out of the world with praise and honor; and that this performance of brave actions, which bring us into danger of death, will alleviate the coming death; and at the same time to leave that reputation behind them to their children and to all their relatives, men or women, which will be of great advantage to them afterward.

And with such discourses did those men incite the young men to this action; and a report having come to them that the king was dead, this was an addition to the wise men's persuasions; so, in the very middle of the day they got up on the place, they pulled down the eagle, and cut it into pieces with axes, while a great number of the people were in the Temple. And now the king's captain, hearing of the undertaking, and supposing it to be a thing of a higher nature than it proved to be, came thither, with a great band of soldiers sufficient to put a stop to the multitude of those who pulled down what was dedicated to God. He fell upon them unexpectedly, as they were engaged in this bold attempt, in a foolish presumption rather than a cautious circumspection, as is usual with the multitude, and while they were in disorder—he caught no fewer than forty of the young men who had the courage to stay behind while the rest ran away, together with the authors of this bold attempt, Judas and Matthias, who thought it an ignominious thing to flee on his approach, and he led them to the king. And when they had come to the king, he asked them if they had been so bold as to pull down what he had dedicated to God. "Yes," said they, "what was contrived we contrived, and what has been performed, we performed; and that with such virtuous courage as becomes men; for we have given our assistance to those things which were dedicated to the majesty of God, and we have provided for what we have learned by hearing the law: and it ought not to be wondered at, if we esteem those laws which Moses had suggested to Him and were taught Him by God, and which he wrote and left behind him, more worthy of observation than your commands. Accordingly we will undergo death, and all sorts of punishments which you can inflict upon us, with pleasure, since we are conscious ourselves that we shall die, not for any unrighteous actions, but for our love of religion." And thus they said, and their courage was still equal to their profession and to the spirit with which they had set about this undertaking. And when the king had ordered them to be bound, he sent them to Jericho, calling together the leaders among the Jews; and when they came, he assembled them in the theater, and, because he could not himself stand he lay upon a couch, and enumerated the many labors he had long endured on their account, and his building of the Temple, and what a vast charge that was for him; while the Hasmoneans, during the 125 years of their government, had not been able to perform so great a work for the honor of God as that was: that he had also adorned it with very valuable donations; on which account he hoped he had left himself a memorial and procured himself a reputation after his death. He then cried out that these men had not abstained from affronting him even in his lifetime, but that, in the very daytime and in sight of the multitude, they had abused him to such a degree as to fall upon what he had dedicated, and in that manner of abuse had pulled it down to the ground. They pretended, indeed, that they did it to affront him; but if any one consider the thing truly, they would find that they were guilty of sacrilege against God.

But the people, on account of Herod's barbarous temper and out of fear that he would be so cruel as to inflict punishment on them, said what was done was done without approbation, and that it seemed to them that the actors might well be punished for what they had done. But as for Herod, he dealt more mildly with the others; but he deprived Matthias of the high-priesthood, and made Joazar, his wife's brother, high priest in his stead. Now it happened that during the time of the high-priesthood of this Matthias, another person was made high priest for a single day, that very day which the Jews observed as a fast. The occasion was this: This Matthias the high priest, on the night before that day when the fast was to be celebrated,[30] seemed in a dream to have intercourse with a woman; and because he could not officiate on that account, Joseph, the son of Ellemus, his kinsman, in his stead performed that sacred office. But Herod deprived this Matthias of the high-priesthood, and burnt alive the other Matthias, who had raised the sedition, with some of his companions. And that very

[30] The story is told a number of times in the Talmud.

night there was an eclipse of the moon.[31]

But now Herod's disease greatly increased in a severe manner, and this by God's judgment upon him for his sins. It was said by those who pretended to divine, and who were endowed with wisdom to foretell such things, that God inflicted this punishment on the king on account of his great impiety; yet, that he was still in hopes of recovering, though his afflictions seemed greater than any one could bear. He sent for physicians, and did not refuse to follow what they prescribed; he went beyond the river Jordan, and bathed himself in warm baths, which, besides their other virtues, were also fit to drink; this water runs into the Dead Sea. And when the physicians once thought fit to have him bathed in a vessel full of oil, it was supposed that he was dying; but, upon the lamentable cries of his domestics, he revived; and having no longer the least hope of recovering, he gave order that every soldier should be paid fifty drachmae; and he also gave a great deal to their commanders, and to his friends, and came again to Jericho, where he grew so choleric that it brought him to do all things like a madman; and though he was near death, he contrived the following wicked designs. He commanded that all the leaders of the entire Jewish nation, wheresoever they lived, should be called to him. Accordingly, there were a great number that came because the whole nation was called, and all men heard of this call, and death was the penalty for such as should disregard the epistles sent to call them. And now the king was in a wild rage against them all, the innocent as well as those who had offered him ground for accusations; and when they came, he ordered them all to be shut up in the hippodrome and he sent for his sister Salome, and her husband Alexas, and spoke thus to them: "I shall die in a little while, so great are my pains; now, death ought to be cheerfully borne and welcomed by all men; but what troubles me is that I shall die without being lamented, and without such mourning as men usually expect at a king's death." He was not unacquainted with the temper of the Jews, and that his death would be very de-

[31] This is the only eclipse mentioned by Josephus. It is of the greatest importance for the determination of the chronology of Herod and the birth of Jesus of Nazareth. It took place on March 13, in the year 4 B.C.E.

sirable and exceedingly acceptable to them because during his life-time they were ready to revolt against him, and to abuse the offer-ings he had dedicated to God: it was therefore their business to resolve to help alleviate his great sorrows on this occasion; if they do not refuse him their consent in what he desires, he shall have a great mourning at his funeral, such as never any king had before him; for then the whole nation would mourn from their very soul, which otherwise would be done in sport and mockery only. He de-sired therefore that as soon as they saw he had given up the ghost, they should place soldiers round the hippodrome, before they knew he was dead; and that they should not declare his death to the multitude till that was done, but that they should give orders to have those in custody shot with their darts; and that this slaugh-ter would cause him not to miss rejoicing on a double account; that since he was dying, they would make him secure that his will would be executed in what he charged them to do; and that he should have the honor of a memorable mourning at his funeral. So he deplored his condition with tears in his eyes, and tested them as to the kindness due from them, as being of his kindred and by the faith they owed to God, and begged that they would not pre-vent him from having this honorable mourning at his funeral. They promised him not to transgress his commands.

Now any one may easily discover the temper of this man's mind, which not only took pleasure in doing what he had done formerly against his relatives, out of love of life but also through those commands of his which savored of inhumanity; he took care when he was departing from this life that the whole nation should be put into mourning and indeed made desolate of their dearest kindred by his order that one out of every family should be slain although they had done nothing that was unjust or against him nor were they accused of any other crimes, although it is usual for those who have any regard for virtue to lay aside their hatred at such a time, even out of respect to those they justly esteemed their enemies.

As he was giving these commands to his relatives, letters came from his ambassadors who had been sent to Rome to Caesar, which announced that Acme [32] was slain by the emperor out of his indignation at the hand she had taken in Antipater's wicked practices; and that as for Antipater himself, the emperor left it to Herod to act as became a father and a king, and either to banish him or take away his life. When Herod heard this, he felt somewhat better, thanks to the pleasure given him by the contents of the letters: he was elated at the death of Acme and at the power given him over his son; but when his pains became very great, he was ready to faint for want of something to eat; so he called for an apple and a knife, since it had been his former custom to pare the apple himself, cut it, and eat it. When he got the knife, he looked about and had a mind to stab himself with it; and he would have done so had not his first cousin, Achiabus, prevented him, holding his hand and crying out loudly. Whereupon a woeful lamentation echoed through the palace, and a great tumult, as if the king were dead. Upon which Antipater, who verily believed his father was deceased, grew bold in his discourse, hoping to be immediately and entirely released from his bonds and to take the kingdom into his hands without further ado; so he discoursed with the jailor about letting him go, promising him great things, both now and hereafter, as if that were the only thing now in question; but the jailor not only refused to do what Antipater asked but informed the king of his intentions and the many solicitations he had had from him. Hereupon Herod, who had formerly no affection nor good will towards his son, after he heard what the jailor said, cried out and beat his head, although he was at death's door, and raised himself up on his elbow, and sent for some of his guards, and commanded them to kill Antipater without further delay, and to do so immediately, and to bury him in an ignoble manner at Hyrcania.

And now Herod altered his testament with the alteration of his mind; he appointed Antipas, to whom he had before left the kingdom, to be tetrarch of Galilee and Perea, and granted the kingdom

---

[32] An accomplice of Antipater (Herod's son) in a conspiracy against the king.

to Archelaus. He also gave Gaulonitis, Trachonitis, Batanaea, and Paneas to Philip, his son and Archelaus's brother, under the name of a tetrarchy; he bequeathed Jamnia, Ashdod, and Phasaelis to Salome, his sister, with five hundred thousand pieces of coined silver. He also made provision for all the rest of his kindred, giving them sums of money and annual revenues, and so left them all in a wealthy condition. He bequeathed also to the emperor ten million pieces of coined money, plus vessels of gold and silver, and costly garments; to Julia, the emperor's wife and to certain others, five millions. After he had done those things he died, the fifth day after he had Antipater slain; having reigned, since he had arranged for Antigonus to be slain, thirty-four years, but thirty-seven since he had been declared king by the Romans. A man he was of great barbarity towards all men equally, a slave to his passion, and above the consideration of what was right; yet he was favored by fortune, as much as any man ever was, for from a private man he became a king; and even when he was surrounded by ten thousand dangers, he got clear of them all, and continued in life till a very old age; as concerns the affairs of his family and children, that in these too, in his own opinion, he was also very fortunate because he was able to conquer his enemies, but, in my opinion, he was very unfortunate indeed.

A census in Palestine. Popular dissatisfaction. Reflections on war and civil strife.

Now Quirinius, a Roman senator who had passed through other magistracies till he became consul, and who was of great dignity, came at this time to Syria, with a few others; he was sent to be a judge of that nation and to make an assessment of their property: Coponius, a man of the equestrian order, was sent with him, to have the supreme power over the Jews. Moreover, Quirinius himself came into Judea, which was not added to the province of Syria, to take an account of their substance and to dispose of Archelaus's money; but the Jews, although in the beginning they took the report of a taxation heinously, yet they dropped any further opposition to it, on the advice of Joazar, the high priest. Being persuaded by Joazar's words, they gave an account of their estates without dispute.

Yet there was one Judas, a Gaulonite, from the city of Gamala, who, together with Saddok, a Pharisee, became anxious to draw the Jews to revolt; both said that this taxation was no better than an introduction to slavery, and they exhorted the nation to assert its liberty, as if they could procure happiness and security for what they possessed, and an assured enjoyment of a still greater good, which was the honor and glory they would thereby acquire for magnanimity. They also said that God would assist them only if they joined with one another in such counsels as might be successful and for their own advantage; and this especially, if they would set about on great exploits and not grow weary in their execution. Men received what the two said with pleasure, and their bold attempt grew. All sorts of misfortunes also sprang from these men, and the nation was infected with this doctrine to an incredible degree; one violent war after another came upon us, and we lost friends who used to alleviate our pains; there were also great robberies and murders of our leaders. This was done in pretense for the public welfare, but in reality for the hopes of personal gain; whence arose seditions, and from them murders, sometimes of their own people out of the anger of these men towards one another and their desire that none of the adverse party should remain, and sometimes of their enemies; a famine also struck us, reducing us to the last degree of despair, as did also the taking and demolishing of cities; nay, the sedition finally grew to such a peak that the very temple of God was burnt down by their enemy's fire. The consequences of these men's conspiring thus together were that the customs of our fathers were altered, and a change was made that added a mighty weight toward bringing all to destruction; for Judas and Saddok, who incited a fourth sect among us, which had a great many followers, filled our civil government with tumult and laid the foundation for our future miseries. This they did by their system of philosophy, with which we were before unacquainted; I shall discourse a little concerning this because the infection which spread from it among the younger people, who were its zealots, brought the public to destruction.

Jewish sects: *I have excluded Josephus's description*
of the Pharisees, Sadducees, and Essenes which sub-
stantially repeats that found in the second book of The
Jewish War, *for which see below, pp. 190 ff.*

But of the fourth sect of Jewish philosophy, Judas the Galilean
was the author. These men agree in all other things with the Pharisaic notions except that they have an inviolable attachment to liberty and say that God is their only Ruler and Lord. They also do
not fear dying any kind of death, nor indeed do they heed the
deaths of their relatives and friends, nor can any such fear make
them call any man Lord; and since this immovable resolution of
theirs is well known, I shall speak no further about it; nor am I
afraid that anything I have said of them be disbelieved, but I rather
fear that what I have said does not do justice to the resolve they
show when they undergo pain. This sect spread rapidly through
the nation in the time of Gessius Florus, our procurator, who by
his abuse of authority caused the Jews to go wild and to revolt
from the Romans.

Pontius Pilate.

But now Pilate, the procurator of Judea, removed the army
from Caesarea to Jerusalem, to make their winter quarters there
and to abolish the Jewish laws. So he brought into the city the emperor's effigies which were upon the ensigns; since our law forbids
the very making of images, the former procurators used to make
their entry into the city with ensigns lacking such ornaments. Pilate was the first to bring such images to Jerusalem and set them
up there; this was done without the knowledge of the people, in
the nighttime; but as soon as they discovered it, they came in multitudes to Caesarea, interceding with Pilate many days to remove
the images; and since they continued to persevere, he ordered his
soldiers on the sixth day to come with their weapons hidden while
he sat on his judgment seat, which was so prepared in the public
place in the city that it concealed the army that lay ready to oppress them; and when the Jews petitioned him again, he signaled

the soldiers to surround them, and threatened that their punishment would be immediate death unless they stopped disturbing him and go home. But they threw themselves upon the ground, laying their necks bare and saying they would take their death very willingly rather than have the wisdom of their laws transgressed; upon which Pilate was deeply affected by their firm resolution to keep their laws inviolable, and he commanded the images to be carried back immediately from Jerusalem to Caesarea.

> *The following is the famous* testimonium de Christo.
> *Its authenticity has long been doubted but it may well*
> *be that though at least part of it owes its origin to*
> *Christian interpolation, there was some mention of*
> *Jesus in Josephus's text.*

Now there was about this time Jesus, a wise man, if it be lawful to call him a man, for he was a doer of wonderful works— a teacher of such men as receive the truth with pleasure. He drew over to him both many of the Jews and many of the Gentiles. He was the Messiah [33]; and when Pilate, on the accusation of the leaders amongst us, had condemned him to the cross, those that loved him from the first did not forsake him, for he appeared to them alive again the third day, as the divine prophets had foretold these and ten thousand other wonderful things concerning him; and the tribe of Christians, so named after him, are not extinct to this day.

> *Many, though not all, scholars regard the following*
> *passage about John the Baptist as authentic.*

Now some of the Jews thought that the destruction of Herod's [34] army came from God, and that very justly, as a punishment for what he did against John, who was called the Baptist; for Herod

---

[33] Would a Pharisee have used this word about Jesus? For the latest and most balanced treatment of the questions concerning the *testimonium,* see S. Pines, *An Arabic Version of the Testimonium Flavianum,* Israel Academy of Sciences and Humanities, Jerusalem, 1971.

[34] Herod, Tetrarch of Galilee, not to be confused with Herod the Great.

slew him, though he was a good man who commanded the Jews to exercise virtue—both righteousness towards one another and piety towards God—and so come to baptism; [35] the washing with water would be acceptable to him, if they made use of it not in order to put away sins but to purify the body; he believed that the soul was thoroughly purified beforehand by righteousness. Now when others came in crowds to him, for they were greatly moved at hearing his words, Herod, who feared lest John's great influence over the people might put them under his power and inclination to raise a rebellion (for they seemed ready to do anything he would advise), thought it best to put him to death so as to prevent any mischief he might cause: Herod would thus not bring himself into difficulties by sparing a man who might make him repent of it after it was too late. Accordingly John was sent as a prisoner, as a result of Herod's suspicious nature, to Macherus, the castle, and was there put to death.

[35] Baptism, i.e., immersion in water, was a ritual custom taken over by the Christians from their Jewish background.

PART FOUR

The Jewish War

The Jewish War *is Josephus's first and most important work. In the preface, part of which follows here, he tells the motives that prompted the writing of this history. He summarizes his account of the historical background of the Jewish revolt, and of the war itself.*

Whereas the war of the Jews with the Romans was the greatest, not only in our times, but, in a manner, of those ever heard of, both of cities against cities, and nations against nations; while some men not involved in the affairs themselves have gotten together by hearsay vain and contradictory stories, and have written them down in a sophistical manner; and while those who were present have given false accounts of things, either out of flattery to the Romans, or hatred towards the Jews; and while their writings contain sometimes accusations and sometimes encomiums but nowhere the accurate truth, I propose, for the sake of those living under the Romans, to translate those books into the Greek tongue, which I had formerly composed in the language of our country [Aramaic] and sent to the Upper Barbarians; I, Joseph, the son of Matthias, by birth a Hebrew, also a priest, and one who at first

185

fought against the Romans myself and was later forced to be present at what happened afterwards.[1]

Now at the time when this great concussion of affairs took place, the affairs of the Romans themselves were in great disorder. Those Jews who favored independence also arose when the times were disturbed; they were also in a flourishing condition having both strength and riches. Since the affairs of the east were then exceedingly troubled, some hoped for gain, while others were afraid of loss; for the Jews hoped that all of their nation beyond the Euphrates would join together with them to raise an insurrection. The Gauls also, in the neighborhood of the Romans, were in motion, nor were the Celtae quiet; but all was in disorder after the death of Nero. The opportunity now offered induced many to aim at the royal power. The soldiery, in the hopes of getting money, also welcomed change.

I therefore thought it absurd to see the truth falsified in affairs of such great consequence, to take no notice of it, and to suffer those Greeks and Romans who were not in the wars to remain ignorant of these things and to read either flatteries or fiction, while the Parthians, the Babylonians, the remotest Arabians, and those of our nation beyond Euphrates, with the Adiabeni, through my work, knew accurately both the origins of the war, what miseries it brought us, and in what manner it ended.

It is true that these writers have the confidence to call their accounts histories; yet they seem to fail in their own purpose as well as to relate nothing that is sound; for they have a mind to demonstrate the greatness of the Romans, while diminishing and lessening the actions of the Jews, not discerning that it is not possible for those who appear to be great to have only conquered those who were little; nor are they ashamed to overlook the length of the war, the multitude of Roman forces who suffered so greatly in it, or the might of the commanders—whose great labors concerning Jerusalem would be deemed inglorious if what they achieved be reckoned but a small matter.

[1] See below. Note that the term "barbarian" in Greek denotes all non-Greek populations. It does not mean "uncivilized."

However, I will not go to the other extreme, out of opposition to those men who extol the Romans, nor will I praise the actions of my countrymen too much; but I will prosecute the actions of both parties with accuracy. Yet I shall suit my language to my passions regarding the affairs I describe; I must be allowed to indulge in some lamentation for the miseries undergone by my own country; for it was our own seditious temper that destroyed it; and it was the tyrants among the Jews who brought the Roman power upon us, who unwillingly attacked us, and occasioned the burning of our holy Temple; Titus Caesar, who destroyed it, is himself a witness; during the entire war, he pitied the people who were under the power of the seditious and often voluntarily delayed the taking of the city, allowing time for the siege, in order to let the originators of the rebellion have opportunity to repent. But if any one makes an unjust accusation against us, when we speak so passionately about the tyrants or the robbers, or sorely bewail the misfortunes of our country, let him indulge my affections herein, though it be contrary to the rules for writing history; because it had so come to pass that our city Jerusalem had reached a higher degree of felicity than any other city under the Roman government, and yet it fell at the end into the sorest of calamities. Accordingly, it appears to me that the misfortunes of all men, from the beginning of the world, are not as considerable as those of the Jews; nor were the authors of those misfortunes foreigners either. This makes it impossible for me to contain my lamentations. But, if any one be inflexible in his censures of me, let him attribute the facts themselves to the historical part, and the lamentations only to the writer himself.

All of Book I and a part of Book II of the War *overlap with the account in* Antiquities *of the history of the Jews between the Hasmonean revolt against the Seleucid domination in the second century and the outbreak of the war with Rome.*

Josephus is one of the prime sources for our knowledge of the sects of the Pharisees, Sadducees, and Essenes. In his Life, *he tells us briefly that as a young*

*man he examined their teachings and found those of
the Pharisees most congenial. In War (II, 119–166;
quoted below) long descriptions of the practices and
tenets of the Essenes are followed by shorter accounts
of those of the Pharisees and Sadducees; these are sup-
plemented by discussions in* Antiquities *(XIII:
171–173 and XVIII: 11–22).*

*The Essenes are said to have cultivated sanctity to
an exceptional degree. We hear of the strength of their
mutual attachment, their frugality and temperance,
their contempt for wealth and pleasure, and their celi-
bacy. They used to adopt other men's children and
bring them up as their own. Josephus tells of their lit-
urgy, their work, their habitations, their discipline,
their charity, their truthfulness, their interests in the
traditions of their ancestors; he describes the organization of their sect, their endurance of suffering, their belief in the immortality of the soul. He knew a great
deal about them, and much of what he writes agrees
with descriptions in Philo.*

*On the Pharisees, too, Josephus provides informa-
tion which, in its essentials, is part of a picture made
familiar by other sources: they were interpreters of the
Law, they related human events to fate and God, but
they also believed that moral choice belonged to man
(compare* Pirkei Avot, *III:19, R. Akiva:* Everything is
foreseen but there is freedom of choice; *and also* Babylonian Talmud, Berakhot, *33b, R. Hanina:* Everything
is in the power of heaven except the fear of heaven; *so
also* Niddah, *16b. The same rabbi is reported as saying*
[Hullin, *7b*]: A man does not hurt his finger in this
world unless it has been decreed above. *And in* Sanhedrin, *29a* [*see also* Yevamot, *114b*] *we find the
statement:* Even if there is a pestilence for seven years,
no man will die before the time appointed for him.) *Josephus states that the Pharisees held the doctrine of the
immortality of the soul together with that of reward for*

*virtue and punishment for wickedness; this is, of
course, familiar to us as fundamental rabbinic teaching.*

Of the Sadducees he reports that they insist on the
observance of the written law only; they deny fate and
think God has no part, nor interest, in evil and suffering. They insist on the freedom of the human will with
respect to the choice between good and evil, and they
deny the doctrines of the immortality of the soul and of
reward and punishment.

It seems clear that in all essentials Josephus provides trustworthy information. Nevertheless, he not
only describes the sects in terms intelligible to the
Greeks, but also classifies and understands them in accordance with a schema modeled on one representing
the attitudes and relationships of the most prominent
Greek philosophical schools of the Hellenistic era. He
states (Life, 12) that he thought of the Pharisees as
similar to the Stoic school. Indeed, even a cursory
reading reveals that the split between Pharisees and
Sadducees is described by Josephus precisely in terms
which can be used in a discussion of the fundamental
differences between Stoics and Epicureans.

Like the Sadducees (as described by Josephus) the
Epicureans denied the immortality of the soul, and reward and punishment after death; they denied the
power of fate and insisted on the freedom of moral
choice. They taught that the gods were not interested in
human sufferings or deeds. Like the Pharisees, the
Stoics believed in fate but, again like the Pharisees,
they emphasized duty and responsibility and, hence,
moral freedom within an otherwise determined universe. Undoubtedly, divisions prevalent in the Hellenic
world were paralleled in contemporary Jewish thought;
but the parallel formulations seem rather too neat. It
seems likely that Josephus's account of the three sects
was affected by his knowledge of Greek schools and
that he applied a scheme derived from the latter to the

*classification and description of phenomena in Jewish
Palestine that did not perhaps entirely conform to the
same pattern.*

*Josephus states that he himself was a Pharisee; and it
is possible that the Epicurean coloring he gives to the
Sadducees may owe something to the traditional enmity
between them and the Pharisees. In this context, it may
be worth noting that in the Pharisaic tradition the
name "Epicurus" came to be the actual word for "heretic"; according to Josephus, the Sadducees were wont
to argue with their teachers* (Apion, *XVIII: 16*) *and
were rude* (War, *II: 106*); *in the Talmud the* Apikoros
(*Epicurus, heretic*) *is similarly characterized* (Nedarim.
23a; Sanhedrin, *99b; see also* Pirkei Avot, *II:19*).

*On the whole, Josephus paints his picture according
to a pattern formed by controversies in the Greek
world. He fits into this framework details which correspond to Palestinian reality; but the choice of those details, their juxtaposition, and the varying emphasis with
which they are reported, owe something both to the
Greek background and to his personal Pharisaic preju-
dices. If this is a fair assessment, it is of interest that
Josephus seems to have known some Sadducean* Halak-
hot (*see A. Schalit on* Antiquities, *III: 89*).

It is also worth noting that (*probably because of the
varying origin of his sources*) *he speaks occasionally in
an unfriendly way about the Pharisees* (*for example,*
War, *I: 110–112;* Antiquities, *XVII: 41*).

There are three sects among the Jews. The followers of the first
are the Pharisees; the second the Sadducees; and the third sect,
who pretend to a severer discipline, are called Essenes. These last
are Jews by birth, and seem to have a greater affection for one another than do the other sects. These Essenes reject pleasures as
evil, but esteem continence and the conquest of passion as virtue.
They neglect wedlock, but choose out other persons' children
while they are pliable and fit for learning; these they esteem to be

their kindred, and train them according to their own customs. They do not absolutely deny the fitness of marriage and the succession of mankind it provides; but they guard against the lascivious behavior of women, and are persuaded that no one of them preserves her fidelity to one man.

These men are despisers of riches, nor is there any one among them who has more than another; for it is a law among them that those who join them must let what they have be common to the whole order—to the degree that among all of them there is no appearance of poverty or excess of riches, but every one's possessions are intermingled with every other's; and so there is, as it were, one patrimony among all the brothers. They consider oil a defilement; and if any one of them be anointed without his approval, it is wiped off his body; for they think keeping a dry skin a good thing, and so too being clothed in white garments. They also have appointed to take care of their common affairs stewards who have no separate business except what is for the use of all.

They have no specific city, but many dwell in every city; and if any of their sect come from other places what they have lies open for them just as if it were their own; and they go to such as they never knew before, as if they had been ever so long acquainted with them. For this reason, when they travel into remote parts, they carry nothing with them except their weapons, for fear of thieves. Accordingly, there is, in every city where they live, one appointed particularly to take care of strangers and to provide them with garments and other necessities. But the habit and management of their bodies are such as children use who are in fear of their masters. Nor do they allow the change of garments or shoes till they are entirely torn to pieces or worn out. Nor do they either buy or sell anything to one another; but every one of them gives what he has to him that needs it, and receives from him in its stead whatever may be useful for himself; and even if no requital is made, they are fully allowed to take what they need from whomsoever they please.

And as for their piety towards God, it is very extraordinary; for before sunrise they speak not a word about profane matters but offer up certain prayers in supplication received from their forefathers. After this they can be sent away by their curators, to exercise some of those arts wherein they are skilled and in which they labor with great diligence till the fifth hour. After this they assemble in one place; and when they have clothed themselves in white veils, they then bathe their bodies in cold water. And after this purification, they meet together in an apartment of their own, into which no one of another sect is permitted to enter; then they go, in a pure manner, into the dining room, as into a certain holy temple, and quietly sit down; the baker lays loaves in order for them; the cook also brings a single plate of one sort of food, and sets it before every one of them; but a priest says grace before meat; and it is unlawful for any one to taste the food before the grace is said. The same priest, after he has dined, says grace again after meat; and when they begin and when they end, they praise God, as He who bestows food upon them; after this they lay aside their white garments, and betake themselves to their labors again till evening; then they return home to supper, in the same manner; and if there are any strangers there, they sit down with them. Nor is there ever any clamor or disturbance to pollute their house, but they give every one leave to speak in turn; this silence thus kept in their house appears to foreigners like some tremendous mystery, the cause of which is their perpetual sobriety and the same settled measure as is sufficient of meat and drink allotted them.

And truly, they do nothing not in accordance with the injunctions of their curators; only two things are done among them at every one's own free will: to assist those in need, and to show mercy; for they are permitted of their own accord to offer succor to such as deserve and need it, and to bestow food on those in distress; but they cannot give anything to their kindred without the curators. They control their anger in a just manner, and restrain their passion. They are eminent for fidelity, and are ministers of peace; whatsoever they say also is firmer than an oath; but swearing is avoided as being worse than perjury; for they say that he who cannot be believed without swearing by God is already condemned. They also take great pains to study the writings of the ancients, and choose out of them what is most for the advantage of their soul and body; and they inquire after such roots and medicinal stones as may cure their diseases.

But now, if any one has a mind to come over to their sect, he is not immediately admitted, but is prescribed their same method of living for a year, though he continues excluded from them; and they give him a small hatchet, a loincloth, and white garment. And when he has given evidence during that time that he can observe their continence, he approaches nearer to their way of living and is made a partaker of the waters of purification; yet he is not even then admitted to live with them; for after this demonstration of his fortitude, his temper is tried two more years, and if he appears worthy they then admit him into their society.

And before he is allowed to touch their common food, he is obliged to take tremendous oaths: that, in the first place, he will exercise piety towards God; and that he will observe justice towards men; and that he will do no harm to anyone, either of his own accord or by the command of others; that he will always hate the wicked and assist the righteous; that he will ever show fidelity to all men, especially those in authority, because no one obtains the government without God's assistance; and that if he be in authority, he will at no time whatever abuse his authority nor endeavor to outshine his subjects, either in his garments or any other finery; that he will be perpetually a lover of truth, and reprove those that tell lies; that he will keep his hands away from theft and his soul from unlawful gains; and that he will neither conceal anything from those of his own sect nor reveal any of their doctrines to others, no, not even though he be compelled to do so at the risk of his life. Moreover, he swears to communicate their doctrines to no one in any other way than as he received them himself; that he will abstain from robbery, and will equally preserve the books belonging to their sect, and the names of the angels. These are the oaths by which they secure their proselytes to themselves.

But those that are caught in any heinous sins are cast out of their society; and he who is thus separated from them often dies in a miserable manner; for as he is bound by the oath he has taken and the customs he has been engaged in, he is not at liberty to partake of that food that he encounters elsewhere, but is forced to eat grass and famish his body with hunger till he perish; for which reason they receive many of them again when they are at their last gasp, out of compassion, thinking the miseries they have endured before coming to the very brink of death to be sufficient punishment for their sins.

But in the judgments they exercise they are most accurate and just; nor do they pass sentence by fewer than a hundred votes of a court. And what is once determined by that number is unalterable. What they most of all honor, after God Himself, is the name of their legislator Moses, whom, if any one blaspheme, he is punished capitally. They also think it a good thing to obey their elders and the majority. Accordingly, if ten be sitting together, no one of them will speak while the other nine are opposed. They also avoid spitting in their midst, or on the right side. Moreover, they are stricter than any other of the Jews in resting from their labors on the seventh day; for they not only ready their food the day before so that they not be obliged to kindle a fire on that day, but they will not remove any vessel from its place, nor move their bowels. Nay, on the other days they dig a small pit, one foot deep, with a mattock (a kind of hatchet given them when they are first admitted); and covering themselves round with their garment that they may not affront the divine rays of light, they ease themselves into that pit, after which they put the earth that was dug out back into the pit; and even this they do only in the more remote places, which they select for this purpose; and even though this easement of the body is natural, yet it is a rule to wash themselves after it, as if it were a defilement.

Now after the time of their preparatory trial is over, they are separated into four classes; and so far are the juniors inferior to the seniors that if the seniors be touched by the juniors, they must wash themselves, as if they had intermixed themselves with foreigners. They are longlived also; many of them living over a hundred years because of the simplicity of their diet and also, I think, because of their regular course of life. They make light of danger and, through the generosity of their mind, are above pain. And as for death, if it be for their glory, they esteem it better than living forever; and indeed our war with the Romans gave abundant evidence of the greatness of their souls under trial: even though they were tortured and disfigured, burnt and torn to pieces, and experienced all kinds of instruments of torment so that they might be forced either to blaspheme their legislator or to eat what was forbidden them, yet they could not be made to do either of them, no, nor once to flatter their tormentors or shed a tear; but they smiled in their very pains, and laughed those to scorn who inflicted their torments, and resigned up their souls with great alacrity, as though expecting to receive them again.

For their doctrine is this: That bodies are corruptible, and that their matter is not permanent; but souls are immortal and continue forever, and that they come out of the most subtle ether and are united to their bodies as in prisons, into which they are drawn by a certain natural enticement; but once they are set free from the bonds of the flesh, they then, as if released from a long bondage, rejoice and mount upward. And like the Greeks, they believe that good souls have their habitations beyond the ocean, in a region that is neither oppressed by storms of rain or snow, or by intense heat, but is refreshed by the gentle breathing of a west wind perpetually blowing from the ocean; while they allot to bad souls a dark and tempestuous den, full of never-ceasing punishments. And indeed the Greeks seem to me to have followed the same notion when they allot the islands of the blessed to their brave men, whom they call heroes and demigods; and to the souls of the wicked, the region of the ungodly, in Hades, where, their fables relate, the wicked are punished. This, then, was their first supposition, that souls are immortal; and from thence those exhortations to virtue and warnings against wickedness are collected, whereby good men are bettered in the conduct of their life by their hope of reward after death, and whereby the vehement inclinations of bad men to vice are restrained by their fear and expectation that even though they lie concealed in this life they will suffer immortal punishment after death. These are the divine doctrines of the Essenes about the soul, which lay an unavoidable bait for those who have once had a taste of their philosophy.

There are also among them those who undertake to foretell things to come by reading the holy books and using several sorts of purifications, and being perpetually conversant in the discourses of the prophets. And it is but seldom that they miss in their predictions.

Moreover, there is another order of Essenes, who agree with the rest as to their way of living, customs, and laws, but differ in the matter of marriage: they believe that by not marrying they cut off the principal part of human life, which is the prospect of succession; nay, rather, that if all men were of the same opinion, the whole race of mankind would perish. However, they try out their spouses for three years; and if they find they are likely to be fruitful, they then actually marry them; but they do not have intercourse with their wives when they are with child, as a demonstration that they do not marry out of regard for pleasure but for the sake of posterity. Now the women go into the baths with some of their garments on, as the men do with something girded about them. And these are the customs of this order of Essenes.

But then as to the two other orders mentioned, the Pharisees are esteemed most skilful in the exact explication [2] of the laws. They ascribe all to fate and to God, and yet allow that to act what is right, or the contrary, is principally in the power of men, even though fate does cooperate in every action.[3] They say that all souls are imperishable but that the souls of good men are only removed into other bodies [4]—while the souls of bad men are subject to eternal punishment.

But the Sadducees, who make up the second order, remove fate entirely, and believe that God is not concerned with our doing or not doing what is evil; and they say that to act what is good or what is evil is subject to man's free exercise of his moral choice. They also deny belief in the immortal duration of the soul and punishments and rewards in Hades. Moreover, the Pharisees are friendly to one another, and favor the exercise of concord and re-

[2] The Hebrew name of the Pharisees is sometimes thought to be derived from the root meaning "to interpret."

[3] Compare *Pirke Avot,* III:19 "Everything is foreseen, yet freedom of moral choice is given to man." Note the similarity to Stoic doctrines.

[4] Reincarnation is a doctrine found considerably earlier among the Greeks. It is probably of Orphic-Pythagorean origin. For an interesting statement of the doctrine read Plato's *Phaedo.*

gard for the public. But the behavior of the Sadducees towards one another is in some degree wild; and their conversation with those of their own party is as barbarous as if they were strangers.

The War with Rome.
The excesses of Gessius Florus, the Roman procurator,
had led to popular unrest and finally to war. In the
winter of 66–67 C.E. *the Jewish authorities in*
Jerusalem appointed local commanders for the various
regions of the country. Josephus was sent to Galilee.
His account in the Life *differs from what we read here.*
There he tells us that he was sent to Galilee to persuade
the rebels to lay down their arms.

So every one of the other commanders administered the affairs of his section with customary alacrity and prudence; as to Josephus, when he came into Galilee his first care was to gain the good will of the people of that country, aware that he should thereby have in general good success, even though he might fail in other matters. And being aware that if he delegated part of his power to the great men, he would make them his fast friends, and that he would gain the same favor from the populace if he executed his commands through persons of their own country with whom they were well acquainted, he selected seventy of the most prudent elders and appointed them to be rulers of all Galilee: he also chose seven judges in every city to hear the lesser quarrels; as to the greater conflicts, those involving life and death, he enjoined that they be brought to him and the seventy elders.

After he had settled these rules for determining cases by law with regard to the people's dealings with one another, Josephus undertook to make provisions for their safety against external violence; and since he knew the Romans would fall upon Galilee, he built walls in proper places around Jotapata, Bersabee, and Salamis; and, in addition, around Caphareccho, Japha, and Sigo, and what they call Mount Tabor, Tericheae, and Tiberias. Moreover, he built walls around the caves near the lake of Gennessar, in the Lower Galilee; the same he did to the places of Upper Galilee, as well as to the rock called the Rock of the Achabri, and to Seph, Jamnith, and Meroth; and in Gaulanitis he fortified Seleucia, Sogane, and Gamala; but as to those of Sepphoris, they were the only people to whom he gave leave to build their own walls because he perceived they were rich and wealthy and ready to go to war, without need of injunction for that purpose. The same with Gischala, which had a wall built around it by John the son of Levi himself, but with the consent of Josephus; but for the building of the rest of the fortresses, he labored with all the other builders and was present to give all necessary orders. He also got together an army out of Galilee, made up of more than a hundred thousand young men, all of whom he armed with the old weapons he had collected and prepared for them.

And after he was convinced that the Roman power had become invincible, chiefly because of their readiness to obey orders and the constant exercise of their arms, he despaired of teaching his men the use of their arms, which was to be mastered by experience; but observing that their readiness to obey orders was due to the multitude of their officers, he divided his army in the Roman manner, appointing a great many subalterns. He also distributed the soldiers into various classes, putting them under captains of tens, of hundreds, and then of thousands; besides these he had commanders of larger bodies of men. He also taught them to give the signals to one another, and to call and recall the soldiers with the trumpets, how to expand the wings of an army and make them wheel about, and after one wing had had success, to turn again and assist those that were hard set and to join in the defense of those who had most suffered. He also continually instructed them in matters concerning the courage of the soul and the hardiness of the body; above all, he readied them for war by declaring to them distinctly the good order of the Romans, and that they were to fight with men who, both by the strength of their bodies and courage of their souls, had conquered the whole earth. He told them he would make trial of the good order they would observe in war, even before it came to any battle, to see whether they would abstain from the crimes in which they used to indulge such as theft, robbery, and plunder, and defrauding their own countrymen; for

wars are best managed when the warriors preserve a good conscience, and those who are evil in private life will have as enemies
not only those who attack them but also God Himself as their an-
tagonist.

And thus did he continue to admonish them. Now he chose for
the war such an army as was sufficient, i.e., sixty thousand footmen
and three hundred and fifty horsemen; besides these, there were
about four thousand five hundred mercenaries in which he put the
greatest trust; he had also six hundred men as body guards. Now
the cities easily maintained the rest of his army, except for the
mercenaries; every one of the cities enumerated before had sent
out half their men to their army, retaining the other half at home
in order to get provisions, to the extent that one part went to the
war and the other to their work: and so those that sent out their
corn were paid for it by those in arms, through that security they
enjoyed.

Now, as Josephus was thus engaged in the administration of the
affairs of Galilee, there arose a treacherous person, a man of Gischala, the son of Levi, whose name was John. His character was
that of a very cunning, very knavish person: for wicked practices
he had not his match anywhere. He was poor at first, and for a
long time his needs were a hindrance to him in his wicked designs.
He was a ready liar, and yet very sharp in gaining credence for his
fictions: he thought it a point of virtue to delude people, and
would delude even those dearest to him. He was a hypocritical
pretender to humanity, but where he had hopes of gain spared no
shedding of blood: he had great ambitions, and fed his hopes with
his mean wicked tricks. He had a peculiar knack for thieving, and
soon gathered certain companions for his impudent practices: at
first there were only a few, but as he proceeded on his evil course,
they became more and more numerous. He took care that none of
his partners be easily caught in their rogueries, but selected those
who had the strongest constitutions of body and the greatest courage of soul together with great skill in martial affairs; thus he got
together a band of four hundred men, who came principally out of
the country of Tyre, vagabonds who had run away from their villages; and by means of these he laid waste all Galilee.

However, John's lack of money had hitherto restrained him in his ambition to command and advance himself; but when he saw that Josephus was highly pleased with his activity, he persuaded him to entrust him with the repairing of the walls of his native city [Gischala]; for this work he got a great deal of money from its rich citizens. After that he contrived a very shrewd trick: pretending that the Jews who dwelt in Syria were obliged to use oil made by others than those of their own nation, he requested Josephus to permit him to send oil to their borders; so he bought four amphorae with such Tyrian money at the price of four Attic drachmai, and sold every half amphora for the same sum: and since Galilee was very rich in oil, particularly at that time, by exporting great quantities and having the sole privilege so to do, he gathered an immense sum of money together, which he immediately used to the disadvantage of him who had given him that privilege; and since he imagined that if he could once overthrow Josephus, he would himself rule Galilee, he gave orders to the robbers under his command to be more zealous in their thievish expeditions; he figured that with the rise of many that desired innovations in the country, he might either catch their general in his snares as he came to the country's assistance and then kill him, or if Josephus should overlook the robbers, John might accuse him of negligence to the people of the country. He spread abroad a report far and near that Josephus was delivering up the administration of affairs to the Romans; and many such plots did John lay in order to ruin him.

Now at the same time certain young men of the village Dabaritta, who kept guard in the Great Plain, laid snares for Ptolemy, Agrippa's and Berenice's steward, and took from him everything he had with him; among those things were a great many costly garments, no small number of silver cups, and six hundred pieces of gold; yet they were not able to conceal what they had stolen, but brought it all to Josephus, in Taricheae. He blamed them for their violence to the king and queen, and deposited what they brought to him with the most powerful man of Taricheae, with the intention of sending the things back to the owners at a proper time; this act of Josephus brought him into the greatest danger;

for those who had stolen the things were indignant with him, both because they received no share for themselves, and because they perceived Josephus's intention to return to the king and queen what had cost them so much effort. They ran away at night to their several villages, declaring to all men that Josephus was going to betray them; they also raised such great disorders in all the neighboring cities that in the morning a hundred thousand armed men came running together; this multitude crowded into the hippodrome at Taricheae and made a very peevish clamor against him; some cried out that they should depose the traitor, others that they should burn him. Now John incited a great many, as did also one Jesus, the son of Sapphias, who was then governor of Tiberias. Then it was that Josephus's friends and his body guards became so frightened by this violent assault of the multitude that all but four of them fled; and since Josephus was asleep, they awakened him because the people were going to set fire to the house; and although those four that remained urged him to run away, he was neither surprised at his being deserted nor at the great multitude that came against him, but leaped out with his clothes rent and ashes sprinkled on his head, his hands behind him, and his sword hanging at his neck. At this sight his friends, especially those from Taricheae, sympathized with his condition; but those in their neighborhood, to whom his government seemed burdensome, reproached him, bidding him produce immediately the money which belonged to them all, and to confess the agreement he had made to betray them; for they imagined, from the clothing in which he appeared, that he could deny nothing of what they suspected concerning him, and that it was in order to obtain pardon that he had put himself entirely into so pitiable a posture; but his humble appearance was designed only as preparatory to a stratagem of his: he thereby contrived to set those that were so angry at him at variance with one another about the things that angered them. However, he promised to confess all: hereupon he was permitted to speak, and he said, "I did neither intend to send this money back to Agrippa, nor to keep it for myself; for I did never esteem one that was your enemy to be my friend, nor did I consider that what would tend to your disadvantage could be my advantage. But, O you people of Taricheae, I saw that your city stood in greater need than others of fortification for your security, and that it needed money for the building of a wall. I was also afraid lest the people of Tiberias and other cities should lay a plot to seize these spoils, and therefore I intended to retain this money, that I might surround you with a wall. But if this does not please you, I will produce what was brought me and leave it to you to plunder it: but if I have conducted myself so well as to please you, do not punish your benefactor."

Hereupon the people of Taricheae loudly commended him, but those of Tiberias, with the rest of the company, called him harsh names, and threatened him; so both sides stopped quarreling with Josephus, and fell to quarreling with one another. So emboldened by the hold he had on his friends, the people of Taricheae, about forty thousand in number, he spoke more freely to the whole multitude, reproaching them greatly for their rashness; he told them that with this money he would build walls around Taricheae, and would also put the other cities in a state of security; for they should not lack money, if they would but agree for whose benefit it was to be procured, and would not allow themselves to be irritated with the one procuring it for them.

Hereupon the rest of the multitude that had been deluded withdrew; but because they went away angry, two thousand of them made an assault upon him in their armors and since he had already gone to his own house, they stood outside and threatened him. On this occasion Josephus again used a second stratagem to escape them; for he ascended to the top of the house, and with his right hand asked them to be silent, saying to them, "I cannot tell what you want, nor can I hear what you say, because of the confused noise you make": but he said he would comply with all their demands if they would but send some of their number in to talk with him about it. And when their leaders heard this, they came into the house. He then led them to the most remote part of the house, and shut the door of that hall where he put them, and then had them whipped till every one of their inward parts appeared naked. In the meantime the masses stood around the house, supposing that he had a long discourse about their demands with those who had gone in. He then had the doors opened immediately, and sent the men out all bloodied, which so terribly frightened those who had before threatened him that they threw down their arms and ran away.

But as for John, his envy grew greater, and he framed a new plot against Josephus; he pretended to be sick and in a letter requested Josephus to give him leave to use the hot baths at Tiberias for the recovery of his health. Hereupon Josephus, who hitherto suspected nothing of John's plots against him, wrote to the governors of the city, asking them to provide lodging and necessaries for John; after he had made use of these favors, John, in two days' time, did what he had come for; some he corrupted with delusive frauds, others with money, and so persuaded them to revolt against Josephus. Silas, who had been appointed guardian of the city by Josephus, wrote to him immediately, informing him of the plot against him; after Josephus received this epistle, he marched with great diligence all night, arriving early in the morning at Tiberias; at this time the rest of the populace met him. But no sooner had Josephus got the people of Tiberias together in the stadium and tried to discourse with them about the letters he had received than John secretly sent some armed men with orders to slay him. But when the people saw that the armed men were about to draw their swords, they cried out; at their cry Josephus turned about, and when he saw that the swords were just at his throat, he jumped down onto the beach; he then seized a ship which lay in the harbor, and leaped into it with two of his guards, and fled away into the middle of the lake.

But now the soldiers accompanying him took up their arms at once, and aimed against the plotters, but Josephus was afraid lest a civil war be started because of the envy of a few men and thus bring the city to ruin; so he sent some of his party to tell them that they should do no more than provide for their own safety; they should not kill anybody nor accuse any for causing the disorder. Accordingly, these men obeyed his orders and were quiet; but the people of the neighboring country, when informed of this plot and the plotter, got together in great multitudes to oppose John. But he forestalled their attempt, fleeing to Gischala, his native city, while the Galileans came running out of their several cities to Josephus; and since they were now many ten thousands of armed men, they cried out that they had come against John, the common plotter against their interest, and would at the same time burn him and that city which had received him. Hereupon Josephus told them that he valued their good will towards him highly, but still he restrained their fury, intending to subdue his enemies by prudent conduct rather than by slaying them; so he excepted by name those of every city who had joined in this revolt with John, and caused public proclamation to be made that he would seize the effects of those that did not forsake John within five days' time and would burn both their houses and their families. Whereupon three thousand of John's party left him immediately, came to Josephus, and threw their arms down at his feet.

John then forsook open attempts and undertook more secret ways of treachery. Accordingly, he sent private messengers to Jerusalem to accuse Josephus of having too great power, and to let them know that he would soon come as a tyrant to their metropolis unless they prevented him. This accusation the people were aware of beforehand, but they did not heed it. However, some of the grandees, out of envy, and some of the rulers also sent money to John secretly so that he might be able to get together mercenary soldiers in order to fight Josephus; they also issued a decree to recall him from his government, but they did not think that decree sufficient; so they sent also two thousand five hundred armed men, led by four persons of the highest rank, that they might withdraw the good will of the people from Josephus. These had been charged that if he would voluntarily come, they should permit him to give an account of his conduct; but if he obstinately insisted upon continuing in his government, they should treat him as an enemy. Now Josephus's friends had sent him word that an army was coming against him, but they gave him no notice beforehand regarding the reason for their coming, that reason being known only among some secret councils of his enemies; and by this means four cities revolted against him immediately, Sepphoris, Gamala, Gischala, and Tiberias. Yet he recovered those cities without war; and when he had routed those four commanders by stratagems and had captured the most powerful of their warriors, he sent them to Jerusalem; and the people of Galilee were very indignant, and zealous to slay not only those forces but those that sent them also, had not those forces prevented this by running away.

Now John was later detained within the walls of Gischala because of his fear of Josephus; but within a few days Tiberias revolted again, its people inviting King Agrippa to return to exercise his authority there; he did not come at the time appointed, but when a few Roman horsemen appeared that day the Tiberians proclaimed the exclusion of Josephus from the city. Now this revolt of theirs was immediately known at Taricheae; and since Josephus had sent out all his soldiers to gather corn, he did not know whether to march out alone against the revolters or to stay where he was, because he was afraid the king's soldiers might stop him if he tarried and might get into the city; for he did not intend to do anything the next day because it was the Sabbath. So he managed to circumvent the revolters by a stratagem; first, he ordered the gates of Taricheae to be shut so that nobody could go out and inform the enemy what stratagem he was planning; he then got together all the ships on the lake, some two hundred and thirty, and in each of them he put no more than four mariners. So he sailed to Tiberias in haste, keeping at such a distance from the city that it was not easy for the people to see the vessels, and ordering the empty vessels to float up and down there while he himself, with only seven of his guards, and those unarmed, went so near as to be seen; but when his adversaries, who were still reproaching him, saw him from the walls, they were so astonished that they supposed all the ships to be full of armed men; they threw down their arms, and by signals of intercession besought him to spare the city.

Upon this, Josephus threatened them terribly, reproaching them that since they were the first to take up arms against the Romans, they should not be spending their force beforehand in civil dissensions and thus doing what their enemies desired above all things; and that besides, they should not be endeavoring so hastily to seize him who took care of their safety: and were they not ashamed to have shut the gates of their city against him that built their walls; that, however, he would allow any intercessors from among them that might make some excuse for them with whom he could reach agreements for the city's security. Hereupon ten of the most powerful men of Tiberias came to him immediately, and after he had taken them into one of his vessels he ordered them to be carried a great way off from the city. He then commanded that fifty others of their senate, men of the greatest eminence, should come to him that they also might give him some security on their behalf. After this, under one new pretense or another, he called forth others, one after another, to make the leagues between them. He then ordered the masters of those vessels which he had thus filled to sail away immediately for Taricheae, and to confine those men in the prison there; in the end he captured their entire senate, consisting of six hundred persons, and about two thousand of the populace, and carried them away to Taricheae.

And then the rest of the people cried out that it was Clitus who was the chief author of this revolt and they desired Josephus to expend his anger upon him alone, but Josephus, whose intention it was to slay nobody, commanded one Levi, belonging to his guards, to go out of the vessel in order to cut off both Clitus's hands; but Levi was afraid to go out alone before such a large body of enemies, and he refused. Now Clitus saw that Josephus was in great passion inside the ship and ready to leap out in order to execute the punishment himself; he begged therefore, from the shore, that he leave him one of his hands, to which Josephus agreed, on condition that he would cut off the other hand; accordingly he drew his sword, and with his right hand cut off his left— so great was his fear of Josephus. And thus he took the people of Tiberias prisoners, regaining the city again with empty ships and seven of his guard. Moreover, a few days afterward he retook Tiberias, which had again revolted with the people of Sepphoris, and gave his soldiers leave to plunder it; but he got all the loot together and restored it to the inhabitants; and the same he did to the inhabitants of Sepphoris: for once he had subdued those cities, he had a mind, by letting them be plundered, to teach them a good lesson, while at the same time he regained their good will by restoring them their money again.

And thus were the disturbances of Galilee quelled, when, upon their ceasing their civil dissensions, they undertook to prepare for the war with the Romans. Now in Jerusalem the high priest Ananus, and as many of the men of power as were not in favor of the Romans, repaired the walls and made a great many warlike instruments, so many that darts and all sorts of armor were to be seen on the anvil in all parts of the city. Even though most of the young men were engaged in exercises, without regularity, and all places were full of tumultuous doings, yet the moderates were exceedingly sad; and a great many, foreseeing the calamities to come, made great lamentations. There were also omens observed that were understood, by such as loved peace, to be forerunners of evils, but those that kindled the war interpreted them to suit their own inclinations; and the very state of the city, even before the Romans came to attack it, was that of a place doomed to destruction. However, Ananus's concern was to lay aside, for a while, the preparations for the war, and to persuade the rebels to consult their own interest and restrain the madness of those who were called zealots; but their violence was too extreme for him.

The emperor Nero appoints Vespasian to the command in Judea.

When Nero was informed of the Romans' lack of success in Judea, an inner consternation and terror, usual in such cases, fell over him; although he outwardly looked very threatening and was very angry, he said that what had happened was due to the negligence of the commander rather than to any valor on the part of the enemy: and since he thought it fitting for him who bore the burden of the whole empire to despise such misfortunes, he now pretended to do so and to have a soul superior to all such sad accidents whatsoever. Yet the disturbance in his soul plainly appeared.

And as he was deliberating to whom he should commit the care of the east, now that it was in such great disarray, and who might be best able to punish the Jews for their rebellion and prevent the same distemper from seizing the neighboring nations also, he found no one but Vespasian equal to the task and able to undergo the great burden of so mighty a war; he was already growing old in the camp, and from his youth he had been trained in warlike exploits: he was also a man who had long ago pacified the west and made it subject to the Romans, after it had been put into disorder by the Germans: by his arms, he had also regained Britain for them, which had been little known before; whereby he made it possible for Nero's father [5] Claudius to have a triumph bestowed on him without any sweat or labor of his own.

So Nero esteemed these circumstances as favorable omens, and saw that Vespasian's age gave him sure experience and great skill, and that he had his sons as hostages for his fidelity to himself, and that their flourishing age would make them fit instruments of their father's prudence. Perhaps also there was some interposition of providence, which was paving the way for Vespasian's later becoming emperor himself. Nero sent this man to take over the command of the armies in Syria, but not without great encomiums and flatteries, such as necessity required and such as might mollify him into complaisance. So Vespasian sent his son Titus to Alexandria, to bring back from there the fifth and tenth legions, while he himself, after passing over the Hellespont, came by land to Syria, where he gathered together the Roman forces, with a considerable number of auxiliaries from the kings in that neighborhood.

After taking Gabara, Vespasian marches to Jotapata. After a long siege, the city is betrayed by a deserter and taken by Vespasian.

So Vespasian marched to the city of Gabara, and captured it upon the first attack because he found it destitute of any considerable number of grown men fit for war. Then he entered it and slew all the youth, the Romans having no mercy for any age what-

[5] Really his step-father.

soever. He also set fire not only to the city itself but to all the surrounding villages and country towns; some of them were quite destitute of inhabitants; and out of some of them he carried the inhabitants as slaves into captivity. As for Josephus, his retiring into that city which he chose as most fit for his security threw it into great fear; for the people of Tiberias did not imagine that he would have run away unless he had entirely despaired of the success of the war; and indeed, on that point, they were not mistaken; for he saw whither the affairs of the Jews were finally tending and was aware that they had but one way of escaping, and that was by repentance. However, although he expected the Romans would forgive him, yet he chose to die many times over rather than betray his country and dishonor that supreme command of the army which had been entrusted him, or to live happily under those against whom he had been sent to fight. He determined, therefore, to give an exact account of affairs in a letter to the leaders of Jerusalem so that he might not, by too much aggrandizing the power of the enemy, make them too timorous, nor by underestimating their power encourage them to resist when they were perhaps disposed to repentance. He also sent them word that if they thought of coming to terms, they must write him an answer at once; or if they resolved upon war, they must send him an army sufficient to fight the Romans. Accordingly he wrote these things and immediately sent messengers to carry his letter to Jerusalem.

Now Vespasian was very eager to demolish Jotapata, for he had received intelligence that the greatest part of the enemy had retired there; and that it was, on other accounts, a place of great security for them. Accordingly he sent both footmen and horsemen to level the road, which was mountainous and rocky, to be traveled not without difficulty by footmen but absolutely impracticable for horsemen. Now these workmen accomplished what they were about in four days' time, and opened a broad way for the army. On the fifth day, Josephus hurriedly traveled from Tiberias to Jotapata, and raised the drooping spirits of the Jews. And a certain deserter told this good news to Vespasian that Josephus had removed himself there, which made him make haste to the city, supposing that by capturing it he should take all Judea, in case he could get Josephus under his power. So he took this news to be of the vastest advantage to him, and believed it to be brought about by the providence of God that he who appeared to be the most prudent of all their enemies had of his own accord shut himself up in a place of certain custody. Accordingly he sent Placidus with a thousand horsemen, and Ebutius a decurion, a person of eminence both in council and in action, to surround the city so that Josephus might not escape secretly.

Vespasian also, the very next day, took his whole army and followed them, and by marching till late in the evening arrived at Jotapata; and bringing his army to the northern side of the city, he pitched his camp on a certain small hill seven furlongs from the city; he still greatly endeavored to be well seen by the enemy so as to put them into a consternation, which was indeed so immediately terrifying to the Jews that not one of them dared go out beyond the wall. Yet the Romans put off the attack at that time because they had marched all day, although they placed a double row of battalions round the city, with a third row beyond them consisting of cavalry, in order to close off every way of exit; making the Jews despair of escaping, this incited them to act more boldly; for nothing makes men fight so desperately in war as necessity.

Now when an assault was made the next day by the Romans, the Jews at first remained outside the walls and opposed them; and they met them, having formed themselves into a camp in front of the city walls. But when Vespasian had set against them the archers and slingers and the whole multitude that could throw a great distance, he permitted them to go to work, while he himself, with the footmen, got up on an acclivity, from which the city might easily be taken. Josephus was then in fear for the city and leaped out, and all the Jewish populace with him; these fell together upon the Romans in great numbers and drove them away from the wall, performing a great many glorious and bold actions. Yet they suffered as much as they made the enemy suffer; for as despair of deliverance encouraged the Jews, so did a sense of shame equally encourage the Romans. The latter had skill as well as strength; the Jews had only courage, which armed them and made them fight furiously. And after the fight had lasted all day, it was put to an end by the coming on of night. They had wounded a great many of the Romans, and killed thirteen of their men; on the Jews' side seventeen were slain and six hundred wounded.

The next day the Jews made another attack upon the Romans, and went outside the walls, and fought a much more desperate battle with them than before; for they had now become more courageous on account of their unexpectedly good opposition the day before; they found the Romans also fighting more desperately because a sense of shame inflamed them into a passion, esteeming their failure of sudden victory to be a kind of defeat. Thus did the Romans try continuously to make an impression upon the Jews till the fifth day, while the people of Jotapata made sallies out and fought at the walls most desperately; nor were the Jews frightened at the strength of the enemy, nor were the Romans discouraged at the difficulties they met in taking the city.

Now Jotapata is almost entirely built upon a precipice, having on all the other sides valleys so immensely deep and steep that those looking down could have their sight fail them before it reaches the bottom. It is only to be approached from the north side, where the greatest part of the city is built on the mountain, since it ends obliquely at a plain. This mountain Josephus had encompassed with a wall when he fortified the city, so that its top might not be capable of being seized by the enemies. The city is covered all around with other mountains, and cannot be seen in any way till a man almost comes upon it. And this was the strong situation of Jotapata.

Vespasian, therefore, in order to try how he might overcome the natural strength of the place as well as the bold defence of the Jews, made a resolution to prosecute the siege with vigor. To that end he called his commanders to a council of war, and consulted with them which way the assault might be managed to the best advantage; and when the resolution was taken to raise a bank against that part of the wall which was practicable, he sent his whole army abroad to gather the materials together. So when they had cut down all the trees on the mountains adjoining the city and had gotten together a vast heap of stones, besides the wood they had cut down, some of them brought hurdles in order to avoid the effects of the darts shot from above them. These hurdles they spread over their backs, and so were little hurt or not at all by the darts thrown upon them from the wall, while others pulled the neighboring hillocks to pieces and perpetually brought fresh earth to them; so that while they were busy three sorts of ways, nobody was idle. However, the Jews cast great stones from the walls upon the hurdles which protected the men, with all sorts of darts also; and the noise even of what could not reach them was still so terrifying that the workmen were impeded.

Vespasian then set the engines for throwing stones and darts around the city; the number of the engines was 160 in all; and he bade them fall to work and dislodge those on the wall. At the same time engines intended for that purpose simultaneously threw lances upon them with great noise and stones of the weight of a talent thrown by the engines prepared for that purpose, together with fire and a vast multitude of arrows, which made the wall so dangerous that the Jews not only did not dare come on it, but dared not come to those parts within the walls which were penetrated by the engines; for the multitude of Arabian archers, as well also as all those who threw darts and slung stones, fell to work at the same time as the engines. Yet the others did not lie still when they could not throw at the Romans from a higher place; for they then made sallies out of the city like private robbers, in groups, and pulled away the hurdles that covered the workmen, and killed them when they were exposed; and when those workmen gave way, they cast away the earth that composed the bank, and burnt the wooden parts of it together with the hurdles, till at length Vespasian perceived that the intervals between the works were of disadvantage to him; for those spaces of ground afforded the Jews a place for assaulting the Romans. So he united the hurdles and at the same time joined one part of the army to the other, thus preventing the excursions of the Jews.

And when the bank was now raised and brought nearer than ever to the battlements belonging to the walls, Josephus thought it would be entirely wrong if he could make no contrivances to oppose theirs which might help the city's preservation; so he got his workmen together and ordered them to build the wall higher; and when they said this was impossible to do while so many darts were being thrown at them, he invented a sort of cover for them. He bade them fix piles and stretch raw hides of newly killed oxen in front of them so that those hides might intercept the stones that were thrown and quench the fire by the moisture within them; and these he set in front of the workmen; and behind them these workmen went on with their work in safety, both day and night, raising the wall till it was twenty cubits high. He also built a good number of towers on the wall, and fitted it to strong battlements. This greatly discouraged the Romans, who in their own view had already gotten inside the walls, and now they were astonished at both Josephus's contrivance and the fortitude of the citizens in the city.

And now Vespasian was plainly irritated at the great subtlety of this stratagem and at the boldness of the citizens of Jotapata; for taking heart again on building this wall, they made fresh sallies against the Romans, and every day battled with them in groups, together with such contrivances as robbers use, plundering all that came to hand and setting fire to all the other works; and this went on till Vespasian made his army stop fighting them, resolving to lie round the city and starve them into a surrender, supposing that either they would be forced to petition him for mercy because of lack of provisions or even if they had the courage to hold out till the last they would perish by famine: and he concluded he would conquer them more easily in fighting if he gave them an interlude and then fell upon them after they had been weakened by famine; but still he gave orders that they should guard against their coming out of the city.

Now the besieged had plenty of corn within the city, and indeed all other necessaries, but they lacked water because there was no fountain in the city, the people there usually being satisfied with rain water; yet it is a rare thing in that country to have rain in summer, and at this season, during the siege, they were in great distress for some means of satisfying their thirst; and they were very sad at this time particularly because Josephus, seeing that the city abounded with other necessaries and that the men were of good courage, and being desirous to protract the siege of the Romans longer than they expected, ordered their water to be given them by measure; but this scanty distribution of water by measure was deemed by them as harder to bear than its total lack; and their not being able to drink as much as they wanted made them more desirous of drinking than they otherwise might have been; nay, they were so disheartened as if they had reached the last degree of thirst. Nor were the Romans unacquainted with their state for when they stood over against them, beyond the wall, they could see them running together and taking their water by measure, which made them throw their javelins thither, the place being within their reach, and kill a great many of them.

Hereupon Vespasian hoped that their receptacles of water would shortly be emptied, and that they would be forced to deliver up the city to him; but Josephus being minded to break his hope gave command that they should wet a great many of their clothes, and hang them out around the battlements till the entire wall was suddenly all wet with the running down of the water. At this sight the Romans were discouraged and in consternation when they saw them able to throw away in sport so much water, when they had supposed them not to have enough to drink themselves. This made the Roman general despair of taking the city through their lack of necessaries, and to betake himself again to arms, and to try to force them to surrender, which was what the Jews greatly desired; for as they despaired of either themselves or their city being able to escape, they preferred death in battle to one by hunger and thirst.

However, Josephus contrived another stratagem to get what they needed. There was a certain rough and uneven place that could hardly be ascended and on that account was not guarded by the soldiers; so Josephus sent out certain persons along the western parts of the valley, with letters to whomever he pleased of the Jews outside the city, and procured from them an abundance of whatever necessaries they lacked inside the city; he enjoined them also to creep along past the guard as they came into the city, and to cover their backs with sheepskins having their wool on them so that anyone spying them at night might believe them to be dogs.

This was done till the watch perceived their contrivance, and surrounded that rough place themselves.

And now Josephus perceived that the city could not hold out
long, and that his own life would be in danger if he remained
there; so he consulted how he and the most powerful men of the
city might fly out of it. When the multitude understood this, they
approached and begged him not to overlook them because they
depended entirely on him and him alone; there was still hope of
the city's deliverance if he would stay with them because everybody would bear any suffering with great cheerfulness on his account, and in that case there would be some comfort for them
also, even though they be captured: that it became him neither to
fly from his enemies nor to desert his friends nor to leap out of
that city, as out of a ship sinking in a storm, into which he had
come when it was quiet and calm; by going away he would be the
cause of drowning the city because nobody would then venture to
oppose the enemy when he, upon whom they wholly depended,
was gone.

Hereupon Josephus suppressing any mention of his own safety,
told them that he would go out of the city for their sakes; if he
stayed with them, he should be able to do them little good while
they were in a safe condition; and that once they were captured,
he should only perish with them to no purpose; but that if he were
freed from this siege, he would be able to bring them very great
relief; for that he would immediately gather the Galileans in great
multitudes, and draw the Romans off their city by another war.
He did not see what advantage he could bring to them now by
staying among them; it would only provoke the Romans to besiege
them more heavily, esteeming it a most valuable thing to capture
him; but once they were informed that he had fled the city, they
would greatly lessen their efforts against it. But this plea did not
move the people, but inflamed them the more to hang around him.
Accordingly, both the children and the old men, and the women
with their infants, came mourning to him, and fell down before
him; all of them caught hold of his feet and held him fast, and besought him, with great lamentations, to share their fortune with
them; and I think they did this, not because they envied his deliv-

erance, but because they hoped for their own; for they could not imagine they should suffer any great misfortune provided Josephus remained with them.

Now, Josephus thought that if he resolved to stay, it would be ascribed to their entreaties; and if he resolved to go away by force, he should be put into custody. His sympathy also for the people and their lamentations had much broken his eagerness to leave them; so he resolved to stay, and arming himself with the common despair of the citizens, he said to them, "Now is the time to begin to fight in earnest, when there is no hope of deliverance left. It is a brave thing to prefer glory before life, and to set about some such noble undertaking as may be remembered by posterity." Having said this, he fell to work immediately and made a sally, and dispersed the enemies' outguards, and ran as far as the Roman camp itself, and pulled to pieces the coverings of their tents that were on their banks, and set fire to their works. And in this manner he never stopped fighting, neither the next day nor the day after, but went on for a considerable number of days and nights.

When he saw the Romans distressed by these sallies (although they were ashamed to be made to run away by the Jews; and when at any time they made the Jews run away, their heavy armor would not let them pursue them far; while the Jews, when they had performed any action and before they could be hurt themselves, still retired into the city), Vespasian ordered his armed men to avoid their attack, and not to fight it out with men under desperation, since nothing is more courageous than despair; but that their violence would be quenched when they saw they failed in their purpose, just as fire is quenched when it lacks fuel; and that it was most proper for the Romans to gain their victories as cheaply as they could since they are not forced to fight but only to enlarge their own dominions. So he repelled the Jews in great measure by the Arabian archers, the Syrian slingers, and by those that threw stones at them, nor was there any letup of their numerous offensive engines. Now the Jews suffered greatly from those engines without being able to escape them; and when those engines threw their stones or javelins a great distance, and the Jews were within their reach, they pressed hard against the Romans and fought desperately, without sparing either soul or body, one part in turn succoring another.

When, therefore, Vespasian saw himself besieged by these sallies of the Jews, and when his banks were now not far from the walls, he determined to make use of his battering-ram. This battering-ram is a vast beam of wood like the mast of a ship; its forepart is armed with a thick piece of iron at its head, so carved as to be like the head of a ram, whence its name. This ram is slung in the air by ropes passing over its middle, and is hung from another beam, like the balance in a pair of scales, and braced by strong beams passing on both sides in the nature of a cross. When this ram is pulled backward by a great number of men with united force, and then thrust forward by the same men, it batters the walls, with a mighty noise, with that iron part which is prominent; nor is there any tower so strong or walls so broad that can resist any more than its first batteries, but all are forced to yield to it in the end. This was the experiment which the Roman general undertook when he was eagerly bent upon capturing the city; he found that lying in the field so long was to his disadvantage because the Jews would never leave him in peace. So these Romans brought the several engines for galling an enemy nearer to the walls that they might reach those who were on the wall, and endeavored to frustrate their attempts; these threw stones and javelins at them; in like manner the archers and slingers both came together closer to the wall. This brought matters to such a pass that none of the Jews dared mount the walls, and then the other Romans brought the battering-ram that was cased with hurdles all over, and in the upper part was secured with skins that covered it, and this both for their own security and that of the engine. Now, at the very first stroke of this engine, the wall shook and a terrifying clamor was heard from the people within the city as if they were already captured.

And now when Josephus saw this ram still battering the same place and that the wall would quickly be thrown down by it, he resolved to avoid for a while the force of the engine. With this plan he gave orders to fill sacks with chaff and to hang them down in front of that place the ram was battering so that the stroke might be averted, or the place feel the strokes less because of the yielding nature of the chaff. This contrivance very much delayed the attempts of the Romans because, move their engine to what section they pleased, those above it moved their sacks and placed them over against the strokes it made so that the wall was no way hurt, and this by diverting the strokes, till the Romans made an opposing device of long poles, and by tying hooks at their ends, cut off the sacks. Now, when the battering-ram had thus recovered its force, and the newly built wall was giving way, Josephus and those about him had immediate recourse to fire in order to defend themselves; whereupon they took what materials they had that were dry and made a sally three ways, setting fire to the machines and the hurdles and the banks of the Romans themselves; nor did the Romans know how to come to their own assistance, being at once in consternation at the Jews' boldness and unable because of the flames to help themselves; the materials being dry with their bitumen and pitch and brimstone, the fire caught hold of everything immediately; and what had cost the Romans a great deal of trouble was in one hour consumed.

And here a certain Jew appeared worthy of our mention and commendation; the son of Sameas, he was called Eleazar, and was born at Saba, in Galilee. This man took up a stone of vast bigness and threw it down from the wall upon the ram, and this with such great force that it broke off the engine's head. He also leaped down and picked up the head of the ram from their very midst, and without any concern carried it to the top of the wall, and this while he stood as a fit target to be pelted by all his enemies. Accordingly, he received the strokes upon his naked body and was wounded by five darts; nor did he pay attention to any of them while he climbed to the top of the wall, where he stood in sight of them all as an example of the greatest boldness; after which, writhing under his wounds, he fell down together with the head of the ram. Next to him, two brothers showed their courage; their names were Netir and Philip, both from the village Ruma, and both Galileans also; these men leaped upon the soldiers of the tenth legion and fell upon the Romans with such a noise and force as to disorder their ranks and put to flight all upon whom they made their assaults.

After these men's performances, Josephus and the rest of the people took a great deal of fire and burnt both the machines and their coverings together with the works belonging to the fifth and the tenth legions, which they put to flight; others followed them immediately, and buried those instruments and all their materials under ground. However, towards evening the Romans erected the battering-ram again against that part of the wall which had suffered before; there a certain Jew defending the city against the Romans hit Vespasian's foot with a dart, wounding him slightly, the distance being so great that no mighty impression could be made by the dart thrown from so far off. However, this caused the greatest disorder among the Romans; for when those who stood near him saw his blood, they were disturbed, and when a report went abroad through the whole army that the general was wounded, most of them left the siege and came running together with surprise and fear to the general; and at their head came Titus, out of his concern for his father, so that the multitude were in great confusion, out of the regard they had for their general and because of the agony of his son. Yet the father soon put an end to the son's fear and to the disorder of the army; rising above his pains and endeavoring soon to be seen by all who had been frightened over him, he incited them to fight the Jews more briskly; for now everybody was willing to expose himself to danger immediately in order to avenge their general; and then they encouraged one another with loud voices and ran hastily to the walls.

But still Josephus and those with him, even though they were shot down dead one upon another by the darts and stones of the engines, did not desert the wall, but fell upon those who managed the ram, under the protection of the hurdles, with fire and iron weapons and stones; and they could do little or nothing, but kept falling perpetually, since they were seen by those whom they could not see, for the light of their own flame shone around them, making them a most visible target for the enemy in the daytime; at the same time the engines could not be seen at a great distance, and so what was thrown at them could hardly be avoided; for the force with which these engines threw stones and darts allowed them to hurt several at a time, and the violent noise of the stones cast by the engines was so great that they carried away the pinnacles of the wall and broke off the corners of the towers; for no body of men could be so strong as not to be overthrown down to the last rank by the largeness of the stones. And any one may understand the force of the engines by what happened that very night; one of those who was standing near Josephus and the wall had his head carried away by such a stone, and his skull flung as far as three furlongs; that same day also, a woman with child had her belly so violently struck just as she came out of her house that the infant was carried half a furlong. The noise of the instruments themselves was very terrifying; so too the sounds of the darts and stones they threw; so too that noise the dead bodies made when they were dashed against the wall; and dreadful indeed was the clamor which these things raised among the women within the city, which was echoed back at the same time by the cries of those who were slain; meanwhile the whole space of ground whereon they fought ran with blood and the wall might have been covered over by the bodies of the dead carcasses; the mountains also contributed to increase the noise by their echoes; nor was there on that night anything of terror lacking that could affect either one's hearing or one's sight; yet did a great part of those that fought so hard for Jotapata fall manfully, as did a great part of the wounded. However, the morning watch came before the wall yielded to the machines employed against it, though it had been battered without cease. However, those within covered their bodies with armor and raised works over against that part which was thrown down before those machines were laid by which the Romans were to ascend into the city.

In the morning Vespasian got his army together in order to take the city by storm, after a little recreation following their hard work the night before; and as he was desirous of drawing off those opposing him from the places where the wall had been thrown down, he made the most courageous of the horsemen get off their horses, and placed them in three ranks over against those ruins of the walls, but covered with their armor on every side and with poles in their hands, so that they might begin their ascent as soon as the instruments for such ascent were laid. Behind them he placed the flower of the footmen; but the remainder of the horsemen he ordered to extend themselves over against the wall, on the whole hilly countryside, in order to prevent any of them from escaping out of the city after it was taken; and behind these he placed the archers, commanding them to have all their darts ready to shoot. The same command he gave to the slingers and to those in charge of the engines, ordering them to take up other ladders and have them ready to lay upon those parts of the wall which were yet untouched so that the besieged might be engaged in trying to hinder their ascent and so leave off guarding the parts that had been thrown down while the rest of them would be overborne by the darts cast at them and so allow his men to enter the city.

But Josephus, understanding the meaning of Vespasian's contrivance, placed the old men, together with those that were tired out, at the sound parts of the wall, expecting no harm from those quarters, but put, at the place where the wall was broken down, the strongest of his men and, in front of them, six men by themselves, among whom he took his share of the first and greatest danger. He also gave orders that when the Roman legions made a shout they should stop their ears so that they might not be frightened by it, and that, to avoid the multitude of the enemies' darts, they should bend down on their knees and cover themselves with their shields, and that they should retreat a little backward for a while till the archers would have emptied their quivers; but that, when the Romans should lay their instruments for ascending the walls, they should leap out on the sudden and with their own instruments meet the enemy, and that every one should strive to do his best in order not just to defend his own city, as if it were possible to be preserved, but in order to avenge it after it was already destroyed; and that they should set before their eyes how their old men were to be slain and their children and wives to be killed immediately by the enemy. And that they would beforehand spend all their fury on account of the calamities coming upon them, and pour it out on the perpetrators.

And thus did Josephus dispose of both his bodies of men. As for the useless part of the citizens, the women and children, when they saw their city encompassed by the three-fold army (for none of the usual guards that had been fighting before were removed), and not only the walls thrown down but their enemies with swords in their hands, and also the hilly countryside above them shining with their weapons and the darts in the hands of the Arabian archers, they made a final and lamentable outcry over the destruction, as if the misery were not only threatened but had actually come upon them already. But Josephus ordered the women to be shut up in their houses lest they render the warlike actions of the men too effeminate by making them pity their condition, and commanded them to hold their peace, threatening them if they did not, while he placed himself before the breach where his allocation was; for all those who brought ladders to the other places, he took no notice of them but earnestly waited for the shower of arrows that was to come.

And now the trumpeters of the several Roman legions sounded together and the army made a terrible shout; and the darts, as by order, flew so fast that they intercepted the light. However, Josephus's men remembered his charges: they stopped their ears at the sounds and covered their bodies against the darts; and as to the engines that were ready to go to work, the Jews ran out upon them before those that were to have used them had gotten to them. And now, on the ascending of the soldiers, there was a great conflict and many actions of the hands and soul were exhibited, while the Jews did earnestly endeavor, in their extreme danger, not to show less courage than those who, without being in danger, fought so stoutly against them; nor did they stop struggling with the Romans till they either fell down dead themselves or killed their antagonists. But the Jews grew weary with defending themselves continually, and had not enough men to take their places to succor them—while, on the side of the Romans, fresh men were still succeeding those that were tired; and still new men soon got up on the machines for ascent in the place of those thrust down; those encouraging one another and joining side to side with their shields, which were a protection to them, they became a body of men not to be broken; and as this band thrust away the Jews, as though they were themselves but one body, they began already to mount the wall.

Then did Josephus take council in this utmost distress and gave orders to pour scalding oil upon those whose shields protected them. Whereupon they soon got it ready, there being many who brought it, and what they brought being a great quantity also, and poured it on all sides upon the Romans, and threw down upon them their vessels while they were still hissing from the heat of the fire; this so burnt the Romans that it dispersed that united band, who now tumbled down from the wall with horrid pain, for the oil did easily run down the whole body from head to foot, under their entire armor, and fed upon their flesh like flame itself, its fat and unctuous nature rendering it soon heated and but slowly cooled; and as the men were cooped up in their headpieces and breastplates, they could no way get free from that burning oil; they could only leap and roll about in their pain as they fell down from the bridges they had laid. And as they were thus beaten back and retired to their own party, who still pressed them forward, they were easily wounded by those behind them.

However, in this ill success of the Romans, their courage did not fail them, nor did the Jews lack prudence to oppose them; for the Romans, although they saw their own men thrown down and in miserable condition, yet they were vehemently bent against those that poured the oil upon them, while every one reproached the man before him as a coward and as one hindering him from exerting himself; and meanwhile the Jews made use of another stratagem to prevent their ascent and poured boiling fenugreek upon the boards in order to make them slip and fall down; by this means neither could those coming up nor those going down stand on their feet; but some fell backward upon the machines on which they ascended and were trodden upon; many fell down on the bank they had raised and after they had fallen upon it were slain by the Jews; for once the Romans could not remain on their feet, the Jews, freed from fighting hand to hand, had the leisure to throw their darts at them. So the general called off those soldiers in the evening that had suffered so sorely, of whom the number of the slain was not a few and that of the wounded still greater; but of the people of Jotapata no more than six men were killed, although more than three hundred were carried off wounded.

Hereupon Vespasian comforted his army for what had happened, and he found them angry indeed, but wanting action rather than any further exhortations, he gave orders to raise the banks still higher and to erect three towers, each fifty feet high, which they were to cover with plates of iron on every side so that they might be both firm by their weight and not easily liable to be set on fire. These towers he set upon the banks and placed upon them such as could shoot darts and arrows, with the lighter engines for throwing stones and darts also; and besides these he set there the stoutest men among the slingers, who unable to be seen by reason of the height they stood on and the battlements protecting them, might throw their weapons against those on the wall who were easily seen by them. Hereupon the Jews, not being easily able to escape those darts thrown down on their heads nor to avenge themselves on those whom they could not see, and perceiving that the height of the towers was so great that a dart thrown by their hand could hardly reach it, and that the iron plates around them made it very hard to reach them by fire, they ran away from the walls, and fled hastily out of the city, and fell on those that shot at them. And thus did the people of Jotapata resist the Romans, but a great number of them were killed every day, without their being able to inflict the same evil upon their enemies; nor could they keep them out of the city without endangering themselves.

But as the people of Jotapata still held out manfully and bore up under their miseries beyond all that could be hoped for, on the forty-seventh day of the siege the banks cast up by the Romans had risen higher than the wall; on that day a certain deserter went to Vespasian, and told him how few were left in the city, and how weak they were, and that they had become so worn out with perpetual watching and fighting that they could not now oppose any force that came against them, and that they might be taken by stratagem, if any one would attack them during the last watch of the night, when they thought they might have some rest from their hardships and, as they were thoroughly weary, the watch used to fall asleep. Accordingly his advice was that they should make their attack at that hour. But Vespasian had a suspicion about this deserter, knowing how faithful the Jews were to one another and how much they scorned any punishments that could be inflicted on them; he knew that one of the people of Jotapata had undergone all sorts of torments, and though they made him pass through a fiery trial in his examination, he would tell them nothing of the affairs within the city, and as he was being crucified, he smiled at them! However, the probability in the narration itself did partly confirm the truth of what the deserter told them, and they thought he might probably be speaking the truth. Moreover, Vespasian thought they would not suffer greatly even if the report was a sham; so he commanded them to keep the man in custody, and prepared the army for taking the city.

According to this resolution they marched without making any noise, at the hour told them, to the wall; and it was Titus himself that first got up on it, with one of his tribunes, Domitius Sabinus, and a few of the fifteenth legion. Then they cut the throats of the watch and entered the city very quietly. After these came Cerealis the tribune and Placidus, leading those under them. Now after the citadel was taken and the enemy were in the very middle of the city, and when it was already day, the capture of the city was still not known by those who held it; a great many of them were fast asleep, and a great mist, by chance fallen over the city, prevented those that got up from distinctly seeing their situation till after the whole Roman army had entered. As they were being killed, they perceived the city was captured. As for the Romans, they so well remembered what they had suffered during the siege that they spared none nor pitied any, but drove the people down the precipice from the citadel and slew them as they drove them down; at which time the difficulties of the place prevented those still able to fight from defending themselves; for as they were distressed in the narrow streets and could not keep their feet secure along the precipice, they were overpowered by the crowd of those fighting them who came down from the citadel. This provoked a great many, even among those chosen men around Josephus, to kill themselves with their own hands; for when they saw that they could kill none of the Romans, they resolved to prevent being killed by the Romans and got together in great numbers, in the furthermost parts of the city, and killed themselves.

However, those of the watch who perceived they were being taken and ran away as fast as they could, went up into one of the towers on the north side of the city, and for a while defended themselves there; but since they were surrounded by a multitude of enemies, they tried to use their right hands when it was too late, and at length they cheerfully offered their necks to be cut off by those who stood over them. And the Romans might have boasted that the conclusion of that siege was without blood on their side, if there had not been a centurion, Antonius, who was slain at the taking of the city.

And on this day the Romans slew all the populace that appeared openly; but on the following days they searched the hiding places and fell upon those that were underground and in the caverns, and went thus through every age, with the exception of the infants and women, of whom they gathered together twelve hundred as captives; and as for those that were slain at the taking of the city and in the earlier fights, they numbered some forty thousand. So Vespasian gave order that the city should be entirely demolished, and all the fortifications burnt down. And thus was Jotapata taken, in the thirteenth year of the reign of Nero.[6]

> *At the capture of Jotapata, Josephus hid in a cave with some companions, agreed with them on collective suicide, and, by a trick, escaped. Captured by the Romans, he was brought before Vespasian, to whom he claims to have prophesied that he would soon become emperor. He was kept a prisoner but treated kindly. The account of his escape, capture and confrontation with Vespasian is given above, pp. 45 ff.*
>
> *The surrender of the city of Gischala; John flies from it to Jerusalem. Notice in this chapter Josephus's venom against John of Gischala, and his ascription of humanitarian motives to his protector Titus.*

[6] July, 67 C.E.

Now no place in Galilee remained to be captured but the small city of Gischala, whose inhabitants still desired peace; for they were generally farmers, and applied themselves to cultivating the fruits of the earth. However, there were a great number that belonged to a band of robbers, already corrupted, who had crept in among them; and some of the governing sector of the citizens belonged to this crowd. It was John, the son of Levi, that drew them into the rebellion and encouraged them in it. He was a cunning knave, and had a temperament that could put on various shapes; very rash in expecting great things, and very sagacious in bringing about what he hoped for. It was known to everybody that he was fond of using war as a means of thrusting himself into authority; and he kept the seditious among the people of Gischala under his management so that the populace, who would otherwise have been ready to send ambassadors to surrender, waited in battle array for the coming of the Romans. Vespasian sent Titus against them with a thousand horsemen, but withdrew the tenth legion to Scythopolis, while he returned to Caesarea with the two other legions so that they might refresh themselves after their long and hard campaign, thinking that the plentiful supplies in those cities would fortify their bodies and spirits against the difficulties they were to go through later; for he saw that there would be a necessity for great effort at Jerusalem, which was not yet taken, because it was the royal city and the principal city of the whole nation; and because those that had run away from the war in other places had all gathered there. It was also naturally strong, and the walls built around it worried him not a little. Moreover, he esteemed its men to be so courageous and bold that even without consideration of the walls it would be hard to subdue them; for this reason he took care of and exercised his soldiers beforehand for the work, just like athletes before their contests.

Now Titus, as he rode up to Gischala, found it would be easy for him to take the city on the first attack; but he knew that if he took it by force, the populace would be destroyed by the soldiers without mercy. By now he was already satiated with the shedding of blood, and pitied the major part, who would perish without distinction, together with the guilty. He rather preferred that the city be surrendered up to him on terms. Accordingly, when he saw the wall full of those men belonging to the corrupt party, he said to them that he could not but wonder what it was they depended on when they alone remained to fight the Romans, after every other city had been captured by them; especially when they had seen cities much better fortified than theirs overthrown by a single attack; while as many as have entrusted themselves to the security of the Romans' right hands, which he now offers them without regard to their former insolence, enjoy their own possessions in safety; while they had hopes of recovering their liberty, they might be pardoned; but their continuing in their opposition when they saw that to be impossible was inexcusable; if they would not comply with such humane offers and right hands for security, they would experience such a war as would spare nobody, and would soon be made aware that their wall would be but a trifle when battered by the Roman machines; by depending on this, they would demonstrate themselves to be the only Galileans that were no better than arrogant slaves and captives.

Now none of the populace could make a reply, for they dared not so much as get up on the wall, which was all taken up by the robbers, who also guarded the gates in order to prevent any of the rest from getting out to propose terms of submission, or from receiving any of the horsemen in the city. But John answered Titus that for himself he was content to hearken to his proposals, and that he would either persuade or force those that refused them. Yet, he said, Titus ought to have such regard for the Jewish law as to grant them leave to celebrate that day, the seventh day of the week, on which it was unlawful not only to use their arms but even to discuss peace; and that even the Romans were not ignorant that the period of the seventh day required them to cease from all labors; and that he who should compel them to transgress the law would be as guilty as those compelled to transgress it: and that this delay could be to his advantage; for why should anybody think of doing any thing in the night unless it was to fly away, which he might prevent by placing his camp around them. They would think it a great point gained if they not be obliged to trans-

gress the laws of their country; and it would be a right thing for
him, who planned to grant them peace, without their expecting
such a favor, to preserve inviolable the laws of those he saved.

Thus did this man trick Titus, not so much out of regard for the
seventh day as for his own preservation, for he was afraid lest he
be quite deserted if the city were taken. Now this was the work of
God, who therefore preserved this John, that he might bring on
the destruction of Jerusalem; also it was His work that Titus
agreed to this pretended delay and that he pitched his camp further away from the city at Cydessa. This Cydessa was a strong inland village of the Tyrians, which had always hated and made war
against the Jews; it also had a great number of inhabitants and
was well fortified, which made it an appropriate place for enemies
of the Jewish nation.

In the night time, when John saw that there was no Roman
guard around the city, he seized the opportunity directly, and taking with him not only the armed men around him but a considerable number of those that had little to do together with their families, he fled to Jerusalem. And indeed, though the man was
making haste to get away and was tormented with fears of being
taken captive or of losing his life, yet he decided to take out of the
city along with him a multitude of women and children, as far as
twenty furlongs; but as he proceeded further on his journey, he
left them behind and they made sad lamentation; for the further
every one had gone from his own people, the nearer they thought
themselves to be to their enemies. They were also frightened at the
thought that those who would carry them into captivity were near
at hand, and they turned back at the mere noise they themselves
made in their hasty flight, as if those from whom they fled were already upon them. Many also lost their way; and the pushing of
those aiming to go forward caused them to knock down many others. Indeed a miserable destruction was made of the women and
children; some took courage to call their husbands and kinsmen
back, and beseech them, with the bitterest lamentations, to wait
for them; but John, who cried out to them to save themselves and
fly away, prevailed. He said also that if the Romans should seize

those left behind, they would take their revenge on them for it. So this multitude that ran away was dispersed abroad, according to how fast each was able to run.

Now the next day Titus came to the wall to make the agreement; whereupon the people opened their gates and came out to him with their children and wives, and made acclamations of joy to him, as to one who had been their benefactor and had delivered the city out of custody; they also informed him of John's flight and besought him to spare them, and to come in and punish the rest of those who had favored resistance; but Titus, paying not too much heed to the supplications of the people, sent part of his horsemen to pursue John, though they could not overtake him because he had already reached Jerusalem; they also slew six thousand of the women and children who had departed with him but who had returned and brought with them almost three thousand.

However, Titus was greatly displeased that he was not able to bring John, who had deluded him, to punishment; yet he had enough captives as well as the corrupted part of the city to appease his anger. So he entered the city in the midst of acclamations of joy; and after he had given orders to the soldiers to pull down a small part of the wall, as of a city taken in war, he repressed those that had disturbed the city by threats rather than by executions; for he thought that many, out of their own animosities and quarrels, would accuse innocent persons if he should attempt to distinguish those deserving punishment from the rest; and that it was better to leave a guilty person alone with his fears than to destroy with him any one who did not deserve it; probably such a one, through fear of the punishment he had deserved, might be taught prudence and be ashamed of his former offenses after he had been forgiven, whereas the punishment of those put to death could never be retrieved. However, he placed a garrison in the city for its security, by means of which he could restrain those who favored resistance and leave those peaceably disposed in greater security. And thus was all Galilee captured; but this not before it had cost the Romans great effort.

Dissension among the Jews in Jerusalem.

Now, upon John's entry into Jerusalem, the whole body of the people were in an uproar; ten thousand of them crowded around every one of the fugitives who had come to them, inquiring of them what miseries had happened abroad; their breath was so short and hot and quick that in itself it revealed their great distress; yet they talked boastfully under their misfortunes, pretending that they had not fled from the Romans but had come thither in order to fight them with less hazard; they said it would have been unreasonable and fruitless for them to expose themselves to desperate hazards for the sake of Gischala and other such weak cities, whereas they ought to store up their weapons and their zeal and reserve them for their capital city. But when they related the capture of Gischala and their own decent departure, as they pretended, from that place, many of the people understood that it was no better than a flight; and especially when the people were told of those who had been made captives, they were in great confusion, guessing those things to be clear indications that they too should be captured; as for John, he was very little concerned about those whom he had left behind, but went about among all the people, persuading them to go to war. He affirmed that the affairs of the Romans were in weak condition, and he extolled his own power. He also jested about the ignorance of the unskillful, as if those Romans, even if they were to put on wings, could never fly over the wall of Jerusalem since they had encountered such great difficulties in taking the villages of Galilee and had broken their engines of war against their walls.

These harangues by John corrupted a great many of the young men and puffed them up for the war; but among the most prudent and those wiser in years there was not a man who did not foresee what was coming, and they made lamentations on that account, as if the city were already undone. And there was confusion among the people. But then it must be observed that the multitude who had come from the country were in discord before the Jerusalem dispute began. There were disorders and civil wars in every city; and all those who were not being harassed by the Romans turned their hands against one another. There was also a bitter contest between those desiring war and those desiring peace. At first this quarrelsomeness took hold of private families who could not agree among themselves, after which those people who were the dearest broke all restraints with regard to one another, each one associating with those of his own opinion and ready to stand in opposition to the other; as a result, disagreements arose everywhere; those who by their youth and boldness favored resistance and desired war seemed too rash to the aged and the prudent men; and all the people everywhere began to indulge themselves in plundering; after which they got together in bodies to rob the people of the country, to the extent that for barbarity and iniquity those of the same nation did in no way differ from the Romans; nay, it began to seem a much lighter thing to be ruined by the Romans than by themselves.

Now the Roman garrisons which guarded the cities, partly out of their uneasiness to take such trouble upon themselves and partly out of the hatred they bore the Jewish nation, did little or nothing to relieve the miserable, so that the captains of these troops of robbers, after being satiated with plunders in the country, came together from all sides to form a great band; and all together crept into Jerusalem, which had now become a city without a governor and in accordance with the ancient custom, received without distinction all belonging to their nation; and they received those men because it was supposed that those who came so quickly into the city came out of kindness to help them, even though these very men, in addition to the disruption they started, were also the direct cause of the city's destruction; since they were an unprofitable and useless multitude, they depleted those provisions beforehand which might otherwise have been sufficient for the fighting men. Moreover, besides bringing on the war, they were the cause of trouble and famine in the city.

Besides these, there were other robbers who came out of the country and into the city and, joining those who were worse than themselves, engaged in every kind of barbarity; they did not measure their courage by their rapines and plunderings only, but went as far as murdering men, and that not at nighttime or privately or with regard for ordinary men, but openly in the daytime, beginning with the most eminent persons in the city. The first man they meddled with was Antipas, of royal lineage and one of the most powerful men in the whole city since the public treasures were committed to his care; they captured and confined him, as they did next Levias, a person of great note, and Sophas, both of whom were also of royal lineage. And besides these, they did the same to the leaders of the country. This caused terrible consternation among the people; and every one contented himself with taking care of his own safety, as they would do if the city had been taken in war.

But they were not satisfied with the bonds into which they had put the aforementioned men; nor did they think it safe to keep them in custody long since they were very powerful men, who had numerous families of their own able to avenge them. In fact, they thought the general populace might perhaps be so moved at these unjust proceedings as to rise in a body against them. It was therefore resolved to have them slain. Accordingly, they sent one John, the most bloody-minded of them all, to perform that execution: this man was also called "the son of Dorcas," in the language of our country. Ten men went with him into the prison, their swords drawn, and they cut the throats of those in custody there. The grand lying excuse made for so flagrant an excess was that these men had held conferences with the Romans regarding a surrender of Jerusalem to them; and so they said they had slain only those who were traitors to their common liberty. On the whole, they grew even more insolent after this bold prank, as though they had been the benefactors and saviors of the city.

Now the people had arrived at that degree of misery and fear and these robbers to that degree of madness that the latter undertook to appoint high priests. So after annulling the succession of those families out of whom the high priests used to be named, they ordained certain unknown and ignoble persons for that office so that they might have their assistance in their wicked undertakings; for such as obtained this highest of all honors without desert were forced to comply with those who bestowed it on them. They also set the leaders at odds with one another, through several sorts of contrivances and tricks, and won the opportunity to do as they pleased because of the quarrels of those who might otherwise have obstructed their measures; till at length, satiated with their unjust actions towards men, they transferred their contumelious behavior to God Himself, and came into the sanctuary with polluted feet.

And now the multitude were going to rise against them; for Ananus, the oldest of the high priests, had persuaded them to do so. He was a very prudent man and might perhaps have saved the city if he could but have escaped the hands of those that plotted against him. Those men made the Temple of God a stronghold for themselves and a place whither they might resort in order to avoid the troubles they feared from the people; the sanctuary had now become a refuge and a shop of tyranny. They also mixed gambling among the miseries they introduced, which was more intolerable than what they did; for in order to test the submissiveness of the people and how far their own power extended, they undertook to dispose of the high-priesthood by casting lots for it, whereas it used to descend by succession in a family. The excuse they gave for this strange attempt was an ancient practice, saying that of old it had been determined by lot; but in truth it was no better than a dissolution of an undeniable law, and a cunning contrivance to seize the government, invented by those who presumed to appoint governors of their own choice.

Hereupon they sent for one of the pontifical clans and cast lots as to which should be the high priest. By fortune, the lot so fell as to demonstrate their iniquity in the plainest manner, for it fell upon one whose name was Phannias, the son of Samuel, from the village Aphtha. He was a man not only unworthy of the high-priesthood, but who did not really know what the high-priesthood was; such a mere rustic was he; yet did they haul this man, without his consent, out of the country, as if they were acting a play upon the stage, and adorned him with a counterfeit face; they also put on him the sacred garments, and instructed him what he was to do on every occasion. This horrid piece of wickedness was sport and pastime for them, but caused the other priests, seeing their law made a jest of, to shed tears and sorely lament the dissolution of such a sacred dignity.

Now the people could no longer bear the insolence of this procedure, but did come together zealously in order to overthrow that tyranny; and indeed Gorion, the son of Josephus, and Simeon,[7] the son of Gamaliel, encouraged them, going up and down when they were assembled in crowds and when they saw them alone, to bear no longer but to inflict punishment on these pests and plagues of their freedom, and to purge the Temple of its bloody polluters. The best esteemed also of the high priests, Jesus, the son of Gamala, and Ananus, the son of Ananus, bitterly reproached the people for their sloth and incited them against the zealots; for that was the name they went by, as if they were zealous in good undertakings, rather than zealous in the worst actions.

When the multitude was assembled and every one was indignant at these men's seizing the sanctuary, at their plunder and murders, but had not yet begun their attacks upon them (the reason being that they imagined it to be a difficult thing to suppress these zealots, as was indeed the case), Ananus stood in their midst and casting his eyes frequently towards the Temple, with a flood of tears in his eyes, he said, "Certainly, it had been good for me to die before seeing the house of God full of so many abominations, or these sacred places that ought not to be trodden upon at random filled with the feet of these blood-shedding villains; yet do I, who am clothed with the vestments of the high-priesthood, and am called by that most venerable name of high priest, still live, and am too fond of living, and cannot endure undergoing a death which would be the glory of my old age; if I must, I will go alone, and, as if in a desert, give up my life for God's sake; for to what purpose is it to live among a people insensible of their calamities, and where no notion remains of any remedy for their miseries? for when you are seized, you bear it! and when you are beaten, you are silent! and when the people are murdered, nobody dare so much as utter a groan openly! O bitter tyranny that we are under!

"But why do I complain of the tyrants? Was it not you and

[7] Simeon, son of Gamaliel, well-known in rabbinic sources, is mentioned favorably by Josephus in the Life, 190 ff., in spite of the fact that he was an old friend of John of Gischala and had agitated against Josephus in Jerusalem when the latter had been in command in Galilee. Jesus, the son of Gamala, had been a friend of Josephus. (See Life, 204).

your sufferance of them that have nourished them? Was it not you that overlooked those that first got together, for they were then but few, and by your silence made them grow to be many; and by conniving with them when they took arms in effect armed them against yourselves? You ought then to have prevented their first attempts, when they fell to abusing the leaders of the city; but by neglecting to do that in time, you have encouraged these wretches to plunder men. When houses were pillaged, nobody said a word, which was why they carried off the owners of those houses; and when they were hauled through the middle of the city, nobody came to their assistance. They then proceeded to put those into bonds whom you had betrayed into their hands.

"I do not say how many and of what characters those men were whom they thus served, but certainly they were such as had been accused by no one, condemned by no one; and since nobody rescued them when they were in bonds, the consequence was that you saw the same persons slain. We have seen this also; so that the best of the herd of animals, as it were, were led to be sacrificed while nobody said one word or moved his right hand for their preservation. Will you bear, therefore, will you bear to see your sanctuary trampled? and will you lay steps for these profane wretches which they may mount to higher degrees of insolence? Will you not pluck them down from their exaltation? for even by this time, they would have proceeded to higher enormities had they been able to overthrow anything greater than the sanctuary. They have seized upon the strongest place of the whole city; you may call it the Temple, if you please, though it is like a citadel or fortress. Now, while you have tyranny in so great a degree walled in, and see your enemies over your heads, to what purpose is it to take counsel? and what have you to support your minds withal? Perhaps you are waiting for the Romans, that they may protect our holy places: are our affairs brought to that pass? and have we reached that degree of misery that our enemies themselves are expected to pity us?

"O wretched creatures! will you not rise up and turn upon those that strike you? You may observe in wild beasts themselves that they will avenge themselves on those that strike them. Will you not call to mind, every one of you, the calamities you yourselves have suffered? nor lay before your eyes what afflictions you yourselves have undergone? and will not such things sharpen your souls to revenge? Is therefore that most honorable and most natural of our passions utterly lost, I mean the desire for liberty? Truly, we are in love with slavery, and in love with those that lord it over us, as if we had received that principle of subjection from our ancestors! yet did they undergo many and great wars for the sake of liberty, nor were they so far overcome by the power of the Egyptians, or the Medes, but that they still did what they thought fit, notwithstanding their commands to the contrary. And what occasion is there now for a war with the Romans? (I meddle not with determining whether it be an advantageous and profitable war or not.) What excuse is there for it? Is it not so that we may enjoy our liberty? Besides, shall we not bear the lords of the habitable earth to be lords over us rather than bear tyrants of our own country? Although I must say that submission to foreigners may be borne, because fortune has already doomed us to it, while submission to wicked people of our own nation is too unmanly and brought upon us by our own consent.

"However, since I have had occasion to mention the Romans, I will not conceal a thing that, while I am speaking, comes into my mind and affects me considerably; it is this, that though we should be taken by them (God forbid the event should be so!) yet we can undergo nothing that will be harder to be borne than what these men have already brought upon us. How then can we avoid shedding tears when we see the Roman donations in our temples, while we withal see those of our own nation taking our spoils and plundering our glorious capital, and slaughtering our men, from which excesses those Romans themselves would have abstained? to see those Romans never going beyond the bounds allotted to profane persons nor venturing to break in upon any of our sacred customs; nay, having horror on their minds when they view from the distance those sacred walls, while some that have been born in this very country and brought up in our customs and are called Jews do walk about in the midst of the holy places at the very time when their hands are still warm with the slaughter of their own countrymen. Besides, can any one be afraid of a war with such foreign enemies as will have comparatively much greater moderation than our own people have? For truly, if we may suit our words to the things they represent, it is probable one may hereafter find the Romans to be the supporters of our laws, and those within our people to be their subverters. And now I am persuaded that every one of you here is satisfied that these overthrowers of our liberties deserve to be destroyed and that nobody can so much as devise a punishment they have not deserved for what they have done, and that you are all provoked against them by their wicked actions, from which you have suffered so greatly.

"But perhaps many of you are frightened by the multitude of those zealots and their audaciousness, as well as by the advantage they have over us in their being in a higher place than we are; for these circumstances, occasioned as they are by your negligence, will become still greater by being still longer neglected; for their multitude is every day augmented by every evil man's running away to those like himself, and their audaciousness is therefore inflamed because they meet with no obstruction to their designs. As for their higher place, they will make use of it for engines also if we give them time to do so; but be assured of this, that if we go up to fight them they will be made tamer by their own consciences, and whatever advantages they have in the height of their situation they will lose by the opposition of their reason; perhaps also God Himself, who has been affronted by them, will make what they throw at us return against themselves, and these impious wretches will be killed by their own darts; let us but make our appearance before them and they will come to nothing. However, it is a right thing, if there should be any danger in the attempt, to die before these holy gates and to expend our very lives, if not for the sake of our children and wives, yet for God's sake and for the sake of His sanctuary. I will assist you both with my counsel and with my hand, nor shall any sagacity of ours be wanting for your support; neither shall you see that I will be sparing of my body."

By these means Ananus encouraged the multitude to turn against the zealots, although he knew how difficult it would be to disperse them because of their great number and their youth and their courage, but chiefly because of their consciousness of what they had done, since they would not yield, having no hope for pardon in the end for their excesses. However, Ananus resolved to undergo whatever sufferings might come upon him rather than overlook things, now that they were in such great confusion. So the multitude cried out to him to lead them against those he had described in his exhortation; and every one was most readily disposed to run any hazard whatsoever on that account.

Now while Ananus was selecting his men and putting those suited for his purpose into fighting array, the zealots got information of his undertaking (for there were some who went and told them what the people were doing) and were irritated by it; and leaping out of the Temple in crowds, and by parties, they spared none whom they met. Upon this, Ananus quickly gathered the populace, who were more numerous indeed than the zealots but inferior to them in arms because they had not been regularly put into fighting array: but the alacrity that everybody showed made up for their defects, the citizens stronger in their anger than in their arms, and with a degree of courage derived from the Temple more forceful than any multitude whatsoever; and indeed these citizens felt it was not possible for them to dwell in the city unless they could cut off the robbers in it. The zealots also realized that unless they prevailed there would be no punishment too bad to be inflicted on them. So their conflicts were conducted by their passions; and at first they only cast stones at each other in the city and in front of the Temple, and threw their javelins from the distance; but when either of them was too strong for the other, they made use of their swords; and great slaughter took place on both sides, and a great number were wounded. As for the dead bodies of the people, their relatives carried them off to their own houses; but when any one of the zealots was wounded he went into the Temple defiling that sacred floor with his blood, since it may be said that it was their blood alone that polluted our sanctuary.

Now in these conflicts the robbers always sallied out of the Temple and were too strong for their enemies; but the populace grew very angry, and becoming more and more numerous, reproached those that drew back; those behind would not provide room for those retreating but forced them forward again till at length they made their whole body turn against their adversaries; the robbers could no longer oppose them, but were forced gradually to retire into the Temple. When Ananus and his party fell into it at the same time together with them, this horribly frightened the robbers because it deprived them of the first court; so they fled into the inner court immediately and shut the gates. Now Ananus did not think it fitting to make any attack against the holy gates, although the others threw their stones and darts at them from above. He also deemed it unlawful to introduce the multitude into that court before they were purified; he therefore selected by lot six thousand armed men and placed them as guards in the cloisters; so there was a succession of such guards one after another, and every one was forced to serve in turn.

Now it was John who, as we told you, had run away from Gischala and who was the cause of all those being destroyed. He was a man of great craft, and bore in his soul a strong passion for tyranny, and from the distance served as the adviser in these actions; and indeed at this time he pretended to be of the people's opinion, and went all about with Ananus when he consulted the leaders every day, and at night also when he went round the watch; but he divulged their secrets to the zealots; and everything that the people deliberated about was by this means known to their enemies even before they had fully agreed among themselves; and in order not to be brought under suspicion, he cultivated the greatest friendship possible with Ananus and with the leaders of the people; yet did this overdoing of his turn against him, for he flattered them so extravagantly that he was but the more suspected; and his constant attendance everywhere, even when he was not invited to be present, made him strongly suspected of betraying their secrets to the enemy; for they plainly perceived that they understood all the resolutions taken against them in their consultations. Nor was there anyone whom they had so much reason to suspect of that betrayal as this John; yet it was not easy to get rid of him, so powerful had he grown through his wicked practices. He was also supported by many of those eminent men who were to be consulted in all important matters; it was therefore thought reasonable to oblige him to give them assurance on oath of his good will; accordingly, John readily took an oath that he would be on the people's side, and would not betray any of their counsels or practices to their enemies, and would assist them in overthrowing those that attacked them both by his hand and his advice. So Ananus and his party believed his oath, and did now receive him in their consultations without further suspicion; nay, so far did they believe him that they sent him as their ambassador into the Temple to the zealots with proposals of accommodation; for they were very desirous to avoid as much as possible the pollution of the Temple, and that no one of their nation be slain therein.

But now this John, as if his oath had been made to the zealots and in confirmation of his good will to them and not against them, went into the Temple, and stood in their midst, and spoke as follows: that he had run many hazards on their account, in order to let them know everything that was secretly contrived against them by Ananus and his party; but that both he and they should be cast into the most imminent danger unless some providential assistance were provided them. Ananus no longer delayed but had prevailed on the people to send ambassadors to Vespasian to invite him to come immediately and take the city; and that he had announced a fast against them for the next day so that they might obtain admission into the Temple on religious grounds, or gain it by force and fight with them there; that he did not see how long they could either endure a siege or how they could fight against so many enemies. He added further that it was by the providence of God that he himself had been sent as an ambassador to them for a reconciliation; for Ananus did therefore offer them such proposals so that he might come upon them when they were unarmed: that they ought to choose one of these two methods, either to intercede with those who besieged them to spare their lives or to provide themselves some outside assistance; that if they nourished hopes of pardon in the event they were captured, they had forgotten what desperate things they had done if they could even suppose that as soon as they repented those who had suffered at their hands would immediately be reconciled to them; those that have done injuries, even though they pretend to repent, are frequently hated by the others for that sort of repentance; and that the sufferers, once they get the power into their own hands, are usually even more severe with the perpetrators; that the friends and kindred of those who had been destroyed would always be laying plots against them, and that a large body of people were very angry on account of their gross breaches of their laws.

Dissension among the zealots. John tyrannizes over the rest.

By this time John was beginning to tyrannize, and thought it beneath him to accept barely the same honors that others had; and joining to himself by degrees a group of the most wicked of them all, he broke off from the rest of the faction. This was brought about by his disagreeing with the opinions of others, and giving out injunctions of his own in a very imperious manner; so that it was evident he was setting up an absolute power. Now some submitted to him out of their fear of him, and others out of their good will to him; for he was shrewd in enticing men to him, both by deluding them and threatening them. Nay, there were many who thought they would be safer themselves if the causes of their past insolent actions should now be reduced to one head, and not to a great many. His activity was so great both in action and counsel that he had many guards around him; yet there was a great group of his antagonists who left him; among them envy of him weighed heavily since they thought it a great burden to be in subjection to one who was formerly their equal. But the main reason that moved men against him was the dread of monarchy, for they could not hope easily to put an end to his power once he had obtained it; and yet they knew that he would always hold this excuse against them, that they had opposed him when he first advanced. So the sedition was divided into two groups, and John reigned in opposition to his adversaries; they watched one another, nor did they at all, or at least very little, meddle with arms in their quarrels; but they fought earnestly against the people, and contended with one another as to which of them should bring home the greatest prey. But because the city had to struggle against three of the greatest misfortunes—war, and tyranny, and sedition—it appeared, by comparison, that the war was the least troublesome of them all to the populace. Accordingly they ran away from their own houses to foreigners, and obtained that protection from the Romans which they despaired of obtaining among their own people.

These things were told Vespasian by deserters; for although the seditious watched all the passages out of the city, and destroyed all, whoever they were, that entered, yet there were some who concealed themselves, and, after they had fled to the Romans, tried to persuade the general to come to their city's assistance and save the remainder of the people, informing him withal that it was on account of the people's good will towards the Romans that many of them had already been slain, with the survivors in danger of the same treatment. Vespasian did indeed already pity the calamities of these men, and arose, in appearance, as though he were going to besiege Jerusalem—but in reality to deliver them from the worse siege they were already under. However, he was obliged first to overthrow what remained elsewhere and to leave nothing behind him outside of Jerusalem that might interrupt him in that siege.

After some further indecisive warfare Vespasian was preparing to march upon Jerusalem when, in June 68 C.E., he heard of the death of the Emperor Nero.

Vespasian was getting ready to march with all his army directly to Jerusalem when he was informed that Nero was dead, after having reigned for about thirteen years and eight months. Wherefore Vespasian put off his expedition against Jerusalem, and stood waiting to see whither the empire would be transferred after the death of Nero. Moreover, when he heard that Galba had been made emperor, he attempted nothing till Galba sent him some directions about the war: however, he sent his son Titus to him, to salute him and to receive his commands about the Jews. Upon the very same errand did King Agrippa sail along with Titus to

Galba; but as they were sailing in their long ships near the coasts of Achaia, for it was wintertime, they heard that Galba was slain before they could get to him and after he had reigned seven months and as many days. After him, Otho took the government, undertaking the management of public affairs. So Agrippa resolved to go on to Rome without fear because of the change in government; but Titus, by a divine impulse, sailed back from Greece to Syria, arriving in great haste at Caesarea, to his father. And now they were both in suspense about public affairs, the Roman Empire being then in a fluctuating condition; and they did not go on with their expedition against the Jews, but thought that to make any attack upon foreigners was now unseasonable because of the solicitude they felt for their own country.

> *The soldiers, both in Judea and Egypt, proclaim Vespasian emperor.*

But now sedition and civil war prevailed, not only over Judea but in Italy also; for Galba had been slain in the middle of the Roman market place; then Otho was made emperor, and fought against Vitellius, who set himself up as emperor also because the legions in Germany had chosen him: but when he gave battle to Valens and Cecinna, who were Vitellius's generals, Otho gained the advantage on the first day; but on the second day Vitellius's soldiers gained the victory; and after much slaughter and after hearing of this defeat and after he had managed the public affairs three months and two days, Otho slew himself. Otho's army also went over to Vitellius's generals, and he came himself down to Rome with his army; but in the meantime Vespasian moved from Caesarea and marched against those places in Judea which had not yet been overthrown. So he went up to the mountainous country, and took those two districts that were later called Gophna and Acrabattene. After this he took Bethel and Ephraim, two small cities; and when he had put garrisons into them, he rode as far as Jerusalem, taking many prisoners and captives along the way.

But once Vespasian had overthrown all the places near Jerusalem, he returned to Caesarea, where he heard of the troubles in

Rome and that Vitellius was emperor. This made him indignant, although he well knew how to be governed as well as to govern, and he could not with satisfaction acknowledge as his lord one who had acted so madly and had seized the government as if it were absolutely destitute of a governor. And since this sorrow of his was violent, he was not able to bear his torments nor apply himself further in other wars while his own native country was being laid waste; but then, as much as his passion incited him to avenge his country, so much was he restrained by the consideration of his distance from it; fortune might prevent him and do a world of mischief before he could sail the seas to Italy himself, especially since it was still winter; so he restrained his anger, as vehement as it was at that time.

But now his commanders and soldiers met in several companies, and consulted openly about changing public affairs; and, out of their indignation, they cried out how "at Rome there are soldiers that live comfortably, and even when they have not ventured so much as to hear the name of war they ordain whom they please for our governors, and in hopes of gain make them emperors; while you, who have gone through so many labors and have aged under your helmets, give leave to others to use such power when you have among yourselves one more worthy to rule than any whom they have set up. Now what more just opportunity shall they ever have of requiting their generals if they do not make use of the one now before them? There is so much more just reason for Vespasian's being emperor than for Vitellius's just as they are themselves more deserving than those that made the other emperor; for they have undergone as great wars as have the troops that come from Germany; nor are they inferior in war to those who brought that tyrant to Rome nor have they undergone smaller labors; for neither will the Roman senate nor people tolerate such a lascivious emperor as Vitellius, if he be compared with their chaste Vespasian; nor will they endure a most barbarous tyrant instead of a good governor, nor choose one that has no child to preside over them instead of him that is a father, since the advancement of men's own children to dignities is certainly the greatest security kings can have for themselves. If therefore we estimate the capacity of governing from the skill of a person in years, we ought to have Vespasian—or if from the strength of a young man, we ought to have Titus; by this means we shall have the advantage of both their ages, for they will provide strength to those who shall be made emperors, having already three legions plus other auxiliaries from the neighboring kings, and will have further all the armies in the east to support them, also those in Europe, besides such auxiliaries as they may have in Italy itself; that is, Vespasian's brother and his other son Domitian, the latter of whom will bring in a great many young men of dignity, while the former is entrusted with the government of the city, which office will be no small means of Vespasian's obtaining the government. Upon the whole, the case may be such that if we ourselves make further delays the senate may choose an emperor, whom the soldiers, who are the saviors of the empire, will hold in contempt."

These were the discourses the soldiers held in their several companies; after which they got together in a great body, and, encouraging one another, they declared Vespasian emperor and exhorted him to save the government which was now in danger. Now Vespasian had for a considerable time been concerned about the public, yet he did not intend to set himself up as governor, though his deeds showed him to deserve it, since he preferred the safety of a private life to the dangers in a state of such dignity; but when he refused the empire, the commanders insisted the more earnestly upon his acceptance; and the soldiers came around him, their drawn swords in their hands, and threatened to kill him unless he would now live according to his dignity. And after he had shown his reluctance a great while and had endeavored to thrust away this dominion from himself, he at length, being unable to persuade them, yielded to their solicitations to salute him as emperor.

So upon the exhortations of the other commanders that he accept the empire, and upon that of the rest of the army, who cried out that they were willing to be led against all his opponents, he was first intent upon gaining dominion over Alexandria, knowing that Egypt was of the greatest consequence in obtaining the entire government because of its supplying corn to Rome; by becoming master of that corn, he hoped to dethrone Vitellius, should he aim to keep the empire by force (for he would not be able to support himself once the populace in Rome should be in want of food); and because he was anxious to join the two legions in Alexandria to the other legions with him. He also realized that he should then have that country as a defense for himself against the uncertainty of fortune; for Egypt is difficult to enter by land, and has no good harbors by sea.

Justly, therefore, did Vespasian desire to obtain that government in order to corroborate his attempts upon the whole of the empire; so he immediately sent to Tiberius Alexander,[8] then governor of Egypt and Alexandria, and informed him what the army had put him up to, and how he, having been forced to accept the burden of the government, was desirous to have him as confederate and supporter. Now as soon as Alexander had read this letter, he readily obliged the legions and the people to take the oath of fidelity to Vespasian; both of them willingly complied with him, being already acquainted with the courage of the man from his conduct in their neighborhood. Now fame carried abroad more quickly than one could have thought this news that he was emperor over the east, whereupon every city held festivals and celebrated sacrifices and oblations for such good news; the legions also in Moesia and Pannonia, who had been in commotion shortly before on account of the insolent attempt of Vitellius, were very glad to take the oath of fidelity to Vespasian, on his coming to the empire. Vespasian then moved from Caesarea to Berytus, where many missions came to him from Syria and other provinces, bringing with them from every city crowns and the congratulations of the people. Mucianus came also, who was the governor of the province, and told him with what alacrity the people had received the news of his advancement, and how the people of every city had taken the oath of fidelity to him.

Josephus is freed.

[8] A nephew of the Jewish philosopher Philo of Alexandria. He abandoned Judaism, became procurator of Judea, prefect of Egypt, and a senior staff officer under Titus during the siege of Jerusalem.

So Vespasian's good fortune brought him success everywhere, and the public affairs were, for the greatest part, already in his hands; whereupon he considered that he had not arrived at the government without divine providence, but that a righteous kind of fate had brought the empire under his power; for as he called to mind the other signs, which had been numerous everywhere, that foretold he should obtain the government, so did he remember what Josephus had said to him when he ventured to foretell his coming to the empire while Nero was alive; so he was much concerned that this man was still in bonds. He then called for Mucianus, together with his other commanders and friends, and first informed them what a valiant man Josephus had been and what great hardships he had made him undergo during the siege of Jotapata. After that he related those predictions of his which he had then suspected to be fictitious, suggested out of Josephus's fear, but which had in time been demonstrated to be divine.

"It is a shameful thing," said he, "that this man who had foretold my coming to the empire beforehand and was the minister of a divine message to me should still be retained in the condition of captive or prisoner." So he called for Josephus, and commanded that he be set at liberty; whereupon the commanders promised themselves glorious things because of this requital Vespasian had made to a stranger. Titus was then present with his father, and said, "O father, it is but just that the scandal should be taken off Josephus, together with his iron chain; for if we do not barely loose his bonds but rather cut them to pieces, he will be like a man that has never been bound at all." That is the usual method for those who have been bound without cause. This advice was agreed to by Vespasian also; so a man entered and cut the chain to pieces; Josephus received this testimony of his integrity as a reward, and was moreover esteemed a person of credit for his future as well.

After taking measures to secure his rule, Vespasian went to Rome. His son Titus was left in command and sent to the siege of Jerusalem. With the enemy before the gates, civil war raged within the city. The advance

of Titus caused the warring factions to settle, temporar-
ily, their differences, and to bethink themselves of the
defense of their city against the Romans.

Whereas hitherto the several parties in the city had been clash-
ing against one another perpetually, this foreign war, now suddenly come upon them in a violent manner, put the first stop to
their contentions; and, as the seditious with astonishment now saw
the Romans pitching three different camps, they began to think of
an awkward sort of concord, and said to one another, "What are
we doing here when we allow three fortified walls to be built to
coop us in so that we shall not be able to breathe freely? The
enemy is securely building a kind of city to oppose us, while we
sit still within our own walls and become spectators of what they
are doing, our hands idle and our armor laid by, as if they were
doing something that was for our good and advantage. We are, it
seems," so did they cry out, "courageous only against ourselves
while the Romans are likely to gain the city without bloodshed
through our sedition."

Thus did they encourage one another after they had gotten together, and took their armor immediately and ran out against the
tenth legion, and fell upon the Romans with great eagerness and
with a prodigious shout as they were fortifying their camp. These
Romans were found in different groups in order to perform their
several works, and on that account had in great measure laid aside
their arms; for they thought the Jews would not venture to make a
sally against them; and even had they been so disposed, they supposed their sedition would have distracted them. So the Romans
were put into disorder unexpectedly; some left the work they were
doing and immediately marched off, while many ran for their
arms but were smitten and slain before they could turn back
against the enemy. The Jews grew more and more numerous, encouraged by the good success of those who first made the attack;
and since they had such good fortune, they seemed, both to themselves and the enemy, to be many more than they really were.
Their disorderly way of fighting at first brought the Romans to a
standstill, since they had been used to fighting skillfully and in

good order by keeping their ranks and obeying the orders given them; for this reason the Romans were caught unexpectedly and were obliged to give way to the assaults made upon them. Now whenever any of these Romans were overtaken and turned back against the Jews, they put a stop to their progress; and, when the Jews were not sufficiently careful of themselves in the vehemency of their pursuit, they were wounded by them; but as more and more Jews sallied out of the city, the Romans were at length brought into confusion and put to flight, and they ran away from their camp.

In fact, things looked as though the entire legion were in danger, had Titus not been informed of their situation and sent help to them immediately. So he reproached them for their cowardice, and brought those back who were running away, and fell himself upon the Jews on their flank with his own select troops, and slew a considerable number and wounded more of them, and put them all to flight, making them run away hastily down the valley. Now as these Jews suffered greatly in the declivity of the valley, so, after they had gotten over it, they turned around and stood over against the Romans, having the valley between them, and fought with them there. Thus they continued the fight till noon; but a little after noon Titus put those that came with him and those belonging to the cohorts to the assistance of the Romans in order to prevent the Jews from making any more sallies, and then he sent the rest of the legion to the upper part of the mountain to fortify their camp.

This march of the Romans seemed to the Jews to be a flight; and as the watchman, who was placed on the wall, gave a signal by shaking his garment, there came out a fresh multitude of Jews with such mighty violence that one might compare it to the running of the most terrible wild beasts. To say the truth, none of those opposing them could sustain the fury with which they made their attacks; but, as if they had been cast out of an engine, they broke the enemies' ranks to pieces; they were put to flight and ran away to the mountain, none but Titus himself and a few others being left in the midst of the acclivity.

Now those others, who were his friends, hated the danger they were in but were ashamed to leave their general, earnestly exhorting him to give way to these Jews who are fond of dying, and not to run into such dangers in front of those who ought to stay in front of him; to consider his fortune and not, by taking the place of a common soldier, to venture to turn back upon the enemy so suddenly; and this because he was general in the war and lord of the habitable earth, on whose preservation all public affairs depended. These persuasions Titus seemed not even to hear, but he opposed those that ran upon him and smote them on the face; and when he had forced them to go back, he slew them: he also fell upon great numbers as they marched down the hill, and thrust them forward; while those men were so terrified by his courage and his strength that they could not retreat directly into the city but opened up the way to him on both sides, and then pressed after those that fled up the hill; thus did he still attack their flank and put a stop to their onrush.

In the meantime, disorder and terror fell again upon those who were fortifying their camp at the top of the hill when they saw those below running away as if the whole legion were dispersed; they thought that the sallies of the Jews were clearly irresistible and that Titus himself had been put to flight; they took it for granted that, had he remained, the rest would never have fled. Thus they were surrounded on every side by a kind of panic and fear, and some dispersed themselves one way and some another, till certain of them saw their general in the very midst of a battle; and being greatly concerned for him, they loudly proclaimed his danger to the entire legion; and now shame made them turn back, and they reproached one another that by deserting their imperial commander they had done worse than run away. So they used their greatest force against the Jews, and going down from the hillside, they drove them in heaps into the bottom of the valley. Then did the Jews turn around and fight them; but since they were themselves withdrawing and now, because the Romans had the advantage of the ground and were above the Jews, they drove them into the valley. Titus also pressed against those near him, and sent the legion again to fortify their camp, while he and those with him opposed the enemy and kept them from doing further mischief; if

I may be allowed neither to add anything out of flattery nor to diminish anything out of envy but to speak the plain truth, Titus did twice deliver that entire legion when it was in jeopardy and gave them a quiet opportunity to fortify their camp.

After further fighting the Romans succeeded in capturing two of the walls. Titus now decided to suspend the siege in order to give the defenders of Jerusalem an opportunity for reflection. During this interval Josephus was commissioned to address his compatriots and invite them to surrender.

A resolution was now taken by Titus to relax the siege for a while and so afford the partisans an interval for deliberation, and to see whether the demolishing of their second wall would not make them a little more compliant, or whether they were not afraid of a famine because the spoils they had gotten by plunder would not be sufficient for long. He made use of this relaxation for his own designs. Accordingly, when the usual appointed time for distributing subsistence money to the soldiers came, he ordered the commanders to put the army into battle array in full view of the enemy, and then give every one of the soldiers his pay. So the soldiers, according to custom, removed the covers from their arms and marched with their breast-plates, and the horsemen led their horses in their fine trappings. Then the places in front of the city shone very splendidly for great distances; nor was there anything so pleasant to Titus's own men or so terrifying to the enemy as that sight; for the whole old wall and the north side of the Temple were full of spectators, and the houses also were filled with people looking at them; nor was there any part of the city which was not covered with their multitudes; nay, a very great consternation seized the hardiest of the Jews themselves when they saw the entire army in one place, together with the splendor of their arms and the orderliness of their men; and I cannot but think that the partisans would have changed their minds at that sight had not the crimes they had committed against the people been so horrid that they despaired of forgiveness by the Romans. Since they expected death by torture to be their punishment if they did not continue the defense of the city, they thought it better to die in war. Fate also prevailed over them that the innocent were to perish with the guilty, and the city was to be destroyed with its warring factions.

Then Titus did not omit having the Jews exhorted to repentance. He mixed good counsel with deeds, and being aware that exhortations are frequently more effective than arms, he tried to persuade them to surrender the city, now practically captured, and thereby save themselves. He sent Josephus to speak to them in their own language; for he imagined they might yield to persuasion by one of their own countrymen.

So Josephus went around the wall, trying to find a place that was beyond reach of their darts and yet within their hearing; and he besought them, in many words, to spare themselves, their country and their Temple, and not to be more obdurate in these cases than foreigners themselves; for the Romans, who had no relation to those things, had a reverence for their sacred rites and places, even though they belonged to their enemies, and had till now kept their hands off them, while those brought up with them, and who, if they were to be preserved, would be the only people to benefit, seemed in a hurry to have them destroyed. Certainly they had seen that their strongest walls were demolished and only the weakest still remained. They must know that the Roman power was invincible and that they were accustomed to serve the Romans. If fighting for liberty was right, that ought to have been done in the beginning; but for those who had once fallen under the power of the Romans and had submitted to them for so many long years, to pretend to shake off that yoke now was the work of those who had a mind to die miserably and not of those who were lovers of liberty.

Besides, men may well enough grumble over the dishonor of having ignoble masters over them, but they ought not to do so to those who have all things under their command: for what parts of the world exist that have escaped the Romans, unless it be those of no value because of their violent heat or violent cold? It is evident that fortune has on all sides gone over to them; and that God, after having gone around the nations granting dominion, is now settled in Italy. Moreover, it is a strong and fixed law, even among brute beasts as well as among men, to yield to those who are too strong for them; and to suffer those to have dominion who are too strong for the rest in battle. For this reason their forefathers, who were far superior to them both in soul and body, had submitted to the Romans; they would not have tolerated this had they not known that God was with them.

As for themselves, on what can they depend since the greatest part of their city is already captured, and since those within are under greater miseries than if they were taken, even though their walls are still standing? The Romans are not unacquainted with the famine in the city, whereby the people are already consumed, and so too will the fighting men be in a short time; for even if the Romans leave off the siege and do not fall on the city with their swords, there was still an insuperable war inside, which would augment every hour unless they were able to wage war against famine or conquer their natural appetites. He added further how right it was to change their conduct before their calamities became incurable, and to have recourse to such advice as might preserve them while the opportunity was offered them to do so. The Romans would not remember their past actions to their disadvantage unless they persevered in their insolent behavior to the end because they were naturally mild in their conquests, preferring what was profitable to what their passions dictated. Their profit in this case would lie in not leaving the city empty of inhabitants nor the country a desert; on this account Titus now offered them his right hand for their security. Whereas, if he took the city by force, he would not save any one of them, especially if they rejected his offers; for the walls that were already taken assured them that the third wall would quickly be taken also; and though their fortifications might prove too strong for the Romans to break through, yet the famine would fight for the Romans against them.

While Josephus was thus exhorting the Jews, many of them derided him from the wall, and many reproached him; nay, some threw their darts at him. But when he could not persuade them by good frank advice, he turned to the histories of their own nation. And he cried out, "O miserable creatures! Are you so unmindful of those that used to assist you that you will fight with your weapons and your hands against the Romans? When did we ever conquer any other nation by such means? And when was it that God, who is the Creator of the Jewish people, did not avenge them when they were injured? Will you not recall the prodigious things done for your forefathers and this holy place, and how great enemies of yours were subdued by Him for you? I even tremble myself in declaring the works of God before your ears that are unworthy to hear them: however, listen to me that you may know how you fight not only against the Romans but against God Himself. In olden times there was a king of Egypt who was also called Pharaoh: he came with a prodigious army of soldiers and seized Sarah, the mother of our nation. What did Abraham our progenitor then do? Did he defend himself from this injurious person by war, although he had 318 captains under him and an immense army under each of them? Indeed, he deemed them to be no number at all without God's assistance, and only spread out his hands towards this holy place, which you have now polluted, and counted on Him instead of his own army as his invincible supporter. Was not Sarah sent back without defilement to her husband the very next evening—while the king of Egypt fled away, reverencing this place which you have defiled by shedding here the blood of your countrymen? And he also trembled at those visions which he saw in the night, and bestowed both silver and gold on the Hebrews as on a people beloved of God. Shall I say nothing, or shall I mention the removal of our fathers into Egypt? After they had been abused tyrannically and had fallen under the power of foreign kings for four hundred years, they might have defended themselves by war and fighting, but yet they did nothing but commit themselves to God. Who is there that does not know that Egypt was overrun with all sorts of disease? that their land did not bring forth its fruit? that the Nile ran dry? that the ten plagues of Egypt followed one upon another? and that, by those means, our fathers were sent away, under a guard, without bloodshed and without danger because God led them as His peculiar servants?

"Moreover, did not the land of the Philistines groan under the ravage the Syrians made when they carried away our sacred ark?

as did their idol Dagon and also that entire nation that carried it away, who were smitten with a loathsome disease in the secret parts of their bodies, when their very bowels came down together with what they had eaten, till those hands that stole it away were obliged to bring it back again, with the sound of cymbals and timbrels, and other oblations, in order to appease the anger of God for their violation of His holy ark. It was God who then became our general, and accomplished these great things for our fathers, and this because they did not meddle with war and fighting but committed it to Him to rule over their affairs. And Sennacherib, king of Assyria, when he brought along with him all Asia and surrounded this city with his army, did he fall by the hands of men? Were not those hands lifted up to God in prayers, without meddling with their arms, when an angel of God destroyed that prodigious army in one night; when the Assyrian king, as he rose next day, found a hundred fourscore and five thousand dead bodies, and when he, with the remainder of his army, fled away from the Hebrews, though they were unarmed and did not pursue them!

"You are also acquainted with our slavery in Babylon, where the people were captives for seventy years; yet they were not delivered into freedom again before God made Cyrus His gracious instrument to bring it about; accordingly they were set free by him, and did again restore the worship of their Deliverer at His temple.

"And, to speak in general, we can produce no example wherein our fathers succeeded in war or failed when they committed themselves to God without war. When they stayed at home they conquered, as pleased their Judge; but when they went out to fight they were always disappointed: for example, when the king of Babylon besieged this very city and our king Zedekiah fought against him, contrary to the predictions made to him by Jeremiah the prophet, he was at once taken prisoner and saw the city and the Temple demolished. Yet how much greater was the moderation of that king than that of your present governors, and that of the people then under him than your own at this time! For when Jeremiah cried out aloud how very angry God was at them because of their transgressions, and told them that they should be taken prisoners unless they surrender their city, neither did the king nor the people put him to death. But you (to pass over what you have done within the city, which I am unable to describe as your wickedness deserves), you abuse me and throw darts at me when all I have done is to exhort you to save yourselves; you are provoked when you are reminded of your sins, and cannot bear the very mention of those crimes which you every day perpetrate.

"For another example, when Antiochus, who was called Epiphanes, and had been guilty of many indignities against God, lay before this city, and our forefathers met him in arms, they then were slain in the battle, this city was plundered by our enemies, and our sanctuary was made desolate for three years and six months.

"What need have I to bring any more examples! Indeed, what can it be that has stirred up an army of the Romans against our nation? Is it not the impiety of the inhabitants? Whence did our servitude commence? Was it not derived from the rebellions among our forefathers, when the madness of Aristobulus and Hyrcanus, and our mutual quarrels, brought Pompey upon this city, and when God reduced those under subjection to the Romans who were unworthy of the liberty they had enjoyed? After a siege, therefore, of three months, they were forced to surrender, although they had not been guilty as you have of such offenses with regard to our sanctuary and our laws; and this when they had much greater advantages to gain from going to war than you have. Do not we know to what end came Antigonus, the son of Aristobulus, under whose reign God arranged that this city be captured again on account of the people's offenses? When Herod, the son of Antipater, brought upon us Sosius, and Sosius brought upon us the Roman army, they were then surrounded and besieged for six months, until, as punishment for their sins, they were captured and the city plundered by the enemy.

"Thus it appears that arms were never given to our nation, but that we are always doomed to be fought against and to be captured; for I suppose that those who inhabit this holy place ought to commit the disposal of all things to God, to disregard the assistance of men and resign themselves to their Arbitrator, who is above.

"As for you, what have you done of those things that are recommended by our legislator! And what have you not done of those things that he has condemned! How much more sinful are you than those who were so quickly captured! You have not avoided even those sins which are usually done in secret; I mean thefts, and treacherous plots against men, and adulteries. You are quarreling about plunder and murders, and invent strange ways of wickedness. Nay, the Temple itself has become the receptacle of all, and this divine place is polluted by the hands of those of our own country; this place has yet been revered by the Romans when it was at a distance from them, when they have allowed many of their own customs to be replaced by our law. And, after all this, do you expect Him whom you have so impiously abused to be your supporter? To be sure then you have a right to be petitioners, and to call upon Him to assist you, so pure are your hands! Did your King Hezekiah lift up such hands in prayer to God against the king of Assyria when he destroyed that great army in one night? And do the Romans commit such wickedness as did the king of Assyria that you have reason to hope for like vengeance upon them? Did not that king accept money from our king on condition that he should not destroy the city, and yet, contrary to his pledge, he came down to burn the Temple? While the Romans demand no more than the accustomed tribute which our fathers paid to their fathers; and if they may but once obtain that, they neither aim to destroy this city nor to touch this sanctuary; nay, they will grant you besides that your posterity shall be free and your possessions secure, and will preserve your holy laws inviolate.

"And it is plain madness to expect that God should appear as well disposed towards the wicked as towards the righteous; since He knows when it is proper to punish men for their sins immediately, accordingly He broke the power of the Assyrians the very first night they pitched their camp. Wherefore, had He judged that our nation was worthy of freedom or the Romans of punishment,

He would immediately have inflicted punishment upon those Romans, as He did upon the Assyrians, when Pompey began to meddle with our nation, or when after him Sosius came up against us, or when Vespasian laid waste Galilee, or lastly, when Titus first came near this city; although Pompey and Sosius not only suffered nothing, but took the city by force; as did Vespasian go from the war he made against you to become emperor; and as for Titus, those springs that were formerly almost dried up while under your power, since he has come, now run more plentifully than before; you know that Siloam, as well as all the other springs outside the city, failed to such an extent that water was sold by measures; whereas they now have such a great quantity of water for your enemies that it is sufficient not only for drink both for themselves and their cattle, but also for watering gardens.

"The same wonderful sign you had also experienced formerly, when the forementioned king of Babylon made war against us and took the city and burned the Temple, even though I believe the Jews of that age were not so impious as you are. Wherefore I cannot but suppose that God has fled from His sanctuary, and stands on the side of those against whom you fight. Now, even a man, if he be but a good man, will fly from an impure house and will hate those that are in it; and are you persuaded that God, who sees all secret things and hears what is most private, will abide with you in your iniquities? Now what crime is there, I pray you, that is so much as kept secret or concealed by you! nay, what is there that is not open to your very enemies! for you show your transgressions in a pompous manner, and vie with one another as to which of you shall be more wicked than another; and you make a public demonstration of your injustice as if it were virtue!

"However, there is still a chance for your preservation, if you are willing to accept it; and God is easily reconciled to those that confess their faults and repent of them. O hardhearted wretches as you are! cast away all your arms and take pity on your country already going to ruin; return from your wicked ways, and have regard for the excellency of that city which you are going to betray, for that excellent Temple with the donations of so many countries in it. Who could bear to be the first to set the Temple on fire! who could be willing that these things should cease to exist! and what is there more worthy of preservation! O senseless creatures, more stupid than the stones themselves! And if you cannot look at these things with discerning eyes, at least have pity on your families, and set before your eyes your children, and wives, and parents, who will be gradually consumed either by famine or by war.

"I am aware that this danger will extend to my mother and wife, and to that family of mine who have been by no means ignoble, and indeed to one that has been very eminent in former times; and perhaps you may imagine that it is on their account only that I give you this advice: if that be all, kill them; nay, take my own blood as a reward, if it may but procure your preservation; for I am ready to die if you will but return to a sound mind after my death."

Famine and misery in the city.

As Josephus was speaking thus in a loud voice, the rebels would neither yield to what he said nor did they deem it safe for them to alter their conduct; but as for the people, they had a great inclination to desert to the Romans; accordingly, some of them sold what they had, even their most precious treasures, for very small sums, and swallowed down pieces of gold that they might not be found by the robbers; and when they had escaped to the Romans, they emptied their bowels and then had the wherewithal to provide plentifully for themselves. Titus let a great number of them go away into the country, whither they pleased. And the main reason they were so ready to desert was that now they would be freed from those miseries which they had endured in that city, and yet they would not be in slavery to the Romans. However, John and Simon, with their followers, watched these men's going out more carefully than they did the coming in of the Romans; and if any one did but offer the slightest shadow of suspicion of such an intention, his throat was cut immediately.

But for the wealthy, it proved all the same whether they stayed in the city or attempted to get out of it, for they were equally destroyed in either case; for every rich person was put to death under the pretext that he was going to desert—but in reality so that the robbers might take what he had. The madness of the partisans grew together with their famine, and both those miseries daily became more and more inflamed. There was no corn to be seen anywhere, but the robbers went running into and searching men's private houses; and then, if they found any, they tortured them for having denied they had any; and if they found none, they tortured them worse because they supposed they had more carefully concealed it. The proof they used as to whether they had any or not was based on the bodies of these miserable wretches; if they were in good shape, they supposed they were in no want at all of food; but if they were wasted, they walked off without searching any further: nor did they think it proper to kill the latter because they saw they would very soon die for want of food. Many sold what they had for one measure of wheat, if they were richer; but of barley, if they were poorer. Then they shut themselves up in the innermost rooms of their houses and ate the corn they had gotten; some did so without grinding it because of the extremity of their need, while others baked bread out of it, as necessity and fear dictated: a table was nowhere laid for a distinct meal, but they snatched the food out of the fire, half-cooked and ate it hastily.

It was now a miserable situation, and a sight to bring tears to our eyes, for while the powerful had more than enough food, the weak were suffering for lack of it. Famine is hard on all other emotions, and destructive to nothing so much as to decency; for what was otherwise worthy of reverence was now despised; children pulled the very morsels that their fathers were eating out of their mouths, and, what was even more to be pitied, so too did the mothers pull the food from the mouths of their infants; and when those most dear to them were perishing in their arms, they were not ashamed to take from them the very last drops that might preserve their lives; and while they ate in this manner, yet they were not secure in so doing; for the partisans everywhere came down upon them suddenly, and snatched away from them what they had taken from others; for when the latter saw any house shut up, this was a signal to them that the people within had gotten some food;

whereupon they broke open the doors and ran in, taking pieces of what they were eating almost out of their very throats, and this by force: the old men, who held their food fast, were beaten; and if the women hid what they had in their hands, their hair was torn for so doing; nor was any pity shown either to the aged or to infants; they lifted children up from the ground as they clung to the morsels they had gotten, and dashed them down on the floor; but they were even more barbarously cruel to those that had forestalled their coming in and had actually swallowed what they were going to seize.

They also invented terrible methods of torture to discover where any food was, and a man was forced to bear what it is terrible even to hear, in order to make him confess that he had only one loaf of bread, or reveal where a handful of barley meal was hidden. And this was done even when these torturers were not themselves hungry; their actions would have been less barbarous if forced by necessity; but they were done to keep their madness in exercise, and so as to store up provisions for themselves for the coming days. These men also went to meet those who had crept out of the city by night, as far as the Roman guards, to gather some plants and herbs that grew wild; and just when those people thought they had cleared the enemy, the marauders snatched from them what they had brought, even after they entreated them, in the tremendous name of God, to give them back some part of what they had gathered; they gave them not a crumb, and made them feel lucky to be only despoiled and not killed as well.

Such were the afflictions which the lower classes suffered from these tyrants' guards; as for the men of dignity and wealth, they were carried before the tyrants themselves; some were falsely accused of laying treacherous plots and so were destroyed; others were charged with plots to betray the city to the Romans: but the favorite device was to pay an informer to affirm that they were resolved to desert to the enemy. And he who was utterly despoiled by Simon was sent back again to John; whereas of those who had been already plundered by John, Simon got what remained. They drank each other's health in the blood of the populace, and divided the dead bodies of the poor creatures between them; so that even though, on account of their ambition for domination, they contended with each other, yet they agreed very well in their wicked practices.

It is therefore impossible to go over every instance of these men's iniquity in detail. I shall therefore speak my mind briefly: That, from the beginning of the world, never did any other city ever suffer such miseries nor did any age ever breed a generation more fruitful in wickedness than this. In the end, they brought the Hebrew nation into contempt in order that they might themselves appear comparatively less impious in the eyes of strangers. They confessed what was true, that they were the slaves, the scum, and the spurious and abortive offspring of our nation, while they over-threw the city themselves, and forced the reluctant Romans to gain a melancholy reputation by acting gloriously against them, and did almost draw that fire against the Temple which they seemed to think came too slowly; and, indeed, when they saw that Temple burning from the upper city, they were neither troubled, nor did they shed any tears on that account, though these passions were found among the Romans themselves.

> *The siege continued, and so did the sufferings of the*
> *people of Jerusalem, beset by factions within the city*
> *and by the enemy around the walls. The ring was*
> *growing tighter; by August, 70 c.e., sacrifices could no*
> *longer be offered in the Temple.*

And now Titus gave orders to his soldiers to dig up the founda-tions of the tower of Antonia and make a ready passage for his army to come up. He had Josephus brought to him (for he had been informed that on that very day the sacrifice called "the daily sacrifice" had not been offered to God for want of men to offer it, and that the people were grievously troubled at this) and com-manded him to say the same things to John that he had said before—that if he had any malicious inclination to fight, he might come out with as many of his men as he pleased in order to fight and without the danger of destroying either his city or Temple. But he wanted him not to defile the Temple nor thereby offend

God, and that he might, if he wished, offer the sacrifices, which were now discontinued, by any of the Jews whom he should select.

Upon this, Josephus stood in a place where he might be heard not just by John but by many more, and declared to them, in the language of the Jews, what Titus had charged him. He earnestly prayed them to spare their own city and to prevent that fire which was just ready to seize the Temple, and to offer their usual sacrifices to God therein. At these words of his, great sadness and silence were observed among the people. But the tyrant himself cast many reproaches on Josephus, with imprecations besides; and at last he added that he did never fear the capture of the city because it was God's own city.

In answer to this, Josephus said, in a loud voice: "To be sure, you have kept this city wonderfully pure for God's sake! The Temple also continues entirely unpolluted! Nor have you been guilty of any impiety against Him, for whose assistance you hope! He still receives His accustomed sacrifices! Vile wretch that you are! If any one should deprive you of your daily food, you would esteem him to be your enemy; but you hope to have that God for your supporter in this war whom you have deprived of His everlasting worship! and you impute those sins to the Romans, who to this very day take care to have our laws observed, and almost compel still to be offered to God those sacrifices which you have had stopped! Who is there that can avoid groans and lamentations at the amazing change in this city, since it is foreigners and enemies who now correct that impiety which you have brought about; while you, who are a Jew educated in our laws, have become a greater enemy to them than the others!

"But still, John, it is never dishonorable to repent and amend what has been done wrong, even in the last extremity. And I venture to promise that the Romans shall still forgive you. And take notice that I, who make this exhortation to you, am one of your own nation; I, who am a Jew, do make this promise to you. And it will become you to consider who I am that give you this counsel, and whence I am derived; for while I am alive I shall never be in such slavery as to abandon my own kindred or forget the laws of our forefathers. You are indignant with me again, and clamor against me, and reproach me; indeed, I cannot deny that I am worthy of worse treatment than all this because, in opposition to fate, I make this kind invitation and endeavor to force deliverance upon those whom God has condemned. And who does not know what the writings of the ancient prophets contain—for they foretold that this city should be captured when somebody shall have begun the slaughter of his own countrymen! And are not both the city and the entire Temple now filled with the dead bodies of your countrymen? It is God therefore, God Himself, who is bringing on this fire to purge that city and Temple by means of the Romans, and who is going to pluck up this city, which is full of your pollutions."

As Josephus spoke these words with tears in his eyes, his voice was intercepted by sobs. However, the Romans could not but pity his affliction and marvel at his behavior. Except for John, and those with him, they were only the more exasperated against the Romans on this account, and were desirous to get Josephus also under their powers: yet that discourse influenced a great many of the better sort; and truly some of them were so afraid of the guards set by the partisans that they tarried where they were, but still were sure that both they and the city were doomed to destruction. Some also, watching for a proper opportunity when they might quietly get away, fled to the Romans. Now Titus not only received these men very kindly in other respects, but, knowing they would not willingly follow the customs of other nations, he also sent them to Gophna, requesting them to remain there for the present; he told them that when he had finished with this war, he would restore each of them to their possessions again: so they cheerfully retired to that small city allotted them, without fear of danger. But since they did not appear, the partisans gave out the word that these deserters had been slain by the Romans—which was done in order to deter the rest from running away out of fear of like treatment. This trick of theirs succeeded for a while, for the rest were hereby deterred from deserting.

However, after Titus had recalled those men from Gophna, he gave orders that they should go round the wall, together with Josephus, and show themselves to the people; upon which a great many fled to the Romans. These men also gathered in a great number together, and stood before the Romans, and besought the seditious, with groans, and tears in their eyes, to open up the city entirely to the Romans, and so save their own place of residence; if they would not agree to such a proposal, they should at least depart from the Temple, and so save the holy house for their own use; for the Romans would not venture to set the sanctuary on fire, except under the most pressing necessity. Yet did the partisans oppose them more and more; and while they cast loud and bitter reproaches against these deserters, they also set their engines for throwing darts, and javelins, and stones, upon the sacred gates of the Temple, at due distances from one another, so that all the space round about the Temple might be compared to a burying ground, so great was the number of dead bodies therein; so might the holy house itself be compared to a citadel. Accordingly, these men rushed in their armor upon these holy places that were otherwise unapproachable, and while their hands were still warm with the blood of their own people; nay, they proceeded to such great transgressions that the very same indignation which Jews would naturally have against Romans, had they been guilty of such abuses against them, the Romans now had against Jews because of their impiety in regard to their own religious customs. Nay, indeed, there were none of the Roman soldiers who did not look with horror upon the holy house, and worshipped it, and wished that the robbers would repent before their miseries became incurable.

Now Titus was deeply affected by this state of things, and reproached John and his party: "Have you not, vile wretches that you are, by our permission, put up this partition-wall before your sanctuary? Have you not been allowed to put up the pillars belonging thereto, at due distances, and to engrave on it in Greek, and in your own letters, this prohibition that no foreigner should go beyond that wall? Have we not given you leave to kill such as go beyond it, even though he be a Roman? And what do you do now, you pernicious villains? Why do you trample upon dead bodies in this Temple? and why do you pollute this holy house with the blood both of foreigners and Jews themselves? I appeal to the gods of my own country, and to every god that ever had any regard for this place (for I do not suppose it to be now regarded by any of them); I also appeal to my own army and to those Jews now with me, and even to you yourselves, to testify that I do not force you to defile your sanctuary; and if you will but change the place whereon you fight, no Roman shall either come near your sanctuary or offer any affront to it; nay, I will endeavor to preserve your holy house for you, whether you will or not."

This appeal was of no avail. The siege continued. Famine and degradation spread in the city. Destruction of the Temple.

And now two of the legions had completed their banks on the eighth day of the month of Ab. Whereupon Titus gave orders that the battering-rams should be brought and set over against the western edifice of the inner temple; for before these were brought, the firmest of all the other engines had battered the wall for six days in succession without ceasing, without making any impression on it; but the largeness and firm connection of the stones were superior to that engine and to the other battering-rams also. Other Romans did indeed undermine the foundations of the northern gate, and, after a world of pains, removed the outermost stones, yet the gate was still upheld by the inner stones and stood still undamaged; till the workmen, despairing of all such attempts by engines and crows, brought their ladders to the cloisters.

Now the Jews did not interrupt them; but when they had gotten up, they fell upon them and fought with them; some of them they thrust down, throwing them backwards headlong; others they met and slew; they also beat many of those that went down the ladders again, slaying them with their swords before they could bring their shields to protect them; nay, some of the ladders they threw down from above when they were full of armed men. A great slaughter was also made of the Jews at the same time, while those that bore the ensigns fought hard for them, deeming it a terrible thing that would redound to their great shame if they permitted them to be taken. Yet the Jews at length got possession of these engines, and destroyed those that had gone up the ladders, while the rest were so intimidated by what those suffered who were slain that they withdrew, although none of the Romans died without having given good service before his death. Of the seditious, those that had fought bravely in the former battles did the same now; so too did Eleazar, the brother's son of Simon the tyrant. But when Titus perceived that his efforts to spare a foreign temple wrought havoc among his soldiers and caused their death, he gave order to set the gates on fire. . . .

When the Jews saw this fire all about them, their spirits sank, together with their bodies, and they were so amazed that not one of them made any haste either to defend himself or to quench the fire, but they stood like mute spectators. However, they did not so grieve at the loss of what was now burning as to grow wiser thereby for the time to come; but as though the holy house itself had been on fire already, they whetted their passions against the Romans. This fire prevailed during that day and the next also; for the soldiers were not able to burn all the cloisters at one time, but only in sections.

But then, the next day, Titus commanded part of his army to quench the fire, and to make a road for the easier marching up of the legions. He himself gathered the commanders together, proposing to them that they give their advice as to what should be done about the holy house. Now some of these thought it would be best to act according to the rules of war and demolish it; the Jews would never leave off rebelling while that house was standing. Others were of the opinion that if the Jews would leave it and not store their arms in it, he might save it; but if they got up on it and fought any more, he might burn it because it must then be looked upon not as a holy house but as a citadel; and that the impiety of burning it would then belong to those that forced this to be done, and not to them.

But Titus said that "although the Jews should get up on that holy house and fight us from there, yet we ought not to avenge ourselves on inanimate things, instead of on the men themselves." He was not in any event in favor of burning down so vast a work as that because this would be a mischief to the Romans themselves, since it would be an ornament to their government as long as it continued. Then this assembly was dissolved after Titus had given orders to the commanders that the rest of their forces should lie still; but that they should make use of those who were most courageous in this attack. So he commanded that the chosen men that were taken out of the cohorts should make their way through the ruins, and quench the fire.

Now it is true that on this day the Jews were so weary and in such a state of consternation that they refrained from any attack. But on the next day they gathered their whole force together, and ran, very boldly, upon those that guarded the outer court of the Temple, through the east gate, and this about the second hour of the day. These guards received their attack with great bravery; by covering themselves with their shields in front, as with a wall, they drew their squadrons close together; yet it was evident that they could not abide there very long but would be overborne by the multitude of those that sallied out against them and by the heat of their passion. However, the commander seeing, from the tower of Antonia, that this squadron was likely to give way, he sent some chosen horsemen to support them. Hereupon the Jews found themselves unable to sustain their attack, and after the slaughter of those in the forefront, many were put to flight; but as the Romans were going off, the Jews turned upon them and fought them; and as those Romans came back upon them, they retreated again, until about the fifth hour of the day they were overcome, shutting themselves up in the inner court of the Temple.

So Titus retired into the tower of Antonia, and resolved to storm the Temple the next day, early in the morning, with his whole army, and to encamp round the holy house; but, as for that house, God had for certain long ago doomed it to the fire; and now that fatal day had come, according to the revolution of ages: it was the tenth day of the month of Ab [9] on which it had formerly been burnt by the king of Babylon; even though these flames took

[9] According to Jeremiah 52:12 ff. the Babylonians burned the First Temple on the tenth of the fifth month (Ab). In 2 Kings 25:8 the date is the seventh of Ab. In later Jewish tradition the two events are both dated on the

their rise from the Jews themselves, and had been occasioned by them; for upon Titus's retiring, the partisans lay still for a little while, and then attacked the Romans again, when those that guarded the holy house fought with those that quenched the fire burning in the inner court of the Temple; but these Romans put the Jews to flight, and proceeded as far as the holy house itself. At this time one of the soldiers, without staying for orders, and without concern or dread at so great an undertaking, and being hurried on by a certain divine fury, snatched something out of the materials on fire, and being lifted up by another soldier, he set fire to a golden window, through which there was a passage to the rooms around the holy house, on the north side. As the flames went upward, the Jews made a great clamor, as so mighty an affliction required, and ran together to prevent it; and now they did not spare their lives any longer, nor suffered anything to restrain their force, since that holy house, for whose sake they kept such a guard about, was perishing.

And now a certain person came running to Titus and told him of this fire as he was resting in his tent after the last battle; whereupon he rose in great haste and ran, as he was, to the holy house in order to stop the fire; after him followed all his commanders, and after them legionaries in great excitement; so there was raised a great clamor and tumult, as was natural after the disorderly commotion of so great an army. Then did Titus, both by calling in a loud voice to the soldiers that were fighting and by giving them a signal with his right hand, order them to quench the fire; but, though he spoke so loud, they did not hear what he said, their ears already dinned by a greater noise; nor did they heed the signal of his hand, since some of them were still distracted with fighting and others with passion; as for the legionaries that came running thither, neither any persuasions nor any threats could restrain their violence, but each one's own passion was his commander at this time; and as they were crowding into the Temple together,

---

ninth of Ab. "A fictitious symmetry between corresponding events in the two sieges has probably been at work" (Thackeray).

many trampled one another, while a great number fell among the ruins of the cloisters, which were still hot and smoking, and were destroyed in the same miserable way as those they had conquered: and after they had come near the holy house, they pretended they did not so much as hear Titus's orders; on the contrary, they encouraged those that were ahead of them to set it on fire. As for the partisans, they were already in too great distress to offer their assistance towards quenching the fire; they were everywhere slain and everywhere beaten; and as for the great part of the people, weak and without arms, they had their throats cut wherever they were caught. Now, around the altar lay dead bodies heaped one upon another; at the steps leading up to it, whither also the dead bodies that were slain above had fallen, there ran a great quantity of their blood.

And now, since Titus was no way able to restrain the fury of the soldiers, and the fire grew larger and larger, he went into the holy place of the Temple with his commanders, and saw it and what was in it, which he found to be far superior to what had been related in accounts by foreigners and not inferior to what we ourselves boasted of and believed about it; but as the flame had not as yet reached to its innermost sections but was still consuming the rooms around the holy house, Titus, supposing that the house itself might yet be saved, came in haste and endeavored to persuade the soldiers to quench the fire, giving order to Liberalius the centurion and one of those spearmen around him, to beat with their staves the soldiers that were refractory and to restrain them; yet their passions were too strong for their respect for Titus and their dread of him who forbade them and too strong also was their hatred of the Jews and a certain vehement inclination to fight them. Moreover, the hope of plunder induced many to go on, being of the opinion that all the places inside were full of money, and seeing that all around it was made of gold; and besides, one of those that went into the place forestalled Titus when he ran so hastily out to restrain the soldiers, and threw the fire upon the hinges of the gate, in the dark; whereupon the flame burst out from inside the holy house itself immediately, forcing the commanders to retire, and Titus with them, and nobody any longer forbade those that were outside to set fire to it; and thus was the holy house burnt down, without Titus's approval.

Now although any one would justly lament the destruction of such a work as this was, since it was the most admirable of all the works that we have seen or heard of both because of its unique structure and its magnitude and also because of the vast wealth bestowed upon it as well as its glorious reputation for holiness; yet might such a one comfort himself with the thought that it was fate that decreed it so to be, which is inevitable both as to living creatures and works and places as well.

While the holy house was on fire, everything was plundered that came to hand, and ten thousand of those that were caught were slain; nor was there pity for age or reverence for rank; children, and old men, and profane persons, and priests, were all slain in the same manner; so that this war encompassed all sorts of men and brought them to destruction—those that made supplication for their lives as well as those that defended themselves by fighting. The flame was also carried a long way and made an echo, together with the groans of those that were slain; and because this hill was high and the works at the Temple very great, one would have thought the whole city on fire. Nor can one imagine anything either greater or more terrible than this noise; for there was at once a shout of the Roman legions, who were marching all together, and a sad clamor of the rebels, who were now surrounded by fire and sword. The people also that were left above were beaten back upon the enemy and under great consternation, and made sad moans at their calamity; the masses also that were in the city joined in the outcry with those that were on the hill; and in addition, many of those worn away by the famine, their mouths almost closed, when they saw the fire of the holy house they exerted their utmost strength and broke out into groans and outcries again.

Yet the misery itself was more terrible than this disorder; for one would have thought the hill itself, on which the Temple stood, seething hot, so filled with fire on every part of it that the blood was larger in quantity than the fire, and those that were slain more numerous than those that slew them; for the ground did nowhere appear visible because of the dead bodies that lay on it; and the soldiers went over heaps of these bodies as they ran upon those who fled from them. And now the multitude of the robbers were thrust out by the Romans, and had much ado to get into the outer court and from thence into the city, while the remainder of the populace fled into the cloister of that outer court. As for the priests, some plucked up from the holy house the spikes that were upon it, with their bases which were made of lead, and shot them at the Romans instead of darts. But since they gained nothing by so doing, and as the fire burst out upon them, they withdrew to the wall that was eight cubits broad, and there they remained; two of those of eminence among them, who might have saved themselves by going over to the Romans or have borne up with courage and taken their fortune with the others, threw themselves into the fire and were burnt together with the holy house; their names were Meirus, the son of Belgas, and Joseph, the son of Daleus.

And now the Romans, judging it to be in vain to spare what was around the holy house, burnt all those places, and also the remains of the cloisters and the gates, with the exception of two: the one on the east side, and the other on the south; both, however, they burnt afterward. They also burnt down the treasury chambers, in which were deposited an immense quantity of money, an immense number of garments, and other precious goods; and, to speak all in a few words, it was there that the entire riches of the Jews were heaped together. The soldiers also came to the rest of the cloisters in the outer court of the Temple, whither the women and children, and a great mixed multitude numbering about six thousand of the people fled. But before Titus had determined anything about these people, or given the commanders any orders relating to them, the soldiers were in such a rage that they set the cloister on fire; by which it came to pass that some of these were destroyed by throwing themselves down headlong, and some were burnt in the cloisters themselves. Nor did any one of them escape with his life.

*The Romans carry their standards to the Temple and
acclaim Titus* imperator. *He addresses the Jews.*

And now the Romans, on the flight of the rebels into the city
and the burning of the holy house itself and all the buildings
around it, brought their ensigns to the Temple, and set them over
against its eastern gate. And there they offered sacrifices and there
did they make Titus *imperator* with the greatest acclamations of
joy. And now all the soldiers had plundered such vast quantities
of spoils that in Syria a pound weight of gold was sold for half its
former value. But as for those priests that still remained on the
wall of the holy house, there was a boy that, out of his great thirst,
requested some of the Roman guards to give him their right hands
as a security for his life, and confessed he was very thirsty. These
guards took pity on his age and his distress, and gave him their
right hands accordingly. So he came down and drank some water,
and filled the vessel he had with him with water, and then fled
away to his own friends; nor could any of those guards overtake
him; but still they reproached him for his perfidiousness.

To which he made this answer: "I have not broken the agreement; for the security I had given me was not for my staying with
you, but only for my coming down safely and taking up some
water; both these things I have performed, and thereupon I think
myself faithful to my pledge." Hereupon those whom the child
had imposed upon admired his cunning, and that on account of his
age. On the fifth day afterward, the priests that were pining away
with famine came down, and when they were brought to Titus by
the guards, they begged for their lives: but he replied that the time
of pardon was over for them; and that this very holy house, on
whose account only they could justly hope to be preserved, was
destroyed; and that it was agreeable to their office that priests
should perish with the house itself to which they belonged. So he
ordered them to be put to death.

But as for the tyrants themselves and those with them, once
they found that they were encircled on every side, and, as it were,
walled round, without any means of escaping, they desired to negotiate with Titus by word of mouth. Accordingly, so great was

the kindness of his nature and his desire to preserve the city from destruction, joined to the advice of his friends who now thought the robbers had calmed, that he placed himself on the western side of the outer [court of the] Temple; for there were gates on that side and a bridge connecting the upper city to the Temple. This bridge lay between the tyrants and Titus, and separated them, while the people stood on each side: those of the Jewish nation around Simon and John, with great hope of pardon, and the Romans around Titus in great expectation as to how he would receive their supplication. So Titus charged his soldiers to restrain their rage and to leave their darts alone, and appointed an interpreter between them.

He first began the discourse, and said: "I hope you, sirs, are now satiated with the miseries of your country, you who have not had any just notions either of our great power or of your own great weakness; but have, like madmen, in a violent and inconsiderate manner, made such attempts as have brought your people, your city, and your holy house to destruction. You have been the men that have never stopped rebelling since Pompey first conquered you, and have, since that time, made open war against the Romans. Have you depended on your multitude, while a very small part of the Roman soldiery has been strong enough for you? Have you relied on the fidelity of your confederates? And what nations are there, beyond the limits of our dominion, that would choose to assist the Jews against the Romans? Are your bodies stronger than ours? Nay, you know that the strong Germans themselves are our servants. Have you stronger walls than we have? Pray, what greater obstacle is there than the wall of the ocean, with which the Britons are encircled, and yet they respect the arms of the Romans? Do you exceed us in courage of soul, and in the sagacity of your commanders? Nay, indeed, you cannot but know that the very Carthaginians have been conquered by us. It can therefore be nothing certainly but the kindness of us Romans which has incited you against us; who, in the first place, have given you this land to possess; and, next, have set over you kings of your own nation; and, in the third place, have preserved the laws of your forefathers for you, and have withal permitted you to live, either by yourselves or among others, as it should please you.

"And, what is our chief favor of all, we have given you leave to gather up that tribute which is paid to God with such other gifts that are dedicated to Him; nor have we called those that carried these donations to account, nor prohibited them; till at length you became richer than we ourselves, even when you were our enemies; and you made preparations for war against us with our own money: nay, after all, while you were enjoying all these advantages, you turned your too great plenty against those that gave it you, and, like merciless serpents, have thrown out your poison against those that treated you kindly. I suppose, therefore, that you might despise the slothfulness of Nero, and, like limbs of the body that are broken or dislocated, you did then lie quiet, waiting for some other time, though still with malicious intent, and have now shown your distemper to be greater than ever, and have extended your desires as far as your impudent and immense hopes would enable you. At this time my father came into this country, not with a design to punish you for what you had done under Cestius but to admonish you; for, had he come to overthrow your nation, he would have run directly to your fountainhead and immediately laid this city waste; whereas he went and burnt Galilee and the neighboring sections, and thereby gave you time for repentance; which instance of humanity you took for proof of his weakness, nourishing your impudence by our mildness.

"After Nero had departed from the world, you did as the wickedest wretches would have done, and encouraged yourselves to act against us because of our civil dissensions, and abused that time when both I and my father were going away to Egypt to make preparations for this war. Nor were you ashamed to raise disturbances against us when we were made emperors, and that after you had experienced how mild we had been when we were no more than generals of the army; but when it fell to us to run the government, and all other people did thereupon lie quiet and even foreign nations sent embassies and congratulated our access to dominions, then did you Jews show yourselves to be our enemies. You sent embassies to those of your nation beyond the Euphrates to assist you to raise rebellions; new walls were built by you around your city, seditions arose, one tyrant contended against another, and a civil war broke out among you; such, indeed, as became none but so wicked a people as you are. I then came to this city, unwillingly sent by my father, and received melancholy injunctions from him. When I heard that the people were disposed to peace, I rejoiced: I exhorted you to stop these proceedings before I began this war; I spared you even when you had fought against me a great while; I gave my right hand as security to the deserters; I observed what I had promised faithfully. When they fled to me, I had compassion on many of those I had taken captive. It was unwillingly that I brought my engines of war against your walls; I always prohibited my soldiers when they were set upon your slaughter from their severity against you.

"After every victory I invited you to peace, as though I had been myself conquered. When I came near your Temple, I again departed from the laws of war and exhorted you to spare your own sanctuary and preserve your holy house. I allowed you a quiet exit from it, and security for your preservation: nay, if you had a mind, I gave you leave to fight in another place. Yet you have despised every one of my proposals, and have set fire to your holy house with your own hands. And now, vile wretches, do you desire to negotiate with me by word of mouth? To what purpose would you save such a holy house as this was, which is now destroyed? What preservation can you now desire after the destruction of your Temple? Yet do you stand still at this very time in your armor; nor can you bring yourselves so much as to pretend to be supplicants even in this your utmost extremity! O miserable creatures! What is it you depend on? Are not your people dead? Is not your holy house gone? Is not your city in my power? And are not your own very lives in my hands? And do you still deem it part of valor to die? However, I will not imitate your madness. If you throw down your arms and deliver up your bodies to me, I grant you your lives; and I will act like a mild master of a family; what cannot be healed shall be punished, and the rest I will preserve for my own use."

To that offer of Titus they made this reply: That they could not accept it because they had sworn never to do so; but they desired they might have leave to go through the wall that had been made around them, with their wives and children; they would go into the desert and leave the city to him. At this Titus grew very indignant that, being in the situation of men already taken captives, they should aspire to make their own terms with him as if they had been conquerors!

So he ordered this proclamation to be made to them that they should no more come out to him as deserters, nor hope for any further security; he would henceforth spare nobody but fight them with his whole army; and they must save themselves as well as they could; for he would henceforth treat them according to the laws of war. So he gave orders to the soldiers both to burn and plunder the city; they did nothing that day, but on the next day they set fire to the repository of the archives, the Acra, the council house, and the place called Ophlas; at which time the fire proceeded as far as the palace of Queen Helena, the lanes also were burnt down, as were also those houses that were full of the dead bodies of those destroyed by famine.

The city of Jerusalem is taken.

And now the partisans rushed into the royal palace, where many had stored their effects because it was so strong, and drove the Romans away from it. They also slew all the people that crowded into it, who numbered about eight thousand four hundred, and plundered them of whatever they had. They also took two of the Romans alive; the one a horseman, and the other a footman. They then cut the throat of the footman, and immediately had him drawn through the whole city, as though revenging themselves on the whole body of the Romans by this one instance. But the horseman said he had something to suggest to them for their own preservation, whereupon he was brought before Simon. But having nothing to say when he was there, he was delivered for punishment to Ardalas, one of his commanders, who bound his hands behind him and put a riband over his eyes, and then brought him out over against the Romans, intending to cut off his head. But while the Jewish executioner was drawing out his sword, the man escaped and ran away to the Romans. Now after he had gotten away from the enemy, Titus could not think of putting him to death; but because he deemed him unworthy of being a Roman soldier any longer because he had been taken alive by the enemy, he took away his arms and ejected him out of the legion to which he had belonged; this, to one that had a sense of shame, was a penalty more severe than death itself.

On the next day the Romans drove the robbers out of the lower city, and set all on fire as far as Siloam. These soldiers were indeed glad to see the city destroyed. But they missed the plunder, because the rebels had carried off all their effects and had withdrawn into the upper city; for they did not yet repent all the mischiefs they had done, but were insolent, as if they had done well; when they saw the city on fire, they appeared cheerful and put on a joyful countenance, in expectation, as they said, of death to end their miseries. Accordingly, since the people were now slain, the holy house burnt down, and the city on fire, there was nothing further left for the enemy to do.

Yet Josephus did not weary, even in this utmost extremity, to beg them to spare what was left of the city; he spoke mainly to them about their barbarity and impiety, and gave them his advice as to how to escape, though he gained nothing more thereby than to be laughed at by them. And since they could not think of surrendering because of the oath they had taken, nor were they strong enough to fight with the Romans any longer, being surrounded on all sides and, in a way, prisoners already, yet they were so accustomed to kill people that they could not restrain their right hands from acting accordingly. So they dispersed themselves in front of the city, and laid themselves in ambush among its ruins to catch those that attempted to desert to the Romans. Accordingly many such deserters were caught by them and were all slain; for these were too weak, by reason of their want of food, to fly away from them; so their dead bodies were thrown to the dogs. Now every sort of death was thought more tolerable than famine, to the extent that, though the Jews despaired now of mercy, yet they would fly to the Romans and would themselves, even of their own accord, fall among the murderous rebels also. Nor was there any place in the city that had no dead bodies in it, but was entirely covered with those that were killed either by famine or rebellion; and all was full of the dead bodies of those who had perished, either by that sedition or by that famine.

So now the last hope which supported the tyrants and that crew of robbers with them was in the caves and caverns underground; whither, if they could once fly, they did not expect to be searched for, but hoped that after the whole city would be destroyed and the Romans departed, they might come out again and escape. This was no more than a dream, for they were not able to lie hid either from God or from the Romans. However, they depended on these underground subterfuges, and set more places on fire than did the Romans themselves; and those that fled out of their houses thus set on fire and into ditches they killed without mercy, and pillaged them also; and if they discovered food belonging to any one, they seized it and swallowed it, together with their blood also; nay, they had now come to fight with one another about their plunder; and I cannot but think that, had not their destruction prevented it, their barbarity would have made them taste even the dead bodies themselves.

But at this time one of the priests, the son of Thebuthus, whose name was Jesus, upon having security pledged him by Titus, that he be preserved on condition that he deliver to him certain of the precious things deposited in the Temple, came out and delivered to him from the wall of the holy house two candlesticks like those that lay inside, with tables, bowls, and platters, all made of solid gold and very heavy. He also delivered to him the veils and the garments with the precious stones, and a great number of other precious vessels used in their sacred worship. The treasurer of the Temple also, whose name was Phineas, was captured, and showed Titus the coats and girdles of the priests, with a great quantity of purple and scarlet, which were there deposited together with a great deal of cinnamon and cassia, and a large quantity of other sweet spices which used to be mixed together and offered daily as incense to God. A great many other treasures were also delivered to him, and not a few sacred ornaments of the Temple; these things delivered to Titus obtained for this man the same pardon that Titus had granted to such as deserted of their own accord.

And now the banks were finished, and the Romans brought their machines against the wall; but for the seditious, some of them, despairing of saving the city, retired from the wall to the citadel; others went down into the subterranean vaults, though still a great many defended themselves against those that brought the engines for the battery; yet did the Romans overcome them by their number and by their strength, and, most importantly, by going cheerfully about their work while the Jews were quite dejected and weakened. Now, as soon as a part of the wall was battered down and certain of the towers yielded to the impact of the battering-rams, those opposing fled, and such a terror fell upon the tyrants as was much greater than the occasion required; for even before the enemy got over the breach they were quite stunned and were in favor of flying away immediately; and now one might see these men, hitherto so insolent and arrogant in their wicked practices, cast down and trembling to the extent that it would bring pity to one's heart to observe the change made in those vile persons.

Accordingly, they ran with great violence upon the Roman wall that surrounded them in order to force away those that guarded it, and to break through it and get away; but when they saw that those who had formerly been faithful to them had gone away (as indeed they had fled whithersoever their great distress had persuaded them to flee) and also that those who came running before the rest told them that the western wall had been entirely overthrown, while others said the Romans had gotten in, and others that they were near and looking for them—which were only the dictates of their fear imposed upon their sight—when they saw all this they fell on their faces and greatly lamented their own mad conduct; and their nerves were so terribly strained that they could not flee; and here one may chiefly reflect on the power of God exercised upon these wicked wretches, and on the good fortune of the Romans; for these tyrants did now wholly deprive themselves of the security in their own power, and came down of their own accord from those towers whence they could have never been taken by force nor indeed by any other way than by famine. And so did the Romans, when they had taken such great pains about weaker walls, achieve by good fortune what they could never have gotten by their engines; for three of these towers were too strong for any mechanical engines whatsoever.

So they now left these towers of themselves, or rather they were ejected from them by God Himself, and fled immediately to that valley under Siloam, where they again recovered from their fear, for a while, and ran violently against that part of the Roman wall which lay on that side; but as their courage was too depleted to make their attacks with sufficient force, and their power was now broken with fear and affliction, they were repulsed by the guards, and dispersing themselves at distances from each other, went down into the subterranean caverns. So the Romans being now masters of the walls, they placed their engines on the towers, and made joyful acclamations for the victory they had gained, having found the end of this war much lighter than its beginning; for when they had gotten onto the last wall, without any bloodshed, they could hardly believe what they found to be true; but seeing nobody to oppose them, they stood in wonder at what such an unusual solitude could mean. But when they went in numbers into the lanes of the city, their swords drawn, they slew those whom they overtook without mercy, and set fire to the houses whither the Jews had fled, and burnt every soul in them, and laid waste a great many of the rest; and when they had come to the houses to plunder them, they found in them entire families of dead men, and the upper rooms full of dead corpses such as had died by famine; they then stood in horror at this sight, and went out without touching any thing.

But although they had this pity for those destroyed in that manner, yet they had not the same for those that were still alive, but they killed everyone they met and obstructed the very lanes with their dead bodies, and made the whole city run with blood to such a degree indeed that the fire of many of the houses was quenched with these men's blood. And truly it so happened that though the slayers left off at evening, yet the fire prevailed throughout the night; and since all was burning, that eighth day of the month came upon Jerusalem, a city that had been liable to so many miseries during this siege that, had it enjoyed as much happiness from its first foundation, would certainly have been the envy of the world. Nor did it deserve these sore misfortunes on any other account as much as for producing such a generation of men as caused this overthrow.

And thus was Jerusalem captured, in the second year of the reign of Vespasian, on the eighth day of the month Gorpieus (Elul). It had been captured five times before, though this was the second time of its desolation; for Shishak, the king of Egypt, and after him Antiochus, and after him Pompey, and after them Sosius and Herod captured the city but preserved it; but before all these the king of Babylon conquered it and made it desolate, one thousand four hundred and sixty-eight years and six months after it was built. But he who first built it was a powerful man among the Canaanites, and is in our tongue called Melchisedek, the Righteous King, for such he really was; on that account he was the first priest of God, and first built a temple there, and called the city Jerusalem, which was formerly called Salem. However, David, the king of the Jews, ejected the Canaanites, and settled his own people therein. It was demolished entirely by the Babylonians, four hundred and seventy-seven years and six months after him. And from King David, the first of the Jews who reigned therein, to this destruction under Titus were one thousand one hundred and seventy-nine years; but from its first building till this last destruction were two thousand one hundred and seventy-seven years; yet neither its great antiquity, nor its vast riches, nor the diffusion of its nation over all the habitable earth, nor the greatness of the veneration paid it on a religious account have been sufficient to preserve it from being destroyed. And thus ended the siege of Jerusalem.

Titus's dispositions after the capture of Jerusalem.
Simon, son of Giora, taken. The triumph in Rome.

Now as soon as the army had no more people to slay or to plunder, because none remained to be the objects of their fury (for they would not have spared any had any other such work re-

mained to be done), Titus gave orders that they should now demolish the entire city and Temple but leave as many of the towers
standing as were of the greatest prominence, and as much of the
wall as enclosed the city on the west side. This wall was spared in
order to provide a camp for such as were to lie in garrison; so too
were the towers also spared in order to demonstrate to posterity
what kind of city it was and how well fortified, and which Roman
valor had nevertheless subdued; but for all the rest of the wall, it
was so thoroughly razed even with the ground by those that dug it
up to the foundation that there was nothing left to make those that
came thither believe it had ever been inhabited. This was the end
to which Jerusalem was brought by the madness of those that favored revolt—a city of great magnificence and of mighty fame
among all mankind.

But Titus resolved to leave there as a guard the tenth legion,
with certain troops of horsemen and companies of footmen. So,
having entirely completed this war, he was desirous to commend
his whole army for the great exploits they had performed, and to
bestow proper rewards on such as had distinguished themselves
therein. He had therefore a great tribunal made for him in the
middle of the place where he had formerly encamped, and stood
upon it with his principal commanders about him, and spoke so as
to be heard by the whole army in the following manner: That he
returned them abundance of thanks for the good will they had
shown him; he commended them for that ready obedience they
had exhibited in this whole war, which had manifested itself in the
many great dangers they had courageously undergone; as also for
that courage they had shown, by which they had thereby augmented by themselves their country's power and had made it evident to all men that neither the multitude of their enemies nor the
strength of their places, nor the largeness of their cities, nor the
rash boldness and brutish rage of their antagonists, were sufficient
at any time to overcome Roman valor. He said further that it was
but reasonable for them to put an end to this war, now that it had
lasted so long, for they had nothing better to wish for when they
entered upon it; and that this redounded to their glory even more,
that all the Romans had willingly accepted as their governors and

the curators of their dominions those whom they had chosen. Accordingly, although he both admired and tenderly regarded them all because he knew that every one had gone as cheerfully about his work as his abilities and opportunities permitted, yet, he said, he would immediately bestow rewards and dignities on those that had fought the most bravely, and with greater force, and had signalized their conduct in the most glorious manner, and had made his army more famous by their noble exploits: and that no one who had been willing to take more pains than another should miss a just retribution for the same; for that he had been exceedingly careful about this matter, and that the more, because he had much rather reward the virtues of his fellow soldiers than punish such as had offended.

Hereupon, Titus ordered to be read the list of all that had performed great exploits in this war; he called them to him by their names and commended them in front of the company, and rejoiced in them in the same manner as a man would have rejoiced in his own exploits. He also put on their heads crowns of gold, and golden ornaments about their necks, and gave them long spears of gold and ensigns made of silver, and elevated every one of them to a higher rank: and besides this, he plentifully distributed among them silver, and gold, and garments out of the spoils and other booty they had taken. So when they had all these honors bestowed on them and he had wished all sorts of happiness to the whole army, he descended, amid great acclamations, and then betook himself to make thank-offerings to the gods, and at once sacrificed a vast number of oxen that stood ready at the altars and distributed them among the army to feast on; and after he had stayed three days among the principal commanders and feasted with them, he sent away the rest of the army to the several places where each would be best situated; but he permitted the tenth legion to stay as a guard in Jerusalem.

And now Titus was informed of the seizure of Simon, the son of Giora, which was made in the following manner: This Simon, during the siege of Jerusalem, was in the upper city; but when the Roman army had gotten within the walls and were laying the city waste, he then took the most faithful of his friends with him;

among them were some stone-cutters, with iron tools belonging to their occupation and as great a quantity of provisions as would suffice them for a long time; and he let himself and them all down into a certain subterraneous cavern that was not visible above ground. Now they went along as far as had been dug of old without disturbance: but where they met with solid earth, they dug a mine under ground, in hopes that they should be able to proceed so far as to rise in a safe place, and by that means escape; but when they came to make the experiment, they were disappointed; for the miners could make but small progress, and that with difficulty because their provisions, though distributed by measure, began to fail them. And now Simon, thinking he might be able to astonish and delude the Romans, put on a white frock and buttoned on a purple cloak and appeared out of the ground in the place where the Temple had formerly been. At first, indeed, those that saw him were greatly astonished, and stood still in their tracks; but afterward they came nearer and asked him who he was. Now Simon would not tell them but bade them summon their captain; and when they ran to call him, Terentius Rufus, who had been left to command the army there, came to Simon and learned the whole truth, and kept him in bonds, and let Titus know that he was captured.

Thus did God bring this man to be punished for that bitter and savage tyranny he had exercised against his countrymen, by those who were his worst enemies; and he was not subdued by violence, but voluntarily delivered himself up to them to be punished, the same act as that on account of which he had so often laid false accusations against many Jews, as if they were falling away to the Romans and had barbarously slain them; for wicked actions do not escape the divine anger, nor is justice too weak to punish offenders, but in time overtakes those that transgress its laws and inflicts its punishments upon the wicked in a much more severe manner. Simon was made aware of this by falling under the indignation of the Romans. His rising out of the ground also led to the discovery at that time of a great number of other rebels who had hidden themselves under ground; as for Simon, he was brought in bonds to Titus, who gave orders that he be held against that triumph which he was to celebrate in Rome on this occasion.

So Titus took the journey he intended into Egypt, and passing over the desert very suddenly, came to Alexandria, and made a resolution to go to Rome by sea. And as he was accompanied by two legions, he sent each of them back to the places whence they had come; the fifth he sent to Mysia; and the fifteenth to Pannonia: as for the leaders of the captives, Simon and John, with the other seven hundred men whom he had selected as being eminently tall and handsome of body, he ordered that they be soon transported to Italy, resolving to produce them in his triumph.

So after he had had a prosperous voyage, the city of Rome behaved in his reception and its meeting him from a distance as it had done in the case of his father. But what made the most splendid appearance in Titus's opinion was when his father met and received him; but still the multitude of the citizens conceived the greatest joy when they saw all three of them together,[10] as they did at this time: nor did many days pass before they determined to have but one triumph that should be common to both of them for the glorious exploits they had performed, although the senate had decreed each of them a separate triumph for himself. So when notice had been given beforehand of the day appointed for this pompous solemnity to be made on account of their victories, not one of the immense population was left in the city but everybody went out so far as to gain a position to stand, leaving only such a passage as was necessary for those who were to be seen.

Now all the infantry marched out beforehand, in the night-time, by companies, and in their several ranks, under their several commanders, and were around the gates not of the upper palaces but those near the temple of Isis; for it was there that the emperors had rested the preceding night. And as soon as it was day, Vespasian and Titus came out crowned with laurel, and clothed in traditional purple habits and then went as far as Octavian's Walks; for there the senate and the principal magistrates and those recorded as of the equestrian order awaited them. Now a tribunal had been erected before the cloisters, and ivory chairs had been set upon it,

[10] Vespasian, Titus, and Domitian.

on which they sat down. Whereupon the soldiery gave them an ac-
clamation of joy immediately, and all gave them attestations for
their valor, while they were themselves without their arms, and
only in their silken garments, and crowned with laurel: then Vespasian accepted these shouts, but since they were disposed to go
on with such acclamations, he gave them a signal to be silent.

And when everybody held their peace, he stood up, and covering the greatest part of his head with his cloak, he began with the
accustomed solemn prayers; the like prayers Titus also chanted;
after these prayers Vespasian made a short speech to all the people, and then sent away the soldiers to a dinner provided for them
by the emperors. Then he withdrew to the Gate of the Pomp, so
called because formal processions always went through that gate;
there they tasted some food, and when they had put on their
triumphal garments and had offered sacrifices to the gods placed
at the gate, they sent the triumph forward by marching through
the theaters that they might be the more easily seen by the masses.

Now it is impossible to describe the multitude and magnificence
of the displays as they deserve, such indeed as a man could not
easily think of as performed either by the labor of workmen, the
variety of riches, or the rarities of nature; for almost all such curi-
osities as the most happy men ever get piecemeal were heaped one
upon another, both admirable and costly in their nature; and all
brought together on that day demonstrated the vastness of the
Roman dominions; for there was to be seen a mighty quantity of
silver, and gold and ivory, made into all sorts of things, which appeared not just as if carried along in pompous show but, as a man
may say, running along like a river. Some parts were composed of
the rarest purple hangings, and so carried along; and others accurately represented what was embroidered by the arts of the Babylonians. There were also precious stones that were transparent,
some set in crowns of gold, and some in other forms; and of these
such a vast number were brought that we could not but learn from
them how vainly we imagined any of them to be rarities. The images of the gods were also carried, being wonderful for their largeness, made with great artifice and great skill; nor were any of
these images of other than very costly materials; and many species

of animals were brought, every one in their own natural ornaments.

Great multitudes of men brought every one of these displays, adorned with purple garments, interwoven all over with gold; those that were chosen to carry these triumphant displays also had about them such magnificent ornaments as were both extraordinary and surprising. Even the great number of captives were not unadorned, the variety and fine texture of their garments concealing from sight the deformity of their bodies. But what afforded the greatest surprise of all was the structure of the pageants that were borne along; for such was their magnitude that he that saw them could not but be afraid that the bearers would not be able to support them firmly enough; for many of them were made so that they were three or even four stories high, one above another. The magnificence also of their structure afforded both pleasure and surprise; for upon many of them were laid carpets of gold. There was also wrought gold and ivory fastened about them all; and many reproductions of the war, in several ways and varied contrivances affording a most lively portraiture; for there was to be seen a happy country laid waste and entire squadrons of enemies slain; while some ran away, some were carried into captivity; walls of great altitude and magnitude were overthrown and ruined by machines; the strongest fortifications were captured, and the walls of most populous cities on the tops of hills seized, and an army pouring itself within the walls; every place was full of slaughter and supplications of the enemies, after they were no longer able to lift up their hands in opposition. Temples set on fire were here represented, and houses overthrown and falling on their owners: rivers also, after coming out of a large and dreary desert, ran down, not into a land cultivated, nor as drink for men or cattle, but through a land still in flames on every side; for to such sufferings had the Jews condemned themselves when they started this war.

Now the workmanship of these representations was so magnificent and lively that it exhibited what had been done to such as did not see it, as if they had been really present there. At the head of each of these pageants was placed the commander of the city that was captured and the manner wherein he was captured. Moreover, a great number of ships followed those pageants; as for the other spoils, they were carried in great plenty. But for those taken in the Temple of Jerusalem, they made the greatest figure of all; that is the golden table, of the weight of many talents; the candlestick also, made of gold, though in its construction different from that which we ordinarily use; for its middle shaft was fixed on a base, and its small branches a great length, having the likeness of a trident in their position, every one with a socket of brass for a lamp at the top. These lamps were seven in number, representing the dignity of the number seven among the Jews; and the last of all the spoils carried was the Law of the Jews. Following these spoils came a great many men, carrying the images of victory, whose structure was entirely of either ivory or gold. Behind them Vespasian marched first, and Titus followed him; Domitian also rode along with them on a horse worthy of admiration, and made a glorious appearance.[11]

Now the final part of this triumphal procession took place at the temple of Jupiter Capitolinus, where on arriving they stood still; for it was the Romans' ancient custom to stay still till somebody brought the news that the general of the enemy was slain. This general was Simon, the son of Giora, who had then been led in this triumph among the captives; a rope had also been put around his head, and he had been drawn into a proper place in the forum and had withal been tormented by those dragging him along; and the law of the Romans required that malefactors condemned to die should be slain there. Accordingly, when it was told that he had met his end and all the people had set up a shout for joy, they then began to offer those sacrifices which they had consecrated, with the prayers used in such solemnities; when they finished, they went back to the palace. As for some of the spectators, the emperors entertained them at their own feast; and for all the rest there were noble preparations made for their feasting at

[11] Some of the vessels taken from the Temple in Jerusalem and carried in the triumphal procession are depicted on the Arch of Titus still standing in Rome.

home; for this was a festival day for the city of Rome, in celebration of the victory won by their army over their enemies.

Jerusalem had been taken in the summer of 70 C.E. *But fighting continued in a number of fortified places for some time. The last of these was Masada, a fortress in the wilderness, built by the high priest Jonathan in the middle of the second century* B.C.E., *and much extended by Herod, who planned it as a refuge for himself in time of need. It was here that the last stand of the Jewish defenders was overcome after fierce resistance and in circumstances of unsurpassed heroism.*

For now it was that the Roman general came, and led his army against Eleazar and those who held the fortress Masada with him; and he soon gained the whole country adjoining, and put garrisons into the most appropriate places: he also built a wall around the entire fortress so that none of the besieged might easily escape: he also set his men to guard its several sections; he also pitched his camp in a convenient place he had chosen for the siege, where the rock belonging to the fortress offered the nearest approach to the neighboring mountain, which was a difficult place for getting enough provisions; for it was not only food that had to be brought from a great distance (to the army), and this with a great deal of pain to those Jews who were appointed for that purpose, but water also had to be brought to the camp because the place had no fountain near it. When therefore Silva, the Roman commander, had ordered these affairs beforehand, he fell to besieging the place; this siege was likely to stand in need of a great deal of skill and pains, by reason of the strength of the fortress, the nature of which I will now describe.

There was a rock not small in circumference, and very high. It was surrounded by valleys of such vast depth that the eye could not reach their bottoms; they were abrupt, and such as no animal could walk upon, except at two places of the rock, where it subsides in order to offer a passage for ascent, though not without difficulty. Now, of the ways that lead to it, one is from the lake of Asphaltitis,[12] towards the sunrise, and another on the west, where the ascent is easier: one of these ways is called the Serpent, resembling that animal in its narrowness and perpetual windings; for it is broken off at the prominent precipices of the rock, and returns frequently into itself, lengthening again little by little, having much ado to proceed forward; and he that would walk along it must first go on one leg and then on the other; there is also nothing but destruction should your feet slip; for on each side there is a vastly deep chasm and precipice, sufficient to quell a man's courage by the terror it inspires. When, therefore, a man has gone along this way for thirty furlongs, the rest is the top of the hill—ending at not a small point but on a plateau on the highest part of the mountain. On this top of the hill, Jonathan the high priest first of all built a fortress and called it Masada; later the rebuilding of this place occupied King Herod to a great degree; he also built a wall around the entire top of the hill, seven furlongs long; it was composed of white stone; its height was twelve cubits, and its breadth eight; there were also erected on that wall thirty-eight towers, each fifty cubits high; from this you might pass into lesser edifices, built on the inside, around the entire wall; for the king reserved the top of the hill, which was of a rich soil and better mold than any valley for agriculture, so that those committed to this fortress for their preservation might not even there be quite destitute of food, in the event they should ever be unable to receive it from outside. Moreover, he built a palace inside at the western ascent: it was within and beneath the walls of the citadel, but inclined to its north side.

Now the wall of this palace was very high and strong, and had at its four corners towers sixty cubits high. The furnishings of the edifices, and the cloisters and baths, were of great variety, and very costly; and these buildings were supported by pillars of single stones on every side: the walls also and the floors of the edifices were paved with stones of several colors. He also had dug, out of the rocks, many great pits as reservoirs for water, at every one of

[12] The Dead Sea.

the places inhabited, both above and around the palace, and in front of the wall; and by this means he endeavored to have water for several uses, as if there had been fountains there.

Here also was a road dug from the palace, and leading to the very top of the mountain, which still could not be seen by those outside the walls; nor indeed could enemies easily make use of the open roads; for the road on the east side, as we have already noted, could not be walked upon, by reason of its nature; as for the western road, he built a large tower at its narrowest place, at no less a distance from the top of the hill than a thousand cubits; this tower could not possibly be passed by, nor could it be easily taken; nor indeed could those that walked along it without any fear (such was its structure) easily get to the end of it; and in such a manner was this citadel fortified, both by nature and by the hands of men, in order to frustrate the attacks of enemies.

As for the stores within this fortress, they were still more wonderful on account of their splendor and long continuity; for here was laid up corn in large quantities, as would nourish men for a long time; here were also wine and oil in abundance, with all kinds of pulse and dates heaped together; all this Eleazar found there when he and his followers took possession of the fortress by treachery. These fruits were also fresh and ripe, and no way inferior to such fruits newly laid in, though it was a little short of a hundred years from the laying in of these provisions by Herod until the time when the place was captured by the Romans; nay, indeed, when the Romans got possession of those fruits that were left, they found them not spoiled all that while: nor should we be mistaken if we supposed that the air was here the cause of their enduring so long, this fortress being so high and so free from the mixture of all earth and muddy particles of matter. Also found here was a large quantity of all sorts of weapons of war, sufficient for ten thousand men, which had been treasured up by that king: there was cast iron, brass, and tin, which show that he had taken great pains to have all things ready here for the greatest occasions; for the report goes that Herod thus prepared this fortress for himself, as a refuge against two kinds of danger: the one for fear of the multitude of the Jews, lest they depose him and restore their former kings to the government; the other danger, greater and more terrible, arose from Cleopatra, queen of Egypt, who did not conceal her intentions, but spoke often to Antony, and desired him to cut off Herod and bestow the kingdom of Judea upon her. And certainly it is a great wonder that Antony never complied with her commands on this point, as he was so miserably enslaved to his passion for her; nor would any one have been surprised if she had been gratified in her request. So the fear of these dangers had made Herod rebuild Masada and thereby leave it for the finishing stroke of the Romans in this Jewish war.

Since therefore the Roman commander Silva had now built a wall on the outside, around this whole place, as we have said already, and had thereby made a most accurate provision to prevent any one of the besieged from running away, he undertook the siege itself, though he found but one single place that would admit the banks he was to raise; for behind that tower which secured the road leading to the palace and to the top of the hill from the west, there was a certain eminency of the rock, very broad and very prominent, but three hundred cubits beneath the highest part of Masada; it was called the White Cliff. Accordingly he got up on that part of the rock, and ordered the army to bring earth; and when they fell to that work with alacrity, an abundance of them together, the bank was raised and made solid for two hundred cubits in height. Yet this bank was not thought sufficiently high for the use of the engines that were to be set upon it; but still another elevated work of great stones compacted together was raised upon that bank: this was fifty cubits, both in breadth and height. The other machines that were now got ready were like those that had been first devised for sieges by Vespasian, and afterwards by Titus. There was also a tower made sixty cubits in height and plated all over with iron, out of which the Romans threw darts and stones from the engines, and soon forced those that fought from the walls of the place to retire, and would not let them lift up their heads above the works. At the same time Silva ordered that great battering-ram which he had made to be brought thither, and to be set against the wall, and to make frequent batteries against it; with some difficulty, it broke down a part of the wall and almost overthrew it. However, the defenders made haste and soon built another wall inside that, which would not be liable to the same misfortune from the machines as the other: it was made soft and yielding, and so was capable of avoiding the terrible blows that affected the other. It was framed in the following manner: They laid together great beams of wood lengthways, one close to the end of another, and the same way in which they were cut: two of these rows were parallel to one another and laid at such a distance from each other as the breadth of the wall required, and earth was put into the space between those rows.

Now, so that the earth might not fall away upon the elevation of this bank to a greater height, they laid other beams over across them, and thereby bound those beams together that lay lengthways. This work was like a real edifice; and when the machines were applied, the blows were weakened by its yielding; and as the materials were shaken closer together by such concussion, the pike by that means became firmer than before. When Silva saw this, he thought it best to endeavor to take this wall by setting fire to it; so he gave order that the soldiers throw a great number of burning torches upon it: accordingly, since it was chiefly made of wood, it soon caught fire; and when it was once set on fire, its hollowness made that fire spread into a mighty flame. Now, at the very beginning of this fire, a north wind that then blew proved terrible to the Romans; for by bringing the flame downward, it drove it upon them, and they were almost in despair of success, fearing their machines would be burnt: but after this, suddenly the wind changed into the south, as if by divine providence; and blew strongly the contrary way and bore the flame and drove it against the wall, which was now on fire through its entire thickness. So the Romans, having now assistance from God, returned to their camp with joy, and resolved to attack their enemies the very next day; on that occasion they set their watch more carefully that night lest any of the Jews run away from them without being discovered.

The speeches of Eleazar ben Yair. He recommends collective suicide.

However, neither did Eleazar once think of flying away, nor would he permit any one else to do so; but when he saw their wall burnt down by the fire, he could devise no other way to escape or offer hope for further courage, and setting before their eyes what the Romans would do to them, their children, and their wives if they got them into their power, he consulted about having them all slain. Now, as he judged this to be the best thing they could do in their present circumstances, he gathered the most courageous of his companions together, and encouraged them to take that course in a speech made to them in the following manner. "Since we, long ago, my generous friends, resolved never to be servants to the Romans, nor to any other than to God Himself, who alone is the true and just Lord of mankind, the time is now come that obliges us to make that resolution true in practice. And let us not at this time reproach ourselves for self-contradiction, while we formerly would not undergo slavery, though it were then without danger; but we must now, together with slavery, choose such punishments as are also intolerable; I mean this, upon the supposition that the Romans once reduce us under their power while we are alive. We were the very first that revolted from them, and we are the last that fight against them; and I cannot but esteem it as a favor that God has granted us that it is still in our power to die bravely, and in a state of freedom, which has not been the case of others who were conquered unexpectedly.

"It is very plain that we shall be captured within a day's time; but it is still possible to die in a glorious manner, together with our dearest friends. This is what our enemies themselves cannot by any means prevent, even though they are very eager to take us alive. Nor can we propose any more to ourselves to fight them and beat them. It might have been proper indeed for us to have wondered at God's purpose much sooner, and at the very first, when we were so desirous of defending our liberty, and when we received such sore treatment from one another and worse treatment from our enemies, and to have been aware that the same God, who had of old taken the Jewish nation into His favor, had now condemned them to destruction; for had He either continued favorable, or been in a lesser degree displeased with us, He would not have overlooked the destruction of so many men, or delivered His most holy city to be burnt and demolished by our enemies. To be sure, we faintly hoped to have preserved ourselves, and ourselves alone, still in a state of freedom, as if we had been guilty of no sins ourselves against God, nor been partners with those of others; we who taught other men to sin.

"Wherefore, consider how God has convinced us that our hopes were in vain, by bringing such distress upon us in our present desperate state, which is beyond all our expectations; for the nature of this fortress, which was in itself unconquerable, has not proved a means of our deliverance; and even while we still have great abundance of food and a great quantity of arms, and other necessities more than we need, we are openly deprived by God Himself of all hope of deliverance; for that fire which was driven upon our enemies did not, of its own accord, turn back upon the wall which we had built: this was the effect of God's anger against us for our manifold sins, which we have been guilty of in a most insolent and extravagant manner with regard to our own countrymen; the punishments for which let us receive not from the Romans but from God Himself, as executed by our own hands, for these will be more moderate than the other. Let our wives die before they are abused, and our children before they have tasted of slavery; and after we have slain them, let us bestow that glorious benefit upon one another mutually, and preserve ourselves in freedom, as an excellent funeral monument for us. But first let us destroy our money and the fortress by fire; for I am well assured that this will be a great grief to the Romans that they shall not be able to capture our bodies, and shall fail of our wealth also: and let us spare nothing but our provisions; for they will be a testimonial when we are dead that we were not subdued for want of necessities; but that, according to our original resolution, we have preferred death to slavery."

This was Eleazar's speech to them. Yet the opinions of all the auditors did not acquiesce to his plan; but although some of them were very zealous to put his advice in practice and were in a manner filled with pleasure at it and thought death to be a good thing, yet those that were most emotional felt pity for their wives and families; and while these men were especially moved by the prospect of their own certain death, they looked wistfully at one another, and by the tears in their eyes, declared their dissent from his opinion. When Eleazar saw these people in such fear, their souls dejected at so prodigious a proposal, he was afraid lest perhaps these emotional persons should, by their lamentations and tears, enfeeble those that heard what he had said courageously; so he did not leave off exhorting them, but stirred himself up, recollecting appropriate arguments for raising their courage; he undertook to speak more briskly and fully to them concerning the immortality of the soul. So he uttered a groan of lamentation, and fixing his eyes intently on those that wept, he spoke thus: "Truly, I was greatly mistaken when I thought I was listening to brave men who have struggled hard for their liberty, and to those resolved either to live with honor or else to die; but I find that you are such people as are no better than others, either in virtue or in courage, and are afraid of dying though you be delivered thereby from the greatest miseries, while you ought to make no delay in this matter, nor to expect anyone to give you good advice; for the laws of our country, and of God Himself, have, from ancient times, and as soon as ever we could use our reason, continually taught us, and our forefathers have corroborated the same doctrine by their actions and their bravery of mind, that it is life that is calamity to men, and not death; for this last offers our souls their liberty and sends them into their own place of purity, where they are to be liberated from all sorts of misery; for while souls are tied down to a mortal body, they are partakers of its miseries; and really, to speak the truth, they are themselves dead; for the union of what is divine to what is mortal is disagreeable. It is true, the power of the soul is great even when it is imprisoned in a mortal body; for by moving it in a way that is invisible, it makes the body a sensible instrument, and causes it to advance further in its actions than mortal nature could otherwise do. However, once it is freed from that weight which draws it down to the earth and is connected with it, it obtains its own proper place, and does then become a partaker of that blessed power and those abilities which are then every way incapable of being hindered in their operations. It continues invisible, indeed, to the eyes of men, as does God Himself; for certainly it is not itself seen, while it is in the body; for it is there in an invisible manner, and when it is freed from it it is still not seen. It is this soul which has one nature, and an incorruptible one at that; but yet it is the cause of the change made in the body; for whatsoever it be which the soul touches, that lives and flourishes; and from whatsoever it is removed, that withers away and dies; such a degree is there in it of immortality. Let me produce the state of sleep as a most evident demonstration of the truth of what I say; wherein souls, when the body does not distract them, have the sweetest rest depending on themselves and conversing with God, by their alliance to Him; they then go everywhere, and foretell many future events beforehand; and why are we afraid of death, while we are pleased with the rest we have in sleep? and how absurd a thing is it to pursue liberty while we are alive, and yet to deny it to ourselves where it will be eternal!

"We, therefore, who have been brought up in a discipline of our own, ought to become an example to others of our readiness to die; yet if we do not stand in need of foreigners to support us in this manner, let us regard those Indians who profess the exercise of philosophy; for these good men do but unwillingly undergo the time of life, and look upon it as a necessary servitude, and make haste to let their souls loose from their bodies; nay, when no misfortune presses them to it nor drives them upon it, these have such a desire of a life of immortality that they tell other men beforehand that they are about to depart; and nobody prevents them, but every one thinks them happy men and gives them messages to be carried to their familiar friends that are dead; so firmly and certainly do they believe that souls converse with one another in the other world. So when these men have heard all such commands that were to be given them, they deliver their body to the fire; and, in order to get a separation of their soul from the body in the greatest purity, they die in the midst of hymns of commendations made to them; for their dearest friends conduct them to their death more readily than do any of the rest of mankind conduct their fellow citizens when they are going a very long journey, who, at the same time, weep for themselves, but look upon the others as happy persons, so soon to be made partakers of the immortal order of beings. Are we not, therefore, ashamed to have lower notions than the Indians? and by our own cowardice to lay a base reproach upon the laws of our country, which are so much desired and imitated by all mankind?

"But put the case that we had been brought up under another persuasion, and taught that life is the greatest good which men are capable of, and that death is a calamity; however, our present circumstances ought to be an inducement to us to bear such calamity courageously, since it is by the will of God, and by necessity, that we are to die; for it now appears that God has made a decree against the whole Jewish nation that we are to be deprived of this life which we would not make a due use of; for do not ascribe your present condition to yourselves, nor think the Romans the true reason that this war we have had with them has become so destructive to us all: these things have not come to pass by their power, but a more powerful cause has intervened and made us offer them an occasion for their appearing to be conquerors over us. What Roman weapons, I pray you, were those by which the Jews of Caesarea were slain? On the contrary, when they were no way disposed to rebel but were all the while keeping their seventh day festival and did not so much as lift up their hands against the citizens of Caesarea, yet did those citizens run upon them in great mobs, and cut their throats and the throats of their wives and children, and this without any regard to the Romans themselves, who never took us for their enemies till we revolted from them. But some may be ready to say that truly the people of Caesarea always had a quarrel against those that lived among them, and that when an opportunity offered itself, they only satisfied their old rancor. What then shall we say to those of Scythopolis, who ventured to wage war with us on account of the Greeks? they were slain, they and their whole families, in the most inhumane manner, which was all the requital made them for the assistance they had offered the others; for that very same destruction which they had prevented from falling upon the others, they suffered themselves from them, as if they had been ready to be the actors against them.

"It would be too long for me to speak at this time of every destruction brought upon us: you must know that there was not a single Syrian city which did not slay its Jewish inhabitants and were not more bitter enemies to us than the Romans themselves: nay, even those of Damascus, once they were able to allege no tolerable crime against us, filled their city with the most barbarous slaughter of our people and cut the throats of eighteen thousand Jews, along with their wives and children. And as to the multitude of those slain in Egypt, and that by torture also, we have been informed they were more than sixty thousand; indeed, being in a foreign country and so naturally having nothing with which to oppose their enemies, they were killed in the aforementioned manner.

"As for all those of us who have waged war against the Romans in our own country, had we not sufficient reason to have sure hopes of victory? For we had arms, and walls, and fortresses so prepared as not to be easily captured, and courage not to be moved by any dangers in the cause of liberty, which encouraged us all to revolt from the Romans. But then, these advantages sufficed us but for a short time and only raised our hopes, while they really appeared to be the origin of our miseries; for all we had has been taken from us, and all has fallen under our enemies, as if these advantages were only to render their victory over us the more glorious and not disposed to preserve those by whom these preparations had been made.

"And as for those already dead in the war, it is reasonable we should esteem them blessed, for they are dead in defending and not in betraying their liberty; but as to the multitude of those now under the Romans, who would not pity their condition? and who would not make haste to die before suffering the same miseries with them? Some were put upon the rack and tortured with fire and whippings, and so died. Some were half devoured by wild beasts, and yet were preserved alive to be devoured by them a second time, in order to afford laughter and sport to our enemies; and such of those as are still alive are to be looked on as the most miserable, who, being so desirous of death, could not achieve it.

"And where is now that great city, the metropolis of the Jewish nation, which was fortified by so many walls, which had so many fortresses and large towers to defend it, which could hardly contain the instruments prepared for war, and which had so many ten thousands of men to fight for it? Where is this city that was believed to have God Himself inhabiting therein? It is now demolished to its very foundations, and has nothing but that monument of it preserved, I mean the camp of those that destroyed it which still dwells upon its ruins; some unfortunate old men also lie upon the ashes of the Temple, and a few women are there preserved alive by the enemy, to our bitter shame and reproach. Now, who is there that revolves these things in his mind and yet is able to bear the sight of the sun, though he might live out of danger? Who is there so much his country's enemy or so unmanly and so desirous of living as not to repent that he is still alive? And I cannot but wish that we had all died before we had seen that holy city demolished by the hands of our enemies, or the foundations of our holy Temple dug up in so profane a manner.

"But since we had a generous hope that deluded us, that we might perhaps have been able to avenge ourselves on our enemies, though it has now become vanity and has left us alone in this distress, let us make haste to die bravely. Let us take pity on ourselves, our children, and our wives, while it is in our power to show pity to them; for we are born to die, as well as those whom we have begotten; nor is it in the power even of the most happy to avoid it. But for abuses and slavery, and the sight of our wives led away in an ignominious manner, with their children, these are not such evils as are natural and necessary among men; although such as do not prefer death to those miseries when it is in their power so to do, must undergo even them, on account of their own cowardice. We revolted from the Romans with great pretensions to courage; and when, at the very last, they invited us to preserve ourselves, we would not comply with them. Who will not, therefore, believe that they will certainly be in a rage against us, in case they take us alive? Miserable will then be the young men strong enough in their bodies to sustain many tortures! Miserable also will be those of elder years who will not be able to bear those calamities which young men might sustain! A man will be obliged to hear the voice of his son imploring the help of his father, when his hands are bound! But certainly our hands are still at liberty, and have a sword in them! Let them be subservient to us in our glorious design; let us die before we become slaves under our enemies, and let us go out of the world, together with our children and our wives, in a state of freedom.

"This it is that our laws command us to do; this it is that our wives and children desire at our hands; nay, God Himself has brought this necessity upon us; while the Romans desire the contrary, and are afraid lest any of us die before we are captured. Let us therefore make haste, and instead of affording them so much pleasure as they hope for in getting us under their power, let us leave them an example which shall at once cause their astonishment at our death, and their admiration of our hardiness therein."

The defenders of the fortress are persuaded by Eleazar; they kill one another. Only two women and five children survive.

Now as Eleazar was proceeding in this exhortation, they all cut him off short, and made haste to do the work, being filled with an unconquerable ardor of mind and moved by a demoniacal fury. So they went their ways, one still endeavoring to be before another, thinking that this eagerness would be a demonstration of their courage and good conduct, if they could avoid appearing in the last class: so great was their zeal to slay their wives and children, and themselves also! Nor indeed, when they came to the work itself, did their courage fail them, as one might imagine it would have done; but they held fast to the same resolution, without wavering, which they had taken on hearing Eleazar's speech, while yet every one of them still retained his natural passion of love for himself and his family, because the reasoning they went upon appeared to them very just, even with regard to those dearest to them; for the husbands tenderly embraced their wives and took their children into their arms, and gave the longest parting kisses to them, with tears in their eyes. Yet at the same time they completed what they had resolved, as if they had been executed by the hands of strangers, and they had nothing else for their comfort but their necessity to carry out this execution in order to avoid that prospect of the miseries they were to suffer from their enemies.

Nor was there any one of these men that scrupled to act his part in this terrible execution, but every one of them dispatched his dearest relations. Miserable men indeed were they whose distress forced them to slay their own wives and children with their own hands, as the lightest of those evils before them. So being unable to bear their grief any longer, and esteeming it an injury to those they had slain to live even the shortest space of time after them, they presently laid all they had in a heap and set fire to it. They then chose ten men by lot from among them to slay all the rest; every one of these laid himself down beside his wife and children on the ground and threw his arms about them, and they offered their necks to the stroke of those who by lot carried out that melancholy office: and when these ten had, without fear, slain them all, they made the same rule for casting lots for themselves, that he whose lot it was should first kill the other nine, and after kill himself. Accordingly, all these had courage sufficient to be no way behind one another in doing or suffering; so, for a conclusion, the nine offered their necks to the executioner, and he who was the last of all took a view of all the other bodies lest perchance some or other among so many slain should need his assistance to be fully dispatched; and when he perceived that they were all slain, he set fire to the palace, and with the great force of his hand ran his sword entirely through himself, and fell down dead near his own relations.

So these people died with this intention that they would leave not so much as one soul among them all alive to be subject to the Romans. Yet there was an old woman, and another who was kin to Eleazar and superior to most women in prudence and learning, with five children, who had concealed themselves in caverns under ground, and had carried water thither for their drink, and had hidden there when the rest were intent upon the slaughter of one another. Those others were nine hundred and sixty in number, the women and children being withal included in that computation.

Now the Romans expected that they should be fought in the morning, when accordingly they put on their armor, and laid bridges of planks upon their ladders from their banks, in order to make an assault upon the fortress, which they did; but they saw nobody as an enemy, only a terrible solitude on every side, with a fire within the place as well as a complete silence. So they were at a loss to guess what had happened. At length they made a shout, as if at a blow given by the battering-ram, to test whether they could bring anyone out that was within; the women heard this noise and came out of their underground cavern, and informed the Romans what had been done; and the second of them clearly described both what was said and what was done, and the manner of it; yet the Romans did not easily heed such a desperate undertaking, and did not believe it could be as the women said; they also attempted to put the fire out, and quickly cutting themselves a way through it came within the palace, and so met up with the multitude of the slain, but could take no pleasure in the fact even though it were done to their enemies. Nor could they do other than wonder at the courage of the Jews' resolution and the immovable contempt of death which so great a number of them had shown when they went through with such an action as that was.

And here we shall put an end to our history, wherein we earlier promised to deliver the same with all accuracy to those desirous of understanding in what manner this war of the Romans with the Jews was managed. Of which history, how good its style must be left to the determination of the readers; but for the agreement with the facts, I shall not scruple to say, and boldly, that truth has been my sole aim through its entire composition.

Further Reading

Index

Further Reading

I. About the Present Translation

The present selection is taken, with modifications, from the translation by William Whiston, first published in 1737 and reprinted many times since. Among currently available editions is the following:

Life and Work of Flavius Josephus translated by William Whiston, Holt, Rinehart, and Winston, 1957.

William Whiston, son of a clergyman, was born in 1667. He studied mathematics in Cambridge. He was an industrious scholar of wide learning and varied interests. A gifted and hard-working mathematician, he was appointed Newton's deputy in 1701 and his successor in the Lucasian Professorship of Mathematics in 1703. Like Newton he encompassed a curious combination of scientific and theological interests. *The Dictionary of National Biography,* which says of him that he had an acute but ill-balanced intellect, praises him for his simple-minded honesty; his single-minded and stubborn adherence to heretical opinions concerning the Christian faith led in 1710 to his being deprived of his professorship at Cambridge.

The writer of his biography in the *D.N.B.* thinks it not unlikely that Whiston was more or less in Goldsmith's mind when he wrote *The Vicar of Wakefield.* His interest in Josephus was, of course, colored by his deep and abiding interests in biblical and theological questions. These interests included a belief in the approaching restoration of the Jews to Palestine; he also thought that the Tartars were the ten lost tribes. He died in 1752. For further information on this engaging figure see the *D.N.B.* article mentioned above.

II. Other Editions of Josephus

The standard Greek text of Josephus is that of B. Niese, Berlin 1887–1895, reprinted (unchanged) in 1955.

Life, Against Apion, Jewish War, Jewish Antiquities, 9 vols. Complete text of Josephus together with an English translation, edited, translated, and annotated by H. St. J. Thackeray, Ralph Marcus, Allen Wikgren, and L. H. Feldman, Harvard University Press, 1926–1965.

This edition is at once the most easily accessible, the most accurate, and because of its full and learned annotation, the most useful for English-speaking readers. It includes also full indices, special appendices, and much valuable bibliographical material.

Jerusalem and Rome: The Writings of Josephus, edited by Nahum N. Glatzer, Meridian Books, 1960. The story of Judaea from 134 B.C.E. to 73 C.E., based on accounts in *The Jewish War, Antiquities,* and other works.

The Second Jewish Commonwealth: From the Maccabaean Rebellion to the Outbreak of the Judaeo-Roman War, edited by Nahum N. Glatzer, Schocken, 1971. Comprises Books XII:iv–XX of *Jewish Antiquities,* translated by Whiston, as revised by A. R. Shilleto, 1889.

The Jewish War, translated by G. A. Williamson, Penguin, 1959.

III. Works About Josephus

Thackeray, H. St. J., *Josephus, The Man and the Historian,* Ktav, New York, 1929, republished 1968.

This is a scholarly, balanced and fair-minded treatment of a subject that has aroused passionate partisanship in many of those who have written about it.

Notices of other general works, editions, translations, etc. of the complete corpus of Josephus's writings and of individual works, as well as of specialized treatment of particular problems, are to be found in: Ralph Marcus, *Selected Bibliography (1920–1945) of the Jews in the Hellenistic Roman Period, Proceedings of the American Academy for Jewish Research,* XVI (1946–1947), pp. 97 ff.; and L. H. Feldman, *Studies in Judaica, Scholarship on Philo and Josephus* (1937–1962), published by Yeshiva University, New York, pp. 26 ff.

Index

313